Miguel de Cervantes Saavedra, Thomas Shelton

The History of Don Quixote of the Mancha

Translated from the Spanish of Miguel de Cervantes by Thomas Shelton

Miguel de Cervantes Saavedra, Thomas Shelton

The History of Don Quixote of the Mancha
Translated from the Spanish of Miguel de Cervantes by Thomas Shelton

ISBN/EAN: 9783337186937

Printed in Europe, USA, Canada, Australia, Japan

Cover: Foto ©Andreas Hilbeck / pixelio.de

More available books at **www.hansebooks.com**

THE TUDOR
TRANSLATIONS

EDITED BY

W. E. HENLEY

THE HISTORY OF
DON QUIXOTE
OF THE MANCHA

TRANSLATED FROM THE SPANISH
OF MIGUEL DE CERVANTES BY

THOMAS SHELTON

ANNIS 1612, 1620

With Introductions by

JAMES FITZMAURICE-KELLY

VOLUME III

LONDON

Published by DAVID NUTT

IN THE STRAND

1896

Edinburgh: T. and A. CONSTABLE, Printers to Her Majesty

TO

GILBERT PARKER

THIS GREETING

FROM THE BEYOND

INTRODUCTION

TO THE SECOND PART

HE publication of *Don Quixote* gave Cervantes rank among the foremost European figures. From the outset he was accepted as a cosmopolitan. While Shakespeare was still unknown without London and Stratford, while Lope de Vega's fame was yet Peninsular, the new masterpiece was printing in Italy and in the Low Countries. And the author took frank pleasure in his popularity. By the mouth of that credible witness, Sansón Carrasco—'a 'notable Wag-halter, leane-faced, but of a good understand-'ing '—he vaunts his vogue. 'Upon my knowledge,' quoth the Salamantine graduate, 'at this day, there bee printed 'above twelve thousand copies of your History: if not, let 'Portugal, Barcelona, and Valencia speak, where they have 'beene printed, and the report goes, that they are now 'printing at Antwerp, and I have a kinde of ghesse, that 'there is no Nation or Language where they will not bee 'translated.' Nor do the numbers alleged in the Sixteenth Chapter lose in Shelton's ungrudging hands :—'I have 'merited to be in the Presse, in all or most nations of the

Cervantes in Europe

ix

THE SECOND PART OF THE

'world: **thirty thousand volumes of** my History have been
' printed, and thirty thousand millions more are like **to** bee if
' Heaven permit.' Since but a month is supposed to pass
between the close of the First Part and the opening of the
Second, the literal commentator labours greatly to account
for the distribution of twelve—not to say thirty—thousand
copies in so brief a time. And, at first blush, it seems
that Cervantes must certainly err in detail. Assuredly no
edition of his book appeared at Antwerp in the writer's life-
time: but read Brussels for Antwerp—a confusion not inconceivable, as far away as Madrid is—and the boast is
justified. A Barcelona reprint of 1605 were **a** rarity indeed; yet time may vindicate **this** first announcement.
Gayangos and Vedia, the Spanish translators **of** Ticknor,[1]
had rumour of a copy dated 1605—printed **at** Barcelona **or**
Pamplona—in the library of a Hague collector. If the bruit
be true, Cervantes approves his exactitude. **Yet** with all
his self-glory he returned not hastily to **his** theme. 'Though
' **in shew** a Father, yet in truth but **a** step-father to *Don*
' *Quixote*': thus he proclaims **himself** when the piece opens,
and so **in** effect **he** remains **till the** drop falls. 'Forse altro
canterà **con** miglior plettro'—**in** such phrase, borrowed from
Orlando, does **he** challenge rivalry; and, by his dalliance,

he tempts fate. **He** was enamoured of other emprises; *Don
Quixote* **was to** be **the** stepping-stone to success in every
kind: **the** pastoral, **the** short story, 'scene individable or
poem unlimited.' The Prince of Courtesy and the Flower
of Esquires must wait.

[1] *Historia de la literatura española* (Madrid, 1851-56), iv. p. 410.

x

HISTORIE OF DON QUIXOTE

I

So far as concerns authentic, published work, Cervantes remains silent for eight whole years, save for the punctual harvest of sonnets. Yet one cannot suppose him idle, and his name arrives by side-winds. The christening of the future Philip the Fourth and the mission of Lord Nottingham—better known as Howard of Effingham, Lord High Admiral against the Invincible Armada—are celebrated in an anonymous pamphlet published at Valladolid in 1605 under the style of *Relación de lo sucedido en la Ciudad de Valladolid.* Himself a singer of these glories, Góngora pens a brilliant and venomous sonnet, gibbeting Cervantes as the writer of this trifle; and other testimony upholds the ascription. A graver matter is the arrest of our author in the summer of this year on suspicion of being concerned in the doing to death of one Gaspar de Ezpeleta. The legend that makes of Ezpeleta the lover of Cervantes' bastard daughter, Isabel de Saavedra, is the theme of more than one play and of more than one story;[1] and the incidents are so dramatic that it irks one to find Cervantes released on bail without more said or done. Hereto succeeds a rumour of his ruffling

Achievements

Experiences

[1] There is no foundation for the statement that Cervantes, 'upon his return from Algiers, in 1580, assumed the additional surname of Saavedra.' The Dedication to the *Galatea* (1585) is signed Miguel de Cervantes; the Saavedra is first found in business documents during his stay in Seville. Equally baseless is the assertion that his daughter was 'his constant companion till his death.' Cervantes died in 1616. The Marqués de Molins, in *La Sepultura de Miguel de Cervantes* (Madrid, 1870), brings evidence to show that Isabel became a Trinitarian nun in 1613 under the name of Sor Antonia de San José; her mother, Sor Mariana de San José, apparently joined at the same time. Félix Lope de Vega Carpio's natural daughter, Sor Marcela de San Félix, entered the order in 1621.

THE SECOND PART OF THE

it in gaming-houses, his doxy (married) beside **him**; and the
Memorias de Valladolid[1] reveal him in the act. To the years
1605-8 must be assigned such exploits as the sonnets *Á un
Ermitaño*, to the Conde de Saldaña, *Á un Valentón metido á
pordiosero*, this last being published (without the writer's
name) in the *Poesías varias de grandes Ingenios*, by Josef

Alfay, at Zaragoza, as late as 1654. Doubtful pieces abound:
as the Third Part of the *Relación de lo que pasa en la Cárcel
de Sevilla*, a continuation of a spirited sketch of prison-life
conceived by Cristóbal de Chaves twenty years before the
publication of *Don Quixote*. To this should be added the
*Carta á Don Diego de Astudillo Carrillo, en que se le da
Cuenta de la Fiesta de San Juan de Alfarache, el Dia de Sant
Laureano*, a letter not unworthy of the Master. **Not less**
characteristic are the two anonymous *romances*, **the one**
dedicated to Cortés and the other to the Great Captain,
first printed in Engrava's collection in 1653. The *Entremés
de Doña Justina y Calahorra*, and that better one entitled
De los Mirones, are almost certainly apocryphal, as is also
the *Entremés de los Refranes*: all three ascribed to Cervantes by that solemn wag Adolfo de Castro, who further
guarantees the authenticity of the pastoral *Diálogo entre
Sillenia y Selanio*. A discreeter opinion holds the four for
the pranks of an imitator, seduced by a famous model. That
the author of *Don Quixote* corrected the Madrid reprint of
1608 is a wanton fable and a dangerous deceit; that he

dwelt in the capital from 1609 till his death is certain. On
April 17 of this year he and Antonio Robles y Guzmán
are the first recruits of the Congregación de Esclavos del

---

[1] *British Museum Add. MSS.*, 20,812.

HISTORIE OF DON QUIXOTE

Santísimo Sacramento, founded **five** months earlier by Fray
Alonso de la Purificación; and in 1610 appears the ever-
ready sonnet to Hurtado de Mendoza (already sung as
Meliso among the shepherds of the *Galatea*) in the *Obras del
insigne Cavallero Don Diego de Mendoza*. In 1611 he joins
the new christened Academia Selvaje (once El Parnaso), so
called after its founder, the Francisco de Silva celebrated in
the *Viaje*. Meanwhile he is busied with his twelve *Novelas* *The*
Exemplares, officially approved on August 8, 1612. The *The Exemplary*
most of them masterpieces in little, they alone had sufficed *Novels*
for fame: their influence is widespread, and their descend-
ants multiply in every literature. The adventures of
Rinconete y Cortadillo and the whimsies of *El Coloquio
de los Perros* have travelled the world over as the most
finished expressions of the picaresque genius. With them
journey *El Casamiento engañoso* and *La Tia fingida*, this
last first published at Berlin by Franceson and Wolf in
1818. Its absence from the printed collection of 1613
leaves its authenticity in question: but—who else could
have written it? No suggestion is forthcoming, and, perforce, the story ranks among Cervantes' best. In our own
day *El Licenciado Vidriera*, a marvel of ingenious fantasy,
has had the notable distinction of translation at the hands
of that accomplished Spanish scholar, M. Foulché-Delbosc; Foulché-
an odder chance moved Caspar Ens to transform the tale Delbosc
into Latin,[1] and, disguised as *Phantasio-Cratumenos sive* Caspar Ens

---

[1] *Epidorpidum*, Lib. v. Pausilipus sive tristium cogitationum & molesti-
arum Spongia variis incredibilibus ac iucundis históriis, narrationibus, factis,
dictis tam seriis quam iocosis referta et tam recreandis quam erudiendis animis
accommodata . Coloniæ, Apud Michaelem Demenium, sub signo Nominis
Iesu. Anno MDCLIX. Pp. 56-76.

THE SECOND PART OF THE

Homo Vitreus, **it** was issued **at** Köln in 1659. It **has** been said that *El Licenciado Vidriera* may be taken for the first sketch of *Don Quixote*: the idea is untenable, for internal evidence shows it to have been written after the novelist's return from Valladolid—that is to say, at least a year after the Knight's appearance in print. The germ of *Don Quixote* is to be sought, if anywhere, in the *Entremés de los Romances* (first played, it is said, with Lope's *Noche toledana* in 1604), and especially in the verses which tell the craze of Bartolo :—

> ' De leer el *Romancero*
> Ha dado en ser caballero
> Por imitar los romances,
> Y entiendo que á pocos lances
> Será loco verdadero.'

Middleton finds his account in *La Fuerza de la Sangre* and *La Gitanilla* (this last the heroine of Weber's opera, and the mother of Hugo's Esmeralda). Fletcher rifles the Spaniard with assurance and address. From *Las dos Doncellas* he lifts *Love's Pilgrimage*; from *La Señora Cornelia*, his *Chances*; from *El Casamiento*, his *Rule a Wife and Have a Wife*. And thus, in every land, freebooters of genius exploit the Castilian originals: so that a contemporary, Tirso de Molina, in his *Cigarrales de Toledo*, glories in the fame of ' nuestro español Bocacio'; and Scott, as betrayed by Lockhart, ' said ' that the *Novelas* of that author had first inspired him ' with the ambition of excelling in fiction.'

To readers in 1613 not the least interesting section of the *Novelas* was the preface, with its promise of a sequel to the Knight's adventures and to the Esquire his frolics :—' Verás,

Marginal notes: INTRO-DUCTION; Middleton; Weber; Hugo; Fletcher; Tirso; Sir Walter

xiv

HISTORIE OF DON QUIXOTE

' y con brevedad, dilatadas las hazañas de Don Quixote y
' donaires de Sancho Panza.' But there were other tasks
more pressing. Before 1613 closes, a sonnet to Diego
Rosel y Fuenllana must be despatched to Naples, where Juan
Domingo Roncallolo will produce it in his *Parte primera
de varias Aplicaciones*; and not less urgent are the futile
quatrains to Gabriel Pérez del Barrio Ángulo. This while,
Don Quixote tarries; nay, is superseded in 1614 by the
Viaje del Parnaso, an imitation from the Italian of Cesare *The Journey*
Caporali. Neither in the Dedication to Rodrigo de Tapia[1] *to Parnassus*
(then a boy of fifteen) nor in the Prologue to the Curious
Reader is there mention of the two Manchegans. They
could wait. Of more concern was it to polish the seven
stanzas in Saint Teresa's praise: these and other pieces, of
the like inspiration, to be recited in presence of Lope de
Vega at the Church of Carmen Descalzo in October 1614.
The Curious Reader draws his own inferences from in-
disputable facts. In July 1613 the Second Part had been
promised 'shortly'—' con brevedad.' It interests to observe
that the Governor her Husband dates his famous Letter to
his wife Teresa Panza 'from this Castle the twentieth of
July 1614.' A twelvemonth later than the formal pledge
given, Cervantes reaches his Thirty-Sixth Chapter: and his
book contains a Seventy-Fourth! It seems that Knight
and Squire hung heavy on their creator's hands. More:
there were fame and money for the winning on the boards.
Hence that sorry volume entitled *Ocho Comedias, y ocho* Playwright
Entremeses nuevos (1615), 'sold for a tolerable price.' That Once More

---

[1] Seven years later, Lope de Vega dedicated *El Ingrato arrepentido* to this
same Rodrigo de Tapia.

THE SECOND PART OF THE

the Licensers dallied with *Don Quixote* gives our author no pang : to the last his part of stepfather is played with perfection. And so he passes onward to fresh adventures, with the brief announcement that Don Quixote, booted and spurred, is on the road to kiss the feet of his Excellency, the Conde de Lemos.

The First Part, appearing in 1605, had succeeded as no classic but *Childe Harold* has succeeded since ; and the public looked for a sequel. As Shelton delivers the report :—
' Some more Ioviall than Saturnists, cry out ; Let 's have
' more Quixotismes : Let Don Quixote assault, and Sancho
' speake, let the rest bee what they will, this is enough.' But we have seen Cervantes absorbed in other work to which *Don Quixote* must give place. Add that his posthumous romance—' a book that dares to vie with Heliodorus '—*los*

Dreams

Trabajos de Persiles y Sigismunda, occupied him. Both the *Novelas* and the *Comedias* promise a new masterpiece to be called *Las Semanas del Jardín* ; and in the *Comedias* there is mention of a play, *El Engaño á los Ojos*, a certain triumph (if the author mistake not): so he declares himself, punning on the title :—' que (si no me engaño) le ha de dar contento.' In *Persiles*—with the death-rattle in his throat—he announces the appearance of *Las Semanas*, and *El famoso Bernardo*, and

The Second
Galatea

La Segunda Parte de la Galatea. That shepherdess was long a-coming. Promised in 1585 at the end of her First Part, she is pledged to reappear in the Sixth Chapter of the First *Don Quixote* (1605) ; the covenant is ratified in the Prologue to the Second Part (1615); and in the Dedication of *Persiles y Sigismunda* she is promised for the fourth and last time. Of these four conceptions—the *Semanas*, the *Engaño*, the

HISTORIE OF DON QUIXOTE

Bernardo, the second *Galatea*—not **one** was to take life.
Cervantes died as he had lived, brave, confident, and blithe,
prodigal of promises and invincible in hope. It delights us
to forget that our own calendar was unreformed, and to
assert that he died on the same day with Shakespeare : April
23, 1616. Like Saul and Jonathan, they 'were lovely and
' pleasant in their lives, and in their death they were not
' divided : they were swifter than eagles, they were stronger
' than lions.'

Cervantes sleeps at Madrid in the Trinitarian Convent
of the Calle de Cantarranas.[1] A year after his death
appeared the *Persiles,* with its incomparable Dedication and
Prologue.[2] 'One foot already in the stirrup,' he mounts for
the last ride. So, the instinct undimmed by pain, he quotes
with glee from an old *romance* :—

> ' Puesto ya el pié en el estribo,
> Con las ansias de la muerte,
> Gran senor ésta te escribo.'

Some hundred years later, the same note of immitigable

---

[1] The story of Cervantes' remains being hawked to and fro between the
Calle de Cantarranas and the Calle del Humilladero is another idle invention.
The convent in the Calle de Cantarranas was founded by Francisca Romero
in 1612 ; the nuns moved to the Calle del Humilladero in 1639, but returned
within two years to the Calle de Cantarranas. The facts are accurately given
by Pascual Mádoz, *Diccionario geográfico - estadístico - histórico de España*
(Madrid, 1846-50), and completely refute the current legend, which is due
to a rare slip of Navarrete's (1819), mechanically reproduced by other
biographers.

[2] The epitaph on Cervantes, which prefaces the *Persiles,* is by Francisco de
Urbina, brother-in-law of Lope de Vega. This fact lends colour to the
notion that Cervantes' mother, Lenor de Cortinas (of Barajas), and Lope's
first mother-in-law, Magdalena de Cortinas (also of Barajas), were cousins in
some degree.

THE SECOND PART OF THE

INTRO-
DUCTION
Henry
Fielding
gaiety and the same courteous air of dignity and valour
recur in the *Journal of a Voyage to Lisbon*. Like Cervantes,
Fielding too died of dropsy, and his reproduction of the great
Cervantesque manner places Captain Richard Veal nigh on
a level with that student met on the road between Esquivias
and Madrid. With the completion of the *Persiles*, the
writer's work ends: his sonnets to Juan Yagüe and to
the nun Alfonsa González de Salazar are of little moment.
His *Bernardo* and the rest are lost. Henceforth, the dust
of immortality settles on him.

II

Avellaneda
He had lived long enough to learn that no writer, however great, can afford to palter with his pledges and to trifle
with his fame. In the summer of 1614 Felipe Roberto of
Tarragona issued a small quarto entitled *Segundo Tomo del
Ingenioso Hidalgo Don Quixote de la Mancha que contiene su
tercera Salida: y es la quinta Parte de sus Aventuras.* Its
avowed author was the Licentiate Alonso Fernández de
Avellaneda, 'natural de la villa de Tordesillas.' The name
is assumed, nor can the puzzle of authorship be solved. It is
lightly said that the publication of this sham sequel was
purely malicious. But this is doubtful. If imitation be the
sincerest form of flattery, then was Avellaneda no enemy

As He Seemed
to Salvá
but a devotee. His 'fecundity of invention' is unwarily
admitted by a difficult critic like Salvá. His book was

Le Sage
hailed a triumph by Le Sage, who found the second Sancho
'plus original même que celui de Cervantes': and he manifests his good faith by producing a sleek Gallic version

Pope
that inspired six lines in Pope's *Essay on Criticism* :—

HISTORIE OF DON QUIXOTE

'Once on a time La Mancha's knight, they say,
A certain bard encount'ring on the way,
Discoursed in terms as just, with looks as sage,
As e'er could Dennis, of the Grecian stage ;
Concluding all were desperate sots and fools,
Who durst depart from Aristotle's rules.'

Germond de **Lavigne** has likewise paid his **tribute** to the imitation in **a new French** rendering. The judgment of these three experts **is** not to be dismissed curtly ; and, in truth—considered **as a mere continuation**—Avellaneda's exploit is far from contemptible. That it should lack initiative is a thing **of course ; and** even **the fervid** Lavigne confesses **his hero an** 'imitateur servile.' **Nor** may it be **gainsaid that, de-**spite his **many** merits, he shames his **model by making of** Don Quixote a commonplace lunatic **and of Sancho a plain** buffoon. Yet the plagiary **is persuaded that he carries out** Cervantes' ideas with **conspicuous success.** Accepting the theory of malice, Rosell **and Braunfels plead that Avellaneda** sought to avenge the **insult conveyed in the very name of** Sancho **Panza.** But, in that case, why should he wait nine years to take the field? The facts yield an explanation simpler, and therefore preferable. Cervantes had left his intention in doubt, and his last words are almost an invitation to another writer to continue the chronicle of the Knight Adventurous. Avellaneda took him at his word. Near upon nine years had gone, and still Cervantes lay coy, though, as he tells us, his Second Part was hoped for, and though there had been nine editions of his First. Was not it natural to infer that he had abandoned the chivalrous Alonso, even as he deserted the chaste Galatea? Here was an opportunity neglected ! That it would, sooner or later,

xix

be used was a thing most certain. Then why not by
Avellaneda ? Like enough, Avellaneda had his book already
written when, in the preface to the *Novelas*, the promise of
the genuine sequel, ' shortly,' met his eye. A magnanimous
man had laid his work aside, regretting his lost time. At
least he had been civil to him whose ideas he had pilfered.
But Avellaneda's character was beneath his talent. One of
those footpads, as Viardot says, ' qui injurient les gens qu'ils
détroussent,' he grew furious at seeing the bread taken out

of his mouth.   His preface is the outburst of a balked
schemer, the attempt of a man in the wrong to put himself
right by robustious invective. His profession, borne out by
internal evidence, that his aim and Cervantes' are one, is em-
phatic:—'Tenemos ambos un fin, que es desterrar la perniciosa
lición de los vanos libros de Cavallerías.' But he candidly
avows that his immediate object is money :—' Quéxese de mi
trabajo la ganancia que le quito.' His reference to Lope de
Vega is a blind, or at least an afterthought, of no more
pertinence than his taunts that Cervantes is now ' as old as the
Castle of San Cervantes,' that he is a surly, maimed jail-bird,
for ever in a heat with all and everything, so friendless that he
must needs write his own eulogistic Sonnets Prefatory under
cover of Prester John or the Emperor of Trebizond. The shafts

went home. Cervantes, refusing to ' be-Asse him, be-madman
him, and be-foole him,' bitterly resents the sneer at his age
and his wounds. With his infallible insight, he seizes upon
his enemy's admission, and returns an angry defiance :—' Tell
' him too, that for his menacing, that with his booke he
' will take away all my gain, I care not a straw for him.'
Mayhap there was a real basis for the grievance that

HISTORIE OF DON QUIXOTE

Avellaneda states :—'El ofender á mí.' The rational probability is that he was a petty playwright, hit by a flying
shot in the First Part, who imagined in his self-importance
that the attack on the dramatists was directed at him. But,
as he was buoyed by the hope of booty, there had been no
abusive prologue, had not Cervantes published that he was
about to claim his own. Clearly it had been impolitic to
attack the true author of *Don Quixote*. The less said of *him*,
the greater the chance of passing the spurious continuation
as the true.

III

Critics, commentators, and mare's-nesters at large, have
vainly sought for Avellaneda among the important figures of
the time. More probable is it that he was a needy scribbler
writing to fill his purse, not to gratify his spite ; and the
mystery that enshrouds him is the consequence of his rank
obscurity. Suspicion has fastened on the names of Aliaga, the
King's confessor, and of Lope de Vega. Cervantes says of his
rival that ' his language is Arragonian : for sometimes he
writes without Articles.' Now, Aliaga was an ' Arragonian.'
The difficulty is to find him a grievance in the First Part.
Acquainted with Lope, he was not himself a dramatist : so
the plea is invented that he was aggrieved by the character
of Sancho Panza—his own nickname—which brought upon
him ridicule and contempt. This explanation explains
nothing. Cervantes' offence, if it were ever real, must
have been unwitting. When he was writing *Don Quixote*,
he could never have heard of Aliaga, then a simple monk
unknown outside his convent at Zaragoza. Further : for one
who felt outraged by the creation of Sancho, it was surely

a mad revenge to make Sancho grosser, more disreputable, more offensive! 'The very same Sancho of whom you 'speake,' writes Cervantes as interpreted by Shelton, 'must 'be some notorious rogue, some greedy-gut, and notable 'theefe.' Again, the evidence for the nickname is bad. Aliaga is once called Sancho Panza in a satire by Juan de

Tassis y Peralta Muñatones, Conde de Villamediana, under the date of 1621. But it is not alleged that he was ever so called before or after; and it is obvious that, in this instance, the name was about sixteen years older than its appropria-

tion. Resourceful as ever, Pellicer comes pat with certain verses which, if they prove anything, prove that Aliaga was not Avellaneda. For if, as the ingenious critic assumes, Avellaneda be here referred to as Sancho Panza, it follows that he competed in a poetic tourney at Zaragoza in 1614. Now, it happens that the list of the competitors survives, and Aliaga's name is not contained in it. It may be worth while to refute another argument, most confidently used by supporters of the Aliaga theory. There is alleged to exist a striking identity of style (not apparent to the profane) between Avellaneda's book and the *Venganza*

de la Lengua española, a scurrilous reply to Quevedo's *Cuento de Cuentos*. And the syllogism is eked out with courage.

It is positively known, asserts Rosell—'se sabe de positivo' —that Aliaga wrote the *Venganza*. It is not so. 'Se sabe de positivo' nothing of the kind: for the solid reason that Aliaga had been more than a twelvemonth in his grave when Quevedo issued the *Cuento de Cuentos*. Aliaga died on December 3, 1626: the *Cuento* first appeared at Barcelona in 1629. Again, the *Venganza* quotes that 'infernal libro,'

Quevedo's *Sueños*, which was not published till 1627. So
much for the connexion between Avellaneda and Aliaga on
the one hand and Aliaga and Cervantes on the other.

It remains to consider the case of Lope de Vega. Of all contemporary writers, he was the least open to the temptation
which overcame Avellaneda. The idol of his nation, he could
coin money as he chose : for all his writings sold. But the
essential condition was that they should bear his name. Thus,
he was careful to avow the works of Tomé de Burguillos. **That
he wrote the** spurious continuation of *Don Quixote* for greed
of gain is an absurdity. Had he wished to chasten Cervantes,
he had gone to work very differently. Connected, it may be,
by marriage, the two had been friends till the publication of
the *Dragontea* sonnet in 1602. A breach occurred in 1603,
and it is sought to saddle Lope with the responsibility. Facts
cannot be adjusted to this theory. In the famous letter declaring that nobody is 'so foolish as to praise *Don Quixote*,'
Lope proceeds to say that satire is to him 'as odious as are
my little books to Almendárez or my plays to Cervantes.' It
is to be **noted** that in the *Viaje* Cervantes stoops to flatter
Almendárez—'**su** ilustre musa.' The sonnet—'Lope dicen
que vino'—in the Colombina Library at Seville is adjudged
by Señor **Asensio** to Cervantes; and, despite the thing's
vulgarity, **this** ascription is probable. Barrera proffers a
likely theory : that the sonnet was an impromptu, and was
handed about, and that Lope got wind of it; hence his letter
to the Duque de Sessa (or, some hold, to an anonymous
doctor). Howbeit, the earliest public attack is delivered by
Cervantes. In the Prologue to his First Part he says, with a
sneer which Shelton conveys :—'So likewise shall my Book

' want sonnets at the beginning, at least such sonnets whose
' Authors bee Dukes, Marquesses, Earles, Bishops, Ladies,
' or famous Poets.' The jape is directed at Lope's *Rimas* with
its prefatory pieces by the Príncipe de Fez, the Duque de
Osuna, the Marqués de la Adrada, the Conde de Villamor,
and more nobles: the 'Ladies' being none other than that
Marcela Trillo de Armenta and that Isabel de Figueroa
who wrote preliminary verses for *El Isidro*. Cervantes proclaims his 'invective against Bookes of Knighthood, a subject
' whereof Aristotle never dreamed, Saint Basil said nothing,
' Cicero never heard any word.' By an unlucky coincidence
these three—Aristotle, Saint Basil, Cicero—are quoted by
Lope de Vega in *El Isidro*. 'Neither have I any thing to
' cite on the margent, or note in the end,' scoffs Cervantes,
' and much lesse doe I know what Authors I follow, to put
' them at the beginning as the custome is, by one letter
' of the A B C beginning with Aristotle, and ending in

Parodies
' Xenophon, or in Zoylus or Zeuxis.' A palpable hit!
Lope's *El Isidro* is seamed with ostentatious marginal notes,
and *El Peregrino en su Patria* displays a catalogue of
authors cited in alphabetical array. Nor does Cervantes
stop here. He provides ' an other notable notation, saying

and
' the river Tagus was so called of a king of Spaine, it
' takes its beginning from such a place, and dies in the
' Ocean Seas, kissing first the Walles of the famous Citie
' of Lisborne: And some are of opinion that the sands

Jibes
' thereof are of gold, etc.' This is a precise transcript of a
passage in Lope's *Arcadia*. Cervantes continues:—' If of
' the instability of friends, thou hast at hand Cato freely
' offering his distichon :—

xxiv

HISTORIE OF DON QUIXOTE

> ' " Donec eris *felix* multos numerabis amicos.
> Tempora si fuerint nubila, solus eris." '

The pedant triumphs in his recognition of a passage from
the *Tristia*; but the writer thinks not of Ovid nor of
Dionysius Cato. His point is made when he reminds his
reader that Félix is Lope's name. Once more in the clipped
décimas of Urganda the admonition intrudes :—

> ' No indiscretos hierogli—
> Estampes en el escu—.'

These 'emblems vain' are incontestably the nineteen castles on   Lope's **Arms**
Lope's shield, as given in the *Angélica* and the *Dragontea* of
1602, in the *Arcadia* of 1603, and in the *Peregrino* of 1604.
It smacks of blasphemy to think that Lope's mistress, the
Manchegan Lucinda, is hidden beneath the obvious anagram   His Mistress
of Dulcinea : she with 'a little unsavorie sent, somewhat
rammish and manlike.' But the transformation of the
'Unicus aut peregrinus' of the *Peregrino's* title-page into
the 'Único y solo' of Amadís' burlesque sonnet is patent.
In the Twenty-First Chapter of the Fourth Book, Lope's
worst play, *La Ingratitud vengada*, is excepted from the
general censure. Yet, writes Cervantes, 'strangers, which
' doe with much punctuality observe the method of Comedies,
' hold us to be rude and ignorant.' Thus, with fine adroit-   His Plays
ness, he uses against Lope the very words of the *Arte nuevo
de hacer Comedias* :—

> ' Mas ninguno de todos llamar puedo
> Más *bárbaro* que yo, pues contra el arte,
> Me atrevo á dar preceptos, y me dejo
> Llevar de la vulgar corriente adonde
> Me llamen *ignorante* Italia y Francia.'

THE SECOND PART OF THE

This persistence in attack shows Cervantes' disposition
towards his popular rival. Vainly, in his Second Part,
does he profess that 'I adore his wit, admire his workes,
and'—with a knavish glance at the private life of Lope
who, like himself, was neither saint nor Joseph—'his continuall vertuous imployment.' Good taste apart, there is
no more reason to object to these assaults on Lope than to
condemn Lope's sole ripost. Yet to Cervantes belongs the
credit of publishing the quarrel to the world; and the world
is flattered by the confidence. Contemptuous of brawls,

His Retort
Contemptu-
ous
Lope's resentment is shown mainly by disdainful coldness.
A hundred methods of reply were ready to his hand, for
Cervantes was far from invulnerable; yet we know that in
1612 he speaks kindly of his assailant. But that he wrote
Avellaneda's text (which delivers no assault against Cervantes)
or his preface (which does) is a theory unsupported by a
tittle of evidence. It were as reasonable to charge Cervantes with treachery in the matter of the Conde de Lemos,
to whom Lope had once been private secretary. A stroke of
easy sophistry, and Cervantes is indicted an intriguer: the
fact being that, in each instance, the accusation is ridiculous.
On Cervantes' own showing, his foe was an 'Arragonian':
Lope was a Madrileño. And his accusers refute themselves.
Their first contention is that Avellaneda published with a
deliberate purpose of fraud; their second, that his aim was
to ruin the characters out of spite to their original author.
The two arguments are incompatible: if one be true, the
other must be false. Again, they lay it down that Avellaneda's is the worst book in the world; and, in the next
breath, aver that the most likely man to have written

it was Lope de Vega—save Cervantes himself, the greatest
figure in Spanish literature. In **truth,** the charge against
Lope has nothing to sustain it but the fact that—once, and
once only, in a private letter—that spoiled child of the His Innocence
Spanish public fretted under Cervantes' satire, and pouted
at the vogue of *Don Quixote.* It is most unlikely that,
watched by many toadies and more enemies, he could have
escaped identification for twenty years. Not less unlikely
is a conspiracy of silence among the publishers, the licensers,
the transcribers, printers, and compositors who were in the
secret. **Still** more incredible is it that Pedro de Torres
Rámila **in** his *Spongia* and the host of lampooners should
fail to find the skeleton with their muck-rakes. Lastly, it
is inconceivable that an old soldier of the Armada should
jeer the wounds of an old soldier of Lepanto. That Lope
expressed no displeasure at the attacks on Cervantes is
true: but why should he? Cervantes never rebuked Lope's
ruffianly libellers. Meanwhile the theory-mongers ask you The Madness
to reject **to-day** the nostrum of yesterday. Thus Benjumea of them that
Theorise
in 1861 proves (with much erudition) Avellaneda to be a against
Dominican monk, Blanco de Paz; and in 1875 (with yet Reason
more erudition) reveals him as another Dominican, Andrés
Pérez. Adolfo de Castro—the forger of *El Buscapié,*
modestly fathered by him on Cervantes—first demonstrates
that Avellaneda must be Aliaga and no other; and, later,
holds—('with equal confidence and enthusiasm,' says Señor
Máinez drily)—that the culprit is Juan Ruiz de Alarcón.
Señor Máinez himself thought it certain—'nosotros tenemos
por cierto'—that Lope de Vega was the offender; but that
was in 1876. It remains to say plainly that, if Cervantes

did well to be angry, he had done better to exclude his
irritation from his text. Dignity apart, he has conferred a
factitious importance upon Avellaneda and Avellaneda's book.
The false sequel is still reprinted, and is **read by** many
who take it for a vehicle of grave ridicule, **like** *Joseph
Andrews*; and Cervantes' critics and commentators waste
themselves in a jack-o'-lanthorn chase after a writer of no
great brilliancy, whose sole title to importance is that he
unwittingly obliged Cervantes to complete his masterpiece
and utterly establish his right to immortality.

IV

For assuredly the effect of Avellaneda's appearance was to
The Result hasten his hand. But for the intrusion of the 'Arragonian,'
Don Quixote might have been discarded in favour of *Las
Semanas del Jardín*; or, at best, had remained unfinished
while Cervantes was inventing a final burlesque in the pastoral sort. A trace of this fatuous intention survives in the
Sixty-Seventh Chapter:—'Ile buy sheepe, and all things fit
' for our pastorall vocation, and calling my selfe by the name
' of the Shepheard Quixotiz, and thou the Shepheard Pansino,
' we will walke up and down the Hills, thorow Woods
' and Meadowes, singing and versifying. . . . I beleeve the
' Bachelor Samson, and Master Nicholas the Barber will no
' sooner have seene it, but they will turn shepheards with
' us: and pray God the Vicar have not a minde to enter
' into the sheep-coat too, for hee is a merry Lad and jolly.'
The Second To such pale designs Avellaneda's impertinence put an
Part end, and the true *Don Quixote* was issued in the winter of

xxviii

HISTORIE OF DON QUIXOTE

1615. **The** close is hurried, confused, unworthy of the rest.
Here Cervantes shows at his worst, overcome by temper, mismanaging his characters, neglecting them solely that 'the ' world shall see what a lyar this moderne Historiographer ' is.' The screed of abuse is tedious. Cervantes so far loses his self-respect as to credit his enemy with a Second Edition, a slip that misled Ebert. He denounces the 'filthy and obscene things' in his rival's work. 'Let it,' he clamours, 'let it be cast into the very lowest pit of Hell.' And the very Devil **himself** declares that 'it is so vile a Book that, had I my ' self expressly composed it, I could never have encountred ' worse.' But the essential part of the story is unaffected. To the Fifty-Ninth Chapter no book was ever more successful in disproving the truth of Sansón Carrasco's report that 'Second Parts are never good.' The enchantments of the Trifaldi are plainly modelled after *Esplandián* and *Lisuarte*, the Fifth and Seventh of the *Amadís* series; but, on the whole, the burlesque of *Amadís* is less close, the plan is ampler, the variety of incident is richer, and the development shows a finer sense of finish. Considered as an exercise in style, the Second Part outshines the First at all points. The episode of Marcela, with its reasonings borrowed from Castiglione's *Il Cortigiano*, is spotted with *cultismo*, as also are many of the speeches of Cardenio and Dorotea. Save in copies of verses or in speeches like the Trifaldi's, intended to bring contempt upon Góngora and his horde of verbal contortionists, the mincing affectations of the *culto* sect are mostly absent from the Second. As the burlesque of the Knight-Errantries is let drop, so the verbose parodies of Feliciano de Silva and his brethren vanish with

e

INTRO-
DUCTION

Construction

them. Again, the construction is incomparably more solid, and the improvement reacts upon the writing. The author admits that his interminable insertions are a fault in art, and henceforth he prepares his episodes and incidents with a vigilant eye for probability, conviction, and dramatic effect. That is a sound judgment which holds the First Part wealthier in broad farce, the Second in the higher comedy. But, in a letter to Southey (August 19, 1825), Lamb blasphemes

Charles Lamb

contrariwise :—'Marry, when somebody persuaded Cervantes ' that he meant only fun, and put him upon writing that ' unfortunate Second Part with the confederacies of that ' unworthy duke and most contemptible duchess, Cervantes ' sacrificed his instinct to his understanding.' Apart from metaphysical differences between instinct and understand-

Characters

ing, the portrait of the Duchess—the Master's sole great lady—ranks among the Master's triumphs. Ginés de Pasa-monte reappears, more brilliant, more witty in intention, ' his left eye, and halfe his cheeke covered with a patch of ' green Taffata,' his 'prophesying Ape and the Motion of ' Melisendra' both at hand. The loss of Palomeque is more than repaid by the discovery of the great Carrasco, Bachelor, 'Knight of the Looking-glasses' and of the White Moon. To him succeeds the not less sapient Graduate of Osuna, Doctor Pedro Recio de Agüero, rich in precedents and aphorisms from 'Hypocrates our master, North-starre and light of Physick.'

The Knight

A notable development is offered in Don Quixote's case. Cervantes has lived with his hero so long that he has learned to honour and to love him, and to spare him the ignominious buffetings and discomfitures of the First

xxx

HISTORIE OF DON QUIXOTE

Part. **The Knight is** still the matchless madman, crazed
on the single·point of chivalry, intimate with the heroic
warriors of historic repute, and prompt to describe them as
he knew those paladins in the flesh. Thus, of the master
of them all:—'I may say, that with these very eyes I
' have beheld Amadis de Gaul, who was a goodly tall man, His Amadís
' well complectioned, had a broad beard, and blacke, an
' equall countenance betwixt milde and sterne, a man of
' **small** discourse, slow to anger, and soone appeased.' Or,
take Reinaldos de Montalbán, as he knew him :—'Broad- His Reinaldos
' **faced, his** complexion high, quick and full eyed, very
' exceptious and extremely cholericke, a lover of theeves and
' debaucht company.' And the reminiscence of Roland is
precise, minute as intimacy warrants :—'Of a meane stature, His Roland
' broad-shouldered, somewhat bow-legged, Abourne Bearded,
' his body hayrie, and his lookes threatning.' Save for his
one slight foible, the Ingenious Gentleman is the happiest
wit of all La Mancha. None meeter than he for acute discourse with Don Diego, the 'Knight of the Green Cassock';
none apter and readier for criticism on the Laws of Gloss-
ing, wherein his subtlety drives the young poet Lorenzo to
declare :—'I desire to catch you in an absurdity, but cannot :
for still **you slip** from mee like an Eele.' Even in his
maddest moments, the second Don Quixote shows himself a
thought more critical, more exigent of proof, more sensible
to sight. In the First Part, the slashed wine-bag **was** ques-
tionless a decapitated Giant; in the Second, the **Dulcinea**
fabled by Sancho remains—what she **was**—'a Countrey-
' wench, and not very well-favoured, for shee **was blub-fac'd,**
' and flat-nosed.' The Knight develops a **genuine human**

THE SECOND PART OF THE

weakness in his bedizenment of what had passed in Montesinos' Cave. Much frequenting of Sancho Panza's company
has led him to this pass; and his own remark on Sancho's
great recital proves him of uneasy conscience:—'Sancho,
' since you will have us beleeve all that you have seen in
' Heaven, I pray beleeve all that I saw in Montesino's Cave,
' and I say no more.' But the final triumph of Cervantes'
The Squire art is the admirable, deathless, Sancho Panza. And that
this personage was a peculiar favourite with his creator is
shown by the violent contempt which Cervantes pours on
Avellaneda's caricature. 'Pray God,' says the true man
on hearing of his counterfeit, 'pray God, as he calls mee
Glutton, he say not that I am a Drunkard too.' His
noble mendacity is never at fault: in fact, it furnishes
the principal motive of the Second Part. From chapter
to chapter he develops to the perfection of maturity, less
clownish, more convincing, always preparing himself for his
high destiny in Barataria. And his belief in the mirage
of the Island and its Governorship is fed by cunning fore-
tastes of joy. There is that blissful abode of four days
at the Castle of the Knight of the Green Cassock, where
Sancho 'liked wondrous well of Don Diego's plentifull
provision.' There is, again, the Wedding Feast of the
rich Camacho, the invention which was to link the name
Mendelssohn of Cervantes with that of Mendelssohn:—'Six halfe
' Olive - buts, and every one was a very Shambles of
' meat, they had so many whole sheepe soking in them
' which were not seen, as if they had beene Pigeons, the
' flayed Hares, and pulled Hens that were hung upon the
' trees, to bee buried in the pots, were numberlesse; birds

HISTORIE OF DON QUIXOTE

'and fowle of divers sorts infinite.' And both Man and Master take their honourable entertainment by the Duke and Duchess as confirmation strong of their inimitable vocation.

Done on a higher level of art, the development of the Second Part proceeds logically from the First; and the increased urbanity of treatment, tone, and episode justifies —were justification needed—the change of Don Quixote's title from *Hidalgo* to *Caballero*. The humour remains **Humour** simple and direct as ever, self-contained, unmoved, and grave. Cervantes is little skilled in the humour which blends pathos and laughter by means of minute touches and subtle innuendo. His great effects are broad and ample; they spring from the contrasts of incongruous circumstance viewed in the dry light of satiric observa- tion. A master of unwinking irony, he lives by virtue of Qualities his general truthfulness, his brilliant colour, his inexhaust- ible invention of situation, his transfiguring vision, his achievement in portraiture, and his noble simplicity. Ideas he has none; or if he have, they are mostly wrong. He remains **what he** was at the outset: a man of genius, a rare contriver of incident, a Spaniard penetrated with **the average** sentiment and opinion of his age. A con- summate artist in humorous transcription, he presents a living picture of manners, untinctured by sham philosophy and sham poetry. To the ineffectual critic there remains the task of solving imaginary mysteries. It cannot be too strongly emphasised that Cervantes offers an image of life, not a fatuous conundrum. In the First Part he approves himself the brilliant student **of nature** with a turn for

INTRO-DUCTION

Failings

eloquent commonplace, as in the excellent tirade on the exercises of Arms and Letters. And in the Second Part he shows no intellectual—as opposed to artistic—progress. It is in perfect keeping with his character and his view of life that he should hate the Moors, and should applaud their expulsion. That is Cervantes the citizen, as we know him, and should wish him to be. His appreciation of their picturesque value is always present to Cervantes the writer, the observer of whim, custom, and social ritual. A certain

Melancholy

undertone of melancholy has been perceived in his Second Part, and the ingenious would explain it by assuming that he foresaw his country's decline. Nothing in the world is less likely. Like most humorists of the first order, he was a Tory to the marrow, and by consequence his country was to him invincible and impregnable. Such dejection as he displays is rather due to increasing age and failing health than to political discouragement. The farcical spirit was an essential in his genius; but, even so, it dwindled with his strength. But, though at whiles he moralise with that touch of sadness natural to a man of many years and trials,

Dignity and Gentleness

for whom life is only retrospect, the absence of bitterness from his general estimate is, as Señor Valera notes, conspicuous. No single character of his brain is wholly mean or odious; and, as his heroes flaunt their foibles, so do his villains blunder into virtue unawares. He has found life a good estate and a gallant show: and so he has the courage to present it. In so much, posterity is his debtor everlast-

Reward

ingly. And he has his reward: as universal, generic types, Don Quixote and Sancho Panza rank with Shakespeare's men, and Homer's.

xxxiv

HISTORIE OF DON QUIXOTE

His reputation was no more to make. The *Aprobación* of Márquez Torres to the Second Part is evidence of fame. On February 25, 1615, the members of the French Embassy fell in with Sandoval's chaplain :—'Scarce did they hear 'Miguel de Cervantes' name when they rehearsed the esteem 'in which his works were held both in France and in border- 'ing realms—the *Galatea* (which one of them had almost 'by heart), the First Part of this, and the *Novelas*.' Oudin's French version of 1614 had made Don Quixote a Parisian, and a translation of the Second Part was in demand. Accordingly in 1618, 'traduicte fidelement en nostre Langue par F. de Rosset,' at Paris, in the Rue Saint-Jacques, there Rosset was published by Jacques de Clou and Denis Moreau the *Seconde Partie de l'histoire de l'ingenieux et redovtable Cheualier, Dom-Qvichot de la Manche*. Nor was the Knight of Knights forgotten in England. An entry in the Register of the Stationers' Company indicates a false alarm. Edward '5° Decembris, 1615. Master Blount. Entred for his Blount 'Copie vnder the hande of Master Sanford and Master 'Swinhoe warden. The second part of Don Quixote vjᵈ.' This cannot, however, be a rendering of the true Second Part, since—finally licensed by Doctor Gutierre de Cetina on November 5, 1615—it was not given to the public till, at earliest, the very close of the year. In any case, it is a sheer impossibility that the book could have been printed off, sent from Madrid to London, and translated between November 5 and December 5 of the same year. Even the brilliant Shelton needed 'the space of forty daies' for his rendering of the First **Part; and the** Second is of

equal length. The copy delivered to Master Sanford
and Master Swinhoe in December, 1615, was unquestion-
ably Avellaneda's counterfeit (published the year before),
which had imposed on Master Thomas Shelton as on
Master Edward Blount. That no such translation is
known is to be explained by the abandonment of the enterprise on the appearance of the authentic work. But the
'vj^{d}' paid for the counterfeit is made to serve by the frugal

Blount. The Second Part—with a Reprint of the First—
was published in 1620.[1] Its Epistle Dedicatory to Bucking-
ham declares it for 'a bashfull stranger, newly arrived in
'English, having originally had the fortune to be borne
'commended to a Grande of Spain'—the Conde de Lemos—
'and, by the way of translation, the grace to kisse the hands
'of a great Ladie of France.' The great Ladie of France is
manifestly none other than the Duchesse de Luynes to whom
Rosset dedicated his rendering with this compliment :—'l'ay
'de volontez de faire paroistre que vous estes toute la gloire
'de notre siecle, de mesme que toute la honte du passé, et
'la plus grande enuie du futur.'

The absence from the title-page of Shelton's name has led
some to declare that the first English translation of the

---

[1] The *princeps* of 1612 and the reprint of 1620 are easily distinguished.
The first contains twelve unnumbered leaves of prefatory matter, 549 pages of
text, and two final leaves unnumbered ; the second has thirteen preliminary
unnumbered leaves, 572 pages of text, and two final leaves unnumbered. The
princeps is divided into parts—first, second, third, and fourth ; the 1620 edition
substitutes 'booke' for 'part,' to avoid confusion between the First and
Second Parts on one side, and the parts of the First Part on the other. That
useful distinction is maintained in the present reprint. Further, in the *princeps*
each page is enclosed in black lines, which in the first reprint are confined to
the headlines.

HISTORIE OF DON QUIXOTE

Second Part came from another hand than his; and the contention is supported by the assertion that the later effort shows some diminution of dash and spirit. The original Spanish has the same charge to answer, and the translation perforce reflects its qualities. No contemporary ever doubted that the Englishing was Shelton's work, and the reprints of 1652-72 and 1731 (as well as Stevens's botch of 1700-6) bear Shelton's name. But more convincing proof of his responsi-

bility exists in the absolute identity of mannerism and in the fact that the same errors of rendering appear in both parts. *Trance* is a case in point: the translator never chances upon the right word, which is 'emergency.' As in the First Part 'este tan impensado trance' = 'this unexpected trance,' so in the Second 'este último y forzoso trance' = 'this last and forcible trance'; and 'el rigoroso trance nunca visto' is naturally given as 'the rigorous trance never seen,' for was not 'all the trances of warfare' the foregoing equivalent of 'todos los trances de la guerra'? So the same blunder recurs in one chapter upon another. And as with *trance* and 'trance,' so with *sucesos* and 'successes.' Where 'otros sucesos' was accepted as 'other successes,' 'deste suceso' inevitably finds favour as 'out of this successe.' Again, take *desmayarse*. The translator of the First Part was fain to be content with his 'mutable and dismaied traytresse,' and the Second follows with an exact servility: so that 'dió muestras de desmayarse' is delivered as 'shee made shew of dismaying,' and 'la desmayada Altisidora' takes place as 'the dismayed Altisidora.' In both Parts *discreto* figures as 'discreet,' *honestad* as 'honesty,' *suspensos* as 'suspended,' and *admirados* as

f

THE SECOND PART OF THE

'admired'; and in no case does the translator vary from his self-imposed convention. Who but Shelton could so 'fig you like the bragging Spaniard'? That the two Parts come from two hands is manifestly incredible.

As with the First Part, it is possible to identify the text upon which Shelton worked. Writing in *The Quarterly Review* (January 1886), Froude selects a passage in the First Chapter which he scorns as typical of the Sheltonian method. He quotes the rendering of 'que por sólo este pecado que hoy comete Sevilla' (in Shelton = 'that for this dayes offence I will eat up all Sevill'); and he forthwith resolves that 'Shelton, working with extreme haste, mistook *comete* for *comeré*.' Now, this is the kind of desperate guesswork to which the raw amateur is given. Belied as 'acute' and 'ingenious,' it passes for sound doctrine with the vulgar, and takes place as a Fortieth Article. The example chosen in derision of Shelton proves a happy illustration of Froude's own methods. To none but a ferocious partisan—as Froude was ever—would it have seemed a heinous crime had Shelton been convicted of misreading a single letter in a single word; but in truth he did nothing of the kind, and the instance serves but to show—not the translator's but—the commentator's ineptitude. Comparative textual criticism was not for Froude; and he had probably been staggered by the rendering in Rosset:—'Ie deuoreray Seuille, pour le peché qu'elle commet.' It becomes clear, not that Shelton translated from Rosset (as some have feigned) but, that both Shelton and Rosset translated from a common text, and reproduced its error. And so it was. For his First Part Shelton had worked from the Edition given out at Brussels

xxxviii

HISTORIE OF DON QUIXOTE

in 1607 by Roger Velpius. The English market derived its
Castilian books by way of the Low Countries—not straight
from Spain. The practice endured, and for his Second Part
Shelton used the reprint—the first ever issued—published,
with a *Permiso* dated February 4, 'En Bruselas Por Huberto
Antonio, impresor jurado cerca del Palacio, 1616.' And
there (p. 8) the clause denounced by Froude stands a monu-
ment to Shelton's integrity and to his critic's uninquiring
ignorance :—'Que por solo este pecado que oy comerè
Seuilla.'

In one respect a change is to be noted in Shelton's attitude
to his original. Grown older, more critical, and more in-
dependent, in his shoulder-notes he reveals himself a man
of reading, and even of difficult taste ; but his annotations
are not always final. Cervantes writes :—'Y sé, como dice
el gran Poeta castellano nuestro,' and quotes three lines from
Garcilaso de la Vega's elegy on Alva's brother, Bernar-
dino de Toledo. Not content with transcribing the phrase as
'And I know what our great Castilian Poet said,' Shelton
volunteers the tidings that the verses are Boscán's, ignoring
the fact that Boscán, though he wrote in Castilian, was a
Catalan. A like mishap befalls the obliging Scholiast in
the Eighteenth Chapter. Entering Don Diego de Miranda's
house, Don Quixote notes the Tobosan wine-jars in the
cellar, and exclaims :—

> '¡ O dulces prendas, por mi mal halladas !
> Dulces y alegres cuando Dios queria.'

The verses are quoted from Garcilaso de la Vega's tenth
sonnet, in imitation of Virgil's 'Dulces exuviæ, dum fata
deusque sinebant.' Shelton, never **at** a loss, declares them

'A beginning of a sonnet in *Diana de Monte Mayor*, which
D. Q. heere raps out upon a sodaine.' One has a suspicion
that 'Monte Mayor' has been transformed from a man to the
title of a pastoral; but curious inquiry were rash! The
commentary grows in force and liberality. Don Quixote
enlarges on the honourable treatment due to soldiers

Patriotism   grown grey under arms:—'Neither are they dealt with-
'all like those mens Negars, that when they are olde
'and can doe their Masters no service, they (under colour of
'making them free) turne them out of doores, and make them
'slaves to hunger, from which nothing can free them but
'death.' The translator's patriotic gorge rises at the
recorded infamy, and forthwith appears the peremptory
note:—'He describes the right subtill and cruell nature of
his damned Country-men.' In the margin of the Forty-
Fourth Chapter the idea recurs with a variant:—'He
'describes the right custome of his hungry countrey men in
'generall.' And a shoulder-note to the Fifty-Ninth Chapter
applauds 'a good Character, of a lying, beggarly, vaine-
glorious Spanish Oast.' The spirit of nationalism glows
at the simple statement that 'encogió Sancho los hombros,'
or 'Sancho shrunk his shoulders' (as who should say
shrugged them); and there arrives a spirited comment on
'the Spaniards lowsie humility.' These are instances out
of many.

Idiosyncrasies   There are other tokens of a fearless mind. In Montesinos'
Cave the companion of the spell-bound Dulcinea seeks to
borrow six *reales* (or, as the large-handed Shelton renders
the account, 'three shillings') 'upon this new Cotton Petticote'; and Don Quixote, who had but four *reales*—say ten

pence at par—upon him, vows to **disenchant** his fair, and
' not to be quiet, till I have travelled all the seven partitions
' of the world, more punctually then Prince Don Manuel
' of Portugall.' Dom Pedro seems the likelier man : he whose
travels in Europe and the East, recounted by his companion
Gomez de Sancto Estevan, were published, more than a
century later (1554) at Lisbon. The book was as popular
in Spanish **as** in Portuguese, and undoubtedly it had its
place **in** Don Quixote's library. The rover, Dom Pedro,—
brother **of** Prince Henry the Navigator and of Ferdinand,
the *Príncipe Constante* of Calderón's play,—was grandson of
John of Gaunt ; and you love to think that Cervantes, foresee-
ing an English translator, introduced the name with intent
to conciliate a national prejudice. The wile failed. Shelton
bites his thumb at Portugal, deposes Dom Pedro, and proclaims his own creature, Manuel, instead. At sight of the
words ' lelilíes al uso de moros,' the patriot is not content
with rendering ' Moorish cries '; he drives the point home
with a marginal parallel :—' Like the cries of the Wild Irish.'
His fastidious taste rejects more than one petty quip. In
the Forty-first Chapter the Knight tells his Esquire that
' aunque **tonto,** eres hombre verídico '—' though thou beest
a fool, yet **I** think thou art honest '—or, more exactly,
' true blue.' The reply shows that *verídico* is taken for **a**
diminutive of *verde* :—' No soy verde, sino moreno, dijo
Sancho ; pero aunque fuera de mezcla, cumpliera mi
palabra.' Preserving the point of the jest, the answer
should read :—' I am not blue, but brown ; yet, were
I piebald, I 'd keep my word.' Shelton examines the
passage frowningly, rejects it with disgrace, **and** passes

sentence:—'Heere I left out a line or two of a dull
' conceit; so it was no great matter; for in English it could
' not bee expressed.' Familiar with Italian models only,
he boggles at Spanish assonants; and, being engaged

on Don Quixote's song—*Suelen las Fuerzas del Amor*
—he is forced to annotate that 'These verses and the
' former of Altisidora are made to bee scurvy on purpose
' by the Author, fitting the occasions and the subjects, so
' he observes neyther verse nor rime.' In the Sixty-ninth
Chapter are introduced two octaves sung by the 'Carkeise
of a goodly Youth clad like a Romane': the first written
by Cervantes himself, the second lifted from Garcilaso de la
Vega's Third Eclogue. That Shelton can have ignored the
provenance is well-nigh impossible since, in the next Chapter,
Don Quixote pointedly questions the owner of the 'Carkeise':
—'What have the Stanza's of Garcilasse to doe with the
death of this Damozell?' But, with the testimony that the
youth 'sung these two Stanza's following,' honour is satisfied,
and judgment follows in these terms:—'Which I likewise
' omit as being basely made on purpose, and so not worth
' the translation.'

Of an idiom Shelton will sometimes show a brutal disdain,
as in the Tenth Chapter. Sancho bungles the proverb:—
'Do pensáis que hay tocinos no hay estacas'; or 'where you
' think there are flitches, there are no pegs.' The English
version puts the point aside with 'Sweet meat must have
sowre sauce.' A few lines later, Sancho uses the saying,
' Oxte, puto, allá darás rayo,' abbreviating the general form:
' —allá daras rayo en casa de Tamayo.' Góngora employs the
catch as a refrain and Lope (it is said) as the title of a play;

xlii

HISTORIE OF DON QUIXOTE

but Shelton is satisfied to write 'Ware Hawk, ware Hawk,'
without more exertion. Again, the translator trips when con-
fronted with :—'¡ Xo! que te estrego, burra de mi suegro.'
A variant of the same occurs in the First Act of the *Celestina*:
—'¡ Xo! que te estriego, asna coja.' Mabbe gives it precisely Mabbe
as 'I will curry you for this geare, you lame Asse.' But
Shelton fares ill. A glance at Rosset's 'Fais que ie t'estrille, Rosset
asnesse de mon beau pere' had perhaps enabled him to
anticipate Mabbe. The precaution omitted, he frankly
surrenders, and the proverb remains a puzzle to all
English translators of *Don Quixote* till Ormsby solves it. Ormsby
The daughter of Diego de la Llana, discovered wander-
ing at midnight 'clad in a man's habit,' explains to the
Governor Sancho Panza that she and her brother sallied
forth 'guiados de nuestro mozo y desbaratado discurso.'
The obvious meaning is 'urged by our young and reckless
impulse'; but the trap is baited with the word *mozo*, which
is used indifferently as adjective or noun. Jervas, succeeding Jervas
Shelton, stumbles into the ditch, and doggedly avows that
'guided by our footboy and our own unruly fancies, we
traversed the whole town.' His warier predecessor scents
the difficulty, and ignores the phrase.

To point to his shortcomings is an easy task, for his fine
carelessness is always constant. What though 'justa literaria' Intrepidity
appear as a 'true study' in one place if it be rightly given
in another? What though 'Buen corazón quebranta mala
ventura' be cut down to 'Faint heart never, etc.'? What
though 'un conejo albar' be presented as 'a perboyled Coney,'
comida as a 'Comedy,' *mostrenco* as 'a Setting-dogg,' *par
Diez* as 'by ten'? The pedant may enlarge the list at will,

xliii

THE SECOND PART OF THE

and rectify with his *podenco* or *comedia*. For those 'not in
the humour to play at Boyes play'—so Shelton reads it—
it is a more grateful task to note his many successes,
his feats of daring, his flights of invention, his bursts of

humour. 'Yo os lo vestiré como un palmito,' says Teresa
Panza; and, with a visible twinkle, comes the sentence 'Ile
clad him like a Date-leafe.' 'Que me matan si nos ha de
suceder cosa buena esta noche,' declares the Knight; and
the peevishness remains in the familiar :—'Hang me, if we
have any good fortune this night.' 'Mi oíslo me aguarda' is
Sancho's excuse to the Bachelor Carrasco when first he learns
that his exploits are in print. And Shelton bubbles with
merriment as he transcribes 'my Pigs-nie staies for me.'
Oíslo fascinates him, and in the Seventieth Chapter he offers
a variant of the earlier achievement. 'Mientras estoy
cavando, no me acuerdo de mi oíslo' is Sancho's unromantic
admission. The interpretation runs :—'Whilest I am digging
or delving, I never thinke on my Pinkaney at all.' If *oíslo*
soar to 'Pigs-nie' and to 'Pinkaney,' *plática* is ennobled as
'enterparlie.' Nor is the store of gifts exhausted. 'Esotros
badulaques, y enredos, y revoltillos,' writes Cervantes;
'Your other slabber-sawces, your tricks and quillets,' echoes
Shelton. And he overtops himself in his inspired announcement of 'the fearefull Low-Bell-Cally horrour that Don
Quixote received in Processe of his Love,' as in his conver-
sion of 'aquella canalla gatesca encantadora y cencerruna'
to 'that Cattish-Low-Belly Enchanting crue.' The Mirror
of Honour recites the qualities that denote the Perfect
Knight and Happy Warrior, leaving his listener to decide :—
'Si es ciencia mocosa la que aprende el caballero que la

xliv

HISTORIE OF DON QUIXOTE

' estudia y profesa.' *Mocosa*, a **word** of dread, has no
terrors for the Northerner who bluffly inquires 'Whether
' it be a sniveling Science that the Knight that learnes it
' professeth?' And he remains undaunted when 'Discre-
' tion it selfe was a Snotty-nose to her' is substituted for
' Digamos ahora que la discreción era mocosa.' Upon other
the like victories of bright and faithful audacity our
modern prudery draws a veil.

Turn we to the statelier Shelton, who sang the Age of
Gold in the First Part, and he awaits us, a thought more
restrained. The Second Part has no such *locus classicus* to
boast, for it excels rather in pointed dialogue than in formal
soliloquy; but even here occasions offer to the artist's hand.
Judge him, then, when to the Priest, who called him 'Don
Coxcombe' and 'good-man Dull-pate,' the copesmate of
Amadís makes his **Great** Remonstrance:—' Is it happily
' **a** vaine plot, or time ill spent, to range thorow the
' world, not seeking it's dainties, but **the** bitternesse of
' **it,** whereby good men aspire to the **seat** of immor-
' tality? If your Knights, your Gallants, or Gentlemen
' should **have** called me Cox-comb, I should have held it
' **for an affront** irreparable; but that your poore Schollers
' account mee a madde-man, that never trod the paths of
' Knight Errantry, I care not a chip; a Knight I am, a
' Knight I 'le die, if it please the most Highest. Some goe
' by the spacious field of proud ambition, others by the
' way of servill and base flattery, a third sort by deceitfull
' hypocrisie, and few by that of true Religion: But I by
' my starres inclination goe in the narrow path of Knight-
' Errantry; for whose exercise **I despise** wealth, but not

g

'honor. I have satisfied grievances, rectified wrongs,
'chastised insolencies, overcome Gyants, trampled over
'Sprites; I am enamoured, onely because there is a
'necessity Knights Errant should bee so, and though I
'be so, yet I am not of those vicious Amorists, but of
'your chaste Platonicks. My intentions alwaies aime at a
'good end, as, to doe good to all men, and hurt to none:
'If he that understands this, if he that performes it, that
'practiseth it, deserve to be called foole, let your Greatnesses
'judge, excellent Duke and Duchesse.'

Thus Shelton acquits himself in presence of the madman's
debonair phrase; nor falls he a whit behind in his entreat-
ment of Sancho's pithier tags and curter periods. 'Know

'now, Teresa, that I am determined thou goe in thy Coach,
'for all other kinde of going, is to goe upon all foure. Thou
'art now a Governour's wife, let's see if any body will gnaw
'thy stumps. I have sent thee a greene hunter's sute, that
'my Lady the Duchesse gave me, fit it so, that it may serve
'our daughter for a Coate and Bodies. My master Don
'Quixote, as I have heard say in this Country, is a mad wise
'man, and a conceited Coxcombe, and I am ne're a whit
'behinde him. Wee have beene in Montesinos Cave, and
'the sage Merlin hath laid hands on me for the disenchanting
'my Lady Dulcinea del Toboso, whom you there call Aldonsa
'Lorenzo, with three thousand and three hundred lashes
'lacking five, that I give my selfe, she shall be dis-enchanted
'as the Mother that brought her forth: but let no body
'know this; for put it thou to descant on, some will cry
'white, others blacke. . . . God Almighty hath not yet
'beene pleased to blesse mee with a Cloke-bag, and another
  xlvi

'hundred Pistolets as those you wot of: but be not grieved,
'my Teresa, there's no hurt done, all shall be recompenced
'when we lay the Government a bucking.' So Shelton
manifests himself an exquisite in the noble style, an expert in
the familiar; and with such effect as no man has matched
in English.

VI

Cervantes himself was a severe critic—not to say a Cervantes on
good hater—of translations. In his First Part he spares Translations
not Jiménez de Urrea and his fellows, but informs them
roundly that 'they can never arrive to the height of
'that Primitive conceit, which they [the originals] bring
'with them in their first birth.' And, in the Second, he
maintains his thesis with a more caustic deliberation:—
'The translating out of easie languages, argues neither wit
'nor elocution, no more then doth the copying from out of
'one Paper into another; yet I inferre not from this, that
'translating is not a laudable exercise: for a man may be
'far worse employed, and in things lesse profitable.' So the
matter presents itself—and naturally—to the mind of an
original genius; yet to the reviled translator belongs an His Debt to
honourable **esteem.** Consider a moment the diminution of his Translators
Cervantes' **fame** were his gay, melancholy book to be read
solely in Spanish! To Shelton, Oudin, Rosset, and their
followers is due the universal acceptance of his perennial
renown. As no writer has tempted more interpreters, so
none owes them more. And most he owes to Shelton, lord Shelton
of the golden Elizabethan speech, accomplished artificer in above All
style, first of foreigners to hail him **for** the Master that he

was, first to present him—and that with the grand air—to the company of the universal world.

His Second Part lagged not behind his First. That *Don Quixote* greatly throve in England is history. Ben Jonson's *Execration upon Vulcan* cites it as in vogue, and in Drayton's *Nymphidia* :—

> 'Men talk of the adventures strange
> Of Don Quixoit, and of their change
> Through which he armèd oft did range
> Of Sancho Panza's travel.'

Nor was the fashion less abroad. A fragmentary German version by Pahsch Basteln von der Sohle appeared at Cöthen in 1621 ;[1] Lorenzo Franciosini's First Part in Italian was published at Venice in 1622, the Second in 1625; Lambert van den Bos gave the story in Dutch at Dordrecht in 1657. Then for a hundred years, though Spanish, English, and French presses are busy with reprints or new renderings, there is a pause elsewhere till Charlotte Dorothea Biehl does the book into Danish. Then the tide flows again, and collectors now boast a shelf of translations (more or less complete) in some twenty European languages: Bohemian, Catalan, Croatian, Finnish, Greek, Hungarian, Polish, Portuguese, Roumanian, Serbian, Swedish, and what not. A list of editions would fill a large volume : all attempts in this kind, as yet revealed, are simply puerile, and those that purport

---

[1] But there is earlier proof of German vogue. At a Dessau baptismal festival, held on October 27-28, 1613, six or seven characters taken from *Don Quixote* figured in the procession ; and a series of illustrations (signed by Andreas Bretschneider) was published in 1613-14 at Leipzig 'durch Justum Jansonium Danum.'—*An Iconography of Don Quixote*, 1605-1895, by H. S. Ashbee, F.S.A. (privately printed, 1895), p. 132.

HISTORIE OF DON QUIXOTE

to be complete are the very worst. A final Bibliography
is preparing by Señor D. Leopoldo Ruis y Llosellas, who has dedicated a lifetime of labour to the task. Not till it appears can the extent of the immortal book's diffusion be accurately judged. Versions are reported to exist in Oriental tongues; and, sixteen years since, Adolfo Riva-deneyra in his *Viaje al interior de Persia*, mentioned a transfiguration of Cervantes in the speech of Ḥāfiz and Sa'dī done expressly through the Russian by order of the Shah. A fragment in Provençal is found among the *Œuvres* of André-Jean-Victor Gelu, and in Basque there is another.[1] Fernández de Navarrete mentions an ancient Latinising by a German; and indubitably there is a Latin verse rendering of 'the marriage of the rich Camacho and the successe of poor Basilius' included in the *Parva Poëmata latina, seu Ludicra literaria* of Raymundo del Busto **Valdés**, dedicated 'amplissimo viro, Marchioni de Pidal,' under the style of *Nuptiæ Camachii*.

Persian
Russian
Provençal
Basque

Latin

In England Cervantes has been translated times out of counting by men like Jervas, Smollett, Ormsby—the soundest scholar of them all; while his critics and commentators— 'by one letter of the A B C'—run from Bowle to Watts and Webster. Shelton's secular fame ensured him the attention of that impudent buccaneer, Captain John Stevens, who mangled and despoiled him in the reprint of 1700-6. 'For-' merly made English by **Thomas** Shelton; now Revis'd,

English

---

[1] Julien Vinson, *Bibliographie de la Langue Basque* (Paris, 1891), No. 557; *Don Quichotte Manchako aitoren-seme ispiritutsua Michel de Cervantes Saavedra deitzen denas*, xlii capitulua (Bi-garren partea)—(s.t.l.ni.d. : 1882) in-8, 4 pp. tiré à un très petit nombre d'exemplaires. Traduction d'après le français, de la fin du chapitre, depuis les mots : ' Primeramente, oh hijo !'

HISTORIE OF DON QUIXOTE

' Corrected and partly new Translated from the Original,'
the artificial monster perished at birth.   But Shelton lives.
His successors have merits to which he makes no pretence ;
yet he may well survive them.   For his work is literature,
sane and strong and beautiful.   A great poet once wrote
of a fervent admirer of Cervantes that he knew

> ' no version done
> In English more divinely well '

than Fitzgerald's of 'Umar Khaiyām.   And, with small
abatement, as much may be said for our first and best
interpretation of *Cervantes*.

JAMES FITZMAURICE-KELLY.

NOTE

*The text of the Second Part
is reprinted from the
Editio Princeps of
1620*

THE SECOND PART OF

THE HISTORY OF THE

VALOROUS AND WITTY

KNIGHT-ERRANT

DON QUIXOTE

OF THE MANCHA

WRITTEN IN SPANISH BY

MICHAEL CERVANTES

AND NOW TRANSLATED

INTO ENGLISH

1620

GEORGE MARQUESSE BUCKINGHAM

Viscount Villiers, Baron of Whaddon,

Lord High Admirall of England; Iustice in Eyre of all his Majesties Forrests, Parkes, and Chases beyond Trent, Master of the Horse to his Majestie, and one of the Gentlemen of his Majesties Bed-chamber, Knight of the most noble Order of the Garter, and one of his Majesties most Honourable Privy Counsell of England and Scotland.

Right Noble Lord,

YOUR humble servant hath observ'd in the multitude of books that have past his hands, no small varietie of Dedications; and those severally sorted to their Presenters ends: Some, for the meere ambition of Great names: Others, for the desire, or need of Protection; Many, to win Friends, and so favour, and opinion; but Most, for the more sordid respect, Gaine.

3

THE SECOND PART OF THE

This humbly offers into your Lo: presence, with none of these deformities: But as a bashfull stranger, newly arrived in English, having originally had the fortune to be borne commended to a Grande of Spaine; and, by the way of translation, the grace to kisse the hands of a great Ladie of France, could not despaire of lesse courtesie in the Court of Great Brittaine, then to bee received of your Lo: delight; his study being to sweeten those short starts of your retirement from publique affaires, which so many, so unseasonably, even to molestation trouble.

By him who most truely honours,
and humbly professes all duties
to your Lordship.

ED. BLOUNT.

HISTORIE OF DON QUIXOTE

THE AUTHORS PROLOGUE TO THE READER

 *OW God defend! Reader, Noble or Pleb-eyan, what ere thou art: how earnestly must thou needs by this time expect this Prologue, supposing that thou must find in it nothing but revenge, brawling, and rayling upon the Authour of the second 'Don Quixote,' of whom I onely say as others say, that he was begot in Tordesillas,* and borne in Tarragona? the truth is, herein I meane not to give thee content. Let it be never so generall a rule, that injuries awaken and rouze up choler in humble brests, yet in mine must this rule admit an exception: Thou, it may be, wouldst have mee be-Asse him, be-madman him, and be-foole him, but no such matter can enter into my thought; no, let his owne rod whip him; as hee hath brewed, so let him bake; else where he shall have it: and yet there is somewhat which I cannot but resent, and that is, that he exprobrates unto me my age, and my *mayme, as if it had been in my power, to hold   Time backe, that so it should not passe upon mee, or if my mayme had befalne me in a Taverne, and not upon the most famous * occasion which either the ages past or present have seene, nor may the times to come looke for the like: If my wounds shine not in the eyes of such as behold them; yet shall they be esteemed at least in the judgement of such as know how they were gotten. A Souldiour had rather be dead in the battell, then free by running away: and so is it with me, that should men set before me and facilitate an impossibilitie,

*He lost one of his hands.

*At the Battell of Lepanto.

5

THE SECOND PART OF THE

I should rather have desired to have beene in that prodigious action; then now to bee in a whole skinne, free from my skarres, for not having been in it. The skarres which a Souldiour shewes in his face and brest, are starres which leade others to the Heaven of Honor, and to the desire of just praise: and besides it may be noted, that it is not so much mens pens which write, as their judgements; and these use to be better'd with yeeres. Nor am I insensible of his calling me Envious, and describing me as an ignorant. What Envy may be, I vow seriously, that of those two sorts, that are; I skill not but of that Holy, Noble, and ingenuous Envy, which being so, as it is, I have no meaning to abuse any Priest; especially, if he hath annexed unto him the Title of FAMILIAR of the Inquisition: and if he said so, as it seemes by this second Author, that he did, he is utterly deceived: For I adore his wit, admire his workes, and his continuall vertuous imployment; and yet in effect I cannot but thanke this sweet Senior Author, for saying that my Novelles are more Satyrick, then Exemplar; and that yet they are good, which they could not be, were they not so quite thorow. It seemes, thou tellest me, that I write somewhat limited, and obscurely, and containe my selfe within the bounds of my modestie, as knowing, that a man ought not adde misery to him that is afflicted, which doubtlesse must needs be very great in this Senior, since he dares not appeare in open field, in the light, but conceales his Name, faines his Countrey, as if hee had committed some Treason against his King. Well, if thou chance to light upon him, and know him, tell him from mee, that I hold my selfe no whit aggrieved at him: for I well know what the temptations of the Divell are; and one of the greatest is, when hee puts into a mans head, that he is able to compose and print a booke, whereby he shall gaine as much Fame as money, and as much money as Fame. For confirmation hereof, I intreat thee, when thou art disposed to be merry and pleasant, to tell him this Tale.

There was a Mad-man in Sevill, which hit upon one of the prettiest absurd tricks that ever mad-man in this world lighted on, which was: Hee made him a Cane sharpe at one end, and

6

HISTORIE OF DON QUIXOTE

then catching a Dogge in the street, or elsewhere, hee held fast
one of the Dogges legges under his foot, and the other hee
held up with his hand. Then fitting his Cane as well as he
could, behinde, he fell a blowing till hee made the Dogge as
round as a Ball: and then, holding him still in the same
manner, hee gave him two clappes with his hand on the belly,
and so let him goe, Saying to those which stood by (which
alwayes were many) how thinke you, my Masters, Is it a
small matter to blow up a Dogge like a Bladder? and how
thinke you, Is it a small labour to make a Booke? If this
Tale should not fit him: then, good Reader, tell him this
other; for this also is of a Mad-man and a Dog. In Cordova
was another Mad-man, which was wont to carry on the top
of his head, a huge piece of Marble, not of the lightest, who
meeting a masterlesse Dogge, would stalke up close to him:
and on a sudden, downe with his burden upon him: the Dogge
would presently yearne, and barking and yelling run away,
three streets could not hold him. It fell out afterwards among
other Dogges (upon whom hee let fall his load) there was a
Cappers Dogge, which his Master made great account of, upon
whom hee let downe his great stone, and tooke him full on the
head: the poore batter'd Curre cryes pittifully. His Master
spies it, and affected with it, gets a meat-yard, assaults the
mad-man, and leaves him not a whole bone in his skinne; and
at every blow that he gave him, he cryes out, Thou Dogge,
Thou Thiefe, my Spaniell! Saw'st thou not, thou cruell
Villaine, that my Dogge was a Spaniell? And ever and
anon repeating still his Spaniell, he sent away the Mad-man
all blacke and blue. The Mad-man was terribly skarred here-
with, but got away, and for more then a moneth after never
came abroad: At last out hee comes with his invention againe,
and a bigger load then before: and comming where the Dogge
stood, viewing him over and over againe very heedily; he had
no minde, he durst not let goe the stone, but onely said, Take
heed, this is a Spaniell. In fine, whatsoever Dogges he met,
though they were Mastifs or Fysting-Hounds, hee still said
they were Spaniels. So that after that, he never durst throw
his great Stone any more. And who knowes but the same may

7

THE SECOND PART OF THE

befall this our Historian, that hee will no more let fall the
prize of his wit in Bookes? for in being naught, they are
harder then Rockes: tell him too, that for his menacing, that
with his booke he will take away all my gaine; I care not a
straw for him: but betaking my selfe to the famous Interlude
of Perendenga: I answere him, Let the Old man my Master
live, and Christ bee with us all. Long live the great Conde
de Lemos (whose Christianity and well-knowne Liberalitie
against all the blowes of my short fortune, keepes me on foote)
and long live that eminent Charitie of the Cardinall of Toledo,
Don Bernardo de Sandoval y Rojas. Were there no printing
in the world, or were there as many Bookes printed against
mee, as there are letters in the Rimes of Mingo Revulgo;
these two Princes, without any sollicitation of flatterie, or any
other kinde of applause, of their sole bounty have taken upon
them to doe me good, and to favour me; wherein I account
my selfe more happy and rich, then if fortune, by some other
ordinary way, had raised me to her highest: Honour, a Poore
man may have it, but a Vicious man cannot: Poverty may
cast a mist upon Noblenes, but cannot altogether obscure it:
but as the glimmering of any light of it selfe, though but
thorow narrow chinkes and Cranyes, comes to be esteemed by
high and Noble spirits, and consequently favoured. Say no
more to him; nor will I say any more to thee: but onely
advertise that thou consider, that this Second part of 'Don
Quixote,' which I offer thee, is framed by the same Art, and
cut out of the same cloth that the first was: in it I present
thee with Don Quixote enlarged, and at last dead and buried,
that so no man presume to raise any farther reports of him;
those that are past are enow: and let it suffice that an honest
man may have given notice of these discreet follies, with purpose not to enter into them any more. For plenty of any
thing, though never so good, makes it lesse esteemed: and
scarsitie (though of evill things) makes them somwhat
accounted of. I forgot to tell thee that thou mayst
expect 'Persiles,' which I am now about to finish;
as also the Second part of 'Galatea.'

8

HISTORIE OF DON QUIXOTE

A SUMMARY TABLE

of that, which this second part of the famous
History of the valourous Don Quixote
de la Mancha doth containe.

THE SECOND PART OF THE

HISTORIE OF DON QUIXOTE

HISTORIE OF DON QUIXOTE

THE SECOND PART
OF DON QUIXOTE

CHAPTER I

How the Vicar and the Barber passed their time
with Don Quixote, touching his infirmity.

ID HAMET BENENGELI tels us in the
second part of this History, and Don
Quixote his third sally, that the Vicar
and Barber were almost a whole moneth
without seeing him, because they would
not renew and bring to his remembrance
things done and past. Notwithstanding,
they forbore not to visit his Neece and
the olde woman, charging them they should bee carefull to
cherish him, and to give him comforting meats to eat, good
for his heart and braine, from whence in likeli-hood all his
ill proceeded. They answered, that they did so, and would
doe it with all possible love and care : For they perceived
that their Master continually gave signes of being in his
entire judgement ; at which the two received great joy, and
thought they tooke the right course, when they brought
him inchaunted in the Oxe-Waine (as hath beene declared
in the first part of this so famous, as punctual History.) So
they determined to visit him, and make some triall of his
amendment, which they thought was impossible ; and agreed
not to touch upon any point of Knight Errantry ; because
they would not endanger the ripping up of a sore, whose
stitches made it yet tender.

At length they visited him, whom they found set up in
his bed, clad in a Waste-coat of greene bayes, on his head a
red Toledo bonet, so dried and withered up, as if his flesh

15

CHAPTER
I

How the
Vicar and
the Barber
passed their
time with
Don Quixote,
touching his
infirmity.

had beene mommied. He welcommed them, and they asked him touching his health: of it and himselfe he gave them good account, with much judgement and elegant phrase, and in processe of discourse, they fell into State-matters, and manner of Government, correcting this abuse, and condemning that; reforming one custome, and rejecting another; each of the three making himselfe a new Law-maker, a moderne Lycurgus, and a spicke and span new Solon; and they so refined the Common-wealth, as if they had clapped it into a forge, and drawne it out in another fashion then they had put it in. Don Quixote in all was so discreet, that the two Examiners undoubtedly beleeved, he was quite well, and in his right minde. The Neece and the old woman were present at this discourse, and could never give God thankes enough, when they saw their Master with so good understanding: But the Vicar changing his first intent, which was, not to meddle in matters of Cavallery, would now make a thorow triall of Don Quixotes perfect recovery; and so now and then tels him newes from Court, and amongst others, that it was given out for certaine, that the Turke was come downe with a powerfull Army, that his designe was not knowne, nor where such a clowd would dis-charge it selfe: and that all Christendome was affrighted with this terrour he puts us in with his yeerely Alarme: Likewise, that his Majesty had made strong the coasts of Naples, Sicilie, and Malta. To this (sayd Don Quixote) his Majesty hath done like a most politique Warrior, in looking to his Dominions in time, lest the enemy might take him at unawares: but if my counsaile might prevaile, I would advise him to use a prevention, which he is farre from thinking on at present. The Vicar scarse heard this, when hee thought with himselfe; God defend thee, poore Don Quixote: for mee thinkes thou fallest headlong from the high top of thy madnesse, into the profound bottome of thy simplicity. But the Barber presently being of the Vicars minde, askes Don Quixote what advice it was he would give? for peradventure (sayd he) it is such an one as may bee put in the roll of those many idle ones that are usually given to

16

HISTORIE OF DON QUIXOTE

CHAPTER
I

How the
Vicar and
the Barber
passed their
time with
Don Quixote,
touching his
infirmity.

Princes. Mine, Good-man Shaver (quoth Don Quixote) is no such. I spoke not to that intent (replyed the Barber) but that it is commonly seene, that all or the most of your projects that are given to his Majesty, are either impossible, or frivolous, either in detriment of the King or Kingdome. Well, mine (quoth Don Quixote) is neither impossible, nor frivolous; but the plainest, the justest, the most manageable and compendious, that may bee contained in the thought of any Projectour. You are long a telling us it, Mr. Don Quixote, sayd the Vicar. I would not (replyed hee) tell it you heere now, that it should bee earely to morrow in the eares of some privy Councellour, and that another should reap the praise and reward of my labour. For mee (quoth the Barber) I passe my word, heere and before God, to tell neither King nor Keisar, nor any earthly man what you say: an oath I learnt out of the Ballad of the Vicar, in the Preface whereof he told the King of the theefe that robbed him of his two hundred double pistolets, and his gadding mule. I know not your histories (sayd Don Quixote) but I presume the oath is good, because I know Mr. Barber is an honest man. If he were not (sayd the Vicar) I would make it good, and undertake for him, that he shall be dumb in this busines, under paine of excommunication. And who shall undertake for you, Mr. Vicar (quoth Don Quixote)? My profession (answered he) which is to keep counsaile. Body of me, (sayd Don Quixote) is there any more to be done then, but that the King cause proclamation to bee made, that at a prefixed day, all the Knights Errant that rove up and downe Spaine, repaire to the Court? and if there came but halfe a doozen, yet such an one there might bee amongst them, as would destroy all the Turkes power. Harken to me, Hoe, and let me take you with mee: doe yee thinke it is strange, that one Knight Errant should conquer an army of two hundred thousand fighting men, as if all together had but one throat, or were made of sugar-pellets? But tell me, how many stories are full of those marvels? You should have brave Don Belianis alive now, with a pox to me, for Ile curse no other; or some

3 : C

17

THE SECOND PART OF THE

CHAPTER
I

How the
Vicar and
the Barber
passed their
time with
Don Quixote,
touching his
infirmity.

one of that invincible linage of Amadis de Gaul: for if any of these were living at this day, and should affront the Turke, I'faith I would not be in his coat: but God will provide for his people, and send some one, if not so brave a Knight Errant as those formerly, yet at least that shall not be inferiour in courage; and God knowes my meaning, and I say no more. Alasse (quoth the Neece at this instant) hang me, if my master have not a desire to turne Knight Errant againe. Then cryed Don Quixote, I must die so, march the Turke up and downe when he will, and as powerfully as he can, I say againe, God knowes my meaning. Then sayd the Barber, Good Sirs, give me leave to tell you a briefe tale of an accident in Sevil, which because it fals out heere so pat, I must needs tell it. Don Quixote was willing, the Vicar and the rest gave their attention, and thus he began.

In the house of the mad-men at Sevil, there was one put in there by his kindred, to recover him of his lost wits, hee was a Bachelour of Law, graduated in the Canons at Osuna, and though he had beene graduated at Salamanca, yet (as many are of opinion) he would have beene mad there too; this Bachelor after some yeeres imprisonment, made it appeare that hee was well and in his right wits, and to this purpose writes to the Arch-Bishop, desiring him earnestly, and with forcible reasons, to deliver him from that misery in which hee lived, since by Gods mercy, he had now recovered his lost understanding: and that his kindred, onely to get his wealth, had kept him there, and so meant to hold him still wrongfully till his death. The Arch-Bishop, induced by many sensible and discreet lines of his, commanded one of his Chaplaines to informe himselfe from the Rector of the house, of the truth; and to speake also with the mad-man, that if he perceived he was in his wits, hee should give him his liberty. The Chaplaine did this, and the Rector said that the party was still mad, that although hee had sometimes faire intermissions, yet in the end he would grow to such a raving, as might equall his former discretion (as hee told him) he might perceive by

18

HISTORIE OF DON QUIXOTE

CHAPTER
I

How the
Vicar and
the Barber
passed their
time with
Don Quixote,
touching his
infirmity.

discoursing with **him.** The Chaplaine would needes make
triall, and comming to him, talked with him an houre and
more, and in all that time the mad-man never gave him a
crosse, nor wilde answer, but rather spoke advisedly, that the
Chaplaine was forced to beleeve him to be sensible enough ;
and amongst the rest he told him, the Rector had an inckling against him, because hee would not lose his kindreds
Presents, that hee might say he was madde by fittes : withall
hee said, that his Wealth was the greatest wrong to him
in his evill Fortune, since to enjoy that, his enemies de-
frauded him, and would doubt of Gods mercie to him, that
had turned him from a Beast to a Man. Lastly, hee spoke
so well, that **hee** made the Rector to bee suspected, and his
kindred thought covetous and damnable persons, and himselfe so discreet, that the Chaplaine determined to have him
with him, that the Arch-Bishop might see him, and be
satisfied of the truth of the businesse. With this good
beliefe, the Chaplaine required the Rector to give the
Bachelor the clothes hee brought with him thither : who
replied ; desiring him to consider what he did, for that
the party was still madde : but the Rectors advice prevailed
nothing with the Chaplaine, to make him leave him ; so hee
was forced to give way to the Arch-bishops order, and to
give him his apparell, which was new and handsome : and
when the madde man saw himselfe civilly cladde, and his
mad-mans weedes off, hee requested the Chaplaine, that in
charity he would let him take his leave of the mad-men his
companions. The Chaplaine told him that hee would likewise **accompany him, and see** the madde-men that were in
the **house. So up they went,** and with them some others
there present, **and the Bachelor** being come to a kinde of
Cage, where **an** outragious mad-man lay, (although as then
still and quiet,) he said, Brother, if you will command me
ought, I am going to my house ; for now it hath pleased
God, of his infinite goodnesse and mercy, without my
desert, to bring me to my right minde : I am now well and
sensible, for unto Gods power nothing is unpossible. Be
of good comfort, trust in him, that since he hath turned
19

THE SECOND PART OF THE

CHAPTER
I

How the
Vicar and
the Barber
passed their
time with
Don Quixote,
touching his
infirmity.

mee to my former state, he will doe the like to you, if you trust in him. I will be carefull to send you some dainty to eat, and by any meanes eat it; for let me tell you what I know by experience, that all our madnesse proceeds from the emptinesse of our stomacks, that fills our brains with aire: Take heart, take heart; for this dejecting in misery, lessens the health, and hastens death. Another madde-man in a Cage over-against, heard all the Bachelors dis-course, and raysing himselfe upon an olde Matresse upon which hee lay starke naked, asked aloud, who it was that was going away sound and in his wits. The Bachelor re-plied: It is I, brother, that am going, for I have no need to stay heere any longer; for which I render infinite thankes to God, that hath done me so great a favour. Take heed what you say, Bachelor, reply'd the madde-man, let not the Devill deceive you; keepe still your foot, and be quiet heere at home, and so you may save a bringing backe. I know (quoth the Bachelor) I am well, and shall need to walke no more stations hither. You'r well, said the mad-man. The event will try; God be with you: but I sweare to thee by Iupiter, whose Majesty I represent on earth, that for this dayes offence, I will eat up all Sevill, for de-livering thee from hence, and saying thou art in thy wits: I will take such a punishment on this City, as shall be re-membred for ever and ever, Amen. Knowest not thou, poore rascall Bachelor, that I can doe it, since (as I say) I am thundering Iupiter, that carry in my hands the scorch-ing bolts, with which I can, and use to threaten and destroy the world? But in one thing onely will I chastise this ignorant Towne; which is, That for three yeers together there shall fall no raine about it, nor the liberties thereof, counting from this time and instant hence-forward, that this threat hath beene made. Thou free? thou sound, thou wise, and I mad, I sicke, I bound? as sure will I raine, as I meane to hang my selfe. The standers by gave atten-tion to the mad-man: but our Bachelor turning to the Chaplaine, and taking him by the hand, said, Be not afraid, Sir, nor take any heed to this mad-mans words:

20

HISTORIE OF DON QUIXOTE

CHAPTER
I

How the
Vicar and
the Barber
passed their
time with
Don Quixote,
touching his
infirmity.

for if he be Iupiter and will not raine, I that am Neptune
the Father and god of the waters, will raine as oft as I list,
and need shall require. To which (quoth the Chaplaine)
Nay, Mr. Neptune, it were not good angring Mr. Iupiter,
I pray stay you here still, and some other time, at more
leisure and opportunitie, we wil returne for you againe.
The Rector and standers by began to laugh, and the
Chaplaine grew to bee halfe abashed the Bachelor was
unclothed, there remained, and there the Tale ends.

Well ; is this the Tale, Mr. Barber (quoth Don Quixote)
that because it fell out so pat, you could not but relate it ?
Ah, goodman Shavester, goodman Shavester, how blind is
he that sees not light through the bottome of a Meale-sive ?
and is it possible that you should not know, that comparisons made betwixt wit, and wit, valour and valour, beauty
and beauty, and betwixt birth and birth, are alwayes odious
and ill taken ? I am not Neptune, god of the waters, neither
care I who thinks me a wise man, (I being none) onely I
am troubled to let the world understand the errour it is in,
in not renewing that most happy Age, in which the Order
of Knight Errantry did flourish : But our depraved times
deserve not to enjoy so great a happines, as former Ages,
when Knights Errant undertook the defence of Kingdomes,
the protection of Damosels, the succouring of Orphans, the
chastizing the Proud, the reward of the Humble. Most of
your Knights now-a-daies, are such as russle in their silkes,
their cloth of gold and silver, and such rich stuffes as these
they weare, rather then Maile, with which they should arme
themselves. You have no Knight now that will lye upon
the bare ground, subject to the rigour of the ayre, armed
Cap a Pie : None now that upright on his stirrops, and
leaning on his Launce, strives to be head-sleepe (as they
say your Knights Errant did :) You have none now, that
comming out of this wood, enters into that mountaine, and
from thence tramples over a barren and desart shore of the
Sea, most commonly stormy and unquiet ; and finding at
the brinke of it some little Cock-boat, without Oares, Saile,
Mast, or any kinde of tackling, casts himselfe into it with

21

CHAPTER
I

How the
Vicar and
the Barber
passed their
time with
Don Quixote,
touching his
infirmity.

undanted courage, yeelds himselfe to the implacable waves of the deepe Maine, that now tosse him as high as Heaven, and then cast him as low as hell, and he exposed to the inevitable tempest, when he least dreames of it, findes himselfe at least three thousand Leagues distant from the place where he embarqued himselfe: and leaping on a remote and unknowne shore, lights upon successes worthy to be written in brasse, and not parchment. But now sloth triumphs upon industry, idlenesse on labour, vice on vertue, presumption on valour, the Theorie on the Practice of Armes, which onely lived and shined in those golden Ages, and in those Knights Errant. If not, tell me, who was more vertuous, more valiant, then the renowned Amadis de Gaul? more discreet then Palmerin of England? more affable and free, then Tirante the White? more gallant then Lisuart of Greece? a greater hackster, or more hacked then Don Belianis? more undaunted then Perion of Gaule? who a greater undertaker of dangers then Felismarte of Hircania? who more sincere then Esplandian? who more courteous then Don Cierongilio of Thracia? who more fierce then Rodomant? who wiser then King Sobrinus? who more couragious then Renaldo? who more invincible then Roldan? who more comely, or more courteous then Rogero? from whom the Dukes of Ferrara at this day are descended (according to Turpin in his Cosmography.) All these Knights, and many more (Master Vicar) that I could tell you, were Knights Errant, the very light and glory of Knight-hood. These, or such as these, are they I wish for, which if it could be, his Majesty would bee well served, and might save a great deale of expence, and the Turke might goe shake his eares. And therefore let me tell you, I scorne to keepe my house, since the Chaplaine delivers mee not, and his Iupiter (as goodman Barber talkes) raines not; heere am I that will raine when I list: this I speake, that goodman Bason may know I understand him.

Truly Mr. Don Quixote (said the Barber) I spoke it not to that end, and so help mee God, as I meant well, and you ought not to resent any thing. I know well enough

22

HISTORIE OF DON QUIXOTE

CHAPTER
I
How the
Vicar and
the Barber
passed their
time with
Don Quixote,
touching his
infirmity.

whether I ought or no, Sir, replyed Don Quixote. Then
(quoth the Vicar) well, goe to: I have not spoken a word
hitherto, I would not willingly remaine with one scruple
which doth grate and gnaw upon my conscience, sprung
from what Mr. Don Quixote hath here told us. For this
and much more you have full liberty, good Master Vicar
(said Don Quixote) and therefore tell your scruple, for sure
it is no pleasure to continue with a scrupulous conscience.
Under correction (quoth the Vicar) this it is, I can by no
means be perswaded that all that troope of Knights Errant
which you named, were ever true, and really persons of flesh
and bone in this world: I rather imagine all is fiction,
tales, and lies, or dreames set downe by men waking, or to
say trulier, by men halfe asleepe. There's another error
(quoth Don Quixote) into which many have falne, who
believe not that there have beene such Knights in the
world: and I my selfe many times in divers companies,
and upon severall occasions, have laboured to shew this
common mistake, but sometimes have failed in my purpose,
at others not; supporting it upon the shoulders of Truth,
which is so infallible, that I may say, that with these very
eyes I have beheld Amadis de Gaul, who was a goodly tall
man, well complectioned, had a broad beard, and blacke,
an equall countenance betwixt milde and sterne, a man of
small discourse, slow to anger, and soone appeased: and
just as I have delineated Amadis, I might in my judgement
paint and decipher out as many Knights Errant, as are in
all the Histories of the world: for by apprehending, they
were such as their histories report them, by their exploits
they did, and their qualities; their features, colours, and
statures may in good Philosophy be guessed at. How bigge,
deare Mr. Don Quixote (quoth the Barber) might Gyant
Morgante be? Touching Gyants (quoth Don Quixote)
there be different opinions whether there have beene any
or no in the world: but the holy Scripture, which cannot
erre a jot in the truth, doth shew us plainely that there
were, telling us the story of that huge Philistine Golias, that
was seven cubits and a halfe high, which is an unmeasur-

23

able greatnesse. Besides, in the Ile of Sicilia, there have beene found shanke-bones, and shoulder-bones so great, that their bignesse shewed their owners to have beene Gyants, and as huge as high towers, which Geometry will make good. But for all this, I cannot easily tell you how big Morgante was, though I suppose he was not very tall; to which opinion I incline, because I finde in his history, where there is particular mention made of his Acts, that many times hee lay under a roofe: And therefore since hee found an house that would hold him, tis plaine, he could not be of extraordinary bignesse. Tis true (quoth the Vicar) who delighting to heare him talke so wildely, asked him what he thought of the faces of Renaldo of Montalban, Don Roldan and the rest of the twelve Peeres of France, who were all Knights Errant. For Renaldo (quoth Don Quixote) I dare boldly say, he was broad-faced, his complexion high, quicke and full eyed, very exceptious and extremely choler-icke, a lover of theeves and debaucht company. Touching Rolando, or Rotolando, or Orlando, for histories afford him all these names, I am of opinion, and affirme that hee was of a meane stature, broad-shouldred, somwhat bow-legged, Abourne bearded, his body hairie, and his lookes threatning, dull of discourse, but affable and well behaved. If Orlando (said the Vicar) was so sweet a youth as you describe him, no marvell though the faire Angelica disdained him, and left him, for the handsome, briske and conceited beard-budding Medor, and that she had rather have his softnesse, then tothers roughnesse. That Angelica (quoth Don Quixote) was a light huswife, a gadder, and a wanton, and left the world as full of her fopperies, as the reports of her beauty: shee despised a thousand Knights, a thousand both valiant and discreet, and contented herselfe with a poore beardlesse Page, without more wealth or honour, then what her famous singer Ariosto could give her in token of his thankfulnesse to his friends love, either because hee durst not in this respect, or because hee would not chaunt what befell this Lady, after her base prostitution, for sure her carriage was not very honest: So he left her when he said,

24

HISTORIE OF DON QUIXOTE

And how Catayes scepter she had at will,
Perhaps, some one will write with better quill.

And undoubtedly this was a kinde of prophesie, for Poets **How the**
are called Vates, that is, South-sayers : and this truth hath **Vicar and**
beene cleerely seene, for since that time, a famous Anda- **the Barber**
luzian Poet wept, and sung her teares : and another famous **passed their**
and rare Poet of Castile her beauty. But tell mee, Mr. Don **time with**
Quixote (quoth the Barber) was there ever any Poet that **Don Quixote,**
wrote a Satyre against this faire Lady, amongst those many **touching his**
that have written in her praise ? I am well perswaded (quoth **infirmity.**
Don Quixote) that if Sacripant or Orlando had beene Poets,
they had trounced the Damosell : for it is an ordinary thing
amongst Poets once disdained, or not admitted by their fained
Mistresses, (fained indeed, because they faine they love them)
to revenge themselves with Satyres and Libels ; a revenge
truely unworthy noble spirits : but hitherto I have not heard
of any infamatory verse against the Lady Angelica, that
hath made any hurly burly in the world. Strange, quoth
the Vicar. With that they might heare the Neece and
the olde woman (who were before gone from them)
keepe a noyse without in the Court : so they
went to see what was the matter.

CHAPTER II

Of the notable fray that Sancho Panca had with the Neece and the old woman, and other delightfull passages.

THE Story sayes, that the noyse which Don Quixote, the Vicar and the Barber heard, was of the Neece and the old woman, that were rating Sancho Panza, that strove with them for entrance to see Don Quixote, who kept the doore against him. What will this bloud-hound have heere? sayd they, Get you home to your own house, for you are he and none else, that doth distract and ring-lead our Master, and carry him astray. To which (quoth Sancho) Woman of Satan, I am hee that is distracted, ring-led, and carried astray, and not your Master: twas he that led mee up and downe the world, and you deceive your selves and understand by halves: he drew me from my house with his conycatching, promising mee an Island, which I yet hope for. A plague of your Islands (replied the Neece) cursed Sancho: and what be your Islands? is it any thing to eat, good-man glutton, you cormorant, as you are? Tis not to eat (quoth Sancho) but to rule and governe, better then foure Cities, or foure of the Kings Iudges. For all that (sayd the olde woman) you come not in heere, you bundle of mischiefe and sacke of wickednesse, get you home and governe there, and sow your graine, and leave seeking after Ilands or Dilands. The Vicar and the Barber tooke great delight to heare this Dialogue betweene the three: But Don Quixote, fearing lest Sancho should out with all, and should blunder out a company of malicious fooleries, or should touch upon poynts that might not be for his reputation, he called him to him, and commanded the women to be silent, and to let him in. Sancho entred, and the Vicar and Barber tooke leave of Don Quixote, of whose recovery they dispaired, seeing how· much he was bent upon his wilde thoughts, and how much he was besotted with his damned Knights Errant. So (quoth the Vicar to the Barber) you shall quickly, Gossip, perceive, when we least thinke of it, that our Gallant takes his flight againe by the river. No doubt, (sayd the Barber) but I wonder not so much at the Knights madnesse, as the Squires simplicity, that believes so in the Ilands, and I thinke all the Art in the world will not drive that out of his noddle. God mend them (sayd the Vicar) and let us expect what issue the multitude of this Knight and Squires absurdities will have: for it seemes they were both framed out of one forge, as it were, for the Masters madnes without the Servants folly, is not worth a chip. Tis true (sayd the Barber) and I should be glad to know their present discourse. I warrant (sayd the Vicar) the Neece and old woman will tell us all when they have done, for they are not so mannerly as not to harken. In the Interim, Don Quixote locked in Sancho, and thus discoursed with him: I am very sorry, Sancho, you should affirme and make good, that I was hee that drew you from your dog-hole cottage, knowing that I willingly left mine, a Palace in comparison; wee went out joyntly, so we marched on, and so we held our whole peregrination; both of us having undergone the same lot, the same fortune; and if once thou wast tossed in a blanket, I have beene banged an hundred times, and heerein have I the advantage of thee. Why, it was very fit (answered Sancho) for (as you hold) misfortunes are more annexed to Knights Errant then to their Squires. Thou art deceived, Sancho, (quoth Don Quixote:) for according to the saying, *Quando caput dolet*, etc. I understand no other language but mine owne, said Sancho. Why I mean (replied Don Quixote) that when the head akes, all the body is out of tune: so that I being thy Lord and Master, am thy head, and thou a part of me, since thou art my servant, in which respect, the ill that toucheth me, must concerne

CHAPTER II

Of the notable fray that Sancho Panca had with the Neece and the old woman, and other delightfull passages.

27

CHAPTER
II

Of the notable
fray that
Sancho
Panca had
with the
Neece and the
old woman,
and other
delightfull
passages.

and grieve thee, and so thine me. Indeed (quoth Sancho) it ought to bee so: but when I was tossed in the blanket, my head stood aloofe, like a part, beholding me fly in the aire, without any feeling my griefe, and since the members are bound to suffer for the head, the head in requitall should also suffer for them. You meane, Sancho (quoth Don Quixote) that I had no feeling of your being tossed? And if you meane so, doe not, neither imagine any such thing: for at that time, I was more vext in spirit, then thou couldst bee in body: but leave we this for the present; for wee shall have leisure to consider and rectifie it: and tell me, friend Sancho, what say the common people of me? In what estimation doe the Gentlemen hold me? In what the Knights and Gallants? What say they of my valour? What of my exployts? What of my affability? What discourse they touching my plot in raising and restoring to the world, the long forgotten order of Knight Errantry? To conclude, I would have thee tell me all that thou hast heard: and you must tell me, without adding to my praise, or diminishing my dispraise, for it is the part of loyall servants, to tell the naked truth to their Masters, in its native colour, without increasing it by flattery, or diminishing it for any other vaine respect; And I would have thee, Sancho, learne by the way, that if the naked truth should come to the eares of Princes, without the apparrell of flattery, we should have another manner of world, and other ages would be called iron, and not ours, and this would bee the golden age. And let mee advise thee, Sancho, that well and discreetly thou tell me the truth of what thou knowest, concerning my demand. I shall with a very good will, Sir, (quoth Sancho) upon condition that you shall not bee angry at what I shall tell you, since you will have the naked truth, without any other clothing then what I have seene her with. By no meanes will I be angry (answered Don Quixote) thou mayst speake freely, Sancho, and without any disguise. Why then, first of all I must tell you, the common people hold you for a notable mad-man, and that I am no lesse Cox-combe. The

28

ordinary Gentle-men say, **that not** containing your selfe **within** the limits of Gentrie, you will needs be-Don your **selfe,** and be a man **of** honour, having but three or foure acres of land, and a rag before, and another behinde. The Knights say, they would not have your poore Squires bee ranked with them, that clout their owne shooes, and take up a stitch in their owne blacke stockings with greene silke. That concernes not me (quoth Don Quixote) for thou seest that I goe alwaies well clad, and never patcht: indeed a little torne sometimes, but more with my armour, then by long wearing. Concerning your valour (quoth Sancho) your affability, your exploits, and your plot, there bee different **opinions:** Some say you are a mad-man, but a merry one: **others,** that you are valiant, but withall unfortunate: a **third** sort, that you are affable, but impertinent: and thus they descant upon us, that they leave neither you nor me a sound bone. Why looke thou, Sancho (quoth Don Quixote) wheresoever vertue is eminent, it is persecuted: few or none of those brave Hero's that have lived, have scaped malicious calumniation. Iulius Cæsar, that most couragious, most wise, most valiant Captaine, was noted to be ambitious, and to be somewhat slovenly in his apparrell and his conditions. Alexander, who for his exploits obtained the **title of Great,** is said to have beene given to drunkennesse: **Hercules, hee** with his many labours, was said to have beene **lascivious and** a Striker: Don Galaor, brother **to** Amadis **de Gaul,** was grudged at for being offensive: **and** his Brother **for a** sheepe-biter. So that, Sancho, since so many worthy **men** have beene calumniated, I may well suffer mine, if it **have** beene **no more** then thou tellest me. Why, there's **the** quiddity **of** the matter, Body of my father, quoth Sancho. Was there any more sayd then? said Don Quixote. There's **more** behinde yet, said Sancho: all that was said hitherto, **is** cakes and white-bread to this: but if you will know all concerning these calumnies, Ile bring you one hither by and by, that shall tell um you all without missing a scrap; for last night Bartholomew Carrasco's **sonne** arrived, that comes from study from Salamanca, and **hath** proceeded Bachelour,

CHAPTER
II
Of the notable
fray that
Sancho
Pança had
with the
Neece and the
old woman,
and other
delightfull
passages.

THE SECOND PART OF THE

CHAPTER
II

Of the notable
fray, etc.

*It should be
Benengeli,
but Sancho
simply mis-
takes, as fol-
loweth in the
next note.

*Berengena
is a fruit in
Spain, which
they boyle
with sod meat,
as we do
carrats, and
here was
Sancho's sim-
plicity in mis-
taking, and to
thinke that
name was
given the
Author for
loving the
fruit.

and as I went to bid him welcome home, he told me that
your History was in print, under the Title of *the most
Ingenious Gentle-man Don Quixote de la Mancha*; and hee
tels mee that I am mentioned too, by mine owne name of
Sancho Pansa, and Dulcinea del Toboso is in too, and other
matters that passed betwixt us, at which I was amazed, and
blessed my selfe how the Historian that wrote them, could
come to the knowledge of them. Assure thee, Sancho (said
Don Quixote) the Author of our History is some Sage Enchanter: for such are not ignorant of all secrets they write.
Well (said Sancho) if hee were wise and an Enchanter, I
will tell you according as Samson Carrasco told me, for
thats the mans name that spoke with mee, that the Authors
name of this History is Cid Hamete *Berengena. That is
the name of a Moore, sayd Don Quixote. It is very like
(quoth Sancho) for your Moores are great lovers of *Beren-
gens. Sancho (said Don Quixote) you are out in the Moores
sirname, which is Cid Hamete Benengeli, and *Cide* in the
Arabicke signifieth Lord. It may bee so (quoth Sancho)
but if you will have the Bachelour come to you, Ile bring
him to you flying. Friend (quoth Don Quixote) thou shalt
doe mee a speciall pleasure, for I am in suspence with
what thou hast told me, and will not eat a bit till I am
informed of all. Well, I goe for him (sayd Sancho;) And
leaving his Master, went for the Bachelor, with whom
a while after hee returned, and the three had
a passing pleasant Dialogue.

CHAPTER III

The ridiculous discourse that passed betwixt
Don Quixote, Sancho, and the Bachelour
Samson Carrasco.

ON QUIXOTE was monstrous pensative,
expecting the Bachelour Carrasco, from
whom he hoped to heare the newes of
himselfe in print (as Sancho had told
him) and he could not be perswaded
that there was such a History, since yet
the bloud of enemies, killed by him, was
scarse dry upon his sword blade, and
would they have his noble acts of Chivalry already in the
Presse? Notwithstanding, hee thought that some wise man,
or friend, or enemy, by way of enchantment, had committed
them to the Presse: If a friend, then to extoll him for
the most remarkable of any Knight Errant: if an enemy,
to annihilate them, and clap um beneath the basest and
meanest that ever were mentioned of any inferior Squire,
although (thought he to himselfe) no acts of Squire were
ever divulged: but if there were any History, being of a
Knight Errant, it must needs be lofty and stately, famous,
magnificent, and true. With this he comforted himselfe
somewhat, but began to bee discomforted, to thinke that
his Author must be a Moore, by reason of that name of
Cide: and from Moores there could bee no truth expected;
for all of them are Cheaters, Impostors, and Chymists.

He feared likewise, that he might treat of his Love with
some indecency, that might redound to the lessening and
prejudice of his Lady Dulcinea del Toboso's honesty, he
desired that he might declare his constancy, and the decorum that hee had ever kept toward her, contemning
Queenes and Empresses, and Damosels of all sorts, keeping

CHAPTER
III
The ridicu-
lous discourse
that passed
betwixt Don
Quixote,
Sancho, and
the Bachelour
Samson
Carrasco.

distance with violencies of naturall motions. Sancho and Carrasco found him thus tossed and turmoyled in these and many such like imaginations, whom Don Quixote received with much courtesie.

This Bachelour, though his name was Samson, was not very tall, but a notable Wag-halter, leane-faced, but of a good understanding; he was about foure and twenty yeeres of age, round-faced, flat-nosed, and wide-mouthed, all signes of a malicious disposition, and a friend to conceits and merriment, as he shewed it when he saw Don Quixote; for hee fell upon his knees before him, saying, Good Mr. Don Quixote, give me your Greatnesse his hand, for by the habit of St. Peter, which I weare, you are, Sir, one of the most complete Knights Errant, that hath beene, or shall be upon the roundnesse of the earth. Well fare, Cid Hamete Benengeli, that left the stories of your Greatnesse to posterity, and more then well may that curious Author fare, that had the care to cause them to bee translated out out of the Arabicke into our vulgar Castilian, to the generall entertainment of all men.

Don-Quixote made him rise, and sayd; Then it seemes my History is extant, and that he was a Moore, and a wise man that made it. So true it is (quoth Samson) that upon my knowledge, at this day, there bee printed above twelve thousand copies of your History: if not, let Portugal, Barcelona, and Valencia speak, where they have beene printed, and the report goes, that they are now printing at Antwerp, and I have a kinde of ghesse, that there is no Nation or Language where they will not bee translated. One of the things then (quoth Don Quixote) that ought to give a man vertuous and eminent content in, is, to see himselfe living, and to have a good name from every bodies mouth, to be printed and in the Presse. I said with a good name: for otherwise, no death could bee equalled to that life. If it bee for good name (said the Bachelour) your Worship carries the prize from all Knights Errant: For the Moore in his language, and the Christian in his, were most carefull to paint to the life, your gallantry, your great courage in

32

attempting **of** dangers, **your** patience **in** adversities, and **your** sufferance as well **in** misfortunes, as in your wounds, **your** honesty and constancy in the so Platonick loves of your selfe, and my Lady Donna Dulcinea del Toboso. I never (replied Sancho) heard my Lady stiled Don before, onely the Lady Dulcinea del Toboso, and there the History erreth somwhat. This is no objection of moment (said Carrasco.) No truly (quoth Don Quixote) but tell me, Signior Bachelour, which of the exploits of mine are most ponderous in this History.

CHAPTER
III

The ridicu-
lous discourse
that passed
betwixt Don
Quixote,
Sancho, and
the Bachelour
Samson
Carrasco.

In **this** (said the Bachelour) there bee different opinions, **as there** bee different tastes: Some delight in the adventure **of the** winde-mils, that you tooke to be Briareans and **Gyants**: Others in that of the fulling-hammers: This man **in the** description of the two Armies, which afterwards fell out **to** be two flockes of sheepe; That man doth extoll your adventure of the dead man, that was carried to be buried at Segovia: One saith, that that of the freeing of the gally-slaves goes beyond them all: Another, that none comes neere that of the Benitian Gyants, with the combate of the valorous Biscayner. Tell mee (said Sancho) Sr. Bachelour, comes not that in of the Yanguesian Carriers? when our precious Rozinante longed for the forbidden fruit? The wise man (said Samson) left out nothing, he sets downe all most punctually, even to the very capers that Sancho fetcht **in** the blanket. Not in the blanket (replied Sancho) but in **the** aire, more **then I** was willing.

According **to my** thought (sayd Don Quixote) there is no humane History **in** the world, that hath not his changes, especially **those** that treat of Cavallery, which can never bee full of prosperous successes. For all that (replied the Bachelour) there be some that have read your History, that would bee glad the Authors had omitted some of those infinite bastings, that in divers encounters, were given Sr. Don Quixote. I, there (quoth Sancho) comes in the truth of the Story. They might likewise in equity silence them, (said Don Quixote) since those actions that neither change nor alter the truth of the story, are best left out, if they

3 : E   33

THE SECOND PART OF THE

CHAPTER
III

The ridicu-
lous discourse
that passed
betwixt Don
Quixote,
Sancho, and
the Bachelour
Samson
Carrasco.

must redound to the misprizing of the chiefe person of the History. Æneas i'faith was ne're so pitifull, as Virgil paints him out: Nor Ulisses so subtill, as Homer describes him. True it is (sayd Samson) but it is one thing to write like a Poet, and another like an Historian; the Poet may say or sing things, not as they were, but as they ought to have beene: And the Historian must write things, not as they ought to bee, but as they have beene, without adding or taking away ought from the truth.

Well, (said Sancho) if you goe to telling of truths, wee shall finde that this Signior Moore hath all the bastings of my Master and mee; for I am sure they never tooke measure of his Worships shoulders, but they tooke it of all my body too: but no marvell, for as my Master himselfe saith, the rest of the parts must participate of the heads griefe. Sancho, you are a Crackrope (quoth Don Quixote:) I'faith you want no memory, when you list to have it. If I would willingly forget those cudgellings that I have had, the bunches yet fresh on my ribs would not consent. Peace, Sancho (quoth Don Quixote) and interrupt not the Bachelour, whom I request to proceede, and tell mee what is said of mee in the mentioned History. And of mee too (said Sancho) for it is said, that I am one of the principall Parsonages of it. `Personages, and not Parsonages, you would say Sancho (quoth Samson.)ʹ More correcting of words (quoth Sancho)? Goe to this; and we shall not end in all our life-time. ʽHang me, Sancho (said Samson) if you be not the second person in the Story, and you have some, that had as liefe heare you speake, as the best there? though others will not sticke to say, you were too credulous to beleeve, that your government of the Iland offered by Sr. Don Quixote heere present, might be true.

There is yet sun-shine upon the wals (quoth Don Quixote) and when Sancho comes to be of more yeeres, with the experience of them, he will be more able and fit then now, to bee a Governour. By the Masse (said Sancho) if I bee not fit to governe an Iland at these yeeres, I shall never governe, though I come to be as old as Methusalem; the

34

mischiefe is, that the said Iland is delaid I know not how, and **not** that I want braine to governe **it**. Leave all to God, Sancho (said Don Quixote) for all will be well, and perhaps better then you thinke for; and the leaves in the tree moove not without the will of God.

Tis true indeed (said Samson) for if God will, Sancho shall not want a thousand Ilands, much lesse one. I have seene (sayd Sancho) of your Governours in the world, that are not worthy to wipe my shooes, and for all this, they give **um** titles, and are served in plate. Those are not Governours of Ilands (replied Samson) but of other easier Governments: for they that governe Ilands, must bee at **least** Grammarians. For your Gra, I care not, but your **Mare I** could like well enough: but leaving this government **to** Gods hands, let him place me where he pleaseth: I say, Sr. Bachelour Samson Carrasco, that I am infinitely glad that the Author of the History hath spoken of me, in such sort, that the things he speakes of me, do not cloy the Reader, for by the faith of a Christian, if he had spoken any thing of mee not befitting an *old Christian as I am, I should make deafe men heare on't. That were to worke miracles, said Samson. Miracles or not miracles (quoth Sancho) every man looke how hee speaks or writes of men, and set not down each thing that comes into his noddle **in** a mingle-mangle. One of the faults that they say (said Carrasco) **is** in that History, is this; that his Author put **in** it **a** certaine Novell or Tale, intitled the *Curious Impertinent*, not that it was ill, or not well contrived, **but** that it was unseasonable for that place, neither had it **any** thing to doe with the History of Don Quixote.

Ile hold a wager (quoth Sancho) the Dog-bolt hath made a Gallimawfry. Let **me** tell you (said Don Quixote) the Author of my Story is not wise, but some ignorant Prater, that at unawares and without judgement undertooke it, hab-nab, as Orbaneja **the** Painter of Ubeda, who being asked what he painted, answered, As it happens, sometimes he would paint yee **a** Cocke, but **so** unlike, that he was forced to write underneath **it** in Gothish letters, 'This is a

CHAPTER III

The ridiculous discourse that passed betwixt Don Quixote, Sancho, and the Bachelour Samson Carrasco.

*In Spanish *Christiano vieio*, a name they desire to be distinguisht from the Moores by.

35

THE SECOND PART OF THE

CHAPTER
III
The ridicu-
lous discourse
that passed
betwixt Don
Quixote,
Sancho, and
the Bachelour
Samson
Carrasco.

Cocke': and thus I beleeve it is with my History, that it
hath neede of a Coment to make it understood.

No surely (replied Samson) it is so conspicuous, and so
void of difficulty, that children may handle him, youths
may read him, men may understand him, and old men may
celebrate him: To conclude, he is so gleaned, so read, and
so knowne to all sorts of people, that they scarse see a leane
horse passe by, when they say, 'There goeth Rosinante': And
amongst these, Pages are most given to read him: You
have no great mans withdrawing room that hath not a *Don
Quixote* in him, some take him, if others lay him downe,
these close with him, they demand him: Lastly, the Story
is the most pleasing, the least hurtfull for entertainment,
that hath hitherto beene seene; for all over it, there is not
to be seene a dishonest word, or one like one; nor an imagination lesse then Catholike.

He that should write otherwise (quoth Don Quixote)
should write no truths, but lies, and he that doth so, ought
to bee burned, like them that coyne false mony; and I
know not what the Author meant, to put in Novels and
strange Tales, my Storie affording him matter enough; belike, he holds himselfe to the proverbe of chaffe and hay, etc.
Well, Ile tell you, out of mentioning onely my thoughts,
my sighs, my teares, my honest wishes, and my on-sets,
he might have made a greater volume then all Tostatus
works. Indeed, Signior Bachelor, all that I conceive, is,
that to write a History, or any other worke of what sort
soever, a man had need of a strong judgement and a ripe
understanding: To speake wittily, and write conceits, belongs onely to good wits: The cunningst part in a play,
is the Fooles; because he must not be a foole, that would
well counterfet to seeme so: An History is as a sacred
thing, which ought to be true and reall, and where truth
is, there God is, in-asmuch as concerneth truth, howsoever;
you have some that doe so compose and cast their workes
from them, as if they were Fritters.

There is no booke so bad (said the Bachelour) that hath
not some good in it. No doubt of that (said Don Quixote:)

36

HISTORIE OF DON QUIXOTE

but many times it fals out, that those that have worthily hoorded up, and obtained great fame by their writings, when they commit them to the Presse, they either altogether lose it, or in something lessen it. The reason of it (quoth Samson) is this, that as the printed workes are viewed by leisure, their faults are easily espied, and they are so much the more pried into, by how much the greater the Authors fame is: Men famous for their wits, great Poets, illustrious Historians, are alwaies or for the most part envied by them, that have a pleasure and a particular pastime, to judge of other mens writings, without publishing their owne. That's not to bee wondred at (cries Don Quixote) for there bee many Divines that are nothing worth in a pulpit, and are excellent in knowing the defect or excesse of him that preacheth. All this (said Carrasco) Sr. Don Quixote, is right, but I could wish such Censurers were more milde, and lesse scrupulous, in looking on the moats of the most cleere sunne of his workes, whom they bite; for if *aliquando bonus dormitat Homerus*, let um consider how much hee watched, to shew the light of his worke without the least shadow that might bee: and it might bee, that what seemes ill to them, were moles that sometimes increase the beauty of the face that hath them; and thus, I say, that hee that prints a booke, puts himselfe into a manifest danger, being of all impossibilities the most impossible to frame it so, that it may content and satisfie all that shall read it.

The booke that treats of me (quoth Don Quixote) will have pleased very few. Rather contrarie (saies Samson) for as *Stultorum infinitus est numerus*, an infinite number have been delighted with this History, but some found fault, and craftily taxed the Authors memory, in that hee forgot to tell, who was the theefe that stole Sancho's Dapple, for there is no mention there, onely it is inferred that hee was stole, and not long after wee see him mounted upon the same Asse, without knowledge how he was found. They also say, that he forgot to tell what Sancho did with those hundred pistolets, which he found in the Maile in Sierra

CHAPTER
III

The ridiculous discourse that passed betwixt Don Quixote, Sancho, and the Bachelour Samson Carrasco.

37

THE SECOND PART OF THE

CHAPTER
III

The ridicu-
lous discourse
that passed
betwixt Don
Quixote,
Sancho, and
the Bachelour
Samson
Carrasco.

Morena, for he never mentions them more, and there be many that desire to know what became of them, and how he imployed them, which is one of the essential points in the worke.

Master Samson (said Sancho) I am not now for your reckonings or relations, for my stomacke is faint, and if I fetch it not agen with a sup or two of the old Dog, it will make me as gaunt as Saint Lucia; I have it at home, and my Pigs-nie staies for me, when I have dined I am for ye, and will satisfie you and all the world in any thing you will aske me, aswell touching the losse of mine Asse, as the expence of the hundred pistolets: And so without expecting any reply, or exchanging another word, home he goes. Don Quixote intreated the Bachelour to stay and take a pittance with him; The Bachelour accepted the invitement, and so staid dinner: Beside their ordinary fare, they had a paire of houshold Pigeons added; at table they discoursed of Cavallery, Carrasco followed his humour, the banquet was ended, and they slept out the heat: Sancho returned, and the former discourse was renewed.

HISTORIE OF DON QUIXOTE

CHAPTER IV

How Sancho Pansa satisfies the Bachelor **Samson** Carrasco's doubts and demands ; with **other** **accidents** worthy to be knowne and related.

ANCHO came backe to Don Quixotes house, and turning to his former discourse, said : Touching what, **Mr.** Samson desired to know ; who, **how, and** when mine Asse was stolne : **By way of** Answer, I say ; That the very same night wee fled from the Hue and Cry, we entred Sierra Morena, after the unfortunate adventure of the Gally-slaves, and the dead man that was carrying to Segovia ; my Master and I got us into a thicket, where he leaning upon his launce, and I upon my Dapple, both of us well bruized and wearied with the former skirmishes, we fell to sleep as soundly, as if we had beene upon foure feather-beds, especially I, that slept so soundly, that he, whosoever hee was, might easily come and put me upon foure stakes, which he had fastned upon both sides of my pack-saddle, upon which he left me thus mounted, and without perceiving it, got my Dapple from under mee.

This was easie to be done, and no strange accident ; for wee read that the same happened to Sacripant, when being at the siege of Albraca, that famous Theefe Brunelo, with the selfesame slight got his horse from under his legs. Sancho proceeds : It was light day (said he) when I had scarse stretched my selfe, but the stakes failed, and I got a good squelch upon the ground : then I looked for mine Asse, but not finding him, the teares came to mine eyes,

39

CHAPTER IV

How Sancho Pansa satisfies the Bachelor Samson Carrasco's doubts and demands; with other accidents worthy to be knowne and related.

and I made such strange moane, that if the Authour of our History omitted it, let him be assured he forgot a worthy passage. I know not how long after, comming with my Lady the Princesse Micomicona, I knew mine Asse, and that he who rode on him in the habit of a Gipson, was that Gines de Passamonte, that Cheater, that arrant Mischiefe-monger, that my Master and I freed from the Chaine.

The errour was not in this (said Samson) but that before there was any newes of your Asse, the Authour still said, you were mounted upon the selfe-same Dapple. I know not what to say to that (quoth Sancho) but that either the Historian was deceived, or else it was the carelesnesse of the Printer. Without doubt (saith Samson) twas like to bee so: But what became of the Pistolets? Were they spent?

I spent them upon my selfe (quoth Sancho) and on my wife and children, and they have been the cause that she hath endured my Iournies and Careeres, which I have fetched in my Master Don Quixotes service: for if I should have returned empty, and without mine Asse, I should have been welcommed with a pox: and if you'l know any more of me, heere I am, that will answer the King himselfe in person; and let no body intermeddle to know, whether I brought, or whether I brought not; whether I spent, or spent not; for if the blowes that I have had in these voyages were to be paid in money, though every one of them were taxed but at three farthings apiece, an hundred Pistolets more would not pay mee the halfe of them, and let every man looke to himselfe, and not take white for blacke, and blacke for white, for every man is as God hath made him, and sometimes a great deale worse.

Let me alone (quoth Carrasco) for accusing the Author of the History, that if he print it againe, hee shall not forget what Sancho hath said, which shall make it twice as good as it was. Is there ought else, Sr. Bachelour (said Don Quixote) to bee mended in this Legend? Yes Mary is there (said he) but nothing so important as what hath

40

beene mentioned. Perhaps the Author promiseth a second part (quoth Don Quixote)? He doth (said Samson) but saith, hee neither findes nor knowes who hath it, so that it is doubtfull, whether it will come out or no : so that partly for this, and partly because some hold that second parts were never good ; and others, that there is enough written of Don Quixote, it is doubted, that there will bee no second part, although some more Ioviall then Saturnists, cry out ; Let's have more Quixotismes : Let Don Quixote assault, and Sancho speake, let the rest bee what they will, this is enough. And how is the Authour enclined ?

CHAPTER IV

How Sancho Pansa satisfies the Bachelor Samson Carrasco's doubts and demands ; with other accidents worthy to be knowne and related.

To **which** (said Samson) when hee hath found this His-**tory, that** hee searcheth after with extraordinary diligence, **hee** will straight commit it to the Presse, rather for his profit tho, then for any other respect. To this (said Sancho) What ? Doth the Authour looke after money and gaine ? tis a wonder if he be in the right : rather he will be like your false stitching Taylours upon Christmas Eeves : for your hasty work is never well performed : let that Mr. Moore have a care of his businesse, for my Master and I will furnish him with rubbish enough at hand, in matter of adventures, and with such different successes, that he may not onely make one second part, but one hundreth : the poore fellow thinkes belike, that we sleep heere in an hay-mow ; well, let it come to scanning, and hee shall see whether wee bee defective : This I know, that if my Master would take my counsaile, hee should now bee abroad in the Champion, remedying grievances, rectifying wrongs, as good Knights Errant are wont to doe.

No sooner had Sancho ended this discourse, when the neighing of Rozinante came to his eares, which Don Quixote tooke to be most auspicious, and resolved within three or foure dayes after to make another sally, and manifesting his minde to the Bachelor, asked his advice to know which way hee should begin his journey ; whose opinion was, That hee should goe to the Kingdome of Aragon, and to the City of Saragosa ; where, not long after, there were solemne Iusts to **bee** held in honour of Saint George, wherein hee might get

CHAPTER
IV

How Sancho
Pansa satisfies
the Bachelor
Samson
Carrasco's
doubts and
demands;
with other
accidents
worthy to be
knowne and
related.

*Santiago,
y Cierra
España.* As
we use in
England,
Saint George
and the
Victory.

more fame then all the Knights of Aragon, which were above all other Knights. Hee praised his most noble and valiant resolution, but withall desired him to be more wary in attempting of dangers, since his life was not his owne, but all theirs also, who needed his protection and succour in their distresse.

I renounce that, Mr. Samson, (said Sancho) for my Master will set upon an hundred armed men, as a boy would upon halfe a doozen of young Melons; Body of the world, Sr. Bachelour, there is a time to attempt, a time to retire, all must not be *Sainte Iacques, and upon um. Besides, I have heard, and I beleeve from my Master himselfe, (if I have not forgotten) that valour is a meane betweene the two extremes of a Coward and a rash man: and if this be so, neither would I have him fly, nor follow, without there be reason for it: but above all, I wish that if my Master carry me with him, it be upon condition, that he fight for us both, and that I be tied to nothing but waiting upon him, to looke to his clothes and his diet, for this I will doe as nimbly, as bring him water; but to thinke that I will lay hand to my sword, although it be but against base fellowes and poore raskals, is most impossible. I (Mr. Samson) strive not to hoord up a fame of being valiant, but of the best and trustiest Squire that ever served Knight Errant: And if Don Quixote my Master, obliged thereunto by my many services, will bestow any Iland on mee, of those many, his Worship saith, wee shall light upon, I shall be much bound to him: and if he give mee none, I was borne, and one man must not live to relie on another, but on God; and perhaps I shall bee aswell with a peece of bread at mine ease, as to be a Governour; and what doe I know, whether in these kindes of governments, the Devill hath set any tripping-blocke before me, where I may stumble and fall, and dash out my teeth? Sancho was I borne, Sancho must I die; but for all that, if so and so, without any care or danger, Heaven should provide some Iland for me, or any such like thing, I am not so very an Asse as to refuse it, according to the Proverbe, Looke not a given horse in the mouth.

42

HISTORIE OF DON QUIXOTE

Friend Sancho (quoth Carrasco) you have spoken like an Oracle: Notwithstanding, trust in God and Mr. Don Quixote, that he will give you not onely an Iland, but a Kingdome too. I thinke one aswell as tother (quoth Sancho) and let me tell you, Mr. Samson, (said Sancho) I thinke my Masters Kingdome would not bee bestowed on mee in vaine, for I have felt mine owne pulse, and finde my selfe healthy enough to rule Kingdomes and governe Ilands, and thus I have told my Master many times.

Looke yee, Sancho (quoth Samson) Honours change manners, and perhaps when you are once a Governour, you may scarse know your owne mother. That's to be understood (said Sancho) of them that are basely borne, and not of those that have on their soules *foure fingers fat of the old Christian, as I have: No, but come to my condition, which will bee ungratefull to no body. God grant it (quoth Don Quixote) and wee shal see when the Government comes, for me thinks I have it before mine eyes. (Which said) he asked the Bachelour whether he were a Poet, and that he would doe him the favour to make him some verses, the subject of his farewell to his Mistris Dulcinea del Toboso, and withall, that at the beginning of every verse, he should put a letter of her name, that so joyning all the first letters, there might bee read Dulcinea del Toboso? The Bachelour made answer, that though he were none of the famous Poets of Spaine, which they said were but three and an halfe; yet he would not refuse to compose the said meeter, although he found a great deale of difficulty in the composition, because there were seventeen letters in the name; and, if hee made foure staves, of each foure verses, that there would be a letter too much; and if hee made them of five, which they call Decimi, there would be three too little; but for all that, hee would see if hee could drowne a letter; so in foure staves there might be read, Dulcinea del Toboso. By all meanes (quoth Don Quixote) let it be so: for if the name be not plaine and conspicuous, there is no woman will beleeve the meeter was composed for her.

How Sancho Pansa satisfies the Bachelor Samson Carrasco's doubts and demands; with other accidents worthy to be knowne and related.

*To expresse his not being borne a Iew, or Moore.

43

CHAPTER
IV

How Sancho
Pansa satisfies
the Bachelor,
etc.

*The Barber.

Upon this they agreed, and that eight dayes after their departure should be. Don Quixote enjoyned the Bachelour to keep it secret, especially from the Vicar, and *Mr. Nicholas, his Neece, and the old woman, lest they should disturbe his noble and valiant resolution. Carrasco assured him, and so tooke leave, charging Don Quixote he should let him heare of all his good or bad fortune, at his best leisure. So they tooke leave, and Sancho went to provide for their journey.

CHAPTER V

Of the wise and pleasant discourse, that passed betwixt Sancho Pansa and his wife Teresa Pansa, and other accidents worthy of happy remembrance.

HE Translatour of this History, when he came to write this fifth Chapter, saies, that hee holds it for Apocrypha, because Sancho speakes in it after another manner then could be expected from his slender understanding, and speakes things more acutely then was possible for him, yet hee would translate it, for the accomplishment of his promise, and so goes on, as followeth.

Sancho came home so jocund and so merry, that his wife perceived it a flight-shot off, insomuch that shee needs would aske him; Friend Sancho, what's the matter that you are so joyfull? To which he answered: Wife, I would to God I were not so glad as I make shew for. I understand you not, husband, (quoth shee) and I understand not what you meane, that if it pleased God, you would not bee so contented; for though I bee a foole, yet I know not who would willingly be sad.

44

HISTORIE OF DON QUIXOTE

Looke yee, Teresa, (said Sancho) I am jolly, because I am determined to serve my Master Don Quixote, once more, who will now this third time sally in pursuit of his adventures, and I also with him, for my poverty will have it so; besides my hope that rejoyceth me, to thinke that I may finde another hundred Pistolets, for those that are spent: Yet I am sad againe, to leave thee and my children, and if it pleased God that I might live quietly at home, without putting my selfe into those Desarts and crosse-waies, which he might easily grant if he pleased and were willing; it is manifest, that my content might bee more firme and wholesome, since the present joy I have, is mingled with a sorrow to leave thee: so that I said well, I should bee glad if it pleased God I were not so contented.

Fie, Sancho (replied Teresa) ever since thou hast been a member of a Knight Errant, thou speakest so round-about the bush, that no body can understand thee. It is enough (quoth Sancho) that God understands mee, who understands all things, and so much for that: but marke, Sister, I would have you for these three daies, looke well to my Dapple, that hee may bee fit for Armes, double his allowance, seeke out his pack-saddle, and the rest of his tackling; for wee goe not to a marriage, but to compasse the world, and to give and take, with Gyants, Sprights and Hobgoblins, to heare hissing, roaring, bellowing, and bawling: and all this were sweet meat, if we had not to doe with *Yangueses and enchanted Moores.

I beleeve indeede (quoth Teresa) that your Squires Errant gaine not their bread for nothing: I shall therefore pray to our Lord, that he deliver you speedily from this misfortune. Ile tell you, wife (said Sancho) if I thought not ere long to bee Governour of an Iland, I should die suddenly. None of that, Husband (quoth Teresa:) Let the hen live, though it bee with her pip; Live you, and the Devill take all the Governments in the world, without Government were you borne, without Government have you lived hitherto, and without Government must you goe, or bee carried to your grave, when it shall please God. How many be there in

45

CHAPTER
V

Of the wise
and pleasant
discourse, that
passed be-
twixt Sancho
Pansa and his
wife Teresa
Pansa, and
other acci-
dents worthy
of happy re-
membrance.

Chapines.

the world, that live without Governments, yet they live well enough, and well esteemed of? Hunger is the best sawce in the world, and when the poore want not this, they eat contentedly. But harke, Sancho, if you should chance to see a Government, pray forget not mee and your children: little Sancho is now just fifteene yeeres old, and tis fit he goe to schoole, if his uncle the Abbot meane to make him a Church-man: And looke ye to, Mary Sancha our daughter will not die, if we marry her, for I suspect she desires marriage, as much as you your Government, and indeed a daughter is better ill married, then well Paramour'd.

I'good faith (quoth Sancho) if I have ought with my Government, Wife; Mary Sancha shall be so highly married, that she shall be called Lady at least. Not so, Sancho (quoth Teresa) the best way is to marry her with her equall, for if in stead of her pattins you give her *high shooes, if in stead of a course petticoat, a farthingale and silke kirtle, and from little Mal, my Lady Whacham, the girle will not know her selfe, and shee will every foot fall into a thousand errours, discovering the thred of her grosse and course web.

Peace, foole (sayd Sancho) all must bee two or three yeeres practice, and then her greatnesse will become her, and her state fall out pat: howsoever, what matter is it? let her be your Ladiship, and come what will on it. Measure your selfe by your meanes (said Teresa) and seeke not after greater, keepe your selfe to the Proverbe; Let neighbours children hold together: Twere pretty i'faith to marry our Mary with a great Lord or Knight, that when the toy takes him in the head, should new-mould her, calling her milke-maid, Boores daughter, Rocke-peeler: not while I live, Husband: for this forsooth have I brought up my daughter? Get you money, Sancho, and for marrying her, let me alone: Why, there's Lope Tocho, Iohn Tocho's sonne, a sound chopping Lad, wee know him well, and I know, he casts a sheepes eye upon the wench, and tis good marrying her with this her equall, and wee shall have him alwayes with us, and wee shall bee all one: Parent, sonnes, and grandsonnes, and

46

CHAPTER
V

Of the wise
and pleasant
discourse, that
passed be-
twixt Sancho
Pansa and his
wife Teresa
Pansa, and
other acci-
dents worthy
of happy re-
membrance.

sonne in law, and Gods peace and blessing will alwaies be amongst us, and let not me have her married into your Courts and Grand Palaces, where they'l neither understand her, nor she them.

Come hither, Beast (quoth Sancho) Woman of Barrabas, why wilt thou, without any reason, hinder me from marrying my daughter where shee may bring mee grand-sonnes that may be stiled Lordship? Behold, Teresa, I have alwaies heard mine Elders say, That he that will not when hee may, when hee desireth, shall have nay: And it is not fit that whilst good lucke is knocking at our doore, we shut it: let us therefore saile with this prosperous winde. (For this and for that which followeth, that Sancho spoke, the Author of the History sayes, hee held this Chapter for Apocrypha.) Doe not you thinke, Bruit-one (sayd Sancho) that it will be fit to fall upon some beneficiall Government, that may bring us out of want: and to marry our Daughter Sancha to whom I please, and you shall see how you shall bee called Dona Teresa Pansa, and sit in the Church with your carpet and your cushions, and your hung-clothes, in spite of the Gentle-women of the towne? No, no, remaine still as you are, in one estate, without increasing or diminishing, like a picture in hangings; goe to, let's have no more, little Sancha must bee a Countesse, say thou what thou wilt.

What a coyle you keepe! (quoth Teresa) for all that, I feare this Earledome will be my daughters undoing, yet doe what ye will, make her Dutchesse or Princesse; it shall not bee with my consent: I have alwaies loved equality, and I cannot abide to see folkes take upon um without grounds, I was Christned Teresa, without welt or gard, nor additions of Don or Dona, my fathers name was Cascaio, and because I am your wife, they call me Teresa Pansa, for indeed they should have called me Teresa Cascaio: But great ones may doe what they list, and I am well enough content with this name, without putting any Don upon it, to make it more troublesome, that I shall not be able to beare it, and I will not have folke laugh at mee, as they see mee walke in my Countesses apparell, or my Gover-

CHAPTER
V

Of the wise
and pleasant
discourse, that
passed be-
twixt Sancho
Pansa and his
wife Teresa
Pansa, and
other acci-
dents worthy
of happy re-
membrance.

nesses, you shall have them cry straight, Looke how stately
the Hog-rubber goes, she that was but yesterday at her
spindle, and went to Church with the skirt of her coat over
her head in stead of an Huke, to day she is in her Varthin-
gale and her buttons, and so demure, as if we knew her not:
God keepe mee in my seven wits, or my five, or those that I
have, and Ile not put my selfe to such hazards; Get you,
Brother, to bee a Government or an Iland, and take state
as you please, for by my mothers Holy-dam, neither I nor
my daughter will stirre a foot from our village: better a
broken joynt then a lost name, and keepe home, the honest
mayd, to bee doing is her trade, goe you with Don Quixote
to your adventures, and leave us to our ill fortunes; God
will send better, if we be good, and I know not who made
him a Don, or a title which neither his Father nor his
Grandfather ever had.

Now I say (quoth Sancho) thou hast a Familiar in that
body of thine: Lord blesse thee for a woman, and what a
company of things hast thou strung up without head or
feet? What hath your Cascaio, your buttons, or your
Proverbes, or your state, to doe with what I have sayd?
Come hither Cox-combe, foole (for so I may call you, since
you understand not my meaning, and neglect your happinesse) If I should say, my daughter should cast her selfe
downe some Towre, or she should rove up and downe the
world, as did the * Princesse Dona Urraca, you had reason
not to consent: But if in lesse then two trap-blowes, or the
opening and shutting of an eye, I clap yee a Don and Ladiship upon your shoulders, and bring it out of your stubble,
and put it you under barne-cover, and set you in your
state, with more Cushions then the Almohada Moores had
in all their linage: why, will you not consent to that,
that I would have you? Would you know why, Husband
(answered Teresa)? for the Proverbe that sayes; He that
covers thee, discovers thee: Every one passeth his eyes
slightly over the poore, and upon the rich man they fasten
them, and if the said rich man have at any time beene
poore, there is your grumbling and cursing, and your back-

*An *Infanta*
of Spain.

48

HISTORIE OF DON QUIXOTE

biters **never** leave, who swarme as thicke as hives of Bees thorow the streets.

Marke, Teresa (said Sancho) and give eare to my speech, such as peradventure you have not heard in all your life time, neither doe I speake any thing of mine owne, for all I purpose to speake, is sentences of our Preacher, that preached all last Lent in this Towne, who (as I remember) said, that all things that wee see before our eyes present, assist our memory much better, and with more vehemency, then things past.

(All these reasons heere delivered by Sancho, are the second, **for** which the Translatour of the History holds **this** chapter for Apocrypha, as exceeding the capacity of Sancho, who proceeded, saying :)

Whereupon it happens, that when wee see some personage well clad in rich apparrell, and with many followers, it seemes hee mooves and invites us perforce to give him respect : although our memory at that very instant represents unto us some kinde of basenesse, which we have seen in that personage, the which doth vilifie him, bee it either for poverty or linage, both passed over, are not : and that which wee see present, only is. And if this man (whom fortune blotted out of his basenesse, and to whom consequently his father left all height of prosperity) be well-behaved, liberall and courteous towards all men, and contends not with such, as **are** most anciently noble, assure thy selfe, Teresa, all men **will** forget what he was, and reverence him for what hee is, except the envious, whom the greatest scape not. I understand you **not,** Husband (replied Teresa) doe what you will, and doe not trouble me with your long speeches and your Rhetoricke : and if you be revolved to doe what you say. Resolved you must say, Wife (quoth Sancho) and not revolved. I pray dispute not with mee, Husband (sayd Teresa) I speake as it pleases God, and strive not for more eloquence : and I tell you, if you persist in having your Government, take your sonne Sancho with you, and teach him from henceforth to governe ; for it is fit that the sonnes doe inherit, and learne the offices of their fathers.

CHAPTER
V
Of the wise
and pleasant
discourse, that
passed be-
twixt Sancho
Pansa and his
wife Teresa
Pansa, and
other acci-
dents worthy
of happy re-
membrance.

3 : G   49

CHAPTER
V

Of the wise
and pleasant
discourse, that
passed be-
twixt Sancho
Pansa and his
wife Teresa
Pansa, and
other acci-
dents worthy
of happy re-
membrance.

When I have my Government (quoth Sancho) I will send Post for him, and I will send thee monies, for I shall want none, and there never want some that will lend Governours money when they have none: but clothe him so, that hee may not appeare what he is, and may seeme what he must bee. Send you money (quoth Teresa) and Ile clad him like a Date-leafe. So that now (sayd Sancho) wee are agreed that our daughter shall bee a Countesse.

The day that I shall see her a Countesse (said Teresa) will bee my deaths day : But I tell you againe, doe what you will, for we women are borne with this clog, to bee obedient to our husbands, though they be no better then Leekes : And heere she began to weep so heartily, as if her little daughter Sancha had been dead and buried. Sancho comforted her, saying, that though she must bee a Countesse, yet hee would deferre it as long as hee could. Heere their Dialogue ended, and Sancho returned to see Don Quixote, to give order for their departure.

CHAPTER VI

What passed betwixt Don Quixote, his Neece, and the old woman : and it is one of the most materiall Chapters in all the History.

HILST Sancho and his wife were in this impertinent aforesayd discourse, Don Quixotes Neece and olde woman were not idle, and by a thousand signes ghessed, that her Unckle and their Master would a slashing the third time, and returne to the exercising of his (for them) ill Knight Errantry ; they sought by all meanes possible to divert him from so bad a purpose : but all was to no purpose, to preach in a Desart, or to beat cold iron.

HISTORIE OF DON QUIXOTE

Notwithstanding, amongst many other discourses that passed betwixt them, the old woman told him; Truely Master, if you keepe not your foot still, and rest quiet at home, and suffer your selfe to be led thorow mountaines and valleyes, like a soule in Purgatory, seeking after those they call adventures, which I call misfortunes, I shall complaine on you, and cry out to God and the King, that they remedie it. To which, Don Quixote answered; Woman, what God will answer to your complaints, I know not, nor what his Majesty will: onely I know, if I were a King, I would **save** a labour in answering such an infinity of foolish Petitions, **as** are given him daily: for one of the greatest **toyles** (amongst many others that Kings have) is this, to bee **bound** to harken to all, to answer all; therefore I would bee **loth,** that ought concerning mee, should trouble him. Then **(quoth** the old woman) tell us Sir, In his Majesties Court bee **there** not Knights? Yes (answered hee) and many, and good reason, for the adornment and greatnesse of Princes, and for ostentation of the Royall Majesty. Why? would not your Worship (replyed she) bee one of them that might quietly serve the King your Master at Court?

Looke yee, friend (answered Don Quixote) All Knights cannot be Courtiers, nor all Courtiers neither can, nor ought to be Knights Errant; in the world there must bee of all sorts, and though wee bee all Knights, yet the one and the other differ much : For your Courtiers, without stirring out of their chambers, or over the Court thresholds, can travell all the world over, looking upon a Map, without spending a mite, without suffering heat, cold, hunger, or thirst. But wee, the true Knights Errant, with sunne, with cold, with aire, with all the inclemencies of Heaven, night and day, a horse-backe and on foot, doe trace the whole world thorow : And wee doe not know our enemies by supposition, as they are painted, but in their reall being, and at all times, and upon every occasion wee set upon um, without standing upon trifles, or on the lawes of Duello, whether a sword or a lance were longer or shorter, whether either of the parties wore **a** charme, or some hidden deceit, if they shall fight after the

CHAPTER VI

What passed betwixt Don Quixote, his Neece, and the old woman : and it is one of the most materiall Chapters in all the History.

51

CHAPTER VI

What passed betwixt Don Quixote, his Neece, and the old woman : and it is one of the most materiall Chapters in all the History.

Sunnes going downe or no, with other ceremonies of this nature, which are used in single combates betwixt man and man, that thou knowest not of, but I doe. Know further, that the good Knight Errant (although he see ten Gyants, that with their heads, not onely touch, but overtop the clouds, and that each of them hath legs as big as two great towres, and armes like the masts of mighty ships, and each eye as big as a mill-wheele, and more fiery then a glasse-oven) must not be affrighted in any wise, rather with a stayd pace and undaunted courage, hee must set on them, close with them, and if possible, overcome, and make um turne taile in an instant ; yea, though they came armed with the shels of a certaine fish, which (they say) are harder then Diamonds, and though in stead of swords, they had cutting skeines of Damasco steele, or iron clubs with pikes of the same, as I have seene them more then once or twice. All this have I said, woman mine, that you may see the difference betwixt some Knights and others, and it is reason that Princes should more esteeme this second, or (to say fitter) this first Species of Knights Errant (for as we read in their histories) such an one there hath beene amongst them, that hath beene a safe-guard not onely of one Kingdome, but many.

Ah Sir, then said his Neece, beware ; for all is lies and fiction that you have spoken, touching your Knights Errant, whose stories, if they were not burnt, they deserve each of them at least to have a penance inflicted upon them, or some note, by which they might bee knowne to bee infamous, and ruiners of good customes.

I assure thee certainely (quoth Don Quixote) if thou wert not lineally my Neece, as daughter to mine owne Sister, I would so punish thee for the blasphemy thou hast spoken, as should resound thorow all the world. Is it possible that a Pisse-kitchin, that scarce knowes how to make Bone-lace, dares speake and censure the histories of Knights Errant ? What would Sr. Amadis have said if hee should have heard this ? But I warrant hee would have forgiven thee, for hee was the humblest and most courteous Knight of his time ;

HISTORIE OF DON QUIXOTE

CHAPTER
VI

What passed
betwixt Don
Quixote, his
Neece, and
the old
woman: and
it is one of
the most
materiall
Chapters in all
the History.

and moreover, a great Protector of Damozels : but such an
one might have heard thee, that thou mightst have repented
thee ; for all are not courteous, or pitifull, some are harsh
and bruitish. Neither are all that **beare** the name of
Knights, so, truely ; for some are of gold, others of Alchymy,
yet all seeme to be Knights : but all cannot brooke the
touchstone of truth : You have some base Knaves that burst
againe to seeme Knights, and some that are Knights, that kill
themselves in post-haste till they become Peasants : The one
either **raise** themselves by their ambition, or vertue ; the
others fall, either by their negligence, or vice ; and a man
had **need** be wise to distinguish betweene these two sorts of
Knights, so neere in their names, so distant in their actions.

Helpe me God (quoth the Neece) that you should know **so
much** Unckle, as were it in case of necessity, you might step
into a pulpit, and *preach in the streets, and for all that
you goe on so blindely, and fall into so eminent a madnesse,
that you would have us thinke you valiant, now you are old,
that you are strong, being so sickly, that you are **able** to
make crooked things straight, being crooked with yeeres,
and that you are a Knight when you are none ? for though
Gentle-men may bee Knights, yet the poore cannot.

*An usuall
thing in
Spaine, that
a Frier or
Iesuite (when
a fiery zeale
takes him)
makes his
pulpit in any
part of the
street, or
market-place.

You say well, Neece, in that (quoth Don Quixote) and
I could tell thee things concerning linages, that should
admire thee, but because I will not mingle Divinity with
Humanity, I say nothing : Marke yee hoe, to foure sorts
of linages (harken to me) may all in the world be reduc'd, and they **are** these. Some that from base begin-
nings have arrived **at** the greatest honours. Others that
had great beginnings, and so conserve them till the **end.**
Others, that though they had great beginnings, yet they
end pointed **like** a Pyramis, having lessened and annihilated
their beginning, till it ends in nothing. Others there **are
(and** these the **most)** that neither had good beginning, nor
reasonable middle, **and** so they passe away without mention,
as the linage of the common and ordinarie sort of people.
Let the house of the Othomans bee an example to thee **of**
the first, who had **an** obscure beginning, but **rose** to the

53

CHAPTER
VI

What passed
betwixt Don
Quixote, his
Neece, and
the old
woman: and
it is one of
the most
materiall
Chapters in all
the History.

greatnesse they now preserve, that from a base and poore shepheard that gave them their first beginning, have come to this height, in which now we see them. Many Princes may be an instance of the second linage, that began in greatnesse, and was so preserved, without augmentation or diminution, onely kept their inheritance, containing themselves within the limits of their own Kingdomes, peacefully. Thousands of examples there bee of such, as began in greatnesse, and lessened towards their end. For all your Pharaos, your Ptolomies of Ægypt, your Cæsars of Rome, with all the hurrie (if I may so terme them,) of your infinite Princes, Monarchs, Lords, Medes, Assyrians, Persians, Grecians, and Barbarians, all these linages, all these Lordships ended, pointed, and came to nought, aswell they, as those that gave them beginning, for it is not possible to finde any of their successors, and if it were, hee must bee in meane and base estate; with the common sort I have nothing to doe, since they only live, and serve to increase the number of men, without deserving more fame, or elogie of their greatnesse.

Thus much (fooles) you may inferre from all that hath beene said, that the confusion of linages is very great; and that those are the most great and glorious, that shew it in the vertue, wealth, and liberalitie of their owners. Vertue, wealth, and liberality (I say) for that great man that is vicious, will be the more so, by his greatnesse, and the rich man not liberall, is but a covetous begger, for he that possesseth riches, is not happie in them, but in the spending them, not only in spending, but in well spending them. The poore Knight hath no way to shew he is a Knight, but that he is vertuous, affable, well fashioned, courteous, and well-behaved, and officious: not proud, not arrogant, not backebiting, and above all, charitable: for in a penie (that he gives cheerefully to the poore) he shewes himselfe as liberall, as he that for ostentation gives an Almes before a multitude, and there is no man that sees him adorned with these vertues, but although he know him not, he will judge of him, and thinke he is well descended: for if he were not,

54

'twere miraculous, and the reward of vertue hath beene alwaies praise, and the vertuous must needs be praised.

CHAPTER
VI

What passed betwixt Don Quixote, his Neece, and the old woman: and it is one of the most materiall Chapters in all the History.

There be two courses for men to come to be wealthie and noble by, the one is Artes, tother Armes. I have more armes then learning, and was borne (according to my inclination that way) under the influence of the Planet Mars, so that I must of force follow his steps, which I meane to doe in spight of all the world, and it is in vaine for you to strive to perswade me, that I should nill what the heavens will me, fortune ordaines, and reason requires, and above all, my affection desires. Well, in knowing (as I know) the innumerable troubles that are annexed to Knight Errantrie, so I know the infinite goods that are obtained with it. And I know that the path of vertue is very narrow, and the way of vice large and spacious. And I know that their endes and resting places are different, for that of vice, large and spacious endes in death, and that of vertue, narrow and cumbersome endes in life, and not in a life that hath ending, but that is endlesse. And I know what *our great Castillian Poet said,

* Boscan.

> To the high Seate of Immortalitie
> Through crabbed paths, we must our journey take,
> Whence he that falles, can never climbe so hie.

Woe is me (said the Neece) my Master too is a Poet, he knowes every thing; I hold a wager, if he would be a Mason, he would build a house as easily as a cage. I promise thee, Neece (quoth Don Quixote) if these knightly cogitations did not wrap my senses, there is nothing I could not doe, nor no curiositie should scape me, especially cages, and tooth-pickers. By this one knockt at the doore, and asking who was there, Sancho answered, Tis I. The old woman, as soone as she heard him, ranne to hide her selfe, because she would not see him, for she could not abide him. The Neece let him in, and his Master Don Quixote went to receive him with open armes: and they both locked themselves in, where they had another Dialogue as good as the former.

55

THE SECOND PART OF THE

CHAPTER VII

What passed betwixt Don Quixote and his Squire, with other most famous accidents.

HE olde woman, as soone as shee saw her
Master and Sancho locked together, be-
gan to smell their drift, and imagining
that his third sally would result from that
consultation, and taking her mantle, full
of sorrow and trouble, she went to seeke
the Bachelour Samson Carrasco, suppos-
ing, that as he was wel spoken, and a late
acquaintance of Don Quixotes, he might perswade him to
leave his doting purpose; she found him walking in the
Court of his house, and seeing him, she fell downe in a
cold sweate, (all troubled) at his feete. When Carrasco saw
her so sorrowfull and affrighted, he asked her: Whats the
matter? what accident is this? Me thinks thy heart is at
thy mouth. Nothing (said she) Mr. Samson, but my Master
is run out, doubtlesse, he is run out. And where runs he?
said he, hath he broken a hole in any part of his body?
He runnes not out (answered she) but out of the doore of
his madnesse: I meane, sweete sir Bachelour, he meanes to
be a gadding againe, and this is his third time, he hath
gone a hunting after those you call adventures: I know not
why they give um this name. The first time they brought
him us athwart upon an Asse beaten to pieces. The second
time he came clapt up in an Oxe-Wayne, and locked in a
Cage, and he made us beleeve hee was enchaunted, and the
poore soule was so changed, that his mother that brought
him forth, would not have knowne him, so leane, so wan,
his eies so sunke into his head, that I spent above sixe
hundreth egges to recover him, as God is my witnesse, and
all the world, and my hennes that will not let me lye. That

56

HISTORIE OF DON QUIXOTE

CHAPTER
VII

What passed
betwixt Don
Quixote and
his Squire,
with other
most famous
accidents.

I well beleeve (quoth the Bachelor) for they are so good, and so fat, and so well nurtured, that they will not say one thing for another if they should burst for it. Well, is there ought else? hath there any other ill lucke hapned more then this you feare, that your Master will abroad? No Sr., (said she:) Take no care (quoth he) but get you home on Gods name, and get me some warme thing to breakefast, and by the way as you goe, pray me the Orison of Saint Apolonia, if you know it, and Ile go thither presently, and you shall see wonders.

Wretch that I am (quoth shee) the Orison of Saint Apolonia quoth you, that were, if my Master had the tooth-ach, but his paine is in his head. I know what I say (quoth hee) and doe not you dispute with me, since you know I have proceeded Bachelour at Salamanca: doe yee thinke there is no more then to take the degree? (said he.) With that, away she goes: and he went presently to seeke the Vicar, and communicate with him, what shall be said here-after.

At the time that Don Quixote and Sancho were locked together, there passed a discourse betweene them, which the historie tels with much punctualitie, and a true relation.

Sancho said to his Master, I have now reluc't my wife to let me goe with you whither soever you please; reduc'd you would say, Sancho (quoth Don Quixote.) I have bid you more then once (if I have not forgotten) said Sancho, that you doe not correct my words, if so be you understand my meaning, and when you doe not understand them, cry, Sancho, or Divell, I understand thee not: and if I doe not expresse my selfe, then you may correct me, for I am so socible.

I understand thee not, Sancho (quoth Don Quixote) for I know not the meaning of your socible. So socible is (said Sancho) I am so, so. Lesse and lesse doe I understand (said Don Quixote.) Why if you do not understand (said Sancho) I cannot do withall, I know no more, and God be with me. Thou meanest docible I beleeve, and that thou art so pliant, and so taking, that thou wilt appre-

3 : H   57

What passed
betwixt Don
Quixote and
his Squire,
with other
most famous
accidents.

hend what I shall tell thee, and learne what I shal instruct thee in.

Ile lay a wager (said Sancho) you searched and understood me at first, but that you would put me out, and heare me blunder out a hundreth or two of follies. It may bee so (quoth Don Quixote) but what saies Teresa? Teresa bids mee make sure worke with you, and that wee may have lesse saying, and more doing, for great sayers are small doers. A bird in the hand, is worth two in the bush. And I say, a womans advice is but slender, yet he that refuseth it, is a madman. I say so too (quoth Don Quixote:) But say (friend Sancho) proceede, for to day thou speakest preciously.

The businesse is (quoth Sancho) that as you better know then I, wee are all mortall, here to day, and gone to morrow, as soone goes the yong lambe to the roste, as the olde sheepe, and no man can promise himselfe more daies then God hath given him, for death is deafe, and when she knocks at lifes doore, she is in haste, neither threats, nor entreaties, nor Scepters, nor miters can stay her, as the common voice goes, and as they tell us in Pulpits.

All this is true (saide Don Quixote) but I know not where thou meanest to stop. My stoppe is (quoth Sancho) that your Worship allow me some certaine wages by *the moneth, for the time that I shall serve you, and that the said wages be paide me out of your substance, for Ile trust no longer to good turnes, which come either slowly, or meanely, or never, God give mee joy of mine owne. In a word, I must know what I may gaine, little or much: for the henne layes aswell upon one egge as many, and many littles make a mickle, and whilst something is gotten, nothing is lost. Indeede, if it should so happen (which I neither beleeve, nor hope for) that your Worship should give mee the Island you promised me, I am not so ungratefull, nor would carrie things with such extremity, as not to have the rent of that Island prized, and so to discount for the wages I received, cantitie for cantitie. Is not quantitie as much worth as cantitie, friend Sancho? answered Don Quixote. I understand you now, said Sancho, and dare lay any thing that I

*The custome
of Spaine is,
to pay their
servants
wages by the
moneth.

HISTORIE OF DON QUIXOTE

should have said quantitie, and not cantitie: but that's no
matter, seeing you have understood mee. I understand yee
very well (answered Don Quixote) and have penetrated the
utmost of your thoughts, and know very well, what marke
you ayme at, with the innumerable arrowes of your proverbes.

What passed
betwixt Don
Quixote and
his Squire,
with other
most famous
accidents.

Looke yee, Sancho, I could willingly affoord you wages,
if I had found in any Histories of Knights Errant, any example that might give me light, through the least chinke,
of any wages given monethly or yeerely: but I have read
all, or the most part of their Histories, and doe not remember that ever I have read, that any Knight Errant
hath allowed any set wages to his Squire. Only I know,
that all lived upon countenance, and when they least dreamt
of it, if their Masters had had good lucke, they were rewarded, either with an Island or some such thing equivalent,
and at least they remained with honour and title.

If you, Sancho, upon these hopes and additaments have a
minde to returne to my service, a Gods name; but to thinke
that I will plucke the old use of Knight Errantry out of his
bounds, and off the hindges, is a meere impossibility. So
that, Sancho, you may goe home, and tell your Teresa mine
intention; and if that shee and you will rely upon my
favour, *bene quidem*; and if not, let's part friends; for if
my pigeon-house have Comyns, it will want no Doves. And
take this by the way, A good expectation is better then a
bad possession, and a good demand better then an ill pay.
I speake thus, Sancho, that you may see, I know as well as
you, to sprinkle Proverbes like raine-showres. Lastly, let
me tell you, if you will not trust to my reward, and run
the same fortune with me, God keepe you, and make you
a Saint, for I shall not want more obedient Squires, and
more carefull, and not so irksome, nor so talkative as you.

When Sancho heard his Masters firme resolution, hee
waxed clowdy, and the wings of his heart began to stoope;
for hee thought verily his Master would not goe without
him, for all the treasure in the world. Thus being doubtfull and pensative, Samson Carrasco entred, and the Neece

CHAPTER
VII

What passed
betwixt Don
Quixote and
his Squire,
with other
most famous
accidents.

desirous to heare how he perswaded her Master that hee should not returne to his adventures.

In came Samson, a notable Crack-rope, and embracing him as at first, began in this loud key: Oh flower of Chivalrie, bright light of Armes, honour and mirrour of our Spanish nation: may it please almighty God of his infinite goodnesse, that he, or they, that hinder or disturbe this thy third sally, that they never finde it in the Labyrinth of their desires, nor let the ill they wish, for ever be accomplished. And turning to the old woman, he said: You neede no longer pray the Orison of Saint Apolonia, for I know, the determination of the spheres, is, that Don Quixote put in execution his loftie and new designes, and I should much burden my conscience, if I should not perswade and intimate unto this Knight, that hee doe no longer withdraw and hold backe the force of his valerous arme, and the courage of his most valiant minde, for with his delaying he defraudes the rectifying of wrongs, the protection of Orphans, the honor of Damsels, the bulwarke of married women, and other matters of this qualitie, which concern, appertain, depend, and are annexed unto the order of Knight Errantrie. Go on then, my beautifull, my brave Don Quixote, rather to day then to morrow, let your Greatnesse be upon the way, and if any thing be wanting to your journey, here am I to supply with my wealth, with my person, and if neede be, to be thy Magnificence his Squire, which I shall hold a most happy fortune. Then (said Don Quixote) turning to Sancho, Did not I tell thee, Sancho, that I should want no Squires? See who offers himselfe to mee: the most rare Bachelour Samson Carrasco, the perpetuall darling and delighter of the Salamancan schooles, sound and active of body, silent, suffering of heates and coldes, hunger and thirst, with all the abilities that belong to the Squire of a Knight Errant: but heaven forbid, that for my pleasure, I hox and breake off the Columne of learning, the vessell of Sciences, and that I lop off the eminent branch of the liberall Arts: Remaine thou another Samson in thy Countrey, honour it, and those gray haires of thine aged

60

HISTORIE OF DON QUIXOTE

CHAPTER
VII
What passed
betwixt Don
Quixote and
his Squire,
with other
most famous
accidents.

Parents, for I will content my selfe with any Squire, since
Sancho daignes not to attend mee.

I doe daigne, said Sancho, (all tender) and the teares
standing in his eyes, and thus proceeds: It shall not be
sayd, Master, for me, 'No longer pipe, no longer dance';
Nor am I made of hardest oake, for all the world knowes,
and especially my Towne, who the Pansa's were, from whom
I descend; besides, I know and have searched out, by many
good works, and many good words, the desire that your
Worship hath to doe me a kindnesse, and if I have beene
too blame to meddle in reckonings concerning my wages, it
was to please my wife, who when shee once falls into a vaine
of perswading, there's no hammer that doth so fasten the
hoopes of a Bucket as shee doth, till shee obtaine what she
would have; but howsoever, the husband must be husband,
and the wife, wife; and since I am a man every where (I
cannot deny that) I will also bee so at home, in spite of
any: so that there's no more to bee done, but that you
make your will, and set to your Codicill, in such sort, that
it may not bee revolked, and let's straight to our journey,
that Mr. Samsons soule may not suffer; for he saith, his
conscience is unquiet, till hee have perswaded you to your
third sally thorow the world, and I afresh offer my service
faithfully and loyally, aswell and better then anie Squire that
ever served Knight Errant in former times, or in present.

The Bachelour wondred to heare Sancho's manner and
method of speaking: for though in the first history he had
read of his Master, he never thought Sancho had beene so
witty, as they there paint him out, yet hearing him now
mention will and Codicill, revolking in stead of revoking,
he beleeved all that he had read of him, and confirmed him
to be one of the most solemnest Cox-combes of our age,
and said to himselfe, that two such mad men, as Master and
man, were not in all the world agen.

Now Don Quixote and Sancho embraced, and remained
friends, and with the grand Carrasco's approbation and good
will (who was then their Oracle) it was decreed, that within
three daies they should depart, in which they might have

61

CHAPTER
VII

What passed
betwixt Don
Quixote and
his Squire,
with other
most famous
accidents.

time to provide all things necessary for their voyage, and to get an helmet, which Don Quixote said, hee must by all meanes carry. Samson offered him one, for he knew a friend of his would not deny it him, although it were fowler with mould and rust, then bright with smooth steele.

The Neece and the olde woman cursed the Bachelour unmercifully, they tore their haire, scratcht their faces, and as your funerall mourners use, they howled at their Masters departure, as if he had beene a dead man. The designe that Samson had to perswade him to this third sally, was, to doe what the History tels us heereafter, all by the advice of the Vicar and the Barber, to whom he had before communicated it. Well, in those three dayes, Don Quixote and Sancho fitted themselves with what they thought they needed, and Sancho having set downe the time to his wife, and Don Quixote to his Neece, and the olde woman, toward night, without taking leave of any body, but the Bachelor, who would needs bring them halfe a league from the towne, they tooke their way towards Toboso. Don Quixote upon his good Rozinante, and Sancho on his old Dapple, his wallets were stuffed with provant, and his purse with money that Don Quixote gave him for their expences. Samson embraced him, and desired him that he might heare of his good or ill fortune, to rejoyce for the one, or bee sorry for the other, as the law of friendship did require ; Don Quixote made him a promise. Samson returned home, and the two went on towards the famous City of Toboso.

CHAPTER VIII

What befell Don Quixote, going to see his Mistris Dulcinea del Toboso.

LESSED be the powerfull Ala (saith Ala amongst Hamete Benengeli) at the beginning of the Moores, is this eighth Chapter: Blessed bee Ala, as much as which he thrice repeated, and sayd, that amongst the he rendred these benedictions, to see that Turkes. now Don Quixote and Sancho were upon their march, and that the Readers of their delightfull History may reckon, that from this time the exploits and conceits of Don Quixote and his Squire doe begin: Hee perswades them they should forget the former Chivalry of the noble Knight, and fix their eyes upon his Acts to come, which begin now in his way towards Toboso, as the former did in the fields of Montiel, and it is a small request, for so much as he is to performe, so he proceeds, saying:

Don Quixote and Sancho were now all alone, and Samson was scarce gone from them, when Rozinante began to neigh, and Dapple to sigh, which, both by Knight and Squire were held for lucky signes, and an happy presaging, though if the truth were tolde, Dapples sighs and brayings were more then the Horses neighing: whereupon Sancho collected, that his fortune should exceede and over-top his Masters; building, I know not upon what judiciall Astrologie, that sure he knew, although the History sayes nothing of it, onely he would often say, when he fell downe or stumbled, he would have beene glad, not to have gone abroad: for of stumbling or falling came nothing, but tearing his shooes, or breaking a rib, and though he were a foole, yet he was not out in this.

Don Quixote said unto him; Friend Sancho, the night comes on us apace, and it will grow too darke for us, to reach

CHAPTER
VIII
What befell
Don Quixote,
going to see
his Mistris
Dulcinea del
Toboso.

Toboso ere it be day, whither I am determined to goe, before I undertake any adventure, and there I meane to receive a benediction, and take leave of the Peerelesse Dulcinea del Toboso, after which I know and am assured, I shall end and close up every dangerous adventure; for nothing makes Knights Errant more hardy, then to see themselves favoured by their Mistresses. I beleeve it (quoth Sancho) but I doubt you will not speake with her, at least, not see her where you may receive her blessing, if shee give you it not from the mud-wals, where I saw her the first time, when I carried the letter and newes of your madde pranckes, which you were playing in the heart of Sierra Morena.

Were those mud-wals in thy fancie, Sancho, (quoth Don Quixote) where or thorow which thou sawest that never-enough-praised gentlenesse and beauty? They were not so, but galleries, walkes, or goodly stone pavements, or how call yee um? of rich and royall Palaces. All this might bee (answered Sancho) but to me they seemed no better, as I remember. Yet let's goe thither (quoth Don Quixote) for so I see her; let them be mud-wals, or not, or windowes; all is one, whether I see her thorow chincks, or thorow garden-lettices, for each ray that comes from the sunne of her brightnesse to mine eyes, will lighten mine understanding, and strengthen mine heart, and make me sole and rare in my wisdome and valour.

Truely Sir (sayd Sancho) when I saw that sunne, it was not so bright, that it cast any rayes from it, and belike twas, that as she was winnowing the wheat I told you of, the dust that came from it, was like a cloud upon her face and dimmed it. Still doest thou thinke, Sancho (quoth Don Quixote)? Beleeve and grow obstinate, that my Mistris Dulcinea was winnowing, it being a labor so unfit for persons of quality, that use other manner of exercises and recreation, which shew a slight-shoot off their noblenesse? Thou doest ill remember those verses of our Poet, where he paints out unto us, the exercises which those foure Nymphes used in their christall

habitations, when they advanced their heads above the loved *Tagus, and sat in the greene fields working those rich

64

HISTORIE OF DON QUIXOTE

CHAPTER
VIII
What befell
Don Quixote,
going to see
his Mistris
Dulcinea del
Toboso.

embroyderies, which the ingenious Poet there describes unto us, all which were of gold, of purle, and woven with embossed pearles: such was the worke of my Mistris, when thou sawest her, but that the envy, which some base Enchanter beares to mine affaires, turnes all that should give me delight, into different shapes, and this makes me feare, that the Historie of my exploits which is in print (if so be some Wizard my enemie were the Author) that he hath put one thing for another, mingling with one truth a hundreth lies, diverting himselfe to tell tales, not fitting the continuing of a true Historie. **Oh** envie thou roote of infinite evils, thou worme of vertues.

All vices, Sancho, doe bring a kinde of pleasure with them, but envie hath nothing but distaste, rancor and raving. I am of that minde too (said Sancho) and I thinke that in the Historie that Carrasco told us of, that he had seene of us, that my credit is turned topsie turvy, and (as they say) goes a begging. Well, as I am [an] honest man, I never spoke ill of any Enchanter, neither am I so happie as to be envied: true it is, that I am somewhat malicious, and have certaine knavish glimpses: but all is covered and hid under the large cloake of my simplicitie, alwaies naturall to me, but never artificiall: and if there were nothing else in me, but my beliefe (for I beleeve in God, and in all that the Romane Church believes, and am sworne a mortall enemie to the Iewes) the Historians ought to pittie me, and to use me well in their writings: but let um say what they will, naked was I borne, naked I am, I neither winne nor lose, and though they put me in bookes, and carrie me up and downe from hand to hand, I care not a figge, let um say what they will.

'Twas just the same (quoth Don Quixote) that happened to a famous Poet of our times, who having made a malicious Satyre against all the Curtizans, he left out one amongst them, as doubting whether she were one or no, who seeing she was not in the scrowle amongst the rest, tooke it unkindly from the Poet, asking him, what he had seene in her, that he should not put her amongst the rest, and desired him to enlarge his Satyre, and put her in the spare roome: if not,

3 : I   65

CHAPTER
VIII
What befell
Don Quixote,
going to see
his Mistris
Dulcinea del
Toboso.

she would scratch out his eyes: the Poet consented, and set her downe with a vengeance, and shee was satisfied, to see her selfe famous, although indeed infamous. Besides, the tale of the shepherd agrees with this, that set Diana's Temple on fire, which was one of the seven wonders of the world, because he would bee talked of for it; and although there were an Edict, that no man should either mention him by speaking or writing, that he might not attaine to his desire; yet his name was knowne to be Erostratus: the same allusion may be had out of an Accident, that befell the great Emperour Charles the fift with a Knight of Rome.

The Emperour was desirous to see the famous Temple of the Rotunda, which in ancient times was called the Temple of all the Gods, and now by a better stile, of all Saints, and it is the only entire edifice that hath remained of all the Gentiles in Rome, and that which doth most conserve the Glory and Magnificence of it's founders: tis made like an halfe Orange, exceeding large, and very lightsome, having but one window that gives it light, or to say truer, but one round Loover on the top of it: the Emperour looking on the edifice, there was a Romane Knight with him, that shewed him the devices and contriving of that great worke and memorable architecture; and stepping from the Loover, said to the Emperour: a thousand times, mightie Monarch, have I desired to see your Majestie, and cast my selfe down from this Loover, to leave an everlasting fame behind me. I thanke you (said the Emperour) that you have not performed it, and henceforward, I will give you no such occasion to shew your loyaltie, and therefore I command you, that you neither speake to me, nor come to my presence; and for all these words, he rewarded him.

I'le tell you, Sancho, this desire of honour is an itching thing: What do'st thou thinke cast Horatius from the Bridge all arm'd into deepe Tyber? What egged Curtius to lanch himselfe into the Lake? What made Mutius burne his hand? What forced Cæsar against all the South-sayers to passe the Rubicon? And to give you more moderne examples, What was it bored those ships, and left those valorous Spaniards on ground, guided by the most courteous Cortez in the new world?

All these, and other great and severall exploits, are, have bin, and shall be the workes of fame, which mortals desire as a reward, and part of the immortalitie, which their famous artes deserve: though we that be Christian Catholicke Knights Errant, must looke more to the happinesse of another world (which is Eternall in the Ethereall and Celestiall regions) then to the vanitie of fame, which is gotten in this present fraile age, and which, let it last as long as it will, it must have ending with this world which hath its limited time: so that, oh Sancho, our actions must not passe the bounds, that Christian Religion (which wee professe) hath put us in.

In Gyants we must kill pride: envie in generousnesse and noble brests: anger in a continent reposed and quiet minde: ryot and drowzinesse, in temperance and vigilance: lasciviousnesse, in the loyaltie we observe to those that we have made the Mistresses of our thoughts: and sloth, by travelling up and downe the world, seeking occasions, that may make us (besides Christians) famous Knights. These, Sancho, are the meanes, by which the extremes of glory are obtained, which fame brings with it.

All that you have hitherto spoken (quoth Sancho) I understand passing well: but I would faine have you zolve me of one doubt, which even now comes into my head. Resolve, thou would'st say Sancho, (quoth Don Quixote) speake a Gods name, for I 'le answer thee, as well as I can. Tell me, Sr., said Sancho, these Iulies, or Augusts, and all these famous Knights you talke of, that are dead, where are they now? The Gentiles, said he, undoubtedly are in Hell: the Christians, if they were good Christians, either in *Purgatorie, or in Hell. Tis very well, but the Sepulchers where the bodies of these great Lordlings lye interred, have they *silver lampes burning before them, or are their Chappell walles decked with Crutches, winding sheets, periwigs, legges, and waxe eyes? and if not with these, with what? The Sepulchers of the Gentiles (saide Don Quixote) were for the

What befell Don Quixote, going to see his Mistris Dulcinea del Toboso.

*According to the Romish opinion, erronious.

*Relicks that use to be hanged up in the Papists Churches.

THE SECOND PART OF THE

CHAPTER
VIII
What befell
Don Quixote,
going to see
his Mistris
Dulcinea del
Toboso.

most part, sumptuous Temples, the ashes of Iulius Cæsars
bodie were put upon a huge Pyramis of stone, which at this
day, is called Saint Peters needle. The Emperour Adrians
Sepulchre was a great Castle as bigge as a pretty village, it
was called Moles Adriani, and at this day, the Castle of
Saint Angelo in Rome: Queene Artemisia buried her husband Mausolus in a Sepulchre, which was held to be one of
the seven wonders of the world: but none of all these, nor
many others the Gentiles had, were decked with winding
sheetes, nor any kinde of offrings or signes that testified,
they were Saints that were buried in them.

That's it I come to (said Sancho:) and tell me now, which
is more, to raise a dead man, or to kill a Gyant? The
answer is at hand (said Don Quixote:) To raise a dead man.
There I caught you (quoth Sancho) then, the fame of him
that raiseth the dead, gives sight to the blinde, makes the
lame walke, restoreth sicke men, who hath lampes burning
before his Sepulchre, whose Chappell is full of devout people,
which upon their knees adore his Relickes, this man hath
greater renowne, and in another world, then ever any of
your Gentile Emperours, or Knights Errant ever left behind
them.

I grant you that (quoth **Don Quixote**). Wel, answered
Sancho, this fame, these graces, these prerogatives, how call
ye um? have the bodies and Relikes of Saints, that, by the
approbation and license of our holy Mother the Church,
have their lampes, their lights, their winding sheetes, their
crutches, their pictures, their heads of haire, their eyes, and
legges, by which they increase mens devotions, and endeere
their Christian fame; Kings carrie the bodies of Saints, or
their Reliques upon their shoulders, they kisse the pieces of
their bones, and doe decke, and inrich their Chappels with
them, and their most precious altars.

What will you have me inferre from all this, Sancho
(quoth Don Quixote)? I meane (said Sancho) that we
endevour to be Saints, and we shall the sooner obtaine the
fame we looke after: and let me tell you Sr., that yesterday
or tother day, (for so I may say, it being not long since)

68

HISTORIE OF DON QUIXOTE

CHAPTER
VIII
What befell
Don Quixote,
going to see
his Mistris
Dulcinea del
Toboso.

there were two poore barefoote Friers canonized or beatified, and now many thinke themselves happie, to kisse or touch, those yron chaines, with which they girt and tormented their bodies, and they are more reverenced, then is (as I said) Roldans sword in the Armorie of our Lord the King, (God save him:) So that (Master mine) better it is, to be a poore Frier of what order soever, then a valiant Knight Errant: a doozen or two of lashes obtaine more at Gods hands, then two thousand blowes with the launce, whether they be given to Gyants, to Spirits, or Hobgoblins.

Al this is true (answered Don Quixote:) but al cannot be Friers, and God Almighty hath many waies, by which he carries his Elect to heaven: Cavallerie is a religion, and you have many Knights Saints in heaven. That may be (said Sancho) but I have heard, you have more Friers there, then Knights Errant. That is (quoth Don Quixote) because the Religious in number are more then the Knights. But there are many Knights Errant (said Sancho). Many indeede (quoth Don Quixote) but few that deserve the name.

In these and such like discourses they passed the whole night, and the next day, without lighting upon any thing, worth relation, for which, Don Quixote was not a little sorrie: at last, the next day toward night they discovered the goodly Citie of Toboso, with which sight Don Quixotes spirits were revived, but Sancho's dulled, because he knew not Dulcineas house, nor ever saw her in his life, no more then his Master, so that, the one to see her, and the other, because he had not seene her, were at their wits end, and Sancho knew not how to doe, if his Master should send him to Toboso: but Don Quixote resolved to enter the Citie in the night, and till the time came, they staide betweene certaine Okes, that were neere Toboso; and the prefixed moment being come, they entred the citie, where they lighted upon things, things indeede.

69

CHAPTER IX

Where is set downe as followeth.

IDNIGHT was neere spunne out, when Don Quixote and Sancho left the mountaine, and entred the Citie: the towne was all husht, and the dwellers were asleepe, with their legges stretcht at length, (as they say:) the night was brightsome, though Sancho wisht it had beene darker, that he might not see his madnesse: the dogges in the towne did nothing but barke and thunder in Don Quixotes eares, and affrighted Sancho's heart: now and then an Asse braied, Hogs grunted, Cats mewed, whose different howlings were augmented with the silent night: all which the enamoured Knight held to be ominous: but yet he spoke to Sancho, Sonne Sancho (said he) guide to Dulcinea's Palace: it may be, we shall finde her waking. Body of the Sunne (quoth Sancho) to what Palace shall I guide? for where I saw her Highnesse, it was a little house. Belike (quoth Don Quixote) she was retired into some corner of her Palace, to solace her selfe in private with her Damozels, as great Ladies and Princesses use to doe. Sr., (quoth Sancho) since, whether I will or no, you will have my Mistris Dulcinea's house to be a Palace, doe ye thinke neverthelesse, this to be a fit time of night to finde the doore open in? Doe you thinke it fit, that we bounce, that they may heare and let us in, to disquiet the whole towne? are we going to a bodie house thinke yee? Like your whoremasters, that come, and call, and enter, at what houre they list, how late soever it be? First of all, to make one thing sure, let's finde the Palace, replide Don Quixote, and then, Sancho, I'le tell thee what's fit to be done: and looke, Sancho, either my sight failes me, or that great Bulk and shadow that we see, is Dulcinea's Palace.

70

HISTORIE OF DON QUIXOTE

Well, guide on Sr., (said Sancho) it may be it is so, though I'le first see it with my eyes, and feele it with my hands, and beleeve it, as much as it is now day. Don Quixote led on, and having walked about some two hundreth paces, he lighted on the Bulk that made the shadow, and saw a great steeple, which he perceived was not the Palace, but of the chiefe Church in the towne. Then said he, Sancho, we are come to the Church. I see it very well (quoth Sancho) and I pray God, wee come not to our graves: for it is no good signe to haunt Church-yards so late, especially since I told you (as I remember) that this Ladies house is in a little Allie without passage thorow. A poxe on thee blockhead (said Don Quixote) where hast thou ever found, that Kings houses and Palaces have beene built in such Allies? Sr., (quoth Sancho) every country hath their severall fashions: It may be, here, in Toboso, they build their great buildings thus, and therefore pray Sr., give me leave, to looke up and downe the Streets, or Lanes that lie in my way, and it may be, that in some corner I may light upon this Palace (the Divell take it) that thus mockes and misleades us. Speake mannerly, Sr., (quoth Don Quixote) of my Mistrisses things, and let's be merry and wise, and cast not the rope after the bucket.

I will forbeare (said Sancho) but how shall I endure, that you will needs have me be thorowly acquainted with a house, I never saw but once, and to finde it at midnight, being you cannot finde it, that have seene it a million of times? Sirrah, I shall grow desperate (quoth Don Quixote) come hither hereticke. Have not I told thee a thousand times, that I never saw the Peerelesse Dulcinea, nor never crossed the thresholds of her Palace, and that I only am enamoured on her by heare-say, and the great fame of her beautie and discretion? Why now I heare you (said Sancho) and since you say, you have never scene her; nor I neither. That cannot be (said Don Quixote) for you told me at least, that you had seene her winnowing of wheate, when you brought me the answer of the letter I sent by you. Ne're stand upon that (said Sancho) for let me tell you, that I only saw

71

THE SECOND PART OF THE

CHAPTER
IX
Where is
set downe
as followeth.

her by heare-say too, and so was the answer I brought: for
I know her as well, as I can boxe the Moone. Sancho,
Sancho, (said Don Quixote) ther's a time to laugh, and a
time to mourne. Not because I say, I have neither seene,
nor spoken to the Mistris of my soule, shouldst thou say,
thou hast neither seene, nor spoken to her, it being otherwise (as thou knowest.) Being in this discourse, they saw
one passing by um with two Mules, and by the noise the
plough made which they drew upon the ground, they might
see it was some husbandman, that rose by breake of day, to
goe to his tillage, and so it was: as he came, he went singing that Romante, of the batell of Roncesvalles with the
Frenchmen.

In hearing of which (quoth Don Quixote) Sancho, hang
me, if we have any good fortune this night. Doe not you
heare what this Clowne sings? Yes marry doe I (said
Sancho) but what doth the Chase of Roncesvalles concerne
us? Tis no more then if he had sung the Romante of

*As if we
should have
said in Eng-
lish, Chevie
Chase, or
such like.

* Calantos, and all one, for our good or ill lucke in this
business.

By this the ploughman came by them: and Don Quixote
questioned him: Can you tell me, friend (so God reward
you) which is the Palace of the Peerelesse Dulcinea del
Toboso? Sir (answered the yong man) I am a stranger,
and have lived but a while in this towne, and serve a rich
husbandman to till his ground; here over-against, the Vicar
and the Sexton both live, any of them will tell you of this
Lady Princesse, as having a List of all the inhabitants of
Toboso; although I thinke, there is no such Princesse here,
but many Gentlefolkes, each of which may be a Princesse in
her owne house. Why friend (quoth Don Quixote) it may
be, that shee I aske for, is amongst these. It may be so
(said the fellow) and God speede you, for now it begins to
be day peepe: and switching his Mules, he staid for no
more questions.

Sancho seeing his Master in a deepe suspence, and very
malecontent, told him: Sr., the day comes on apace, and it
will not be so fit, that we Sunne our selves in the Streete: it

72

is better to go out of the Citie, and that you shade your selfe in some Grove here abouts, and I will come backe anon, and not leave a by-place in all this towne, where I may search for the House, Castle, or Palace of my Lady, and it were ill lucke, if I found her not: and if I doe, I will speake with her, and let her know, where, and how you doe, expecting, that she give you order and direction, how you may see her, without prejudice to her honour and good name.

Sancho, (said Don Quixote) thou hast spoken a thousand sentences, inclosed in the circle of thy short discourse: The advice that thou hast now given me, I hunger after, and most lovingly accept of it: Come, sonne, let us take shade, and thou shalt returne (as thou sayest) to seeke, to see, and to speake to my Mistris, from whose discretion and courtesie, I hope for a thousand miraculous favours. Sancho stood upon thornes, till he had drawne his Master from the towne, lest he should verifie the lie of the answer, that he had carried him from Dulcinea, to Sierra Morena. So he hastned him to be gone, which was presently done, some two miles from the towne, where they found a forrest, or wood, where Don Quixote tooke shade: and Sancho returned to the Citie to speake with Dulcinea, in which Embassie matters befell him, that require a new attention, and a new beliefe.

CHAPTER X

How Sancho cunningly enchanted the Lady Dulcinea, and other successes, as ridiculous as true.

THE Authour of this history comming to relate that which he doth, in this Chapter sayes; That hee would willingly have passed it over in silence, as fearing not to be beleeved; because heere Don Quixotes madnesse did exceed, and was at least two flight-shoots beyond his greatest that ever was: but for all this feare and suspition, he set it downe as tother acted it, without adding or diminishing the least jot of truth in the History, not caring for any thing that might bee objected against him for a lier, and hee had reason; for truth is stretcht, but never breakes, and tramples on the lie, as oyle doth upon water; and so prosecuting his History, hee sayes, that as Don Quixote had shaded himselfe in the Forrest or Oake-wood neere the Grand Toboso, he willed Sancho to returne to the City, and not to come to his presence, without he had first spoken to his Mistris from him, requesting her, that she would please to be scene by her captiv'd Knight, and to daigne to bestow her blessing on him, that by it, hee might hope for many most prosperous successes, in all his onsets and dangerous enterprizes. Sancho tooke on him to fulfill his command, and to bring him now as good an answer as the former.

Goe, Lad, (sayd Don Quixote) and bee not daunted when thou comest before the beames of the Sunne of Beauty, which thou goest to discover; O happy thou, above all the Squires of the world, be mindfull, and forget not how she entertaines thee; if she blush just at the instant, when thou deliverest my Embassie; if she be stirred and troubled

HISTORIE OF DON QUIXOTE

CHAPTER
X

How Sancho
cunningly
enchanted
the Lady
Dulcinea,
and other
successes,
as ridiculous
as true.

when she heares my name; whether her cushion cannot hold her; if she be set in the rich state of her Authority: and if she stand up, marke her whether she clap somtimes one foot upon another; if she repeat the answer shee gives thee, twice or thrice over; or change it from milde to curst; from cruell to amorous; whether shee seeme to order her haire, though it be not disordered: Lastly, observe all her actions and gestures; for if thou relate them, just as they were, I shall ghesse what is hidden in her heart, touching my love in matter of fact: For know, Sancho, if thou knowest it not, that the actions and outward motions that appeare (when love is in treaty) are the certaine messengers that bring newes of what passeth within. Goe, Friend, and better fortune guide thee then mine, and send thee better successe then I can expect twixt hope and feare, in this uncouth solitude in which thou leavest me.

I goe (said Sancho) and will returne quickely; Enlarge that little heart of yours no bigger then an Hasell-nut, and consider the saying, 'Faint heart never,' etc., 'Sweet meat must have sowre sauce': And another, 'Where wee least thinke, there goes the Hare away.' This I say, because that if to night wee found not the Castle or Palace of my Lady, now by day I doubt not but to finde it, when I least dreame of it, and so to finde her. Beleeve me, Sancho (quoth Don Quixote) thou always bringest thy Proverbes so to the haire of the businesse wee treat of, as God give me no worse fortune then I desire.

This sayd, Sancho turned his backe, and switched his Dapple, and Don Quixote stayd a horse-backe, easing himselfe on his stirrups, and leaning on his lance, full of sorrowfull and confused thoughts, where we will leave him, and wend with Sancho, who parted from his Master no lesse troubled and pensative then he; insomuch, that hee was scarce out of the wood, when turning his face, and seeing that Don Quixote was out of sight, he lighted from his Asse, and resting at the foot of a tree, hee began to discourse thus to himselfe, and say: Now, brother Sancho, I pray let's know whither is your Worship going? To seeke some Asse

75

CHAPTER
X

How Sancho
cunningly
enchanted
the Lady
Dulcinea,
and other
successes, as
ridiculous
as true.

*Mistakes of
simplicity.

that you have lost? No forsooth. Well, what is it you seeke for? I seeke (a matter of nothing) a Princesse, and in her the Sunne of Beauty, and all Heaven withall. And where doe yee thinke to finde this you speake of, Sancho? Where? Why in the Grand City of Toboso. Well, and from whom doe yee seeke her? From the most famous Knight Don Quixote de la Mancha, he that righteth wrongs, *gives the thirsty meat, and the hungry drinke. All this is well: and doe you know her house, Sancho? **My** Master sayes, It is a Royall Palace, or a lofty Towre. **And** have you ever seen her, trow? Neither hee nor I, never. And doe you thinke it were well, that the men of Toboso should know, that you were here to entice their Princesses, and to trouble their wenches, and should come and grinde your ribs with bangs, and leave you never a sound bone? Indeed, belike they should consider that you are commanded, friend, but as a messenger, that you are in no fault, not you. Trust not to that, Sancho, for your Manchegan people are as cholericke, as honest, and doe not love to be jested with. In very deede, if they smell you, you are sure to pay for it. Ware Hawke, ware Hawke: No, no, let me for **anothers** pleasure seeke better bread then's made of wheat; **and I** may as well finde this Dulcinea, as one Mary in *Robena, or a Scholler in blacke in Salamanca: The Devill, the Devill, and none else hath clapt me into this businesse. This Soliloquy passed Sancho with himselfe, and the upshot was this:

*As if wee
should say,
one Ione in
London.

   All things (sayd he) have a remedy but death, under whose yoke wee must all passe in spite of our teethes, when life ends. This Master of mine, by a thousand signes that I have seene, is a Bedlam, fit to be bound, and I come **not a** whit short of him, and am the greater Cox-combe of two, to serve him, if the Proverbe be true that says, 'Like master, like man'; and another; 'Thou art knowne by him that doth thee feed, not by him that doth thee breed.' Hee being thus mad then, and subject, out of madnesse, to mistaking of one thing for another, to judge blacke for white, and white for blacke, as appeared, when he sayd the winde-

76

HISTORIE OF DON QUIXOTE

CHAPTER
X

How Sancho
cunningly
enchanted
the Lady
Dulcinea,
and other
successes, as
ridiculous
as true. ·

mils were Gyants, and the Friers mules, Dromedaries, and the flocks of sheepe, armies of enemies, and much more to this tune; it will not be hard to make him beleeve, that some husband-mans daughter, the first we meet with, is the Lady Dulcinea: and if he beleeve it not, Ile sweare; and if hee sweare, Ile out-sweare him; and if he be obstinate, Ile be so more: and so, that I will stand to my tackling, come what will on it. Perhaps with mine obstinacy I shall so prevaile with him, that hee will send mee no more upon these kinde of messages, seeing what bad dispatch I bring him: or perhaps hee will thinke, that some wicked Enchanter, one of those that he sayes persecute him, hath changed her shape, to vex him.

With this conceit Sancho's spirit was at rest, and hee thought his businesse was brought to a good passe: and so staying there till it grew to be toward the Evening, that Don Quixote might thinke he spent so much time in going and comming from Toboso, all fell out happily for him: for when hee got up to mount upon Dapple, he might see three Countrey-wenches comming towards him from Toboso, upon three Asse-Colts, whether male or female, the Author declares not, though it be likely they were shee-asses, they being the ordinary beasts that those Countrey-people ride on: but because it is not very pertinent to the story, we neede not stand much upon deciding that. In fine, when Sancho saw the three Countrey-wenches, he turned back apace to finde out his Master Don Quixote, and found him sighing, and uttering a thousand amorous lamentations.

As soone as Don Quixote saw him, he sayd; How now, Sancho, what is the matter? May I marke this day with a white or a blacke stone? 'Twere fitter (quoth Sancho) you would marke it with red Oker, as the Inscriptions are upon Professours chaires, that they may plainely read that see them. Belike then (quoth Don Quixote) thou bringest good newes. So good (sayd Sancho) that you need no more but spurre Rozinante, and straight discover the Lady Dulcinea del Toboso, with two Damozels waiting on her, comming to see your Worship. Blessed God! friend Sancho, what

CHAPTER
X

How Sancho
cunningly
enchanted
the Lady
Dulcinea,
and other
successes, as
ridiculous
as true.

sayest thou (quoth Don Quixote)? See thou deceive mee
not with thy false mirth to glad my true sorrow.

What should I get by deceiving you (quoth Sancho) the
rather your selfe being so neere to discover the truth?
Spurre, Sir, ride on, and you shall see our Mistris the
Princesse comming, clad indeede and adorned like her selfe:
She and her Damozels are a very sparke of gold: They are
all ropes of pearle, all Diamonds, all Rubies, all cloth of
gold, ten stories high at least: Their haires hung loose over
their shoulders, that were like so many Sun-beames playing
with the winde, and besides all this, they are mounted
upon three flea-bitten Nackneyes, the finest sight that can
be. Hackneyes thou would'st say, Sancho. Hackney or
Nackney (quoth Sancho) there is little difference: but let
them come upon what they will, they are the bravest Ladies,
that can be imagined, especially, My Ladie the Princesse
Dulcinea that dazels the sences.

Let's go, sonne Sancho (quoth Don Quixote) and for a
reward for this unlookt for good newes, I bequeath thee the
best spoile I get in our first adventure next, and if this content thee not, I give thee my this yeeres Coltes by my three
Mares thou knowest I have to foale in our towne Common.
The Colts I like (quoth Sancho:) but for the goodnesse of
the spoile of the first adventure I have no minde to that.
By this they came out of the wood, and saw the three
Country wenches neere them. Don Quixote stretcht his
eyes, all over Toboso way, and seeing none but the three
wenches, he was somewhat troubled, and demanded of Sancho,
if he had left them comming out of the Citie. How, out of
the Citie (quoth Sancho:) are your eyes in your noddle, that
you see them not comming here, shining as bright as the
Sunne at noone? I see none, said he, but three Wenches
upon three Asses.

Now God keepe me from the Devill (quoth Sancho:) and
is it possible that three Hackneyes, or how call ye um, as
white as a flake of snow, should appeare to you to be Asses?
As sure as may be, you shall pull off my beard if that be so.
Well, I tell you, friend Sancho, tis as sure that they are

HISTORIE OF DON QUIXOTE

CHAPTER
X

How Sancho
cunningly
enchanted
the Lady
Dulcinea,
and other
successes, as
ridiculous
as true.

Hee, or Shee Asses, as I am Don Quixote de la Mancha,
and thou Sancho Pansa; at least to me they seeme so.

Peace, sir (quoth Sancho) and say not so, but snuffe your
eyes, and reverence the Mistris of your thoughts, for now
she drawes neere: and so saying, he advanced to meet the
three Countrey-wenches, and alighting from Dapple, tooke
one of their Asses by the halter, and fastning both his knees
to the ground, sayd, Queene, and Princesse, and Dutchesse
of beauty, let your Haughtinesse and Greatnesse be pleased,
to receive into your grace and good liking, your captiv'd
Knight that stands yonder turned into marble, all-amazed
and without his pulse, to see himselfe before your Magnificent Presence. I am Sancho Pansa his Squire, and he is
the Way-beaten Knight Don Quixote de la Mancha, otherwise called The Knight of the Sorrowfull Countenance.

And now Don Quixote was on his knees by Sancho, and
beheld with unglad, but troubled eyes, her that Sancho
called Queene and Lady; but seeing he discovered nothing
in her but a Countrey-wench, and not very well-favoured,
for shee was blub-fac'd, and flat-nosed; he was in some
suspence, and durst not once open his lips. The wenches
too were astonisht, to see those two so different men upon
their knees, and that they would not let their companion
goe forward. But she that was stayed, angry to heare her
selfe mis-used, broke silence first, saying: Get you out of
the way with a mischiefe, and let's be gone, for wee are in
haste.

To which (quoth Sancho) Oh Princesse and universall
Lady of Toboso, why doth not your magnanimous heart
relent, seeing the Pillar and Prop of Knight Errantry pro-
strated before your sublimated presence? Which when one
of the other two heard, after she had cryed out to her Asse,
that was turning aside, shee said: Look how these Yonkers
come to mocke at poore Countrey-folke, as if wee knew not
how to returne their flouts upon them: get you gone your
way, and leave us, you had best. Rise, Sancho (quoth Don
Quixote) at this instant, for I perceive now, that mine ill
fortune, not satisfied, hath shut up all the passages by which

79

CHAPTER
X

How Sancho
cunningly
enchanted
the Lady
Dulcinea,
and other
successes, as
ridiculous
as true.

any content might come to this my wretched soule within my flesh. Oh thou, the extreme of all worth to bee desired, the bound of all humane gentlenesse, the only remedy of this mine afflicted heart that adores thee, now that the wicked Enchanter persecutes me, and hath put clouds and Cataracts in mine eyes, and for them onely, and none else, hath transformed and changed thy peerelesse beauty and face, into the face of a poore Countrey-wench, if so be now hee have not turned mine too into some Hobgoblin, to make it lothsome in thy sight, look on mee gently and amorously, perceiving, by this submission and kneeling, which I use to thy counterfet beauty, the humility with which my soule adores thee.

Marry-muffe (quoth the Countrey-wench) I care much for your courtings: Get you gone, and let us goe; and wee shall be beholding to you. Sancho let her passe by him, most glad that he had sped so well with his device. The Countrey-wench that played Dulcinea's part, was no sooner free, when spurring her Hackney with a prickle she had at the end of her cudgell, she began to run apace; and the Asse feeling the smart of it more then ordinary, began to wince so fast, that downe came my Lady Dulcinea: which when Don Quixote saw, hee came to help her up, and Sancho went to order and gird her pack-saddle, that hung at the Asses belly; which being fitted, and Don Quixote about to lift his enchanted Mistris in his armes to her Asse, shee being now got upon her legs, saved him that labour; for stepping a little backe, shee fetcht a rise, and clapping both her hands upon the Asses crupper, shee lighted as swift as an Hawke upon the pack-saddle, and sate astride like a man.

Then sayd Sancho: By Saint Roque our Mistris is as light as a Robin-ruddocke, and may teach the cunningst Cordovan or Mexicanian to ride on their Ginets: At one spring shee hath leapt over the crupper, and without spurres makes the Hackney run like a Muske-Cat, and her Damozels come not short of her; for they flie like the winde. And he said true: for when Dulcinea was once on horse-backe, they

HISTORIE OF DON QUIXOTE

all made after her, and set a running for two miles, without
looking behinde them.

Don Quixote still looked after them, but when they were
out of sight, turning to Sancho, he sayd; Sancho, how
thinkest thou? How much Enchanters doe hate mee?
And see how farre their malice extends, and their aime at
mee, since they have deprived me of the happinesse I should
have received, to have seene my Mistris in her true being.
Indeed I was borne to be an example of unfortunate men,
to be the Marke and Butt, at which Ill-Fortunes arrowes
should be sent. And thou must note, Sancho, that these
Enchanters were not content to have changed and transformed my Dulcinea: but they have done it into a shape,
so base and ugly, as of a Country-wench thou sawest, and
withall, they have taken from her, that which is so proper
to her and great Ladies, to wit, her sweet sent of flowres
and Amber: for let me tell thee, Sancho, that when I went
to helpe Dulcinea to her Hackney (which as thou sayest,
seemed to me to be a shee-Asse) she gave me such a breath
of raw garlicke, as pierc'd and intoxicated my braine.

O base rowt, cried out Sancho instantly. Oh dismall and
ill minded Enchanters. I would I might see you all strung
up together like Galls, or like Pilchers in sholes: cunning
you are, much you can, and much you doe it had bin
enough for you, Rascals, to have turned the pearles of my
Ladies eyes, into Corky galls, and her most pure golden
haire, into Bristles of a red Oxes taile, and finally, all her
feature from good to bad, without medling with her breath,
for only by that, we might have ghessed, what was concealed
under that course rinde, though to say true, I never saw her
coursenesse, but her beautie, which was infinitely increased
by a Moale she had upon her lippe, like a Mostacho, with
seven or eight red haires like threeds of gold, and above a
handfull long. To this Moale (quoth Don Quixote) according to the correspondencie that those of the face have, with
those of the body, shee hath another in the Table of her
thigh, that correspondes to the side, where that of her face
is: but haires of that length thou speakest of, are very

How Sancho
cunningly
enchanted
the Lady
Dulcinea,
and other
successes, as
ridiculous
as true.

3 : L   81

much for Moales. Well, I can tell you (quoth Sancho) that there they appeared, as if they had beene borne with her. I beleeve it, friend, replide Don Quixote : for nature could forme nothing in Dulcinea that was not perfect and complete ; and so, though she had a hundreth Moales, as well as that one thou sawest in her, they were not Moales, but Moones and bright starres.

But tell me, Sancho, that which thou didst set on, which seemed to me, to be a packe-saddle, was it a plaine saddle, or a saddle with a backe ? It was (said Sancho) a Ginet saddle, with a field covering, worth halfe a Kingdome, for the richnesse of it. And could not I see all this ? Well, now I say againe, and will say it a thousand times, I am the unhappiest man alive. The crack-rope Sancho had enough to doe to hold laughter, hearing his Masters madnesse, that was so delicately gulled.

Finally, after many other reasons that passed betwixt them both, they gate up on their beasts, and held on the way to Saragosa, where they thought to be fitly, to see the solemnities that are performed once every yeere in that famous Citie. But before they came thither, things befell them, that because they are many, famous and strange, they deserve to be written and read, as shall be seene here following.

HISTORIE OF DON QUIXOTE

CHAPTER XI

Of the strange Adventure that befell **Don** Quixote, with the Cart or Waggon **of** the Parliament of Death.

ON QUIXOTE went on, wonderfull pensative, to thinke what a shrewd tricke the Enchanters had played him, in changing his Mistris Dulcinea into the Rusticke shape of a Country Wench, and could not imagine what meanes he might use to bring her to her Pristine being; and these thoughts so distracted him, that carelesly he gave Rozinante the Reines, who perceiving the libertie he had, stayed every stitch-while to feede upon the greene grasse, of which those fields were full; but Sancho put him out of his Maze, saying: Sr., Sorrow was not ordained for beasts, but men: yet if men doe exceede in it, they become beasts, pray Sr., recollect and come to your selfe, and plucke up Rozinantes Reines, revive and cheere your selfe, shew the courage that befits a Knight Errant. What a Devil's the matter? What faintnesse is this? are we dreaming on a dry Summer? Now Satan take all the Dulcineas in the world, since the well-fare of one only Knight Errant, is more worth then all the Enchantments and transformations in the world.

Peace, Sancho (quoth Don Quixote) with a voice now not very faint: peace, I say, and speake no blasphemies against that Enchanted Lady, for I only am in fault for her misfortune and unhappinesse: her ill plight springs from the envie that Enchanters beare me. So say I too (quoth Sancho) for what heart sees her now, that saw her before, and doth not deplore? Thou mayst well say so, Sancho, repli'd Don Quixote, since thou sawest her, in her just entire

CHAPTER
XI
Of the strange
Adventure
that befell
Don Quixote,
with the Cart
or Waggon
of the Par-
liament of
Death.

beautie, and the Enchantment dimmed not thy sight, nor concealed her fairenesse: against me only, only against mine eyes the force of it's venome is directed.

But for all that, Sancho, I have falne upon one thing, which is, that thou didst ill describe her beautie to me: for if I forget not, thou saydst she had eyes of Pearles, and such eyes are rather the eies of a Sea-Breame then a faire Dames: but as I thinke, Dulcineas eyes are like two greene Emeralds rared with two Celestiall Arkes, that serve them for Eye-browes. And therefore for your pearles, take them from her eyes, and put them to her teeth: for doubtlesse, Sancho, thou mistook'st eyes for teeth. All this may be, said Sancho, for her beauty troubled me, as much as her foulenesse since hath done you; but leave we all to God, who is the knower of all things that befall us in this Vale of teares, in this wicked world, where there is scarce any thing without mix-ture of mischiefe, Impostorship, or villanie.

One thing (Master mine) troubles me more then all the rest; to thinke what meanes there will be, when you over-come any Gyant or other Knight, and command him to present himselfe before the beautie of the Lady Dulcinea, where this poore Gyant, or miserable vanquisht Knight shall finde her. Me thinkes I see um goe staring up and downe Toboso, to finde my Lady Dulcinea, and though they should meete her in the midst of the streete, yet they would no more know her then my father.

It may be, Sancho (quoth Don Quixote) her Enchantment will not extend to take from vanquished and presented Gyants and Knights, the knowledge of Dulcinea: and therefore in one or two of the first I conquer and send, we will make triall, whether they see her or no, commanding them, that they returne to relate unto me what hath befalne them.

I say Sr., (quoth Sancho) I like what you have said very well, and by this device we shall know what we desire; and if so be she be only hidden to you, your misfortune is beyond hers: but so my Lady Dulcinea have health and content, we will beare and passe it over here aswell as we

84

may, seeking our adventures, and let time alone, who is the best Phisician for these and other infirmities.

Don Quixote would have answered Sancho Pansa: but he was interrupted by a waggon that came crosse the way, loaden with the most different and strange personages and shapes, that might be imagined. He that guided the Mules, and served for Wagoner, was an ugly Devill. The Wagons selfe was open without Tilt or Boughes. The first shape that presented it selfe to Don Quixotes eyes, was of Death her selfe, with a humane face, and next her an Angel with large painted wings. On one side stood an Emperour, with a crowne upon his head, to see to of gold. At Deaths feet was the god called Cupid, not blind-folded, but with his Bow, his quiver, and arrowes. There was also a Knight compleatly Arm'd, only he had no Murrion or headpeece, but a hat full of divers colour'd plumes: with these there were other personages of different fashions and faces.

All which seene on a suddaine, in some sort troubled Don Quixote, and affrighted Sancho's heart, but straight Don Quixote was jocund, beleeving, that some rare and dangerous Adventure was offred unto him, and with this thought, and a minde disposed to give the onset to any perill, he got himselfe before the Wagon, and with a loud and threatning voice, cried out: Carter, Coach-man, or Devill, or whatso-e're thou art, be not slow to tell me, who thou art, whither thou goest, and what people these are thou carriest in thy Cart-coach, rather like Charons boate, then Waggons now in use.

To which, the Devill staying the Cart, gently replide, Sr., we are Players of Thomas Angulo's Companie, we have playd a play called the *Parliament of Death*, against this Corpus Christi tyde, in a towne behind the ridge of yonder mountaine, and this afternoone we are to play it againe at the towne you see before us, which because it is so neere, to save a labour of new attiring us, we goe in the same cloathes in which we are to Act. That yong man playes Death: that other an Angel: that woman our Authors wife, the Queene, a fourth there, a Souldier, a fift the Emperour, and I the

CHAPTER
XI

Of the strange
Adventure
that befell
Don Quixote,
with the Cart
or Waggon
of the Par-
liament of
Death.

CHAPTER
XI
Of the strange
Adventure
that befell
Don Quixote,
with the Cart
or Waggon
of the Par-
liament of
Death.

Devill, which is one of the chiefest Actors in the play, for I have the best part. If you desire to know any thing else of us, aske me, and I shall answer you most punctually, for as I am a Devill, nothing is unknowne to me.

/By the faith of a Knight Errant (said Don Quixote) as soone as ever I saw this Waggon, I imagined some strange Adventure towards, and now I say it is fit to be fully satisfied of these apparitions, by touching them with our hands./ God be with you, honest people: Act your play, and see whether you will command any thing wherein I may be serviceable to you, for I will be so most cheerefully and willingly: for since I was a boy, I have loved Maske-shewes, and in my youth, I have beene ravished with Stage-playes.

Whilst they were thus discoursing, it fell out, that one of the company came toward them, clad for the Foole in the Play, with Morrice-bels, and at the end of sticke, he had three Cowes bladders full-blowne, who thus masked, running toward Don Quixote, began to fence with his cudgell, and to thwacke the bladders upon the ground, and to friske with his bels in the aire: which dreadfull sight so troubled Rozinante, that Don Quixote not able to hold him in (for hee had gotten the bridle betwixt his teeth) he fell a running up and down the field, much swifter then his anatomized bones made shew for.

Sancho, that considered in what danger of being throwne downe his Master might bee, leapt from Dapple, and with all speed ran to help him; but by that time he came to him, he was upon the ground, and Rozinante by him, for they both tumbled together. This was the common passe Rozinantes trickes and boldnesse came to. But no sooner had Sancho left his horseback-ship to come to Don Quixote, when the damning Devill with the bladders leapt on Dapple, and clapping him with them, the feare and noyse, more then the blowes, made him fly thorow the field, towards the place where they were to play. Sancho beheld Dapples careere and his Masters fall, and knew not to which of the ill chances hee might first repaire: But yet like a good Squire

86

HISTORIE OF DON QUIXOTE

and faithfull servant, his Masters love prevailed more with him, **then** the cockering of his Asse: though every hoysting of the bladders, and falling on Dapples buttocks, were to him trances and tydings of death, and rather had hee those blowes had lighted on his eye-bals, then on the least haire of his Asses taile.

In this perplexity hee came to Don Quixote, who was in a great deale worse plight then he was willing to see him: and helping him on Rozinante, sayd; Sir, the Devill hath carried away Dapple. What Devill (quoth Don Quixote)? Hee with the bladders, replied Sancho. Well, I will recover him **(sayd** Don Quixote) though he should locke him up **with him in** the darkest and deepest dungeons of Hell: **Follow** me, Sancho, for the waggon goes but slowly, and the **Mules** shall satisfie Dapples losse. There is no neede (sayd Sancho:) temper your choller, for now I see the Devill hath left Dapple, and hee **returnes** to his home, and he sayd true, for the Devill having **falne** with Dapple, to imitate Don Quixote and Rozinante, he went on foot to the towne, and the Asse came backe to his Master.

For all that (sayd Don Quixote) it were fit to take revenge of the Devils unmannerlinesse upon some of those in the waggon, even of the Emperour himselfe. Oh never thinke of any such matter (sayd Sancho) and take my counsell, that is, never to meddle with Players, for they are a people mightily beloved: I have knowne one of um in prison for **two** murders, and yet scap'd Scot-free: Know this, Sir, **that as** they **are** merry Ioviall Lads, **all** men love, esteeme, and helpe them, especially if they be the Kings Players, and all **of** them in their fashion **and** garbe are Gentleman-like.

For all **that** (sayd Don Quixote) the Devill-Player shall not scape **from me** and brag of it, though all mankind help him: and so saying, he gat to the waggon, that was now somewhat neere the towne, and crying aloud, sayd ; Hold, stay, merry Greekes, for Ile make yee know what belongs to the Asses and furniture, belonging to the Squires of Knights Errant. Don Quixotes noyse was such, that those

CHAPTER
XI

Of the strange Adventure that befell Don Quixote, with the Cart or Waggon of the Parliament of Death.

87

THE SECOND PART OF THE

CHAPTER
XI
Of the strange
Adventure
that befell
Don Quixote,
with the Cart
or Waggon
of the Par-
liament of
Death.

of the waggon heard it, and ghessing at his intention by
his speeches, in an instant Mistris Death leapt out of the
waggon, and after her the Emperor, the Devill-Waggoner,
and the Angell, and the Queene too with little Cupid, all
of them were straight loaded with stones, and put themselves in order, expecting Don Quixote with their Peebles
poynts.

Don Quixote, that saw them in so gallant a Squadron,
ready to discharge strongly their stones, held in Rozinantes
reines, and began to consider how he should set upon them,
with least hazard to his person. Whilst he thus stayd,
Sancho came to him, and seeing him ready to give the
on-set, sayd; Tis a meere madnesse, Sir, to attempt this
enterprise: I pray consider, that for your *river-sops, there
are no defensive weapons in the world, but to be shut
up and inlayd under a brazen-bell: and consider likewise,
tis rather rashness then valour, for one man alone to set
upon an Army, wherein Death is, and where Emperors
fight in person, and where good and bad Angels help:
and if the consideration of this be not sufficient, may this
moove you to know, that amongst all these (though they
seeme to be Kings, Princes and Emperours) there is no
Knight Errant.

*Meaning
the stones.

Thou hast hit upon the right, Sancho (sayd Don Quixote)
the very poynt that may alter my determination: I neither
can nor must draw my sword, as I have often told thee,
against any that be not Knights Errant. It concernes
thee, Sancho, if thou meanest to bee revenged for the wrong
done thine Asse, and Ile encourage thee, and from hence
give thee wholesome instructions. There needs no being
revenged of any body (said Sancho) for there is no Christianity in it; besides, mine Asse shall be contented to put
his cause to me, and to my will, which is, to live quietly as
long as Heaven shall afford me life.

Since this is thy determination (sayd Don Quixote) honest,
wise, discreet, Christian-like, pure Sancho, let us leave these
dreams, and seek other better and more reall adventures:
for I see, this Countrey is like to afford us many miraculous

88

ones. So he turned Rozinantes reines, and Sancho tooke his Dapple, Death with all the flying Squadron returned to the wagon, and went on their voyage: And this was the happy end of the wagon of Deaths adventure: thankes to the good advice that Sancho Pansa gave his Master: to whom there happened the day after another Adventure, no lesse pleasant, with an enamoured Knight Errant as well as he.

CHAPTER
XI

Of the strange
Adventure
that befell
Don Quixote,
etc.

CHAPTER XII

Of the rare Adventure that befell Don Quixote, with the Knight of the Looking-Glasses.

DON QUIXOTE and his Squire passed the ensuing night, after their Deaths encounter, under certaine high and shadie trees, Don Quixote having first (by Sancho's entreaty) eaten somewhat of the Provision that came upon Dapple, and as they were at supper, Sancho sayd to his Master; Sir, what an Asse had I beene, had I chosen for a reward, the spoyles of the first adventure which you might end, rather then the breede of the three Mares? Indeed, indeed, a bird in the hand is better then two in the bush.

For all that (quoth Don Quixote) if thou, Sancho, hadst let me give the on-set (as I desired) thou hadst had to thy share, at least, the Empresses golden crowne, and Cupids painted wings, for I had taken um away against the haire, and given um thee. Your Players scepters and Emperours crownes (sayd Sancho) are never of pure golde, but leafe and Tinne.

Tis true (answered Don Quixote) for it is very necessary, that your Play-ornaments bee not fine, but counterfet and

3 M

89

CHAPTER
XII
Of the rare
Adventure
that befell
Don Quixote,
with the
Knight of
the Looking-
Glasses.

seeming, as the Play it selfe is, which I would have thee, Sancho, to esteeme of, and consequently the Actors too, and the Authors, because they are the Instruments of much good to a Commonwealth, being like Looking-glasses, where the actions of humane life are lively represented, and there is no comparison, that doth more truely present to us, what we are, or what we should be, then the Comedy and Comedians : If not, tell mee, hast not thou seene a Play acted, where Kings, Emperours, Bishops, Knights, Dames, and other personages are introduced ? One playes a Ruffian, another the Cheater, this a Merchant, t'other a Souldier, one a crafty Foole, another a foolish Lover : And the Comedy ended, and the apparrell taken away, all the rehearsers are the same they were.

Yes marry have I, quoth Sancho. Why, the same thing (sayd Don Quixote) happens in the Comedy and Theater of this world, where some play the Emperours, other the Bishops; and lastly, all the parts that may be in a Comedy : but in the end, that is, the end of our life, Death takes away all the robes that made them differ, and at their buriall they are equall. A brave comparison (quoth Sancho) but not so strange to me, that have heard it often, as that of the Chesse-play, that while the game lasts, every Peere hath it's particular motion, and the game ended, all are mingled and shuffled together, and cast into a lethern bag, which is a kinde of buriall.

Every day, Sancho (quoth Don Quixote) thou growest wiser and wiser. It must needs bee (sayd Sancho) that some of your wisdome must cleave to me ; for grounds that are dry and barren, by mucking and tilling them, give good fruit : I meane, your conversation hath beene the mucke, that hath beene cast upon the sterill ground of my barren wit ; and the time that I have served you, the tillage, with which I hope to render happy fruit, and such as may not gaine-say or slide out of the paths of good manners, which you have made in my withered understanding.

Don Quixote laughed at Sancho's affected reasons, and it seemed true to him, what hee had sayd touching his reforma-
90

HISTORIE OF DON QUIXOTE

tion : for now and then his talke admired him, although for
the most part, when Sancho spoke by way of contradiction,
or like a Courtier, he ended his discourse with a downefall,
from the mount of his simplicity, to the profundity of his
ignorance : but that, wherein he shewed himselfe most
elegant and memorable, was in urging of Proverbs, though
they were never so much against the haire of the present
businesse, as hath been seene, and noted in all this History.

CHAPTER
XII
Of the rare
Adventure
that befell
Don Quixote,
with the
Knight of
the Looking-
Glasses.

A great part of the night they passed in these and such
like discourses, but Sancho had a great desire to let fall the
Pott-cullices (as he called them) of his eyes, and sleepe ; and
so undressing his Dapple, he turned him freely to graze :
with Rozinantes saddle he medled not, for it was his Masters
expresse command, that whilst they were in field, or slept not
within doores, hee should not unsaddle him, it being an
ancient custome observed by Knights Errant, to take the
bridle and hang it at the saddle-pummell : but beware taking
away the saddle, which Sancho observed, and gave him the
same liberty, as to his Dapple, whose friendship and Rozinantes was so sole and united, that the report goes by tradition
from father to sonne, that the Author of this true History
made particular chapters of it, onely to keepe the decency
and decorum due to so heroike a Story : he omitted it,
although sometimes he forgets his purpose herein, and writes,
that as the two beasts were together, they would scratch one
another, and being wearied and satisfied, Rozinante would
crosse his throte over Dapples necke, at least halfe a yard over
the other side : and both of them looking wistly on the
ground, they would stand thus three dayes together, at least
as long as they were let alone, or that hunger compelled them
not to looke after their provander.

'Tis sayd (I say) that the Author in his Story, compared
them in their friendship, to Nisus and Eurialus, to Pilades
and Orestes, which, if it were so, it may be seene (to the
generall admiration) how firme and stedfast the friendship
was of these two pacificke beasts, to the shame of men, that
so ill know the rules of friendship one to another. For this,
it was sayd, No falling out, like to that of friends. And let

91

CHAPTER
XII

Of the rare
Adventure
that befell
Don Quixote,
with the
Knight of
the Looking-
Glasses.

no man think the Author was unreasonable, in having compared the friendship of these beasts, to the friendship of men; for men have received many Items from beasts, and learnt many things of importance, as the Storks dung, the Dogs vomit and faithfulnesse, the Cranes watchfulnesse, the Ants providence, the Elephants honesty, and the Horse his loyalty.

At length Sancho fell fast asleepe at the foote of a Cork-tree, and Don Quixote reposed himselfe under an Oke. But not long after, a noise behind wakned him, and rising suddainly, he looked and hearkned from whence the noise came, and he saw two men on horsebacke, and the one tumbling from his saddle, said to the other; Alight, friend, and unbridle our horses, for me thinkes this place hath pasture enough for them, and befits the silence and solitude of my amorous thoughts: thus he spoke, and stretcht himselfe upon the ground in an instant, but casting himselfe down, his Armour wherwith he was armed, made a noise: a manifest token that made Don Quixote, thinke hee was some Knight Errant, and comming to Sancho, who was fast asleepe, hee pluck't him by the Arme, and tolde him softly. Brother Sancho, wee have an Adventure. God grant it bee good (quoth Sancho:) and where is this Masters Adventures Worship? Where, Sancho, replide Don Quixote, looke on one side, looke, and there thou shalt see a Knight Errant stretcht, who (as it appeares to me) is not overmuch joyed, for I saw him cast himselfe from his horse, and stretch on the ground, with some shewes of griefe, and as he fell, he crossed his Armes. Why, in what doe you perceive that this is an Adventure (quoth Sancho)? I will not say (answered Don Quixote) that this is altogether an Adventure, but an introduction to it, for thus Adventures begin.

But harke, it seemes he is tuning a Lute, or Viall, and by his spitting and cleering his brest, he prepares himselfe to sing. In good faith you say right (quoth Sancho) and tis some enamoured Knight. There is no Knight Errant (said Don Quixote) that is not so: let us give eare, and by the circumstance, we shall search the Laberynth of his thoughts, if so be he sing, for out of the abundance of the heart, the tongue speaketh. Sancho would have replied to his Master: But the Knight of the woods voice (which was but so so) hindered him, and whil'st the two were astonisht, he sung as followeth.

CHAPTER XII

Of the rare Adventure that befell Don Quixote, with the Knight of the Looking-Glasses.

Sonet.

Permit me, Mistris, that I follow may
  The bound, cut out just to your hearts desire:
To the which, in mine I shall esteeme for aye,
  So that I never from it will retire.
If you be pleas'd, my griefe (I silent) stay,
  And die make reckning that I straight expire,
If I may tell it you; the unusuall way
  I will, and make loves selfe be my supplier.
Fashion'd I am to proofe of contraries,
  As soft as waxe, as hard as Diamond too,
And to Loves lawes, my soule her selfe applies,
  Or hard, or soft, my brest I offer you
Graven, imprint in't what your pleasure is,
  I (secret) **sweare** it never to forgoe.

With a deep-fetcht, heigh, ho: even from the bottome of his heart, the Knight of the wood ended his song: and after some pause, with a grieved and sorrowfull voice uttered these words: Oh the fairest and most ungratefull woman in the world. And shall it be possible, most excellent Casildea de Vandalia, that thou suffer this thy captive Knight to pine and perish, with continuall peregrinations, with hard and painefull labours? Sufficeth not, that I have made all the Knights of Navarre, of Leon, all the Tartesians, all the Castillians confesse thee to be the fairest Lady of the world? I, and **all** the Knights of Mancha too? Not so, (quoth Don Quixote straight) for I am of the Mancha, but never yeelded to that, for I neither could nor ought confesse a thing so prejudiciall to the beautie of my Mistris: and thou seest, Sancho, how much this Knight is wide: but let **us** heare him, it may be, he will unfold himselfe more. Marry will he (quoth Sancho) for he talkes, as if he would lament a moneth together. But it fell out otherwise; for the Knight of the wood, having over-heard that they talked somewhat neere

CHAPTER
XII

Of the rare
Adventure
that befell
Don Quixote,
with the
Knight of
the Looking-
Glasses.

Sereno, the
night-dew
that falles.

him, ceasing his complaints, he stood up, and with a cleere, but familiar voice thus spake, Who's there, who is it? Is it haply some of the number of the contented, or of the afflicted? Of the afflicted (answered Don Quixote.) Come to me then (said he of the wood) and make account, you come to sadnesse it selfe, and to afflictions selfe. Don Quixote, when he saw himselfe answered so tenderly, and so modestly, drew neere, and Sancho likewise. The wailefull Knight laid hold on Don Quixotes arme, saying, Sit downe, Sr. Knight: for to know that you are so, and one that professeth Knight Errantrie, it is enough that I have found you in this place, where solitarines, and the *Sereno beare you companie, the naturall beds, and proper beings for Knights Errant.

To which Don Quixote replide, A Knight I am, and of the profession you speake of, and though disgraces, misfortunes, and sorrowes have their proper seate in my minde : notwithstanding, the compassion I have to other mens griefs, hath not left it : by your complaints I ghesse you are enamoured, I meane, that you love that ungratefull faire one, mentioned in your laments. Whilst they were thus discoursing, they sat together lovingly upon the cold ground, as if by day-breake, their heads also would not breake.

The Knight of the wood demanded, Are you happily enamoured, Sr. Knight? Unhappily I am (quoth Don Quixote) although the unhappines that ariseth from wel-placed thoughts, ought rather to be estemed a happinesse then otherwise. True it is (replide he of the wood) if disdaines did not vexe our reason and understanding, which being unmercifull, come neerer to revenge. I was never (said Don Quixote) disdained of my Mistris. No indeed (quoth Sancho) who was neere them : for my Lady is as gentle as a lambe, and as soft as butter. Is this your Squire (said he of the wood)? He is (said Don Quixote.) I ne're saw Squire (replide he of the wood) that durst prate so boldly before his Master, at least yonder is mine, as bigge as his father, and I can proove he never unfolded his lippes, whensoever I spake.

Well yfaith (quoth Sancho) I have spoken, and may speake

94

before, as, and perhaps : but let it alone, the more it is stirred,
the more it will stinke. The Squire of the wood tooke
Sancho by the hand, saying: Let us goe and talke what we
list Squirelike, and let us leave these our Masters, Let them
fall from their launces and tell of their Loves : for I warrant
you, the morning wil overtake them, before they have done.
A Gods name (quoth Sancho) and Ile tell you who I am, that
you may see whether I may be admitted into the number of
your talking Squires. So the two Squires went apart,
betweene whom there passed as wittie a Dialogue,
as their Masters was serious.

CHAPTER XIII

Where the Adventure of the Knight of the Wood
is prosecuted, with the discreete, rare, and
sweete Coloquie, that passed betwixt
the two Squires.

HE Knights and their Squires were devided;
these telling their lives, they their loves:
and thus sayth the Storie, that the Squire
of the wood said to Sancho, It is a cumbersome life that we leade, Sr., we, I say,
that are Squires to Knights Errant : for
truly we eate our bread with the sweat of
our browes, which is one of the curses,
that God laid upon our first parents. You may say also
(added Sancho) that we eate it in the frost of our bodies :
for who endure more heates and colds, then your miserable
Squires to Knights Errant ? and yet not so bad if we might
eate at all, for good fare lessens care : but sometimes it
happens, that we are two daies without eating, except it be
the ayre that blowes on us. All this may be borne (quoth
95

THE SECOND PART OF THE

Where the
Adventure of
the Knight of
the Wood is
prosecuted,
with the dis-
creete, rare,
and sweete
Coloquie, that
passed be-
twixt the two
Squires.

he of the wood) with the hope we have of reward: for if the
Knight Errant whom a Squire serves, be not too unfortunate,
he shall, with a little good hap, see himselfe rewarded with
the government of some Island, or with a reasonable Earledome. I (said Sancho) have often told my Master, that I
would content my selfe with the government of any Island,
and he is so Noble and Liberall, that he hath often promised
it me. I (said he of the Wood) for my services would be
satisfied, with some Canonrie, which my Master too hath
promised me.

Your Master indeed (said Sancho) belike is an Ecclesiasti-
call Knight, and may doe his good Squires these kindnesses:
but my Master is meerely Lay, though I remember, that
some persons of good discretion (though out of bad intention) counselled him, that he should be an Archbishop:
which he would not be, but an Emperour: and I was in a
bodily feare, lest he might have a minde to the Church, because I held my selfe uncapable of benefits by it: for let me
tell you, though to you I seeme a man, yet in Church matters
I am a very beast. Indeed, Sr., (said he of the Wood)
You are in the wrong: for your Iland-Governments are not
al so special, but that some are crabbed, some poore, some
distastefull; and lastly, the stateliest and best of all brings
with it a heavy burden of cares and inconveniences, which
hee (to whom it falls to his lot) undergoes. Farre better
it were, that we, who professe this cursed slavery, retire
home, and there entertaine ourselves with more delightfull
exercises, to wit, hunting and fishing; for what Squire is
there in the world so poore, that wants his Nag, his brace
of Grey-hounds, or his Angle-rod, to passe his time with, at
his Village?

I want none of this (sayd Sancho:) true it is, I have
no Nag, but I have an Asse worth two of my Masters
Horse: An ill Christmas God send mee, (and let it be the
next ensuing) if I would change for him, though I had foure
bushels of barley to boot: you laugh at the price of my
Dapple, for dapple is the colour of mine Asse: well, Grey-
hounds I shall not want neither, there being enow to spare

96

CHAPTER
XIII

Where the
Adventure of
the Knight of
the Wood is
prosecuted,
with the dis-
creete, rare,
and sweete
Coloquie, that
passed be-
twixt the two
Squires.

in **our towne;** besides, **the sport is best at** another mans charge.

Indeed, indeed, Sr. Squire (sayd he of the Wood) I have proposed and determined with my selfe, to leave these bezelings of these Knights, and returne to my Village, and bring up my children, for I have three, like three Orient-pearles. Two have I (sayd Sancho) that may bee presented to the Pope in person, especially one, a wench, which I bring up to bee a Countesse (God save her) although it grieve her mother. And how olde (asked he of the Wood) is this Lady-Countesse that you bring up so?

Fifteene, somewhat under or over (sayd Sancho) but she is **as long as a** lance, and as fresh **as** an Aprill-morning, and as **sturdy as a** Porter. These are parts (sayd he of the Wood) not **onely** for her **to** be a Countesse, but a Nymph **of** the Greeny **Grove**: Ah whoreson, whore, and what **a** sting the Queane **hath**? To which (quoth Sancho somewhat musty) Shee is no whore, neither was her mother before her, and none **of** them (God willing) shall be, as long as I live: and I pray, **Sir,** speake more mannerly: for these speeches are not consonant from you, that have beene brought up amongst Knights Errant, the flowers of courtesie. Oh (sayd he of the Wood) Sr. Squire, how you mistake, and how little you know what belongs to praising: what? have yee never observed, that when any Knight in the market-place gives the Bul a sure thrust with his lance, or when any body doth a thing well, the common people **use** to say; Ah whoreson whoremaster, how bravely he did **it? so** that, that which seemes to be a dispraise, in that **sence is a** notable commendation, and renounce you those **sonnes and** daughters, that doe not the workes, that may **make their** parents deserve such like praises. I doe re- **nounce** (sayd Sancho) and if you meant no otherwise; **I pray** you clap a whole whore-house **at** once upon my wife **and** children; for all **they** doe or say, are extremes worthy **of** such praises, and so **I** may see them, God deliver **me** out of this mortall sinne, that is, out of this dangerous profession of being **a** Squire, into which I have this second time incurred, being inticed and deceived with the purse

THE SECOND PART OF THE

CHAPTER
XIII

Where the
Adventure of
the Knight of
the Wood is
prosecuted,
with the dis-
creete, rare,
and sweete
Coloquie, that
passed be-
twixt the two
Squires.

of the hundred duckats, which I found one day in the
heart of Sierra Morena, and the Devill cast that bag of
Pistolets before mine eyes: (me thinkes) every foot I touch
it, hugge it, and carry it to mine house, set leases, and
rents, and live like a Prince, and still when I thinke of this,
all the toyle that I passe with this Block-head my Master,
seems easie and tolerable to me, who (I know) is more mad-
man then Knight.

Heereupon (sayd he of the Wood) it is sayd; that, 'All
covet, all lose': And now you talke of mad-men, I thinke,
my Master is the greatest in the world, he is one of them
that cries, 'Hang sorrow'; and that another Knight may
recover his wits, hee'l make himselfe mad, and will seeke
after that, which perhaps once found, will tumble him upon
his snowt. And is hee amorous haply? Yes (sayd hee of
the Wood) hee loves one Casildea de Vandalia, the most
raw and most rosted Lady in the world; but she halts not
on that foot of her rawnesse, for other manner of impostures doe grunt in those entrailes of hers, which ere long will
be knowne.

There is no way so plaine (quoth Sancho) that hath
not some rubbe, or pit, or as the Proverbe goes, In some
houses they seethe beanes, and in mine whole kettles full.
So madnesse hath more companions, and more needie ones
then wisedome. But if that which is commonly spoken be
true, that to have companions in misery is a lightner of it,
you may comfort me, that serve as sottish a Master as
I doe. Sottish but valiant, (answered he of the wood) but
more knave then foole or then valiant. It is not so with
my Master, said Sancho: for he is ne're a whit knave;
rather he is as dull as a Beetle, hurts no-body, does good
to all, he hath no malice, a childe will make him beleeve tis
night at noone day: and for his simplicitie, I love him as
my heart-strings, and cannot finde in my heart, to leave
him for all his fopperies. For all that, Brother and friend
(said he of the wood), if the blinde guide the blinde, both
will be in danger to fall into the pit.

Tis better to retire faire and softly, and returne to our

98

HISTORIE OF DON QUIXOTE

loved homes: for they that hunt after Adventures, doe not
alwaies light upon good. Sancho spit often, and as it
seemed, a kinde of glewy and dry matter: which noted by
the charitable wooddy Squire, he said, Me thinkes, with our
talking, our tongues cleave to our roofes: but I have suppler
hangs at the pummell of my horse, as good as touch: and
rising up, he returned presently with a Borracha of wine,
and a bak't meate, at least halfe a yard long, and it is no
lye, for it was of a Parboiled Cony so large, that Sancho,
when he felt it, thought it had beene of a Goate, and not a
Kid: which being seene by Sancho, he said, And had yee
this with you too, Sr.? Why, what did yee thinke (said
the other) doe you take me to be some hungry Squire? I
have better provision at my horses crupper, then a Generall
carries with him upon a March. Sancho fell to, without
invitation, and champed his bits in the darke, as if he had
scraunched knotted cordes, and said, I marry, Sr., you are a
true Legall Squire, round and sound, Royall and Liberall
(as appeares by your feast) which if it came not hither by
way of Enchantment, yet it seemes so at least, not like me
unfortunate wretch, that only carry in my wallets, a little
Cheese, so hard, that you may breake a Gyants head with
it, and only some doozens of Saint Iohns Weed leaves, and
some few Walnuts, and small nuts, (plentie in the strictnesse
of my Master, and the opinion he hath) and the method
he observes, that Knights Errant must only be maintained
and sustained onely with a little dry fruit, and sallets. By
my faith (Brother) replide he of the wood, my stomacke is
not made to your thistles, nor your stalkes, nor your mountaine roots: let our Masters deale with their opinions, and
their Knightly statutes, and eate what they will, I have my
cold meates, and this bottle hanging at the pummel of
my saddle, will he, or nill he: which I reverence and love
so much, that a minute scarce passeth me, in which I
give it not a thousand kisses and embraces. Which said,
he gave it to Sancho, who rearing it on end at his mouth,
looked a quarter of an houre together upon the Starres:
and when he had ended his draught, he held his necke on

Where the
Adventure of
the Knight of
the Wood is
prosecuted,
with the dis-
creete, rare,
and sweete
Coloquie, that
passed be-
twixt the two
Squires.

99

Where the
Adventure of
the Knight of
the Wood is
prosecuted,
with the dis-
creete, rare,
and sweete
Coloquie, that
passed be-
twixt the two
Squires.

*A place in
Spaine that
hath excellent
wines.

one side, and fetching a great sigh, cryes, Oh whoresoone
raskal, how Catholike it is. Law yee there (said he of the
wood) in hearing Sancho's whoresoone, how you have praised
the wine, in calling it whoresoone? I say (quoth Sancho)
that I confesse, that I know it is no dishonour to call any
bodie whoresoone, when there is a meaning to praise him.
But tell me, Sr., by the remembrance of her you love best,
is this wine of *Ciuidad Reall? A brave taste (said he
of the wood :) it is no lesse, and it is of some yeeres standing
too. Let me alone (said Sancho) you could not but thinke
I must know it to the height. Doe not you thinke it
strange, Sr. Squire, that I should have so great, and so
naturall an instinct, in distinguishing betwixt wines, that
comming to smell any wine, I hit upon the place, the
grape, the savour, the lasting, the strength, with all circumstances belonging to wine? But no marveile, if in
my linage by my fathers side, I had two of the most
excellent tasters that were knowne in a long time in
Mancha: for proofe of which, you shall know what befell
them.

They gave to these two some wine to taste out of a
Hogshead, asking their opinions, of the state, qualitie,
goodnesse or badnesse of the wine: the one of them
prooved it with the tip of his tongue, the other only
smelt to it. The first said, that that wine savoured of
yron. The second said, Rather of goats leather. The
owner protested, the Hogshead was cleane, and that the
wine had no kinde of mixture, by which it should receive
any savour of yron or leather. Notwithstanding, the two
famous tasters stood to what they had said. Time ran
on, the wine was sold, and when the vessell was cleansed,
there was found in it a little key, with a leatherne thong
hanging at it. Now you may see, whether he that comes
from such a race, may give his opinion in these matters.

Therefore I say to you (quoth he of the wood) let us
leave looking after these Adventures, and since we have
content, let us not seeke after dainties, but returne to our
cottages, for there God will finde us, if it be his will.

HISTORIE OF DON QUIXOTE

CHAPTER
XIII

Where the
Adventure of
the Knight of
the Wood is
prosecuted,
etc.

Till my Master come to Saragosa, I meane (quoth Sancho) to serve him, and then weele all take a new course. In fine, the two good Squires talked and dranke so much, that it was fit sleepe should lay their tongues, and slake their thirst, but to extinguish, it was impossible; so both of them fastned to the nigh emptie bottle, and their meate scarce out of their mouthes, fell asleepe : where for the present wee will leave them, and tell what passed betweene the two Knights.

CHAPTER XIV

How the Adventure of the Knight of the Wood is prosecuted.

AMONGST many discourses that passed betweene Don Quixote, and the Knight of the Wood, the History saies, that he of the wood said to Don Quixote, In briefe, Sr. Knight, I would have you know, that my destinie, or to say better, my election enamoured me upon the peerelesse Casildea de Vandalia, Peerelesse I call her, as being so in the greatnesse of her Stature, and in the extreme of her being and beautie. This Casildea (I tell you of) repaide my good and vertuous desires, in employing me (as did the stepmother of Hercules) in many and different perils, promising me at the accomplishing of each one, in performing another, I should enjoy my wishes : but my labours have beene so linked one upon another, that they are numberlesse, neither know I which may be the last to give an accomplishment to my lawfull desires.

Once she commanded me to give defiance to that famous Gyantesse of Sevil, called the Giralda, who is so valiant and so strong (as being made of brasse, and without changing

101

THE SECOND PART OF THE

XIV

How the
Adventure of
the Knight of
the Wood is
prosecuted.

*As if we
should say, **to**
remove the
stones at
Stonage in
Wilt-shire.

place) is the most mooveable and turning woman in the
world. I came, I saw, and conquered her, and made her
stand still, and keepe distance ; for a whole weeke together,
no windes blew, but the North : Otherwhiles she commanded
me to lift up the ancient *stones of the fierce Buls of Guisando : an enterprize fitter for Porters, then Knights : another time she commanded me to go downe and dive in the
Vault of Cabra (a fearefull and unheard of attempt) and to
bring her relation of all that was inclosed in that darke pro-
funditie. I staide the motion of the Giralda, I waied the
Buls of Guisando, I cast my selfe downe the steep Cave, and
brought to light the secrets of that bottome, but my hopes
were dead, how dead ? her disdaines still living, how living ?
Lastly, she hath now commanded me, that I run over all
the Provinces of Spaine, and make all the Knights Errant,
that wander in them, confesse, that she alone goes beyond
all other women in beauty, and that I am the valiantest,
and most enamoured Knight of the world : in which demand
I have travelled the greatest part of Spaine, and have overcome many Knights, that durst contradict me. But that
which I prize and esteeme most is, that I have conquer'd, in
single combate, that so famous Knight Don Quixote de la
Mancha, and made him confesse that my Casildea is fairer
then his Dulcinea, and in this conquest only I make account,
that I have conquer'd all the Knights in the world, because
the aforesaid Don Quixote hath conquered them all, and I
having overcome him, his fame, his glorie, and his honour
hath beene transferred and passed over to my person, and
the Conquerour is so much the more esteemed, by how
much the conquered was reputed : so that the innumerable
exploits of Don Quixote now mentioned, are mine, and passe
upon my account.

Don Quixote admired to heare the Knight of the wood,
and was a thousand times about to have given him the lye,
and had his Thou lyest, upon the point of his tongue : but
hee defer'd it as well as he could, to make him confesse with
his owne mouth that he lyed, and so he told him calmely.
That you may have overcome (Sr. Knight) all the Knights
102

HISTORIE OF DON QUIXOTE

Errant **of** Spaine, **and the** whole world, I grant yee: but
that you have overcome Don Quixote de la Mancha, I doubt
it, it might be some other like him, though few there be so How the
Adventure of
the Knight of
the Wood is
prosecuted.
like. Why not? replide he of the Wood: I can assure you,
Sir, I fought with him, overcame, and made him yeeld.
Hee is a tall fellow, withred faced, lanke and dry in his
limbes, somewhat hoary, sharpe-nosed and crooked; his
mustachoes long, blacke, and falne; hee marcheth under
the name of The Knight of the Sorrowfull Countenance:
he presses the loine, and rules the bridle of a famous horse
called Rozinante, and hath for the Mistris of his thoughts,
one Dulcinea del Toboso, sometimes called Aldonsa Lorenso,
just **as mine,** that because her name was Casilda, and of
Andaluzia, I call her Casildea de Vandalia: and if all these
tokens be not enough to countenance the truth, heere is my
sword that shall make incredulity it selfe believe **it.** Have
patience, Sr. Knight (quoth Don Quixote) and heare what I
shall say. Know, that this Don Quixote you **speake** of, is
the greatest friend I have in this world, and so much that I
may tell you, I love him as well as my selfe, and by the
signes that you have given of him, so punctuall and certaine,
I cannot but thinke it is he whom you have overcome. On
the other side, I see with mine eyes, and feele with my hands,
that it is not possible it should be he, if it be not, that,
as he hath many Enchanters that be his enemies, especially
one, that doth ordinarily persecute him, there be some one
that hath taken his shape on him, and suffered himselfe to
be overcome, to defraud him of the glory which his noble
chivalry hath gotten and layd up for him thorowout the
whole earth. And for confirmation of this, I would have
you know, **that** these Enchanters mine enemies (not two
daies since) transformed the shape and person of the faire
Dulcinea del Toboso, into a foule and base country wench,
and in this sort belike they have transformed Don Quixote:
and if all this be **not** sufficient to direct you in the truth,
here is Don Quixote himselfe, that will maintaine it with his
Armes on foot or on horse-back, or in what manner you
please: and he grasped his sword, expecting what resolution

103

CHAPTER
XIV

How the
Adventure of
the Knight of
the Wood is
prosecuted.

the Knight of the Wood would take, who with a stayed voyce, answered and sayd: A good Pay-master needs no surety: hee that could once, Don Quixote, overcom you when you were transformed, may very well hope to restore you to your proper being. But because it becomes not Knights to doe their feats in the darke like high-way-robbers and Ruffians, let us stay for the day, that the Sunne may behold our actions; and the condition of our combate shall be, that he that is overcome, shall stand to the mercy of the Conquerour, to do with him according to his will, so farre as what he ordaineth shall be fitting for a Knight.

I am over-joyed with this condition and agreement (quoth Don Quixote). And (this sayd) they went where their Squires were, whom they found snorting, and just as they were, when sleep first stole upon them. They wakened them, and commanded they should make their horses ready: for by sun rising, they meant to have a bloudy and unequall single combate. At which newes Sancho was astonisht and amazed, as fearing his Masters safety, by reason of the Knight of the Woods valour, which he had heard from his Squire: but without any reply, the two Squires went to seeke their cattel: for by this the three horses and Dapple had smelt out one another, and were together.

By the way, he of the Wood sayd to Sancho, You must understand, Brother, that your Combatants of Andaluzia use, when they are Sticklers in any quarrell, not to stand idlely with their hands in their pockets, whilst their friends are fighting. I tell you this, because you may know, that whilst our Masters are at it, we must skirmish too, and breake our lances to shivers. This custome, Sr. Squire (answered Sancho) may be currant there, and passe amongst your Ruffians and Combatants you talke of: but with your Squires that belong to Knights Errant, not so much as a thought of it. At least, I have not heard my Master so much as speake a word of any such custome, and hee knowes without booke all the ordinances of Knight Errantry. But let mee grant yee, that tis an expresse ordinance that the Squires fight, whilst their Masters doe so: yet I will not

fulfill that, **but** pay the *penalty that shall **be** imposed upon
such peaceable Squires: for I doe not **thinke**, it will be
above two pound of wax, and I had rather **pay** them, for I
know they will cost me lesse, then the lint that **I** shall spend
in making tents to cure my head, which already I make
account is cut and divided in two: besides, tis impossible I
should fight, having never a sword, and I never wore any.

For that (quoth he of the Wood) Ile tell you a good
remedy, I have heere two linnen bags of one bignesse, you
shall have one, and I the other, and with these equall
weapons, **wee** 'll fight at bag-blowes. Let us doe so and you
will (sayd Sancho) for this kinde of fight will rather serve to
dust, then to wound us. Not so (sayd the other) for within
the bags (that the winde may not carry them to and fro)
wee will put halfe **a** doozen of delicate smooth pebbles, of
equall waight, and so we may bag-baste one another, without
doing any great hurt. Looke ye, body of my father (quoth
Sancho) what Martins **or** Sables furre, or what fine-carded
wooll he puts in **the** bags, not to beat out our brains, or
make Privet of our **bones**: but know, Sir, if they were silke
bals, I would **not** fight: let our Masters fight, and heare on
it in another world, let us drinke and live, for time will bee
carefull to take away our lives, without our striving to end
them before their time and season, and that they drop before
they are ripe. **For** all that (sayd he of the Wood) we must
fight halfe an houre. No, no (sayd Sancho) I will not be so
discourteous **and** ungratefull, as to wrangle with whom **I**
have eaten **and** drunke, let the occasion bee never so small,
how much more I being without choller **or** anger, who the
Devill can barely without these fight?

For this (sayd he of the Wood) **Ile give** you a sufficient
cause, which is, that before wee begin **the** combate, I will
come mee finely **to** you, **and** give you three or foure boxes,
and strike you to my feet, with which I shall awake your
choller, although **it** sleepe like a Dormouse. Against this
cut I have another (quoth Sancho) that comes not short **of**
it, I will take me a good cudgell, and before you waken **my**
choller, I will make you sleepe so soundly with bastinadoing

**CHAPTER
XIV**

How **the**
Adventure of
the Knight of
the Wood is
prosecuted.

*Alluding to
some penalties
enjoyned by
Confessors, to
pay to burne
in candles **in**
the Church.

3: O   105

CHAPTER
XIV

How the
Adventure of
the Knight of
the Wood is
prosecuted.

you, that it shall not wake but in another world, in which it shall be knowne, that I am not hee that will let any man handle my face ; and every man looke to the shaft he shoots : And the best way were to let every mans choller sleepe with him, for no man knowes what's in another, and many come for wooll, that returne shorne, and God blessed the Peace-makers, and cursed the Quarreller ; for if a Cat shut into a roome, much baited and straightned, turne to be a Lyon, God knowes what I that am a man, may turne to : There-fore, from henceforward, Sr. Squire, let mee intimate to you, that all the evill and mischiefe that shall arise from our quarrell, bee upon your head. Tis well (quoth he of the Wood) let it be day, and we shall thrive by this.

And now a thousand sorts of painted birds began to chirp in the trees, and in their different delightfull tones, it seemed they bad good morrow, and saluted the fresh Aurora, that now discovered the beauty of her face, thorow the gates and bay-windowes of the East, shaking from her lockes an in-finite number of liquid pearles, bathing the hearbes in her sweet liquour, that it seemed they also sprouted, and rained white and small pearles : the willowes did distill their savoury Manna, the fountaines laughed, the brookes murmured, the woods were cheered, and the fields were enriched with her comming.

But the brightnesse of the day scarce gave time to dis-tinguish things, when the first thing that offered it selfe to Sancho's sight, was the Squire of the Woods nose, which was so huge, that it did as it were shadow his whole body. It is sayd indeed, that it was of an extraordinary bignesse, crooked in the middest, and all full of warts of a darkish-greene colour, like a Berengene, and hung some two fingers over his mouth : this hugenesse, colour, warts, and crooked-nesse, did so dis-figure his face, that Sancho in seeing him, began to lay about him back-ward and forward, like a young raw Ancient, and resolved with himselfe to endure two hundred boxes, before his choller should waken to fight with that Hobgoblin.

Don Quixote beheld his opposite, and perceived that his

106

HISTORIE OF DON QUIXOTE

CHAPTER
XIV
How the
Adventure of
the Knight of
the Wood is
prosecuted.

helmet was on and drawne, so that he could not see his face, but he saw that he was well set in his body, though not tall; upon his armour he wore an upper garment or cassocke, to see to, of pure cloth of gold, with many Moones of shining Looking-glasses spred about it, which made him appeare very brave and gorgeous, a great plume of greene feathers waved about his Helmet, with others white and yellow, his Lance which he had reared up against a tree, was very long and thicke, and with a steele pike above a handfull long. Don Quixote observed and noted all, and by what he had seene and marked, judged that the sayd Knight must needs be of great strength: But yet he was not afrayd (like Sancho) and with a bold courage thus spoke to the Knight of the Looking-glasses: If your eagernesse to fight, Sir Knight, have not spent your courtesie, for it, I desire you to lift up your Visor a little, that I may behold whether the livelinesse of your face be answerable to that of your disposition, whether vanquisht or Vanquisher you be in this enterprize. Sir Knight (answered he of the Looking-glasses) you shall have time and leisure enough to see me, and if I doe not now satisfie your desire, it is because I thinke I shall doe a great deale of wrong to the faire Casildea de Vandalia, to delay so much time as to lift up my Visor, till I have first made you confesse what I know you goe about. Well, yet while we get a horse-backe (Don Quixote sayd) you may resolve me whether I be that Don Quixote whom you sayd, you had vanquished.

To this I answer you (said he of the Looking-glasses) You are as like the Knight I conquered, as one egge is to another: But, as you say, Enchanters persecute you, and therefore I dare not affirme whether you bee hee or no. It sufficeth (quoth Don Quixote) for mee, that you beleeve your being deceived: but that I may entirely satisfie you, let's to horse, for in lesse time then you should have spent in lifting up your Visor (if God, my Mistrisse, and mine Arme defend me) will I see your face, and you shall see that I am not the vanquisht Don Quixote you speake of.

And heere cutting off discourse, to horse they goe, and

107

THE SECOND PART OF THE

CHAPTER
XIV
How the
Adventure of
the Knight of
the Wood is
prosecuted.

Don Quixote turn'd Rozinante about, to take so much of
the field (as was fit for him) to returne to encounter his
enemie, and the Knight of the Looking-glasses did the like.
But Don Quixote was not gone twenty paces from him,
when he heard that he of the looking-glasses called him.
So the two parting the way, he of the Glasses sayd, Be
mindefull, Sr. Knight, that the condition of our combate
is, that the vanquished (as I have told you before) must
stand to the discretion of the Vanquisher. I know it (sayd
Don Quixote) so that what is imposed and commanded the
vanquished, be within the bounds and limits of Cavallery.
So it is meant, sayd he of the Glasses.

Heere Don Quixote saw the strange nose of the Squire,
and he did not lesse wonder at the sight of it, then Sancho;
insomuch that he deemed him a monster, or some new kinde
of man not usuall in the world. Sancho, that saw his
Master goe to fetch his Careere, would not tarry alone with
Nose-autem, fearing that at one snap with tothers Nose upon
his, their fray would bee ended, that either with the blow,
or it, hee should come to the ground. So he ran after his
Master, laying hold upon one of Rozinantes stirrup leathers,
and when hee thought it time for his Master to turne backe,
he sayd; I beseech your Worship, Master mine, that before
you fall to your encounter, you helpe mee to climbe up yon
Cork-tree, from whence I may better, and with more delight,
then from the ground, see the gallant encounter you shall
make with this Knight.

Rather, Sancho (sayd Don Quixote) thou wouldest get
aloft, as into a scaffold, to see the Buls without danger.
Let mee deale truely (sayd Sancho) the ugly nose of that
Squire hath astonisht me, and I dare not come neere him.
Such an one it is (sayd Don Quixote) that any other but
I, might very well be afrayd of it, and therefore come, and
Ile helpe thee up.

Whilst Don Quixote was helping Sancho up into the
Cork-tree, he of the Looking-glasses tooke up roome for
his Careere, and thinking that Don Quixote would have
done the like, without looking for trumpets sound, or any

HISTORIE OF DON QUIXOTE

CHAPTER
XIV
How the
Adventure of
the Knight of
the Wood is
prosecuted.

other warning-signe, he turned his horses reines (no better to see to, nor swifter then Rozinante) and with his full speede (which was a reasonable trot) hee went to encounter his enemy: but seeing him busied in the mounting of Sancho, hee held in his reines, and stopped in the midst of his Careere, for which his horse was most thankefull, as being unable to moove. Don Quixote, who thought his enemy by this came flying, set spurres lustily to Rozinantes hinderflancke, and made him post in such manner, that the Story sayes, now onely he seemed to run, for all the rest was plaine trotting heeretofore. And with this unspeakable fury, he came where he of the Looking-glasses was gagging his spurres into his horse, to the very hoopes, without being able to remoove him a fingers length from the place, where he had set up his rest for the Careere.

In this good time and conjuncture, Don Quixote found his contrary puzzled with his horse, and troubled with his lance; for either he could not, or else wanted time to set it in his rest. Don Quixote that never looked into these inconveniencies, safely and without danger, encountred him of the Looking-glasses so furiously, that in spight of his teeth hee made him come to the ground from his horse-crupper, with such a fall, that stirring neither hand nor foot, hee made shew as if hee had beene dead. Sancho scarce saw him downe, when hee slid from the Cork-tree, and came in all haste to his Master, who dismounted from Rozinante, got upon him of the Looking-glasses, and unlacing his helmet, to see if he were dead, or if he were alive, to give him aire, he saw: (Who can tell without great admiration, wonder and amaze to him that shall heare it?) he saw (sayes the History) the selfesame face, the same visage, the same aspect, the same phisiognomy, the same shape, the same perspective of the Bachelor Samson Carrasco, and as he saw it, hee cryed aloud, Come Sancho, and behold what thou mayest see, and not beleeve, runne whore-sonne, and observe the power of Magicke, what Witches and Enchanters can doe.

Sancho drew neere, and saw the Bachelour **Samson Car-**

109

CHAPTER
XIV
How the
Adventure of
the Knight of
the Wood is
prosecuted.

rasco's face, and so began to make a thousand crosses, and to blesse himselfe as oft. In all this while the overthrowne Knight made no shew of living. And Sancho sayd to Don Quixote, I am of opinion, Sir, that by all means you thrust your sword down this fellowes throte, that is so like the Bachelour Samson Carrasco, and so perhaps in him, you shall kill some of your enemies the Enchanters. Tis not ill advised (quoth Don Quixote.) So drawing out his sword, to put Sancho's counsell in execution, the Knights Squire came in, his nose being off, that had so dis-figured him, and sayd aloud: Take heede, Sr. Don Quixote, what you doe; for hee that is now at your mercy, is the Bachelor Samson Carrasco your friend, and I his Squire.

Now Sancho seeing him without his former deformity, said to him, And your nose? To which he answered, Here it is in my pocket: and putting his hand to his right side, hee pulled out a pasted nose, and a varnisht vizard, of the manifacture described. And Sancho more and more beholding him, with a loud and admiring voyce said, Saint Mary defend me: and is not this Thomas Cecial my neighbour and my Gossip? And how say you by that? (quoth the un-nosed Squire.) Thomas Cecial I am, Gossip and friend Sancho, and streight I will tell you, the conveyances, sleights and trickes that brought mee hither: in the meane time request and intreat your Master, that he touch not, misuse, wound or kil the Knight of the Looking-glasses, now at his mercy; for doubtlesse it is the bold and ill-advized Bachelor Samson Carrasco our Countryman.

By this time the Knight of the Looking-glasses came to himselfe, which Don Quixote seeing, hee clapt the bare point of his sword upon his face, and said, Thou diest, Knight, if thou confesse not, that the peerelesse Dulcinea del Toboso excells your Casildea de Vandalia in beauty: and moreover, you shall promise (if from this battell and fall you remaine with life) to goe to the Citie of Toboso, and present your selfe from me before her, that she may dispose of you as she pleaseth: and if she pardon you, you shall returne to me; for the tracke of my exploits will bee your guide, and bring you

110

HISTORIE OF DON QUIXOTE

where I am, to tell mee what hath passed with her. These conditions (according to those wee agreed on before the battell) exceed not the limits of Knight Errantrie.

I confesse, said the faln Knight, that the Lady Dulcinea del Toboso's torne and foule shooe, is more worth then the ill-combed haire (though cleane) of Casildea : and here I promise to goe and come from her presence to yours, and give you entire and particular relation of all you require. You shall also confesse and believe (added Don Quixote) that the Knight whom you overcame, neyther was, nor could be Don Quixote de la Mancha, but some other like him, as I confesse and believe, that you, although you seeme to be the Bachelor Samson Carrasco, are not he, but one like him, and that my enemies have cast you into his shape, that I may with-hold and temper the force of my choller, and use moderately the glory of my conquest. I confesse, judge, and allow of all as you confesse, judge, and allow (answered the backe-broken Knight.) Let me rise, I pray you, if the blow of my fall will let mee ; for it hath left me in ill case. Don Quixote helped him to rise, and Thomas Cecial his Squire, on whom Sancho still cast his eyes, asking him questions, whose answeres gave him manifest signes, that hee was Thomas Cecial indeed, as hee said, but the apprehension that was made in Sancho, by what his Master had said, that the Enchanters had changed the forme of the Knight of the glasses into Samson Carrasco's, made him not beleeve what he saw with his eyes. To conclude, the Master and Man remained still in their errour : and he of the glasses and his Squire very moody and ill Errants, left Don Quixote, purposing to seeke some towne where hee might seare-cloth himselfe, and settle his ribbes. Don Quixote and Sancho held on their way to Saragosa, where the story leaves them, to tell who was the Knight of the Glasses and his Nosie Squire.

111

THE SECOND PART OF THE

CHAPTER XV

Who the Knight of the looking-glasses and his Squire were.

DON QUIXOTE was extremely contented, glad, and vaine-glorious, that hee had subdued so valiant a Knight, as hee imagined hee of the Looking-glasses was, from whose knightly word he hoped to know if the Enchantment of his Mistris were certaine, since of necessity the said vanquished Knight was to returne, (on paine of not being so) to relate what had happened unto him: but Don Quixote thought one thing, and he of the Glasses another, though for the present he minded nothing, but to seeke where hee might scare-cloth himselfe. The history then tels us, that when the Bachelor Samson Carrasco advised Don Quixote that he should prosecute his forsaken Cavallery, hee entred first of all into counsell with the Vicar and the Barber, to know what meanes they should use, that Don Quixote might bee perswaded to stay at home peaceably and quietly, without troubling himselfe with his unlucky adventures: from which counsaile by the common consent of all, and particular opinion of Carrasco, it was agreed, that Don Quixote should abroad againe, since it was impossible to stay him, and that Samson should meet him upon the way like a Knight Errant, and should fight with him, since an occasion would not be wanting, and so to overcome him, which would not be difficult, and that there should be a covenant and agreement, that the vanquished should stand to the courtesie of the vanquisher, so that Don Quixote being vanquished, the Bachelor Knight should command him to get him home to his towne and house, and not to stirre from thence in two yeeres after, or till hee should command him to the contrary: the which in all likelihood Don Quixote once vanquished would infallibly accomplish, as unwilling to contradict or bee defective in the Lawes of Knighthood, and it might so be, that in this time of sequestring, he might forget all his vanities, or they might finde out some convenient remedy for his madnesse. Carrasco accepted of it, and Thomas Cecial offered himselfe to be his Squire, Sancho Pansa's neighbour and Gossip, a merry knave and a wittie. Samson armed himselfe (as you have heard) and Thomas Cecial fitted the false nose to his owne, and clapt on his vizard, that he might not be known by his Gossip, when they should meete. So they held on the same voyage with Don Quixote, and they came even just as hee was in the adventure of Deaths Wagon. And at last they lighted on them in the Wood, where what befell them, the discreet Reader hath seene, and if it had not beene for the strange opinion that Don Quixote had, that the Bachelor was not the selfe-same man, he had beene spoyled for ever for taking another Degree, since he mist his marke.

Thomas Cecial that saw what ill use hee had made of his hopes, and the bad effect that his journey tooke, sayd to the Bachelor, Truely, Mr. Samson, we have our deserts: things are easily conceived, and enterprizes easily undertaken, but very hardly performed. Don Quixote mad, we wise, but hee is gone away sound and merry, you are heere bruised and sorrowfull. Let us know then who is the greatest mad-man, hee that is so and cannot doe withall, or hee that is so for his pleasure? To which (quoth Samson) The difference betweene these madde men is, that hee that of necessity is so, will alwaies remaine so, and he that accidentally is so, may leave it when he will. Since it is so (said Thomas Cecial) I that for my pleasure was madde, when I would needes be your Squire; for the same reason I will leave the office, and returne home to my owne house. Tis fit you should (said Samson) yet to thinke that I will doe so, till I have soundly banged Don Quixote, is vaine, and now I goe not about to restore him to his wits, but to revenge my selfe on him: for

CHAPTER
XV

Who the
Knight of
the looking-
glasses and
his Squire
were.

3 : P   113

CHAPTER
XV

Who the
Knight of
the looking-
glasses and
his Squire
were.

the intolerable paine I feele in my ribbes, will not permit mee
a more charitable discourse.   Thus they two went on parly-
ing till they came to a Towne, where by chance they lighted
upon a Bone-setter, who cured the unfortunate Samson.
Thomas Cecial went home and left him, and hee stayed
musing upon his revenge: and the History heereafter
will returne to him, which at present must
make merry with Don Quixote.

CHAPTER XVI

What befell Don Quixote with a discreet
Gentleman of Mancha.

ON QUIXOTE went on his journey with
the joy, content, and gladnesse, as hath
beene mentioned, imagining that for the
late victory, he was the most valiant
Knight that that age had in the world,
he made account that all adventures that
should from thence forward befall him,
were brought to a happy and prosperous
end: he cared not now for any enchantments, or enchanters:
he forgot the innumerable bangs that in the prosecution of
his Chivalrie had been given him, and the stones cast, that
strooke out halfe his teeth, and the unthankefulnesse of the
Galli slaves, and the boldnesse and showres of stakes of the
Yangueses.

In conclusion, he said to himselfe, that if hee could finde
any Art, manner, or meanes how to dis-enchant his Mistresse
Dulcinea, hee would not envy the greatest happinesse or
prosperity that ever any Knight Errant of former times had
obtained.

Hee was altogether busied in these imaginations, when
Sancho told him: How say you Sir, that I have still before

114

mine eyes that ill-favoured, more then ordinary nose of my Gossip Thomas Cecial? And doe you happily, Sancho, thinke that the Knight of the Looking-glasses was the Bachelor Samson Carrasco, and his Squire Thomas Cecial your Gossip? I know not what to say to it (quoth Sancho) onely I know, that the tokens he gave me, of my house, wife, and children, no other could give um mee but he, and his face, (his nose being off) was the same that Thomas Cecials, as I have seene him many times in our Towne, and next house to mine, and his voyce was the same. Let us bee reasonable, Sancho, (said Don Quixote:) Come hither; How can any man imagine that the Bachelor Samson Carrasco, should come like a Knight Errant, arm'd with Armes offensive and defensive, to fight with me? Have I ever given him occasion, that he should dogge mee? Am I his Rival, or is he a Professor of Armes, to envy the glory that I have gotten by them? Why what should I say (answered Sancho) when I saw that Knight (be he who he will) looke so like the Bachelor Carrasco, and his Squire to Thomas Cecial my gossip? and if it were an Enchantment (as you say) were there no other two in the world, they might look like. All is juggling and cunning (quoth Don Quixote) of the wicked Magicians that persecute me, who fore-seeing that I should remaine Victor in this combat, had provided that the vanquisht Knight should put on the shape of my friend Carrasco, that the friendship I beare him might mediate betwixt the edge of my sword, and the rigor of my arme, and temper my hearts just indignation; and so, that he might escape with his life, that with trickes and devices sought to take away mine. For proofe of which, oh Sancho, thou knowest by experience, that will not let thee lye or be deceived, how easie it is for Enchanters to change one face into another, making the beautifull deformed, and the deformed beautifull: and it is not two dayes, since with thine owne eyes thou sawest the beauty and livelinesse of the peerelesse Dulcinea in it's perfection, and naturall conformity, and I saw her in the foulenesse and meanenesse of a course milke-maide, with bleare eyes, and stinking breath, so that

CHAPTER
XVI

What befell Don Quixote with a discreet Gentleman of Mancha.

115

CHAPTER
XVI

What befell
Don Quixote
with a discreet
Gentleman
of Mancha.

the perverse Enchanter, that durst cause so wicked a Metamorphosis, 'tis not much that hee hath done the like in the
shapes of Samson Carrasco and Thomas Cecial, to rob me of
the glory of my conquest. Notwithstanding I am of good
comfort; for in what shape soever it were, I have vanquished
mine enemy. God knowes all (said Sancho) and whereas hee
knew the transformation of Dulcinea had beene a tricke of
his, his Masters Chimera's gave him no satisfaction: but
hee durst not reply a word, for feare of discovering his
cozenage.

Whilest they were thus reasoning, one overtooke them
that came their way, upon a faire flea-bitten Mare, upon
his backe a riding coate of fine greene cloth, welted with
tawny Velvet, with a Hunters cap of the same; his Mares
furniture was for the field, and after the Genet fashion, of
the said tawny and greene, he wore a Moorish Semiter,
hanging at a broad Belt of greene and gold, his buskins
were wrought with the same that his belt was, his spurs
were not gilt, but layd on with a greene varnish, so smooth
and burnisht, that they were more sutable to the rest of his
clothes, then if they had beene of beaten gold. Comming
neere, he saluted them courteously, and spurring his Mare,
rode on: But Don Quixote said to him, Gallant, if you goe
our way, and your haste be not great, I should take it for a
favour that wee might ride together. Truly Sir, said he
with the Mare, I should not ride from you, but that I feare
your horse will bee unruly with the company of my Mare.
You may wel, Sir (said Sancho) you may well reyne in your
Mare: for our horse is the honestest and manerliest horse in
the world; he is never unruly upon these occasions; and
once when hee flew out, my Master and I payd for it with
a witnesse. I say againe, you may stay if you please, for
although your Mare were given him betweene two dishes, he
would not looke at her.

The Passenger held in his reines, wondring at Don Quixotes
countenance and posture, who was now without his helmet,
for Sancho carried it in a Cloke-bag at the pummell of
Dapples pack-saddle: and if hee in the Greene did much

116

HISTORIE OF DON QUIXOTE

CHAPTER
|XVI
What befell
Don Quixote
with a discreet
Gentleman
of Mancha.

looke at Don Quixote, Don Quixote did much more eye him, taking him to be a man of worth; his age shewed him to bee about fifty, having few gray haires, his face was somewhat sharp, his countenance of an equall temper: Lastly, in his fashion and posture, hee seemed to be a man of good quality. His opinion of Don Quixote was, that hee had never seene such a kinde of man before; the lank-nesse of his horse, the talnesse of his owne body, the spare-nesse and palenesse of his face made him admire; his armes, his gesture and composition, a shape and picture, as it were, had not beene seene (many ages before) in that Countrey.

Don Quixote noted well with what attention the Traveller beheld him, and in his suspence read his desire, and being so courteous and so great a friend, to give all men content, before he demanded him any thing, to prevent him, he sayd: This outside of mine that you have seene, Sir, because it is so rare and different from others now in use, may (no doubt) have bred some wonder in you: which you will cease, when I shall tell you, as now I doe, that I am a Knight, one of those (as you would say) that seeke their fortunes. I went out of my Countrey, engaged mine estate, left my pleasure, committed my selfe to the Armes of Fortune, to carry me whither she pleased. My desire was to raise againe the dead Knight Errantry, and long agoe stumbling heere, and falling there, casting my selfe headlong in one place, and rising up in another, I have accomplished a great part of my desire, succouring Widdowes, defending Damozels, favouring married women, Orphans, and distressed children (the proper and naturall office of Knights Errant) so that by my many valiant and Christian exployts, I have merited to be in the Presse, in all or most nations of the world: thirty thousand volumes of my History have beene printed, and thirty thousand millions more are like to be, if Heaven permit. Lastly, to shut up all in a word, I am Don Quixote de la Mancha, otherwise called, The Knight of the Sorrow-full Countenance: And though one should not praise him-selfe, yet I must needs doe it, that is, there being none

117

CHAPTER
XVI

What befell
Don Quixote
with a discreet
Gentleman
of Mancha.

present that may doe it for me: so that, kinde Gentle-man, neither this horse, this lance, nor this shield, nor this Squire, nor all these armes together, nor the palenesse of my face, nor my slender macilency, ought henceforward to admire you, you knowing now who I am, and the profession I maintaine.

This sayd, Don Quixote was silent, and hee with the greene Coat was a great while ere he could answer, as if hee could not hit upon't: but after some pause, hee sayd: You were in the right, Sir Knight, in knowing, by my suspension, my desire: but yet you have not quite remooved my admiration, which was caused with seeing you, for although that, as you say, Sir, that to know who you are, might make me leave wondring, it is otherwise, rather since now I know it, I am in more suspence and wonderment. And is it possible, that at this day there bee Knights Errant in the world? And that there bee true Histories of Knighthood printed? I cannot perswade my selfe, that there are any now that favour widowes, defend Damozels, honour married women, or succor Orphans, and I should never have beleeved it, if I had not in you beheld it with mine eyes: Blessed be Heavens; for with this History you speake of, which is printed of your true and lofty Chivalry, those innumerable falsities of fained Knights Errant will be forgotten, which the world was full of; so hurtfull to good education, and prejudiciall to true Stories.

There is much to be spoken (quoth Don Quixote) whether the Histories of Knights Errant were fained or true. Why, is there any that doubts (sayd he in the Greene) that they bee not false? I doe (sayd Don Quixote) and let it suffice, for if our journey last, I hope in God to let you see, that you have done ill, to bee led with the streame of them that hold they are not true. At this last speech of Don Quixote, the Traveller suspected hee was some Ideot, and expected when some others of his might confirme it: but before they should be diverted with any other discourse, Don Quixote desired to know who he was, since hee had imparted to him his condition and life: Hee in the Greene made

HISTORIE OF DON QUIXOTE

answer ; I, Sir Knight **of** the Sorrowfull Countenance, am a
Gentle-man borne in a towne, where (God willing) wee shall
dine to day : I am well to live, my name is Don Diego de
Miranda, I spend my life with my wife, and children, and
friends : my sports are hunting and fishing : but I have
neither Hawke nor Grey-hounds, onely a tame Cock-Partridge,
or a murdering Ferret, some six doozen of bookes, some
Spanish, some Latine, some History, others Devotion : your
books of Knighthood have not yet entred the threshold of
my doore, I do more turne over your prophane bookes then
religious, if they be for honest recreation, such as may delight
for their language, and admire, and suspend for their invention, although in Spaine there be few of these. Sometimes
I dine with my neighbors and friends, and otherwhiles invite
them : my meales are neat and handsome, and nothing
scarce : I neither love to back-bite my selfe, nor to heare
others doe it : I search not into other mens lives, **or** am a
Lynce to other mens actions, I heare every day a Masse,
part my goods with the poore, without making a muster of
my good deeds, that I may not give way to hypocrisie and
vaine-glory to enter into my heart, enemies that easily cease
upon the wariest brest : I strive to make peace betweene
such as are at ods. I am devoted to our blessed Lady, and
alwayes trust in Gods infinite mercy.

Sancho was most attentive to this relation of the life and
entertainements of this Gentle-man, which seeming to him to
bee good and holy, and that he that led it, worked miracles,
he flung himselfe from Dapple, and in great haste layd hold
of his right stirrup, and with the teares in his eyes often
kissed his feet : which being seene by the Gentle-man, hee
asked him ; What **doe** ye, Brother ? Wherefore be these
kisses ?

Let me kisse **(quoth** Sancho :) for (me thinkes) your Worship is the first **Saint,** that in all the dayes of my life, I ever
saw a horse-backe. I am no Saint (sayd he) but a **great**
sinner, you indeed, Brother, are, and **a** good soule, as your
simplicity shewes you **to** be. Sancho went againe to recover
his pack-saddle, having (as it were) brought into the market-

119

CHAPTER
XVI
What befell
Don Quixote
with a discreet
Gentleman
of Mancha.

place his Masters laughter out of a profound melancholy, and caused a new admiration in Don Diego.

Don Quixote asked him how many sonnes hee had: who told him, that one of the things in which the Philosophers *Summum Bonum* did consist (who wanted **the true** knowledge of God) was in the goods of Nature, **in** those of Fortune, in having many friends, and many vertuous children. I, Sir Don Quixote (answered the Gentle-man) have a sonne, whom if I had not, perhaps you would judge mee more happy then I am, not that he is so bad, but because not so good as I would have him: he is about eighteen yeers of age, six of which he hath spent in Salamanca, learning the tongues Greeke and Latin, and when I had a purpose that he should fall to other Sciences, I found him so besotted with Poesie, and that Science (if so it may bee called) that it is not possible to make him looke upon the Law (which I would have him study) nor Divinity the Queene of all Sciences. I would he were the crowne of all his linage, since wee live in an age, wherein our King doth highly reward good learning: for learning without goodnesse, is like a pearle cast in a Swines snowt: all the day long hee spends in his Criticismes, whether Homer sayd well or ill in such a verse of his Iliads, whether Martial were bawdy or no in such an Epigram, whether such or such a verse in Virgil ought to be understood this way or that way. Indeed, all his delight is in these aforesayd Poets, and in Horace, Persius, Iuvenal, and Tibullus; but of your moderne writers he makes small account: yet for all the grudge he beares to moderne Poesie, hee is mad upon your catches, and your glossing upon foure verses, which were sent him from Salamanca, and that I thinke is his true study.

To all which, Don Quixote answered; Children, Sir, are pieces of the very entrailes of their Parents, so let them bee good or bad, they must love them, as wee must love our spirits that give us life: It concernes their Parents to direct them from their infancie in the paths of vertue, of good manners, and good and Christian exercises, that when they come to yeeres, they may be the staffe of their age, and the glory of

HISTORIE OF DON QUIXOTE

their posterity: and I hold it not so proper, to force them to study this or that Science, though to perswade them were not amisse, and though it be not to study to get his bread (the Student being so happy, that God hath given him Parents able to leave him well) mine opinion should bee, that they let him follow that kinde of study hee is most inclined to, and though that of Poetry be lesse profitable then delightfull, yet it is none of those, that will dishonour the Professour.

Poetry, Signior, in my opinion, is like a tender virgin, young and most beautifull, whom many other virgins, to wit, all the other Sciences, are to enrich, polish, and adorne, she is to be served by them all, and all are to bee authorized by her: but this Virgin will not bee handled and hurried up and downe the streets, nor published in every market-nooke, nor Court-corners. Shee is made of a kind of Alchymie, that he that knowes how to handle her, will quickly turne her into the purest gold of inestimable value, he that enjoyeth her, must hold her at distance, not letting her lash out in uncleane Satyrs, nor in dull Sonnets, she must not by any meanes bee vendible, except in Heroyke Poems, in lamentable Tragedies, or pleasant and artificiall Comedies: Shee must not be meddled with by Iesters, nor by the Ignorant vulgar, uncapable of knowing or esteeming the treasures that are locked up in her; and think not, Sir, that I call here only the common people vulgar, for whosoever is ignorant, be he Potentate or Prince, he may and must enter into the number of the vulgar: so that hee who shall handle and esteeme of Poetry with these Requisites I have declared, he shall be famous, and his name shall be extolled in all the Politique nations of the world.

And wheras, Sir, you say your sonne neglects moderne Poesie, I perswade my selfe he doth not well in it, and the reason is this: Great Homer never wrote in Latine, because he was a Grecian; nor Virgil in Greeke, because he was a Latine: Indeed all your ancient Poets wrote in the tongue which they learnt from their cradle, and sought not after strange languages to declare their lofty conceits. Which

3 : Q   121

THE SECOND PART OF THE

CHAPTER
XVI
What befell
Don Quixote
with a discreet
Gentleman
of Mancha.

being so, it were reason this custom should extend it selfe thorow all nations, and that your German Poet should not be under-valued, because hee writes in his language, nor the Castilian, or Biscayner, because they write in theirs. But your sonne (as I suppose) doth not mislike moderne Poesie, but Poets that are meerely moderne, without knowledge of other tongues, or Sciences, that may adorne, rowze up, and strengthen their natural impulse, and yet in this there may be an errour. For it is a true opinion, that a Poet is borne so, the meaning is, a Poet is naturally borne a Poet from his mothers wombe, and with that inclination that Heaven hath given him, without further study or Art, he composeth things, that verifie his saying that sayd, *Est Deus in nobis*, etc.

Let mee also say, that the naturall Poet, that helps him-selfe with Art, shall bee much better, and have the advantage of that Poet, that onely out of his Art strives to be so: the reason is, because Art goes not beyond Nature, but onely per-fects it, so that Nature and Art mixt together, and Art with Nature, make an excellent Poet. Let this then be the scope of my discourse, Sir, let your sonne proceede whither his Starre cals him: for if he be so good a Student, as he ought to be, and have happily mounted the first step of the Sciences, which is the languages, with them (by himselfe) hee will ascend to the top of humane learning, which appeares as well in a Gentle-man, and doth as much adorne, honour, and en-noble him, as a Miter doth a Bishop, or a loose Cassocke a Civilian. Chide your sonne, if he write Satyrs that may pre-judice honest men, punish him, and teare them: but if he make Sermones, like those of Horace, to the reprehension of vice in generall, as he so elegantly did, then cherish him, for it is lawfull for a Poet to write against envy, and to inveigh against envious persons in his verse, and so against other vices, if so be he aime at no particular person: But you have Poets, that in stead of uttering a jerke of wit, they will venter a being banished to the Ilands of Pontus. If a Poet live honestly, he will bee so in his verses, the pen is the mindes tongue; as the conceits are, which be ingendred in it, such

HISTORIE OF DON QUIXOTE

will the writings be, and when Kings and Princes see the
miraculous Science of Poesie, in wise, virtuous, and grave
Subjects, they honour, esteeme, and enrich them, and even
crowne them with the leaves of that *Tree, which the thunder-
bolt offends not, in token that none shall offend them, that
have their temples honoured and adorned with such crownes.
The Gentle-man admired Don Quixotes discourse, and so
much, that now he forsooke his opinion he had of him, that he
was a Coxcombe.   But in the midst of this discourse, Sancho,
(that was weary of it) went out of the way to beg a little
milke of some shepheards not farre off, curing of their sheepe :
so the Gentleman still maintained talke with Don Quixote,
beeing wonderfully taken and satisfied with his wise discourse.
But Don Quixote lifting up sodainly his eyes, saw that in
the way toward them, there came a Cart full of the Kings
Colours, and taking it to be some rare adventure, hee called
to Sancho for his Helmet.   Sancho hearing himselfe called
on, left the shepheards, and spur'd Dapple apace,
and came to his Master, to whom a rash and
stupendious adventure happened.

CHAPTER
XVI
What befell
Don Quixote
with a discreet
Gentleman
of Mancha.
*The Lawrell.

CHAPTER XVII

Where is shewed the last and extremest hazard, to which the unheard of courage of Don Quixote did or could arrive, with the prosperous accomplishment of the adventure of the Lyons.

HE Historie sayes, that when Don Quixote called to Sancho, to bring him his Helmet, he was buying curds which the Shepheards sold him ; and being hastily layd at by his Master, he knew not what to doe with them, or how to bestow them without losing them, for hee had payed for them ; so hee bethought himselfe, and clapt them into his Masters Helmet, and this good order taken, hee went to see what he would have : who, when he came, sayd, Give mee, friend, that same Helmet, for eyther I know not what belongs to adventures, or that I see yonder is one that will force mee to take Armes. Hee of the greene coat that heard this, turned his eyes every way, and saw nothing but a Cart that came toward them, with two or three small flags, which made him thinke that the said Cart carried the Kings money, and so he told Don Quixote : but he beleeved him not, alwaies thinking that every thing hee saw, was adventure upon adventure : so hee answered the Gentleman, He that is warn'd, is halfe arm'd : there is nothing lost in being provided ; for I know by experience, that I have enemies visible and invisible, and I know not when, nor where, nor at what time, or in what shape they will set upon me : and turning to Sancho, hee demanded his Helmet, who wanting leysure to take the Curds out, was forced to give it him as it was. Don Quixote tooke it, and not perceiving what

124

was in it, clapt it sodainly upon his head; and as the Curds were squeazed and thrust together, the whay began to runne downe Don Quixotes face and beard; at which he was in such a fright, that he cryed out to Sancho, What ailes me, Sancho? for me-thinkes my skull is softned, or my braines melt, or that I sweat from top to toe; and if it be sweat, I assure thee it is not for feare, I beleeve certainely that I am like to have a terrible adventure of this; give mee something (if thou hast it) to wipe on, for this abundance of sweat blindes me. Sancho was silent and gave him a cloth, and with it thankes to God, that his Master fell not into the businesse. Don Quixote wiped himselfe, and tooke off his Helmet to see what it was, that (as hee thought) did be-numme his head, and seeing those white splatches in his helmet, hee put um to his nose, and smelling to them, said, By my Mistresse Dulcinea del Toboso's life, they are Curds that thou hast brought me heere, thou base traitor, and un-mannerly Squire. To which Sancho very cunningly, and with a great deale of pawse, answered. If they be curds, give them me, pray, and Ile eate um: but let the Devill eat um, for he put um there. Should I be so bold as to foule your worships Helmet? and there you have found (as I told you) who did it. In faith Sir, as sure as God lives, I have my Enchanters too that persecute me as a creature and part of you, and I warrant have put that filth there, to stirre you up to choller, and to make you bang my sides (as you use to doe.) Well, I hope this time they have lost their labour, for I trust in my Masters discretion, that he will consider, that I have neyther Curds, nor milke, nor any such thing; for if I had, I had rather put it in my stomacke, then in the Helmet: All this may be (said Don Quixote.)

The Gentleman observed all, and wondred, especially when Don Quixote, after hee had wiped his head, face, beard, and helmet, clapt it on againe, settling himselfe well in his stirrops, searching for his sword, and grasping his Launce, he cried out: Now come on 't what will, for here I am, with a courage to meet Satan himselfe in person.

By this, the Cart with the flags drew neere, in which

CHAPTER
XVII

Where is shewed the last and extremest hazard, to which the unheard of courage of Don Quixote did or could arrive, etc.

125

CHAPTER
XVII
Where is
shewed the
last and
extremest
hazard, to
which the
unheard of
courage of
Don Quixote
did or could
arrive, etc.

there came no man but the Carter with his Mules, and another upon the formost of them. Don Quixote put himselfe forward, and asked; Whither goe ye, my masters? what Cart is this? what doe you carry in it? and what colours be these? To which the Carter answered, The Cart is mine, the Carriage is two fierce Lyons caged up, which the Generall of Oran sends to the King at Court for a Present: these Colours be his Majesties, in signe that what goes here is his. And are the Lyons bigge? sayd Don Quixote. So bigge (said he that went toward the Cart doore) that there never came bigger out of Africa into Spaine, and I am their keeper, and have carried others, but never any so big: they are Male and Female, the Male is in this first grate, the Female in the hindermost, and now they are hungry, for they have not eat to day, and therefore I pray Sir give us way; for we had neede come quickly where wee may meate them. To which (quoth Don Quixote smiling a little) Your Lyon whelps to me? to me your Lyon whelps? and at this time of day? Well, I vow to God, your Generall that sends um this way shall know, whether I be one that am afraid of Lyons. Alight, honest fellow, and if you be the Keeper, open their Cages, and let me your beasts forth; for I'le make um know in the middest of this Champian, who Don Quixote is, in spight of those Enchanters that sent um. Fye, fye, (said the Gentleman at this instant to himselfe) our Knight shewes very well what he is, the Curds have softned his skull, and ripened his braines. By this Sancho came to him and sayd; for Gods love handle the matter so, Sir, that my Master meddle not with these Lyons; for if he doe, they'l worry us all. Why, is your Master so madde (quoth the Gentleman) that you feare, or beleeve hee will fight with wilde beasts? Hee is not mad, sayd Sancho, but hardy. Ile make him otherwise, said the Gentleman; and comming to Don Quixote, that was hastening the Keeper to open the Cages, sayd, Sir Knight, Knights Errant ought to undertake adventures, that may give a likelihood of ending them well, and not such as are altogether desperate: for valour

126

HISTORIE OF DON QUIXOTE

grounded upon rashnesse, hath more madnesse then forti-
tude. How much more, these Lyons come not to assayle
you, they are carried to bee presented to his Majesty, and
therefore 'twere not good to stay or hinder their journey.
Pray get you gone, gentle Sir (quoth Don Quixote) and
deale with your tame Partridge, and your murdring Ferret,
and leave every man to his function : this is mine, and I am
sufficient to know whether these Lyons come against me or
no : so turning to the Keeper, he cried : *By this—good-
man slave, if you doe not forthwith open the Cage, Ile
nayle you with my Launce to your Cart. The Carter that
perceived the resolution of that armed Vision, told him,
Seignior mine, will you be pleased in charity to let me
unyoke my Mules, and to put my selfe and them in safety,
before I unsheath my Lyons ? for if they should kill them,
I am undone all dayes of my life, for I have no other living
but this Cart and my Mules. Oh thou wretch of little
Faith (quoth Don Quixote) light, and unyoke, and doe
what thou wilt, for thou shalt see thou mightest have
saved a labour. The Carter alighted, and unyoaked hastily,
and the keeper cryed out aloud, Beare witnesse, my Masters
all, that I am forced against my will to open the Cages,
and to let loose the Lyons, and that I protest to this
Gentleman, that all the harme and mischiefe that these
Beasts shall doe, light upon him, besides that he pay mee
my wages and due. Shift you sirs for your selves, before
I open, for I am sure they 'l doe mee no hurt. The Gentle-
man perswaded him the second time, that he should not
attempt such a piece of madnesse ; for such a folly was to
tempt God.

To which Don Quixote answered, that he knew what he
did. The Gentleman replyde, That he should consider
well of it, for he knew he was deceived. Well, Sir, (sayd
Don Quixote) if you will not be a spectator of this (which
you thinke Tragedy) pray spurre your Flea-bitten, and put
your selfe in safety. Which when Sancho heard, with
teares in his eyes, he beseeched him to desist from that
enterprize, in comparison of which, that of the Winde-Mils

Where is
shewed the
last and
extremest
hazard, to
which the
unheard of
courage of
Don Quixote
did or could
arrive, etc.

*Voto a tal.
When hee
would seeme
to sweare, but
sweares by
nothing.

127

CHAPTER
XVII

Where is
shewed the
last and
extremest
hazard, to
which the
unheard of
courage of
Don Quixote
did or could
arrive, etc.

•

was Cakebread, and that fearefull one also of the Fulling-Mill, or all the exployts that ever he had done in his life. Looke ye, Sir (said Sancho) heere's no Enchantment, nor any such thing; for I have looked thorow the grates and chinkes of the Cages, and have seen a clawe of a true Lyon, by which clawe I ghesse the Lyon is as big as a mountaine.

Thy feare at least (sayd Don Quixote) will make him as bigge as halfe the world. Get thee out of the way, Sancho, and leave me, and if I die in the place, thou knowest our agreement, repayre to Dulcinea, and that's enough.

To these hee added other reasons, by which hee cut off all hope of his leaving the prosecution of that foolish enter-prize.

Hee of the Greene coate would have hindered him, but hee found himselfe unequally matched in weapons, and thought it no wisedome to deale with a mad-man; for now Don Quixote appeared no otherwise to him, who hastning the Keeper afresh, and reiterating his threats, made the Gentleman set spurs to his Mare, and Sancho to his Dapple, and the Carter to his Mules, ech of them striving to get as farre from the Cart as they could, before the Lyons should be unhampered.

Sancho bewailed his Masters losse; for he beleeved certainely that the Lyon would catch him in his pawes, he cursed his fortune, and the time that ever hee came againe to his Masters service. But for all his wailing and lamenting, he left not punching of Dapple, to make him get farre enough from the Cart.

The Keeper, when he saw those that fledde farre enough off, began anew to require and intimate to Don Quixote, what hee had formerly done: who answered, That hee heard him, and that hee should leave his intimations; for all was needlesse, and that he should make haste.

Whilest the Keeper was opening the first Cage, Don Quixote began to consider, whether it were best to fight on foot, or on horsebacke: And at last he determined it should be on foot, fearing that Rozinante would bee afraid

HISTORIE OF DON QUIXOTE

to looke upon the Lyons: and thereupon hee leap'd from **his** horse, cast by his Launce, buckled his Shield to him, **and** unsheathed his sword faire and softly; with a marvellous courage and valiant heart, he marched toward the Cart, recommending himselfe first to God, and then to his Lady Dulcinea.

And heere is to be noted, that when the Author of the true History came to this passage, hee exclaimes and cries, O strong (and beyond all comparison) couragious Don Quixote! thou Looking-glasse, in which all the valiant Knights of the World may behold themselves: thou new and second Don Manuel de Leon, who was the honor and glory of the Spanish Knights: with what words shall I recount this fearefull exployt? or with what arguments shall I make it credible to ensuing times? or what praises will not fit and square with thee? though they may seeme Hyperboles above all Hyperboles? Thou on foot, alone, undanted and magnanimous, with thy sword onely, and that none of your cutting Foxe-blades, with a Shield, not of bright and shining steele, expectest and attendest two of the fiercest Lyons that ever were bred in African woods. Let thine owne deeds extoll thee, brave Manchegan: for I must leave um here abruptly, since I want words to endeere them.

Heere the Authors exclamation ceased, and the thred of the story went knitting it selfe on, saying:

The Keeper seeing Don Quixote in his posture, and that hee must needs let loose the Male Lyon, on paine of the bold Knight his indignation, he set the first Cage wide open, where the **Lyon** (as is saide) was, of **an** extraordinary bignesse, **fearefull** and ugly to see to. The first thing he did, was to tumble up and down the cage, stretch one pawe, and rowse himselfe, forthwith he yawned, and gently sneezed, then with his tongue some two handfuls long, he licked the dust out of his eyes, and washed his face; which done, **he** thrust his head out of the Cage, and looked round about him, with his eyes like fire coales: a sight and gesture able to make Temerity it selfe afraid. Onely Don Quixote

3 : R

CHAPTER
XVII

Where is
shewed the
last and
extremest
hazard, to
which the
unheard of
courage of
Don Quixote
did or could
arrive, etc.

beheld him earnestly, and wished he would leape out of the Cart, that they might grapple, for hee thought to slice him in pieces. Hitherto came the extreme of his not-heard-of madnesse : but the generous Lyon, more courteous then arrogant, neglecting such childishnesse, and Bravados, after hee had looked round about him (as is said) turned his backe, and shewed his tayle to Don Quixote, and very quietly lay downe againe in the Cage. Which Don Quixote seeing, he commanded the Keeper to give him two or three blowes, to make him come forth. No, not I (quoth the Keeper) for if I urge him, I shall bee the first he will teare in pieces. I pray you, Sir Knight, be contented with your daies worke, which is as much as could in valour be done, and tempt not a second hazard. The Lyons door was open, hee might have come out if he would ; but since hee hath not hitherto, he will not come forth all this day. You have well shewed the stoutnesse of your courage : no brave Combatant (in my opinion) is tyed to more, then to defie his Enemy, and to expect him in field ; and if his contrary come not, the disgrace is his, and he that expected, remaines with the prize.

True it is (answered Don Quixote) friend, shut the dore, and give me a certificate in the best forme that you can, of what you have seene me doe here : to wit, That you opened to the Lyon, that I expected him, and hee came not out ; that I expected him againe, yet all would not doe, but hee lay downe. I could doe no more. Enchantments, avant, God maintaine right and truth, and true Chivalrie : shut (as I bad you) whilest I make signes to them that are fledde, that they may know this exployt from thy relation. The Keeper obeyed, and Don Quixote putting his handkerchiefe on the poynt of his Launce, with which hee had wiped the Curd-showre from off his face, he began to call those that fledde, and never so much as looked behinde them, all in a troope, and the Gentleman the foreman : but Sancho seeing the white cloth, said, Hang mee, if my Master have not van-quished the wilde beasts, since he calls us. All of them made a stand, and knew it was Don Quixote that made the

signe. So lessening their feare, by little and little they drew neere him, till they could plainely heare that he called them. At length they returned to the Cart, and **Don** Quixote said to the Carter; Yoake your Mules againe, Brother, and get you on your way : and Sancho, give him two pistolets in gold, for him and the Lyon-keeper, in recompence for their stay. With a very good will, (said Sancho) but what's become of the Lyons? are they alive or dead? Then the Keeper faire and softly began to tell them of the bickering, extolling, as well as he could, Don Quixotes valour, at whose sight the Lyon trembling, would not, or durst not sallie from the Cage, although the dore were open a pretty while, and that because **hee** had told the Knight, that to provoke the Lyon, **was to** tempt God, by making him come out by force (as he would that hee should be provoked in spight of his teeth, **and** against his will) he suffered the doore to be shut. What thinke you of this, Sancho? (quoth Don Quixote) Can Enchantment now prevaile against true Valour? Well may Enchanters make mee unfortunate, but 'tis impossible they should bereave mee of my valour.

Sancho bestowed the Pistolets, and the Carter yoaked, the Keeper tooke leave of Don Quixote, and thanked him for his kindnesse, and promised him to relate his valerous exploit to the King himselfe, when hee came to Court. Well, if his Majesty chance to aske who it was that did it, tell him, The Knight of the Lyons : for henceforward, I will that my name be trucked, exchanged, turned and changed now, from that I had of The Knight of the sorrowfull Countenance ; and in this I follow the ancient use of Knights Errant, that would change their **names** when they pleased, or thought it convenient.

The Cart went on it's way, and Don Quixote, Sancho, and he in the greene, held on theirs. In all this while, Don Diego de Miranda spoke not a word, being busied in noting Don Quixotes speeches and actions, taking him to bee a wise mad-man, or a mad-man that came somewhat neere a wiseman. Hee knew nothing as yet of the first part of his History, for if hee had read that, he would have left admir-

CHAPTER
XVII

Where is
shewed the
last and
extremest
hazard, to
which the
unheard of
courage of
Don Quixote
did or could
arrive, etc.

*In Spaine
they use with
horse-men,
and foot-men
to course their
Bull to death
in the Market
places.

ing his words and deeds, since he might have knowne the
nature of his madnesse: but for hee knew it not, he held
him to be wise and mad by fits; for what hee spoke, was consonant, elegant, and well delivered: but his actions were
foolish, rash, and unadvised: and (thought hee to himselfe)
What greater madnesse could there be, then to clap on a
helmet full of Curds, and to make us beleeve that Enchanters
had softned his skull? or what greater rashnesse or foppery,
then forcibly to venter upon Lyons? Don Quixote drew him
from these imaginations, saying, Who doubts, Seignior Don
Diego de Miranda, but that you will hold me in your opinion
for an idle fellow, or a mad-man: and no marvell that I be
held so; for my actions testifie no lesse: for all that, I would
have you know, that I am not so mad, or so shallow as I
seeme. It is a brave sight to see a goodly Knight in the
midst* of the Market-place before his Prince, to give a thrust
with his Launce to a fierce Bull. And it is a brave sight to
see a Knight armed in shining armour passe about the Tilt-
yard at the cheerefull Iusts before the Ladies; and all those
Knights are a brave sight that in Military exercises (or such
as may seeme so) doe entertaine, revive, and honour their
Princes Courts: but above all these, a Knight Errant is a
better sight, that by Desarts and Wildernesses, by crosse-
waies and Woods, and Mountaines, searcheth after dangerous
Adventures, with a purpose to end them happily and fortu-
nately, onely to obtaine glorious and lasting Fame. A Knight
Errant (I say) is a better sight, succouring a widdow in
some Desart, then a Court Knight courting some Damozell
in the City. All Knights have their particular exercises:
Let the Courtier serve Ladies, authorize his Princes Court
with liveries, sustaine poore Gentlemen at his Table, appoint
Iusts, maintaine Tourneyes, shew himselfe noble, liberall, and
magnificent, and above all, Religious, and in these he shal
accomplish with his obligation. But for the Knight Errant,
let him search the corners of the world, enter the most intricate Labyrinths, every foote undertake Impossibles, and
in the Desarts and Wildernesse: let him resist the Sunne-
beames in the midst of Summer, and the sharpe rigor of the

132

windes and frosts in **Winter**: Let not Lyons fright him, nor spirits terrifie him, nor Hobgoblins make him quake: for to seeke these, to set upon them, and to overcome all, are his prime exercises. And since it fell to my lot to bee one of the number of these Knights Errant, I cannot but undergoe all that I think comes under the jurisdiction of my profession. So that the encountring those Lyons did directly belong to me, though I knew it to be an exorbitant rashnesse; for well I know, that valour is a vertue betwixt two vicious extremes, as cowardise and rashnesse: but it is lesse dangerous for him that is valiant, to rise to a point of rashnesse, then to fall or touch **upon** the Coward. For as it is more easie for a pro-digall **man** to be liberall, then a covetous, so it is easier for a rash man to be truely valiant, then a Coward to come to true valour. And touching the on-set in Adventures, believe mee Signior Don Diego, it is better playing a good trump then **a** small, for it sounds better in the hearers eares: Such a Knight is rash and hardy, then, such a Knight is fearefull and cowardly.

CHAPTER XVII

Where is shewed the last and extremest hazard, to which the unheard of courage of Don Quixote did or could arrive, etc.

I say, Signior (answered Don Diego) that **all** that you have said and done **is** levelled out by the line of Reason, and I thinke if the Statutes and Ordinances of Knight Errantry were lost, they might be found again in your brest, as in their own Storehouse and Register, and so let us haste, for the day growes on us, let us get to my village and house, where you shall ease your selfe of your former labour; which, though it have not beene bodily, yet it **is** mentall, which doth often redound to the bodies **wearinesse**. I thanke you for your kinde offer, Signior (quoth **Don** Quixote) and spurring on faster, about two **of** the clocke they came to the Village, and Don Diego's house, whom Don Quixote stiled, The Knight of the greene Cassocke.

CHAPTER XVIII

What happened to Don Quixote in the Castle, or Knight of the Greene Cassocke his house, with other extravagant matters.

ON QUIXOTE perceived that Don Diego de Miranda's house was spacious, after the Country manner, and his Armes (though of course stone) upon the dore towards the streete, his wine-celler in the Court, his other sellar or vault in the entry, with many great stone vessels round about, that were of Toboso, which renued the remembrance of his enchanted and transformed Mistresse Dulcinea, so sighing, and not minding who was by, he said,

* O happy pledges, found out to my losse,
  Sweet, and reviving, when the time was once.

O dulces prendas. A beginning of a sonnet in *Diana de Monte Mayor,* which D. Q. heere raps out upon a sodaine.

Oh you Tobosian Tunnes, that bring to my remembrance the sweet pledge of my greatest bitternesse. The Scholler Poet, son to Don Diego, that came out with his Mother to welcome him, heard him pronounce this, and the mother and sonne were in some suspence at the strange shape of Don Quixote, who alighting from Rozinante, very courteously desired to kisse her hands: And Don Diego sayd; I pray, wife, give your wonted welcome to this Gentle-man, Signior Don Quixote de la Mancha, a Knight Errant, and the valiantest and wisest in the world.

The Gentle-woman called Donna Cristina, welcommed him very affectionately, and with much courtesie, which Don Quixote retorted with many wise and mannerly complements, and did (as it were) use the same over againe to the Scholler, who hearing Don Quixote speake, tooke him to bee wondrous

134

HISTORIE OF DON QUIXOTE

wise and witty. Heere the Author paints out unto us all the circumstances of Don Diego his house, deciphering to us all that a Gentle-man and a rich Farmers house may have: but it seemed good to the Translator, to passe over these and such like trifles, because they suited not with the principall scope of this History, the which is more grounded upon truth, then upon bare digressions.

Don Quixote was led into a Hall, Sancho un-armed him, so that now he had nothing on but his breeches, and a Chamois doublet, all smudged with the filth of his Armour, about his necke he wore a little Scholasticall band unstarcht, and without lace, his buskins were Date-coloured, and his shooes close on each side, his good sword he girt to him, that hung at a belt of Sea-wolves skins, for it was thought he had the running of the reines many yeeres, hee wore also a long cloke of good russet-cloth: but first of all, in five or six kettles of water (for touching the quantity there is some difference) hee washed his head and his face, and for all that, the water was turned whey-colour, God a mercy on Sancho's gluttony, and the buying those dismall black curds, that made his Master so white. With the aforesayd bravery, and with a spritely aire and gallantry, Don Quixote marched into another room, where the Scholler stayed for him, to entertaine him till the cloth was layd, for the Mistris of the house, Dona Cristina, meant to shew to her honourable guest, that shee knew how to make much of them that came to her house.

Whilest Don Quixote was dis-arming himselfe, Don Lorenzo had leasure (for that was Don Diego's sonnes name) to aske his father; What doe you call this Gentle-man, Sir, that you have brought with you? for his name, his shape, and your calling him Knight Errant, makes my mother and me wonder. Faith, sonne (quoth Don Diego) I know not what I should say to thee of him, onely I may tell thee, I have seene him play the maddest prankes of any mad-man in the world, and speake againe speeches so wise, as blot out and undoe his deeds; doe thou speake to him, and feele the pulse of his understanding, and since

CHAPTER
XVIII

What happened to Don Quixote in the Castle, or Knight of the Greene Cassocke his house, with other extravagant matters.

thou art discreet, judge of his discretion or folly as thou seest best, though to deale plainely with thee, I rather hold him to be mad then wise.

Heereupon Don Lorenzo (as is sayd) went to entertaine Don Quixote, and amongst other discourse that passed betwixt them, Don Quixote sayd to Don Lorenzo; Signior Don Diego de Miranda, your father, hath told me of your rare abilities and subtill wit, and chiefly that you are an excellent Poet. A Poet perhaps (replide Don Lorenzo) but excellent, by no meanes: true it is, that I am somewhat affectionated to Poesie, and to read good Poets: but not so, that I may deserve the name of excellent, that my father stiles me with. I doe not dislike your modesty (quoth Don Quixote) for you have seldome times any Poet that is not arrogant, and thinkes himselfe to be the best Poet in the world. There is no rule (quoth Don Lorenzo) without an exception, and some one there is, that is so, and yet thinkes not so. Few (sayd Don Quixote:) but tell mee, Sir, what verses bee those that you have now in hand, that your father sayes doe trouble and puzzle you? and if it be some kinde of glosse, I know what belongs to glossing, and should be glad to heare them: and if they bee of your verses for the

Prize, content your selfe with the second reward: For the first goes alwayes by favour, or according to the quality of the person, and the second is justly distributed, so that the third comes (according to this account) to be the second, and the first the third, according to degrees that are given in Vniversities: but for all that, the word first is a great matter.

Hitherto (thought Don Lorenzo to himselfe) I cannot thinke thee mad: proceed we: and hee sayd; It seemes, Sir, you have frequented the Schooles, what Sciences have you heard? That of Knight Errantry (quoth Don Quixote) which is as good as your Poetry, and somewhat better. I know not what Science that is (quoth Don Lorenzo) neither hath it, as yet comne to my notice. Tis a Science (quoth Don Quixote) that containes in it all, or most of the Sciences of the world, by reason that he who professes it, must be

136

HISTORIE OF DON QUIXOTE

skilfull **in the** Lawes, **to** know Iustice Distributive and
Commutative, to give every man his owne, and what belongs
to him : he must be a Divine, to know how to give a reason
cleerly and distinctly of his Christian profession, whersoever
it shall be demanded him : hee must bee a Physician, and
chiefly an Herbalist, to know in a wildernesse or Desart,
what hearbs have vertue to cure wounds : for your Knight
Errant must not bee looking every pissing-while who shall
heale him : He must be an Astronomer, to know in the night
by the starres what a clock tis, and in what part and Climate
of the world he is : He must be skilfull in the Mathematikes,
because every foot he shal have need of them : And to let
passe, that he must be adorned with all divine and morall
vertues ; descending to other trifles, I say, he must learne to
swimme (as they say) fish Nicholas, or Nicolao did : Hee
must know how to shoo a horse, to mend a saddle or bridle :
And comming againe to what went before, hee must serve
God and his Mistris inviolably, he must be chaste in his
thoughts, honest in his words, liberall in his deedes, valiant
in his actions, patient in afflictions, charitable towards the
poore, and lastly, a Defender of truth, although it cost him
his life for it. Of all these great and lesser parts a good
Knight Errant is composed, that you may see, Signior Don
Lorenzo, whether it be a sniveling Science that the Knight
that learnes it professeth, and whether it may not be equalled
to the proudest of them all taught in the Schooles.

If it be **so** (sayd Don Lorenzo) I say this Science goes
beyond them all. If it be so (quoth Don Quixote) ? Why,
let **mee** tell you (sayd Don Lorenzo) I doubt whether there
be **any** Knights Errant now adorned with so many vertues.
Oft **have** I spoken (replide Don Quixote) that which I must
now speake agen, that the greatest part of men in the
world are of opinion, that there be no Knights Errant, and
I thinke, if Heaven doe not miraculously let um understand the truth, that there have been such, and that at this
day there be, all labour will be in vaine (as I have often
found by experience.) I will not now stand upon shewing
you your errour : all I will doe, is to pray to God to deliver

CHAPTER
XVIII
What hap-
pened to Don
Quixote in
the Castle,
or Knight of
the Greene
Cassocke his
house, with
other extrava-
gant matters.

3 : S   137

THE SECOND PART OF THE

**CHAPTER
XVIII**

What happened to Don Quixote in the Castle, or Knight of the Greene Cassocke his house, with other extravagant matters.

you out of it, and to make you understand, how profitable and necessary Knights Errant have beene to the world in former ages, and also would be at present, if they were in request: but now, for our sinnes, sloth, idlenesse, gluttony, and wantonnesse doe raigne. I'faith (thought Don Lorenzo) for this once our ghest hath scaped me: but for all that, he is a lively Asse, and I were a dull foole, if I did not beleeve it.

Heere they ended their discourse, for they were called to dinner: Don Diego asked his sonne, what triall he had made of their ghests understanding: To which he made answer; All the Physicians and Scriveners in the world will not wipe out his madnesse. He is a curious mad-man, and hath neat Dilemma's. To dinner they went, and their meat was such as Don Diego upon the way described it, such as hee gave to his ghests, well drest, savory and plentifull: But that which best pleased Don Quixote, was the marvellous silence thorowout the whole house, as if it had beene a Convent of Carthusians: So (that lifting up his eyes, and grace being sayd, and that they had washed hands) hee earnestly entreated Don Lorenzo to speake his Prize-verses.

To which (quoth he) because I will not be like your Poets, that when they are over-intreated, they use to make scruple of their workes, and when they are not intreated, they vomit um out, I will speake my glosse, for which I expect no reward, as having written them only to exercise my Muse. A wise friend of mine (sayd Don Quixote) was of opinion, that to glosse was no hard taske for any man, the reason being, that the Glosse could ne're come neere the Text, and most commonly the Glosse was quite from the Theame given; besides that, the Lawes of glossing were too strict, not admitting interrogations, of 'Sayd he?' or, 'Shall I say?' Or changing Nounes into Verbes, without other ligaments and strictnesses to which the Glossor is tyed, as you know. Certainely, Signior Don Quixote (said Don Lorenzo) I desire to catch you in an absurdity, but cannot, for still you slip from mee like an Eele. I know not (sayd Don Quixote) what you meane by your slipping. You shall

138

HISTORIE OF DON QUIXOTE

know my meaning (said Don Lorenzo:) but for the present
I pray you harken with attention to my glossed verses, and
to the Glosse, as for example.

What hap-
pened to Don
Quixote in
the Castle,
or Knight of
the Greene
Cassocke his
house, with
other extrava-
gant matters.

> If that my Was, might turne to Is,
> If look't for 't, then it comes compleat,
> Oh might I say, Now, time tis,
> Our after-griefes may be too great.

The Glosse.

> As every thing doth passe away,
> So Fortunes good, that erst she gave
> Did passe, and would not with me stay,
> Though she gave once all I could crave :
> Fortune, 'tis long since thou hast seene
> Me prostrate at thy feet (I wis)
> I shall be glad (as I have beene)
> If that my Was, returne to Is.

The first verse
of the glosse.

> Vnto no honour am I bent,
> No Prize, Conquest, or Victorie,
> But to returne to my content,
> Whose thought doth grieve my memorie ;
> If thou to me doe it restore,
> Fortune ; the rigor of my heat
> Allayd is, let it come, before
> I looke for 't, then it comes compleat.

The second
verse.

> Impossibles doe I desire
> To make time past returne (in vaine)
> No Pow'r on earth can once aspire
> (Past) to recall him backe againe,
> Time doth goe, time runs and flies
> Swiftly, his course doth never misse,
> Hee 's in an errour then that cries,
> Oh might I say, Now, now time 'tis.

The third
verse.

> I live in great perplexitie,
> Sometimes in hope, sometimes in feare,
> Farre better were it for to die,
> That of my griefes I might get cleare ;
> For me to die 'twere better farre,
> Let me not that againe repeat,
> Feare sayes, 'Tis better live long : for
> Our after griefes may be too great.

The fourth
verse.

THE SECOND PART OF THE

**CHAPTER
XVIII**

What hap-
pened to Don
Quixote in
the Castle,
or Knight of
the Greene
Cassocke his
house, with
other extrava-
gant matters.

When Don Lorenzo had ended, Don Quixote stood up
and cried aloud, as if hee had screecht, taking Don Lorenzo
by the hand, and sayd ; Assuredly, generous youth, I thinke
you are the best Poet in the world, and you deserve the
Lawrell, not of Cyprus or Gaeta, as a Poet sayd (God forgive him) but of Athens, if it were extant, Paris, Bolonia,
and Salamanca : I would to God those Iudges that would
deny you the Prize, might bee shot to death with arrowes by
Phœbus, and that the Muses never come within their thresholds. Speake, Sir, if you please, some of your loftier verses,
that I may altogether feele the pulse of your admirable
wit.

How say you by this, that Don Lorenzo was pleased, when
he heard himselfe thus praised by Don Quixote, although
he held him to be a mad-man ? Oh power of flattery, how
farre thou canst extend, and how large are the bounds of
thy pleasing jurisdiction ! This truth was verified in Don
Lorenzo, since hee condiscended to Don Quixotes request,
speaking this following Sonnet to him, of the Fable or
Story of Pyramus and Thisbe.

> The wall was broken by the Virgin faire,
> That op't the gallant brest of Pyramus,
> Love parts from Cyprus, that he may declare
> (Once seene) the narrow breach prodigious.
> There nought but Silence speakes, no voyce doth dare,
> Thorow so strait a straight, be venturous ;
> Yet their mindes speake, Love workes this wonder rare,
> Facilitating things most wonderous.
>
> Desire in her grew violent, and haste
> In the fond Mayd, in stead of hearts delight
> Solicites death : See ! now the Storie 's past,
> Both of them, in a moment (oh strange sight !)
>
> One Sword, one Sepulcher, one Memorie,
> Doth kill, doth cover, makes them never die.

Now thanked bee God (quoth Don Quixote, having heard
this Sonnet) that amongst so many consumed Poets as be,
I have found one consummate, as you are, Sir, which I per-

140

HISTORIE OF DON QUIXOTE

ceive by your well-framed Sonnet. Don Quixote remained foure dayes (being well entertained) in Don Diego's house, at the end of which he desired to take his leave, and thanked him for the kindnesse and good welcome he had received: but because it was not fit that Knights Errant should bee too long idle, hee purposed to exercise his Function, and to seeke after Adventures he knew of; for the place whither hee meant to goe to, would give him plenty enough to passe his time with, till it were fit for him to goe to the Iusts at Saragosa, which was his more direct course: but that first of all he meant to goe to Montesino's vault, of which there were so many admirable tales in every mans mouth: so to search and enquire the Spring and Origine of those seven Lakes, commonly called of Ruydera. Don Diego and his sonne commended his noble determination, and bid him furnish himselfe with what hee pleased of their house and wealth, for that hee should receive it with all love and good will; for the worth of his person, and his honourable profession obliged them to it.

To conclude, the day for his parting came, as pleasing to him, as bitter and sorrowfull to Sancho, who liked wondrous well of Don Diego's plentifull provision, and was loth to returne to the hunger of the forrests and wildernesse, and to the hardnesse of his ill-furnisht wallets, notwithstanding hee filled and stuffed them with the best provision he could. And Don Quixote, as he tooke his leave of Don Lorenzo, sayd; I know not, Sir, whether I have told you heretofore, but though I have, I tell you againe, that when you would save a great deale of labor and paines, to arrive at the inaccessible top of Fames Temple, you have no more to doe, but to leave on one hand the straight and narrow path of Poesie, and to take the most narrow of Knight Errantry, sufficient to make you an Emperour, ere you would say, ' What's this?'

With this Epilogue Don Quixote shut up the Comedy of his madnesse, onely this he added: God knowes, I would willingly carry Signior Don Lorenzo with me, to teach him, what belongs to pardoning the humble, to curbing and

141

THE SECOND PART OF THE

CHAPTER
XVIII
What hap-
pened to Don
Quixote in
the Castle,
or Knight of
the Greene
Cassocke, his
house, with
other extrava-
gant matters.
restraining the proud; vertues annexed to my profession: but
since his slender age is not capable, and his laudible enter-
prises will not permit him, I am onely willing to advize you,
that being a Poet, you may be famous, if you governe your
selfe by other mens judgements, more then by your owne;
for you have no parents that dislike their owne children,
faire or foule, and this errour is more frequent in mens
understandings.

The Father and the Son afresh admired at Don Quixotes oft
interposed reasons, some wise, some foolish, and at his obstinate being bent altogether upon his unlucky Adventures,
which hee aimed at, as the marke and end of his desire, they
renewed againe their kinde offers and complements with
him; but Don Quixote taking his leave of the Lady of
the Castle, mounted his Rozinante, and Sancho
his Dapple; so they parted.

CHAPTER XIX

Of the Adventure of the enamoured Shepheard,
with other, indeed, pleasant Accidents.

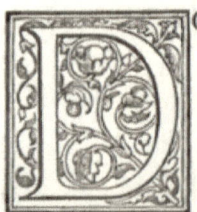

ON QUIXOTE was not gone far from
Don Diego's towne, when hee overtooke
two men that seemed to be Parsons, or
Schollers, with two Husbandmen that
were mounted upon foure Asses. One of
the Schollers had (as it were in a Port-
mantue) a piece of white cloth for Scarlet,
wrapped up in a piece of greene Buckeram,
and two payre of Cotton Stockings: the other had nothing
but two Foiles, and a paire of Pumpes. The Husbandmen
had other things, which shewed they came from some Market
Towne, where they had bought them to carry home to their
village: so as well the Schollers as the Husbandmen fell into

142

HISTORIE OF DON QUIXOTE

CHAPTER
XIX

Of the Adventure of the
enamoured
Shepheard,
with other, indeed, pleasant
Accidents.

the same admiration, that all they had done who first saw
Don Quixote, and they longed to know what manner of
fellow he was, so different from all other men. Don Quixote
saluted them, and after hee asked them whither they went,
and that they had said they went his way, he offered them
his company, and desired them to goe softlyer, for that their
young Asses travelled faster then his horse: and to oblige
them the more, he told them who he was, and of his profession, that he was a Knight Errant, that he went to seeke
Adventures round about the world. Hee told them his
proper name was Don Quixote de la Mancha, but his ordinary
name, The Knight of the Lyons.

All this to the Husbandmen was Heathen Greek, or Pedlers
French: but not to the Schollers, who straight perceived the
weakenesse of Don Quixotes braine: Notwithstanding they
beheld him with great admiration and respect, and one of
them said, Sir Knight, if you goe no set journey, as they
which seeke Adventures seldome doe, I pray goe with us,
and you shall see one of the bravest and most sumptuous
mariages that ever was kept in the Mancha, or in many
leagues round about. Don Quixote asked them if it were
of any Prince (for so hee imagined.) No, Sir, (said hee)
but betwixt a Farmer, and a Farmers daughter: he is the
richest in all the Countrey, and she she fairest alive. Their
provision for this marriage is new and rare, and it is to be
kept in a medow neere the Brides towne. Shee is called,
the more to set her out, Quiteria the faire, and he Camacho
the rich: she is about eighteene yeeres of age, and he two
and twenty, both well mette, but that some nice people,
that busie themselves in all mens linages, will say that the
faire Quiteria is of better parentage then he: but that's
nothing, riches are able to soulder all clefts. To say true,
this Chamacho is liberall, and he hath longed to make an
Arbor, and cover all the Medow on the Top, so that the
Sunne will be troubled to enter to visit the greene hearbs
underneath. He hath also certaine warlike Morrices, as well
of swords, as little jyngling bels; for wee have those in the
towne that will jangle them. For your foot-clappers I say

143

THE SECOND PART OF THE

**CHAPTER
XIX**

Of the Adven-
ture of the
enamoured
Shepheard,
with other, in-
deed, pleasant
Accidents.

nothing, you would wonder to see **um bestirre** themselves:
but none of these, **nor** others I have **told** you of, are like to
make this marriage so remarkeable, as **the** despised Basilius.
This Basilius is a neighbouring swaine of Quiteria's Towne,
whose house was next dore to her Fathers. From hence
Love tooke occasion to renew unto the world, the long forgotten loves of Pyramus and Thysbe; for Basilius loved
Quiteria from a childe, and she answered his desires with
a thousand loving favors. So that it grew a common talke
in the towne, of the love betweene the two little ones.
Quiteria began to grow to some yeeres, and her Father
began to deny Basilius his ordinary accesse to the house;
and to avoyd all suspition, purposed to marry her to the
rich Camacho, not thinking it fit to marry her to Basilius,
who was not so rich in Fortunes goods, as in those of the
minde, (for **to** say truth without envy) he is the activest
youth we have, a famous Barre-pitcher, an excellent Wrastler,
a great Tennis-player, he runnes like a Deere, out-leapes a
shee-goat, and playes at tenne pinnes miraculously, sings like
a Larke, playes upon a Gitterne as if he made **it** speake, and
above all, fenceth as well as the best.

For that slight only (quoth Don Quixote) **the** youth deserves not onely to match with the faire Quiteria, but with
Queene Ginebra her selfe, if she were now alive, in spight of
Lansarote, and all that would gain-say it. There's for my
wife now (quoth Sancho that had beene all this while silent)
that would have every one marry with their equals, holding
her selfe to the Proverbe, that sayes: 'Like to like' (quoth
the Devill to the Collier.) All that I desire, is, that honest
Basilius (for me thinkes I love him) **were** married to Quiteria,
and God give um joy (I was saying) those that go about to
hinder the mariage of two that love well. If all that love
well (quoth Don Quixote) should marry, Parents would lose
the priviledge of marying their children, when and with
whom they ought; and if daughters might chuse their
husbands, you should have some would choose their fathers
servants, and others, any passenger in the street, whom they
thought to be a lusty swaggerer, although hee were a
144

HISTORIE OF DON QUIXOTE

cowardly Ruffian; for love and affection doe easily blinde the eyes of the understanding, which is onely fit to choose, and the state of Matrimony is a ticklish thing, and there is great heed to be taken, and a particular favour to be given from above to make it light happily.

Any man that would but undertake some voyage, if hee be wise, before he is on his way, he will seeke him some good companion. And why should not he doe so, that must travell all his life-time till he come to his resting-place, Death? and the rather if his company must be at bed, and at boord, and in all places, as the wives company must be with the Husband? Your wife is not a commodity like others, that is bought and sold, or exchang'd, but an inseparable accident, that lasts for terme of life. It is a nooze, that beeing fastned about the necke, turnes to a Gordian knot, which cannot be undone but by Deaths sickle.

I could tell yee much more in this businesse, were it not for the desire I have to be satisfied by Master Parson, if there be any more to come of Basilius his story. To which hee answered, This is all, that from the instant that Basilius knew the fair Quiteria was to be maried to the rich Camacho, he was never seene to smile, or talke sensibly; and hee is alwaies sad and pensative, talkes to himselfe: an evident token that hee is distracted: eates little, sleepes much: all he eates, is fruites, and all his sleepe is in the fields, upon the hard ground like a beast; now and then hee lookes up to heaven, and sometimes casts his eyes downeward, so senselesse, as if hee were onely a statue clothed, and the very ayre strikes off his garments. In fine, he hath all the signes of a passionate heart, and we are all of opinion, that by that time Quiteria to morrow gives the, I, it will be the sentence of his death. God forbid (sayd Sancho) for God gives the wound, and God gives the salve: no body knowes what may happen, 'tis a good many houres betweene this and to morrow, and in one houre, nay one minute, a house falls, and I have seene the Sunne shine, and foule weather in an instant; one goes to bed sound at night, and stirres not the next morning: and pray tell me, is there any one

Of the Adventure of the enamoured Shepheard, with other, indeed, pleasant Accidents.

3 : T   145

CHAPTER
XIX
Of the Adven-
ture of the
enamoured
Shepheard,
with other, in-
deed, pleasant
Accidents.

here that can say he hath stayd the course of Fortunes great wheele? No truly, and betweene a womans I, and no, I would be loth to put a pins poynt; for it would hardly enter. Let mee have Mistresse Quiteria love Basilius with all her heart, and I 'le give him a bagge full of good lucke, for your love (as I have heard tell) lookes wantonly with eyes that make copper seeme gold, and poverty riches, and filth in the eyes, pearles. Whither a plague run'st thou, Sancho (quoth Don Quixote)? when thou goest threading on thy Proverbs and thy flim-flams, Iudas him selfe take thee, cannot hold thee: Tell me, Beast, what knowest thou of Fortune, or her wheele, or any thing else? Oh if you understand me not, no marvell though my sentences be held for fopperies: well, I know what I say, and know I have not spoken much from the purpose: but you, Sir, are alwaies the Tourney to my words and actions. Attourney thou wouldest say, God confound thee, thou Prevaricator of language. Doe not you deale with me (said Sancho) since you know I have not bin brought up in Court, nor studied in Salamanca, to know whether I adde or diminish any of my syllables. Lord God, you must not thinke your *Galizian

*One of that
Province that
speake a
bastard lan-
guage to the
Spanish.

can speak like your Toledonian, and they neyther are not all so nimble. For matter of your Court-language (quoth the Parson) 'tis true; for they that are bred in the Tanner-rowes, and the *Zocodover, cannot discourse like them that

walke all day in the high Church-Cloysters; yet all are Toledonians, the language is pure, proper, and elegant, (indeed) only in your discreet Courtiers, let them be borne where they will: Discreet I say, because many are other-wise, and discretion is the Grammar of good language, which is accompanied with practice: I Sir, I thanke God have studied the Canons in Salamanca, and presume sometimes to yeeld a reason in plaine and significant termes. If you did not presume (said the other Scholler) more on your using the foyles you carry, then your tongue, you might have beene Senior in your degree, whereas now you are lagge. Looke you Bachelor (quoth the Parson) you are in the most erroneous opinion of the world, touching the

HISTORIE OF DON QUIXOTE

skill of the weapon, since you hold it frivolous. Tis no
opinion of mine (said Corchuelo) but a manifest truth, and
if you will have me shew it by experience, there you have
foyles commodious: I have an arme, and strength, which
together with my courage, which is not small, shall make
you confesse I am not deceived; alight and keepe your distance, your circles, your corners, and all your Science, I hope
to make you see the starres at noone day with my skill,
which is but moderne and meane, which though it be small,
I hope to God the man is yet unborn that shall make mee
turne my backe, and there is no man in the world, but I 'le
make him give ground. For turning your backe (said the
Skilfull) I meddle not, though perhaps where you first set
your foot, there your grave might be digged, I meane you
might be killed for despising skill. That you shall try (said
Corchuelo) and lighting hastily from his Asse, he snatched
one of the swords that the Parson carried. Not so (sayd
Don Quixote instantly) Ile be the Master of this Fence,
and the Iudge of this undecided controversie, and lighting
from Rozinante, and taking his Launce, he stepped betweene
them till such time as the Parson had put himselfe into
his Posture and distance against Corchuelo, who ranne
(as you would say) darting fire out of his eyes. The two
Husbandmen that were by, without lighting from their
Asses, served for spectators of the mortall Tragedy, the
blowes, the stockados, your false thrusts, your back-blowes,
your doubling-blowes, that came from Corchuelo, were numberlesse, as thicke as hoppes, or haile, he layd on like an
angry Lyon: but still the Parson gave him a stopple for
his mouth, with the button of his foyle, which stopped him
in the midst of his fury, and he made him kisse it, as if it
had been a Relike, though not with so much devotion as
is due to them. In a word, the Parson with pure Stocados
told all the buttons of his Cassocke which he had on, his
skirts flying about him like a fishes tayle. Twice he strooke
off his hat, and so wearied him, that what for despight, what
for choller and rage, he tooke the sword by the hilt, and
flung it into the ayre so forcibly, that **one** of the husband-

CHAPTER
XIX
Of the Adven-
ture of the
enamoured
Shepheard,
with other, in-
deed, pleasant
Accidents.

147

CHAPTER
XIX
Of the Adven-
ture of the
enamoured
Shepheard,
with other, in-
deed, pleasant
Accidents.

men that was by, who was a notary, and went for it, gave testimony after, that he flung it almost three quarters of a mile; which testimony serves, and hath served, that it may be knowne and really seene, that force is overcome by Art.

Corchuelo sate down being very weary, and Sancho comming to him, said; Truely Sir Bachelor, if you take my advice, hereafter challenge no man to fence, but to wrastle, or throw the bar, since you have youth and force enough for it; for I have heard those (that you call your Skilfull men) say, that they will thrust the poynt of a sword through the eye of a needle. I am gladde (quoth Corchuelo) that I came from my Asse, and that experience hath shewed me what I would not have beleeved. So rising up, he embraced the Parson, and they were as good friends as before. So, not staying for the Notary that went for the sword, because they thought hee would tarry long, they resolved to follow, and come betimes to Quiteria's Village, of whence they all were. By the way, the Parson discourses to um, of the excellency of the Art of Fencing, with so many demonstrative reasons, with so many figures and Mathematical demonstrations, that all were satisfied with the rarenesse of the Science, and Corchuelo reduced from his obstinacy.

It began to grow darke: but before they drew neere, they all saw a kinde of heaven of innumerable starres before the Towne. They heard likewise, harmonious and confused sounds of divers Instruments, as Flutes, Tabers, Psalteries, Recorders, hand-Drummes and Bells: and when they drew neere, they saw that the trees of an Arbour, which had been made at the entrance of the towne, were all full of lights, which were not offended by the winde, that then blew not, but was so gentle, that it scarce moved the leaves of the trees. The Musicians were they that made the marriage more sprightly, who went two and two in companies, some dancing and singing, others playing upon divers of the aforesaid instruments: nothing but mirth ranne up and downe the Medow, others were busied in raising skaffolds, that they might the next day see the representations and dances commodiously, dedicated to

148

HISTORIE OF DON QUIXOTE

CHAPTER
XIX
Of the Adven-
ture of the
enamoured
Shepheard,
with other, in-
deed, pleasant
Accidents.

the marriage of the rich Camacho, and the Obsequies of
Basilius.

Don Quixote would not enter the Towne, although the
Husbandmen and the Bachelor entreated him : for he gave
a sufficient excuse for himselfe (as hee thought) that it was
the custome of Knights Errant to sleepe in fields and
forrests, rather then in habitations, though it were under
golden roofes : so hee went a little out of the way,
much against Sancho's will, who remembred the
good lodging hee had in the Castle, or
house of Don Diego.

CHAPTER XX

Of the Marriage of rich Camacho, and the successe of poore Basilius.

CARSE had the silver morne given bright
Phœbus leave, with the ardour of his
burning rayes, to dry the liquid pearles
on his golden lockes, when Don Quixote
shaking off sloth from his drowsie members, rose up, and called Sancho his Squire,
that still lay snorting : which Don Quixote seeing, before he could wake, he said,
Oh happy thou above all that live upon the face of the earth,
that without envy, or being envied, sleepest with a quiet
brest, neyther persecuted by Enchanters, nor frighted by
Enchantments. Sleepe, I say, once againe, nay an hundred
times, sleepe : let not thy Masters jealousie keepe thee
continually awake, nor let care to pay thy debts make
thee watchfull, or how another day thou and thy small,
but streightned family may live, whom neither ambition
troubles, nor the worlds vaine pompe doth weary, since the
bounds of thy desires extend no further then to thinking
149

CHAPTER
XX
Of the Mar-
riage of rich
Camacho, and
the successe
of poore
Basilius.

of thine Asse; for, for thine owne person, that thou hast committed to my charge, a counterpoise and burden that Nature and Custome hath layd upon the Masters. The servant sleepes, and the Master wakes, thinking how he may maintaine, good him, and doe him kindnesses: the griefe that is, to see heaven obdurate in releeving the earth with seasonable moysture, troubles not the servant, but it doth the Master, that must keepe in sterility and hunger, him that served him in abundance and plenty.

Sancho answered not a word to all this, for hee was asleepe, neyther would hee have awaked so soone, if Don Quixote had not made him come to himselfe with the little end of his Lance. At length he awaked, sleepy and drowsie, and turning his face round about, hee said, From this Arbor (if I bee not deceived) there comes a steame and smell rather of good broyled rashers, then Time and Rushes: A marriage that begins with such smells, (by my Holidam) I thinke twill be brave and plentifull.

Away, Glutton (quoth Don Quixote) come and let us go see it, and what becomes of the disdained Basilius. Let him doe what he will (said Sancho) were it not better that he were poore still, and married to Quiteria? There is no more in it, but let the Moone loose one quarter, and shee 'l fall from the clouds: Faith, Sir, I am of opinion, that the poore fellow bee contented with his fortunes, and not seek after things impossible. Ile hold one of mine arms, that Camacho wil cover Basilius all over with sixpences: and if it be so, as tis like, Quiteria were a very foole to leave her bravery and Iewells that Camacho hath, and can give her, and chuse Basilius for his barre-pitching and fencing: In a Taverne they will not give you a pint of wine for a good throw with the barre, or a tricke at fence, such abilities that are worth nothing, have um whoso will for me: but when they light upon one that hath crownes withall, let mee be like that man that hath them: upon a good foundation, a good building may be raised, and mony is the best bottome and foundation that is in the world. For Gods love, Sancho (quoth Don Quixote) conclude thy tedious discourse: with

150

which (I beleeve) if thou wert let alone, thou wouldest neyther eat nor sleepe for talking. If you had a good memory (sayd Sancho) you would remember the articles of our agreement, before we made our last sally from home, one of which was, that you would let me speake as much as I list, on condition that it were not against my neighbor, or against your authority, and hitherto I am sure I have not broken that article.

CHAPTER
XX

Of the Marriage of rich Camacho, and the successe of poore Basilius.

I remember no such article, Sancho, (sayd he) and though it were so, I would have you now be silent, and come with mee ; for now the Instruments we heard over-night begin to cheere the valleyes, and doubtlesse, the marriage is kept in the coole of the morning, and not deferred till the afternoones heat. Sancho did what his master willed him, and saddling Rozinante, with his pack-saddle clapped likewise on Dapple, the two mounted, and faire and softly entred the Arbor. The first thing that Sancho saw, was a whole Steere spitted upon a whole Elme, and for the fire where it was to bee rosted, there was a pretty mountaine of wood, and six pots that were round-about this Bon-fire, which were never cast in the ordinary mold that other pots were, for they were six halfe Olive-butts, and every one was a very Shambles of meat, they had so many whole sheepe soking in um which were not seene, as if they had beene Pigeons, the flayed Hares, and pulled Hens, that were hung upon the trees, to bee buried in the pots, were numberlesse, birds and fowle of divers sorts infinite, that hung on the trees, that the aire might coole them. Sancho counted above threescore skinnes of wine, each of them of above two Arroba's, and as it afterward seemed, of spritely liquor : there were also whole heapes of purest bread, heaped up like corne in the threshing-floores, your cheeses like bricks piled one upon another, made a goodly wall, and two kettles of oyle bigger then a Diers, served to frie their paste-worke, which they tooke out with two strong peeles, when they were fried, and they ducked them in another kettle of honey that stood by for the same purpose : There were Cookes above fifty, men and women, all cleanely, carefull, and cheerfull : In the

Arroba, a measure of 25 pound wayt, which may be some six gallons of wine.

151

CHAPTER
XX

Of the Mar-
riage of rich
Camacho, and
the successe
of poore
Basilius.

spacious belly of the Steere, there were twelve sucking Pigs,
which being sowed there, served to make him more savoury :
the spices of divers sorts, it seemes were not brought by
Pounds, but by Arrobas, and all lay open in a great chest.
To conclude, this preparation for the marriage was rusticall ;
but so plentifull, that it might furnish an Army.

Sancho Pansa beheld all, and was much affected with
it : and first of all, the goodly pots did captivate his desires,
from whence with all his heart hee would have beene glad
to have received a good pipkin full ; by and by he was
enamoured on the skins, and last of all upon the fried
meats, if so be those vast kettles might bee called frying-
pans : so without longer patience, as not being able to
abstaine, he came to one of the busie Cookes, and with
courteous and hungry reasons, desired him, that he might
sop a cast of bread in one of the pots. To which the Cooke
replide ; Brother, this is no day on which hunger may have
any jurisdiction (thanks be to the rich Camacho) alight, and
see if you can finde ever a ladle there, and skimme out a
Hen or two, and much good may they doe you.

I see none (sayd Sancho.) Stay (sayd the Cooke) God
forgive me, What a Ninny tis ! and saying this, he layed
hold of a kettle, and sowsing into it one of the halfe-butts,
he drew out of it three Hens and two Geese, and sayd to
Sancho ; Eat, Friend, and breake your fast with this froth,
till dinner-time. I have nothing to put it in (sayd Sancho.)
Why, take spoone and all (sayd the Cooke) for Camacho's
riches and content will very well beare it.

Whilest Sancho thus passed his time, Don Quixote saw,
that by one side of the Arbour, there came a doozen
Husband-men upon twelve goodly Mares, with rich and
sightly furniture fit for the Countrey, with many little bels
upon their Petrels, all clad in bravery for that dayes solem-
nity, and all in a joynt-troop ran many Careeres up and
downe the medow, with a great deale of mirth and jollity,
crying : Long live Camacho and Quiteria, he as rich, as shee
faire, and shee the fairest of the world. Which when Don
Quixote heard, thought hee to himselfe, It well appeares

HISTORIE OF DON QUIXOTE

that these men have not seene my Dulcinea del Toboso: for
if they had, they would not bee so forward in praising this
their Quiteria.

Of the Mar-
riage of rich
Camacho, and
the successe
of poore
Basilius.

A while after, there began to enter at divers places of the
Arbour, certaine different dances, amongst which there was
one Sword-dance, by foure and twenty Swaines, handsome
lusty Youths, all in white linnen, with their hand-kerchiefs
wrought in severall colours of fine silke, and one of the
twelve upon the Mares asked him that was the fore-man of
these, a nimble Lad, if any of the Dancers had hurt themselves.

Hitherto (sayd he) no body is hurt, wee are all well, God
bee thanked : and straight he shuffled in amongst the rest
of his companions, with so many tricks, and so much flight ;
that Don Quixote, though he were used to such kinde of
dances, yet hee never liked any so well as this. He also
liked another very well, which was of faire young Mayds, so
young, that never a one was under foureteene, nor none
above eighteene, all clad in course greene, their haire partly
filletted and partly loose : but all were yellow, and might
compare with the Sunne, upon which they had garlands of
* Iasmines, Roses, Wood-bine and Hony-suckles, they had
for their guides a reverend olde man, and a matronly woman,
but more light and nimble then could bee expected from
their yeeres.

*Iasmines, a
little sweet
white flower
that growes
in Spaine in
hedges, like
our Sweet
Marjoram.

They danc'd to the sound of a * Zamora bag-pipe, so that
with their honest lookes, and their nimble feet, they seemed
to be the best Dancers in the world. After this there came
in another artificiall dance, of those called Brawles, it con-
sisted of eight Nymphs, divided into two rankes, God Cupid
guided one ranke, and Money the other, the one with his
wings, his Bow, his Quiver and Arrowes, the other was clad
in divers rich colours of gold and silke : The Nymphs that
followed Love, carried a white parchment scrowle at their
backes, in which their names were written in great letters :
the first was Poesie, the second Discretion, the third Nobility,
the fourth Valour. In the same manner came those whom
god Money led, the first was Liberality, the second Reward,

*Zamora, a
towne in
Castile,
famous for
that kinde of
musicke, like
our Lanca-
shire horn-
pipe.

3 : U   153

THE SECOND PART OF THE

CHAPTER
XX
Of the Mar-
riage of rich
Camacho, and
the successe
of poore
Basilius.

the third Treasure, the fourth Quiet Possession; before
them came a woodden Castle, which was shot at by two
Savages clad in Ivie and Canvas, died in greene, so to the
life, that they had well-nigh frighted Sancho. Vpon the
Frontispice, and of each side of the Castle, was written;
'The Castle of good heede': Foure skilfull Musicians played
to them on a Taber and Pipe; Cupid began the Dance, and
after two changes, hee lifted up his eyes, and bent his Bow
against a Virgin that stood upon the battlements of the
Castle, and sayd to her in this manner:

> I am the pow'rfull Deitie,
> In Heaven above and Earth beneath,
> In Seas and Hels profunditie,
> O're all that therein live or breathe.
>
> What 'tis to feare, I never knew,
> I can performe all that I will,
> Nothing to me is strange, or new;
> I bid, forbid, at pleasure still.

The Verse being ended, he shot a flight over the Castle,
and retired to his standing; By and by came out Money,
and performed his two changes; the Taber ceased, and he
spoke:

> Loe I, that can doe more then Love,
> Yet love is he that doth me guide,
> My of-spring great'st on earth, to Iove
> Above I neerest am allide.
>
> I Money am, with whom but few
> Performe the honest workes they ought;
> Yet heere a miracle to shew,
> That without me they could doe ought.

Money retired, and Poetry advanced, who after she had
done her changes aswell as the rest, her eyes fixt upon the
Damozell of the Castle, she sayd:

> Lady, to thee, sweet Poesie
> Her soule in deepe conceits doth send,
> Wrapt up in writs of Sonnetrie,
> Whose pleasing straines doe them commeud.

154

If with my earnestnesse, I thee
Importune not, faire Damozell, soone
Thy envied fortune shall, by mee,
Mount the circle of the Moone.

Poetry gave way, and from Monies side came Liberality, and after her changes, spoke:

To give is Liberalitie,
In him that shunnes two contraries,
The one of Prodigalitie,
Tother of hatefull Avarice.

Ile be profuse in praising thee,
Profusenesse hath accounted beene
A vice, yet sure it commeth nie
Affection, which in gifts is seene.

CHAPTER
XX

Of the Mar-
riage of rich
Camacho, and
the successe
of poore
Basilius.

In this sort both the shewes of the two Squadrons, came in and out, and each of them performed their changes, and spoke their verses, some elegant, some ridiculous, Don Quixote onely remembred (for he had a great memory) the rehearsed one, and now the whole troope mingled together, winding in and out with great spritelinesse and dexterity, and still as Love went before the Castle, he shot a flight aloft, but Money broke gilded bals, and threw into it.

At last, after Money had danc'd a good while, he drew out a great purse made of a Romane Cats skinne, which seemed to be full of money, and casting it into the Castle, with the blow, the boords were dis-joyned, and fell downe, leaving the Damozell discovered, without any defence. Money came with his assistants, and casting a great chaine of golde about her necke, they made a shew of leading her captive: Which when Love and his Party saw, they made shew as if they would have rescued her, and all these motions were to the sound of the Taber, with skilfull dancing, the Savages parted them, who very speedily went to set up and joyne the boords of the Castle, and the Damozell was enclosed there anew: and with this the dance ended, to the great content of the Spectators.

Don Quixote asked one of the Nymphs, Who had so drest and ordered her? Shee answered, A Parson of the towne,

CHAPTER
XX

Of the Mar-
riage of rich
Camacho, and
the successe
of poore
Basilius.

who had an excellent capacity for such inventions. Ile lay a wager (sayd Don Quixote) he was more Basilius his friend then Camacho's, and that he knowes better what belongs to a Satyr then to Even-song; he hath well fitted Basilius his abilities to the dance, and Camacho's riches.

Sancho Pansa that heard all sayd; The King is my Cocke, I hold with Camacho. Well, Sancho (quoth Don Quixote) thou art a very Peasant, and like them that cry, Long live the Conquerour. I know not who I am like (said Sancho :) but I know I shall never get such delicate froth out of Basilius his Pottage-pots, as I have out of Camacho's: and with that shewed him the kettle full of Geese and Hens, and laying hold on one, he fell to it merrily and hungerly, and for Basilius abilities this he sayd to their teeth: So much thou art worth as thou hast, and so much as thou hast, thou art worth. An olde Grandam of mine was wont to say, there were but two linages in the world, Have-much, and Have-little; and she was mightily enclined to the former: and at this day, Master, your Physician had rather feele a having pulse, then a knowing pulse, and an Asse covered with golde makes a better shew then a horse with a pack-saddle. So that I say againe, I am of Camacho's side, the scumme of whose pots are Geese, Hens, Hares, and Conies, and Basilius his, bee they neere or farre off, but poore thin water.

Hast thou ended with thy tediousnesse, Sancho (sayd Don Quixote)? I must end (sayd hee) because I see it offends you, for if it were not for that, I had worke cut out for three dayes. Pray God, Sancho (quoth Don Quixote) that I may see thee dumbe before I die. According to our life (sayd Sancho) before you die, I shall be mumbling clay, and then perhaps I shall bee so dumbe, that I shall not speake a word till the end of the world, or at least till Domes-day.

Although it should bee so, Sancho (sayd hee) thy silence will never be equall to thy talking past, and thy talke to come; besides, tis very likely that I shall die before thee, and so I shall never see thee dumbe, no not when thou drinkest or sleepest, to paint thee out thorowly. In good

faith, **Master** (quoth Sancho) there is no **trusting** in the
raw **bones, I** meane Death, that devoures **lambes** as well
as sheepe, and I have heard our Vicar **say**, she tramples
as wel on the high Towres of Kings, as **the** humble cottages of poore men: this Lady hath more power then
squeamishnesse, she is nothing dainty, shee devoures all,
playes at all, and fils her wallets with all kinde of people,
ages, and preeminences: Shee is no Mower that sleepes in
the hot weather, but mowes at all howers, and cuts aswell
the greene grasse as the hay: she doth not chew, but
swallowes at once, and crams downe all that comes before
her; shee hath a Canine appetite, that is never satisfied,
and though shee have no belly, yet shee may make us thinke
shee is Hydropsicall, with the thirst shee hath to drinke all
mens lives, as if it were a jugge of colde water.

No more, Sancho (quoth Don Quixote) at this instant,
hold while thou art well, and take heed of falling, for certainely thou hast spoken of Death in thy rusticall termes,
as* much as a good Preacher might have spoken. I tell
thee, Sancho, that for thy naturall discretion, **thou** mightst
get thee a Pulpit, and preach thy fine knacks up and downe
the world. Hee preaches well that lives well (sayd Sancho)
and I know no other preaching. Thou needest not (quoth
he:) But I wonder at one thing, that wisdome beginning
from the feare of God, that thou, who fearest a Lizard more
then him, shouldst be so wise? Iudge you of your Knight
Errantry (sayd Sancho) and meddle not with other mens
feares or valors, for I am as pretty a Fearer of God
as any of my neighbours, and so let mee snuffe away this
scum, for all the rest are but idle words, for which we
must give account in another life. And in so saying,
hee began **to** give another assault to the kettle, with
such a courage, that he wakened Don Quixote, that
undoubtedly would have taken his part, if he had
not beene hindered by that, that of neces-
sity must be set downe.

CHAPTER
XX

Of the Mar-
riage of rich
Camacho, and
the successe
of poore
Basilius.

Meaning to
eat his Pen
and the Goose.

CHAPTER XXI

Of the prosecution of Camacho's marriage, with other delightfull accidents.

AS Don Quixote and Sancho were in their discourse mentioned in the former chapter, they heard a great noyse and out-cry, which was caused by them that rode on the Mares, who with a large Carreere and shouts, went to meet the married couple; who, hemmed in with a thousand trickes and devices, came in company of the Vicar, and both their kindreds, and all the better sort of the neighbouring townes, all clad in their best apparell. And as Sancho saw the Bride, he said, In good faith she is not drest like a country wench, but like one of your nice Court Dames: by th'Masse me thinkes her glasse necke-laces she should weare, are rich Corrall; and her course greene of Cuenca, is a *thirty piled velvet; and her lacing that should be white linnen, (I vow by me) is Satten: well looke on her hands that should have their Iette rings, let me not thrive if they be not golden rings, arrant gold, and set with pearles as white as a sillabub, each of them as precious as an eye. Ah whooreson, and what lockes she hath? for if they be not false, I never saw longer, nor fairer in my life. Well, well, finde not fault with her livelinesse and stature, and compare her me to a Date tree, that bends up and downe when it is loaden with bunches of Dates; for so doth she with her trinkets hanging at her hayre and about her necke: I sweare by my soule, she is a wench of mettall, and may very well passe the pikes in Flanders.

Don Quixote laughed at Sancho's rusticke praises, and hee thought, that setting his Mistresse Dulcinea aside, he never saw fairer woman: the beauteous Quitcria was some-

*In stead of three-piled.

158

CHAPTER XXI

Of the prosecution of Camacho's marriage, with other delightfull accidents.

what pale, belike, with the ill night that Brides alwaies have when they dresse themselves for next daies marriage. They drew neere to a Theater on one side of the Medow, that was dressed with Carpets and boughes, where the marriage was to bee solemnized, and where they should behold the dances and inventions. And just as they should come to the place, they heard a great out-cry behind them, and a voyce, saying; Stay a while, rash people as well as hasty: At whose voyce and words they all turned about, and saw that he that spoke, was one cladde (to see to) in a blacke Iacket all welted with Crimson in flames, crowned (as they straight perceived) with a crowne of mournefull Cypresse, in his hand he had a great Truncheon: and comming neerer, hee was knowne by all to be the Gallant Basilius, who were in suspence, expecting what should be the issue of those cryes and words, fearing some ill successe from this so unlooked-for arrivall. Hee drew neere, weary, and out of breath, and comming before the married couple, and clapping his Truncheon upon the ground, which had a steele pike at the end of it: his colour changed, and his eyes fixed upon Quiteria, with a fearfull and hollow voyce, thus spoke:

Well knowest thou, forgetfull Quiteria, that according to the Law of God that wee professe, that whilest I live thou canst not be married to any other: neyther are you ignorant, that because I would stay till time and my industry might better my fortunes, I would not breake that decorum that was fitting to the preserving of thy honesty: but you forgetting all duetie, due to my vertuous desires, will make another Master of what is mine, whose riches serve not onely to make him happy in them, but every way fortunate, and that he may be so to the full, (not as I thinke he deserves it, but as the Fates ordaine it for him) I will with these hands remoove the impossibility or inconvenience that may disturbe him, removing my selfe out of the way. Live, rich Camacho, live with the ungratefull Quiteria many and prosperous yeeres, and let your poore Basilius die, whose poverty clipped the wings of his happinesse, and laid him

159

CHAPTER XXI

Of the prosecution of Camacho's marriage, with other delightfull accidents.

in his grave : and saying this, he layd hold of his Truncheon that he had stuck in the ground, and the one halfe of it remaining still there, shewed that it served for a scabberd to a short Tucke that was concealed in it, and putting that which might be called the hilt on the ground, with a nimble spring, and a resolute purpose, hee cast himselfe upon it, and in an instant the bloudy poynt appeared out of his backe, with halfe the steele blade, the poore soule weltring in his bloud, all along on the ground, runne thorow with his owne weapon. His friends ranne presently to helpe him, greeved with his misery and miserable happe, and Don Quixote forsaking his Rozinante, went also to helpe him ; tooke him in his armes, but found that as yet there was life in him. They would have pulled out the Tucke, but the Vicar there present, was of opinion that it were not best before hee had confessed himselfe ; for that the drawing it out, and his death, would be both at one instant. But Basilius comming a little to himselfe, with a faint and dolefull voyce, said, If thou wouldest, O Quiteria, yet in this last and forcible trance, give me thy hand to be my spouse, I should thinke my rashnesse might something excuse me, since with this I obtained to be thine.

The Vicar hearing this, bad him he should have a care of his soules health, rather then of the pleasures of his body, and that he should heartily aske God forgivenesse for his sinnes, and for his desperate action. To which Basilius reply'd, That he would by no meanes confesse himselfe, if Quiteria did not first give him her hand to be his spouse, for that content would make him cheerefully confesse himselfe. When Don Quixote heard the wounded mans petition, he cried aloud, that Basilius desired a thing very just and reasonable, and that Signior Camacho would be as much honoured in receiving Quiteria, the worthy Basilius his widdow, as if hee had received her from her Fathers side : heere is no more to doe but give one I, no more then to pronounce it, since the nuptial bed of this mariage must be the grave.

Camacho gave eare to all this, and was much troubled,

160

not knowing what to **doe or** say: but Basilius his friends were **so** earnest, requesting him to consent that Quiteria might give him her hand to bee his Spouse, that hee might not endanger his soule, by departing desperately, that they mooved him and enforced him, to say that if Quiteria would, he was contented, seeing it was but deferring his desires a minute longer. Then all of them came to Quiteria, some with intreaties, others with teares, most with forcible reasons, and perswaded her she should give her hand to poore Basilius; and shee more hard then marble, more lumpish then a statue, would not answer a **word,** neyther would she at all, had not the Vicar bid her **resolve** what she would doe, for Basilius was even now ready to depart, and could not expect her irresolute determination. Then the faire Quiteria, without answering a word, all sad and troubled, came where Basilius was, with his eyes even sette, his breath failing him, making shew as if he would die like a Gentile, and not like a Christian. Quiteria came at length, and upon her knees made signes to have his hand. Basilius unjoyn'd his eyes, and looking stedfastly upon her, said, Oh Quiteria, thou art now come to be pittifull, when thy pitty must be the sword that shall end my life, since now I want force to receive the glory that thou givest in chusing mee for thine, **or** to suspend the dolor that so hastily closeth up mine eyes, with the fearefull shade of death. All I desire thee is (oh fatall starre of mine) that the hand thou requirest, and that that thou wilt give me, that it be not for fashion-sake, nor once more to deceive mee, but that thou confesse and say without being forced to it, that thou givest me thy hand freely, as to thy lawfull Spouse, since it were unmerciful in this trance to deceive mee, or to deale falsely with him that **hath** beene so true to thee. In the middest of this discourse **he** fainted, so that all the standers by thought now he **had** beene gone. Quiteria all honest and shamefast, laying hold with her right hand on Basilius **his,** said to him; No force can worke upon my will, and **so I** give thee the freest hand I have to be thy lawfull

CHAPTER XXI

Of the prosecution of Camacho's marriage, with other delightfull accidents.

3 : X   161

CHAPTER
XXI

Of the pro-
secution of
Camacho's
marriage,
with other
delightfull
accidents.

Spouse, and receive thine, if thou give it me as freely, and
that the anguish of thy sodaine accident doe not too much
trouble thee. I give it (said Basilius) lively and couragiously,
with the best understanding that heaven hath endued mee
withall, and therefore take me, and I deliver my selfe as thy
espousall; and I (said Quiteria) as thy Spouse, whether thou
live long, or whether from my armes they carry thee to thy
grave.

This young man (said Sancho) being so wounded, talks
much me thinks, let him leave his wooing, and attend his
souls health, which me thinks appeares more in his tongue,
then in his teeth.

Basilius and Quiteria having their hands thus fastned, the
Vicar, tender-harted and compassionate, powred his blessing
upon them, and prayed God to give good rest to the new-
married mans soule, who as soone as he received this benediction, sodainely starts up, and with an unlook't for agility,
drew out the Tucke which was sheathed in his body. All
the spectators were in a maze, and some of them, more out
of simplicity then curiosity, began to cry out, A Miracle, a
Miracle: but Basilius reply'd, No Miracle, no Miracle; but
a Tricke, a Tricke. But the Vicar, heed-lesse and astonisht,
came with both his hands to feele the wound, and found that
the blade had neyther passed thorow flesh or ribbes, but
thorow a hollow pipe of yron, that he filled with bloud
well fitted in that place, and (as after it was knowne) pre-
pared so, that it could not congeale. At last the Vicar and
Camacho, and all the standers by, thought that they were
mocked and made a laughing-stocke. The Bride made no
great shew of sorrow: rather when she heard say that the
marriage could not stand currant, because it was deceitfull,
she said, that shee anew confirmed it; by which they all
collected, that the business had beene plotted by the knowledge and consentment of them both. At which, Camacho
and his friends were so abashed, that they remitted their
revenge to their hands, and unsheathing many swords, they
set upon Basilius, in whose favor in an instant there were as
many more drawne: and Don Quixote taking the Vantguard

162

HISTORIE OF DON QUIXOTE

on horsebacke, with his Launce at his rest, and well covered with **his** shield, made way thorow um all. Sancho (whom such feates did never please or solace) ranne to the pottage-pot, from whence he had gotten the skimmings, thinking that to be a sanctuary, and so to be respected. Don Quixote cryed aloud, Hold, hold, Sirs; for there is no reason that you should take revenge for the wrongs that Love doth us: and observe, that love and warre are all one: and as in warre it is lawfull to use sleights and stratagems to overcome the enemy: So in amorous strifes and competencies, Impostures and juggling tricks are held for good, to attaine to the wished end, so it bee not in prejudice and dishonour of the thing affected. Quiteria was due to Basilius, and Basilius to Quiteria, by the just and favourable inclination of heaven. Camacho is rich, and may purchase his delight, and whom God hath joyned, let **no** man separate. Basilius hath but this one sheepe, let none offer to take it from him, be he never so power-full: he that first attempts it, must first passe thorow the point of this Launce; at which hee shaked his Launce so strong and cunningly, that hee frighted all that knew him not: But Quiteria's disdaine was so inwardly fixt in Camacho's heart, that he forgot her in an instant; so that the Vicars perswasions prevailed with him, (who was a good discreet and honest-minded man) by which Camacho and his complices were pacified and quieted, in signe of which, **they** put up their swords, rather blaming Quiteria's facility, **then** Basilius his industry. Camacho fram'd this discourse **to** himselfe, That if Quiteria loved Basilius when she was a maide, shee would also have continued her love to him though she **had** beene his wife, and so that hee ought to give God thankes rather for having ridden him of her, then to have given her to him. Camacho then, and those of his crue being comforted and pacified, all Basilius his likewise were so, and Camacho to shew that he stomacked not the jest, nor car'd for it, was willing the feast should goe forward, as if he had beene really married. But neyther Basilius, **nor** his Spouse, **nor** their followers would

CHAPTER
XXI

Of the pro-secution of Camacho's marriage, with other delightfull accidents.

163

CHAPTER
XXI

Of the pro-
secution of
Camacho's
marriage,
with other
delightfull
accidents.

stay, but went to Basilius his towne: for your poore that
are vertuous and discreet, have as well those that will
follow, honour, and uphold them, as the rich theirs, and
such as will flatter them. Don Quixote went with them too,
for they esteemed him to be a man of worth and valor. But
Sancho's mind was in a mist, to see that it was impossible
for him to stay for Camacho's sumptuous feast and sports
that lasted till the evening: so that straighted and sorrowfull, he followed on with his Master that went in Basilius his
squadron, and thus left behind him those flesh-pots of Ægypt,
though hee bore them with him in his minde, whose skumme
which he carried in the kettle being consumed now and ended,
represented unto him the glorious and abundant happinesse hee lost, so that all sad and sorrowfull, though
hungerlesse, without alighting from Dapple,
he followed Rozinante's tracke.

CHAPTER XXII

Of the famous Adventure of Montesinos Cave, which is in the heart of Mancha, which the valerous Don Quixote happily accomplished.

HE married couple made wonderfull much
of Don Quixote, obliged thereunto for
the willingnesse he shewed to defend
their cause, and with his valor they
paraleld his discretion, accounting him a
Cid in Armes, and a Cicero in eloquence.
The good Sancho recreated himselfe three
daies at the Bridegroomes charge, and
now knew that Quiteria knew nothing of the fayned wound-
ing, but that it was a tricke of Basilius, who hoped for the
successe that hath been shewed: true it was, that he had

HISTORIE OF DON QUIXOTE

made some **of his** loving **frends** acquainted with **his** purpose, that they might helpe him at need, and make good his deceit. They cannot be called deceits (quoth Don Quixote) that are done to a vertuous end, and that **the** marriage of a loving couple was an end most excellent : **but** by the way, you must know that the greatest opposite that Love hath, is want and continuall necessity ; for Love **is** all mirth, content and gladsomenes, and the more, when hee that loves, enjoyes the thing loved ; against which, necessity and poverty are open and declared enemies. All this he spoke with a purpose to advise Basilius, that he should leave exercising his youthfull abilities, that although they got him a name, yet they brought no wealth, and that he should looke to lay up somthing now by lawfull and industrious means, which are never wanting to those that will be wary and apply themselves : the honest poore man (if so be the poore man may be called honest) hath a jewell of a faire woman, which if any man bereave him of, dis-honors him and kills her. Shee that is faire and honest, when her husband is poore, deserves to be crowned with Lawrell and triumphant Bayes. Beauty alone attracts the eyes of all that behold it, and the princely Eagles and high flying birds doe stoop to it as to the pleasing Lure but if extreme necessity be added to that beauty, then Kites and Crowes will grapple with it, and other ravenous birds ; but shee that is constant against all these assaults, doth **well** deserve to bee **her** husbands crowne. Marke, wise **Basilius** (proceeds Don Quixote) it **was an** opinion of I know not what sage man, that there **was but** one good woman in the world, and his advice **was, That** every man should thinke that was married, that **his wife was** she, and so he should **be** sure to live contented. I never yet was married, neyther have I any thought hitherto that way ; notwithstanding, I could be able to give any man counsell heerein that should aske it, and how **he** should choose his wife.

First of all I would have him rather respect fame **then** wealth, for the honest woman gets not a good name onely with being good, but in appearing **so** ; for your publike

CHAPTER XXII

Of the famous Adventure of Montesinos Cave, which is in the heart of Mancha, which the valerous Don Quixote happily accomplished.

165

THE SECOND PART OF THE

CHAPTER
XXII
Of the famous
Adventure of
Montesinos
Cave, which
is in the heart
of Mancha,
which the
valerous
Don Quixote
happily
accomplished.

loosenesse and liberty doth more prejudice a womans honesty, then her sinning secretly. If you bring her honest to your house, tis easie keeping her so, and to better her in that goodnesse; but if you bring her dis-honest, tis hard mending her; for it is not very pliable to passe from one extreme into another, I say not impossible : but I hold it to be very difficult.

Sancho heard all this, and said to himselfe, This Master of mine, when I speake matters of marrow and substance, is wont to tell me, that I may take a Pulpit in hand, and preach my fine knacks up and downe the world : but I may say of him, that when hee once begins to thred his sentences, he may not onely take a Pulpit in hand, but in each finger too, and goe up and downe the market places, and cry, Who buyes my ware? The Devill take thee, for a Knight Errant, how wise he is! On my soule I thoght hee had knowne onely what belonged to his Knight Errantry; but he snaps at all, and there is no boat that hee hath not an oare in. Sancho spoke this somewhat aloud, and his Master over-heard him, and asked, What is that thou art grumbling, Sancho? I say nothing, neyther doe I grumble, (quoth hee) I was onely saying to my selfe, that I would I had heard you before I was married, and perhaps I might now have said, The sound man needs no Physician. Is Teresa so bad, Sancho? said Don Quixote. Not very bad, said Sancho, and yet not very good, at least, not so good as I would have her. Thou dost ill, Sancho (quoth Don Quixote) to speake ill of thy wife, who is indeede mother of thy children.

There's no love lost (quoth Sancho :) for she speakes ill of me too, when shee list, especially when shee is jealous, for then the Devill himselfe will not cope with her. Well, three dayes they stayed with the married Couple, where they were welcommed like Princes. Don Quixote desired the skilfull Parson to provide him a Guide that might shew him the way to Montesino's Cave, for he had a great desire to enter into it, and to see with his own eies, if those wonders that were told of it up and down the Countrey were true. The Parson tolde him, that a Cousin-German of his, a

HISTORIE OF DON QUIXOTE

famous Student, and much addicted to bookes of Knight-
hood should goe with him, who should willingly carry him
to the mouth of the Cave, and should shew the famous Lake
of Ruydera, telling him hee would bee very good company
for him, by reason he was one that knew how to publish
books, and direct them to great men.

Of the famous
Adventure of
Montesinos
Cave, which
is in the heart
of Mancha,
which the
valerous
Don Quixote
happily
accomplished.

By and by the young Student comes me upon an Asse
with Foale, with a course packing-cloth, or doubled carpet
upon his pack-saddle. Sancho saddled Rozinante, and made
ready his Dapple, furnished his wallets, and carried the
Students too, aswell provided; and so taking leave, and
bidding all, God bee with you, they went on, holding their
course to Montesino's Cave. By the way Don Quixote
asked the Scholler, of what kinde or quality the exercises of
his profession and study were. To which he answered, that
his Profession was Humanity, his Exercises and Study to
make bookes for the Presse, which were very beneficiall to
himselfe, and no lesse gratefull to the Commonwealth, that
one of his bookes was intituled, *The Booke of the Liveries*,
where are set downe seven hundred and three sorts of
Liveries, with their colours, motto's, and cyphers; from
whence any may bee taken at festivall times and shewes, by
Courtiers without begging them from any body, or distilling
(as you would say) from their owne braines, to sute them to
their desires and intentions; for I give to the jealous, to
the forsaken, to the forgotten, to the absent, the most agree-
able, that will fit them as well as their Puncks. Another
booke I have, which I meane to call the *Metamorphosis, or
Spanish Ovid*, of a new and rare invention: for imitating
Ovid in it, by way of mocking: I shew who the Giralda of
Sevil was, the Angell of the Magdalena, who was the Pipe
of Vecinguerra of Cordova, who the Buls of Guisando, Sierra
Morena, the springs of Leganitos and Lavapies in Madrid;
not forgetting that of Pioio, that of the gilded pipe, and of
the Abbesse, and all this with the Allegories, Metaphors,
and Translations, that they delight, suspend, and instruct
all in a moment. Another booke I have, which I call *A
supply to Polydore Virgil*, concerning the invention of things

167

CHAPTER
XXII

Of the famous
Adventure of
Montesinos
Cave, which
is in the heart
of Mancha,
which the
valerous
Don Quixote
happily
accomplished.

which is of great reading and study, by reason that I doe verifie many matters of waight that Polydore omitted, and declare them in a very pleasing stile; Virgil forgot to tell us who was the first that had a Catarre in the world, and the first that was anoynted for the French disease, and I set it downe presently after I propose it, and authorize it with at least foure and twenty Writers, that you may see whether I have taken good paines, and whether the sayd booke may not be profitable to the world.

Sancho, that was very attentive to the Schollers narration, asked him: Tell me, Sir, so God direct your right hand in the Impression of your bookes: Can you tell mee? (For I know you can, since you know all) who was the first man that scratcht his head, for I beleeve it was our first father Adam? Yes marry was it (sayd he) for Adam, no doubt, had both head and haire, and being the first man in the world, would sometimes scratch himselfe. I beleeve it (quoth Sancho:) but tell me now, Who was the first Vaulter in the world? Truely, Brother (sayd he) I cannot at present resolve you, I will study it when I come to my bookes, and then Ile satisfie you, when wee see one another againe, for I hope this will not be the last time. Well, Sir (sayd Sancho) never trouble your selfe with this, for now I can resolve the doubt: Know, that the first Tumbler in the world was Lucifer, when he was cast out of Heaven, and came tumbling down to Hell.

You say true (quoth the Scholler). And Don Quixote sayd; This answer, Sancho, is none of thine, thou hast heard some body say so. Peace, Sir (quoth Sancho) for if I fall to questions and answers, I shall not make an end between this and morning: And to aske foolish questions, and answer unlikeli-hoods, I want no help of my neighbours. Thou hast spoken more, Sancho, then thou thinkest for (quoth Don Quixote) for you have some that are most busied in knowing and averring things, whose knowledge and remembrance is not worth a button. All that day they passed in these and other delightful discourses, and at night they lodged in a little village, from whence the Scholler told

168

them they had but two little leagues to Montesino's Cave, and that if he meant to enter it, he must be provided of ropes, to tie and let himselfe downe into the depth. Don Quixote sayd, that though it were as deep as Hell, he would see whither it reached: so they bought a hundred fathome of cordage, and the next day at two of the clocke, they came to the Cave, whose mouth is wide and spacious ; but full of briers, and brambles, and wilde fig-trees, and weeds so intricate and thick, that they altogether blinde and dam it up. When they came to it, Sancho and the Scholler alighted, and Don Quixote, whom they tied strongly with the cordage : and whilest they were swathing and binding of him, Sancho sayd to him ; Take heede, Sir, what you doe, doe not bury your selfe alive, and doe not hang your selfe like a bottle to be cooled in some Well ; for it neither concernes nor belongs to you, to search this place worse then a Dungeon.

Binde me and peace (quoth Don Quixote) for such an enterprize as this, Sancho, was reserved for me. Then said the Guide, I beseech you, Signior Don Quixote, that you take heede, and looke about you with an hundred eyes, to see what is within ; for perhaps you may meet with things that will be fit for mee to put in my booke of Transformations. He hath his Instrument in his hand (quoth Sancho) that knowes how to use it.

This sayd, and Don Quixotes binding ended (which was not upon his harnesse, but upon his arming doublet) he said. We did unadvisedly, in not providing our selves of some small bell, that might have beene tied with mee to the same cord, by whose sound, you might know that I were still toward the bottome and alive : but since there is now no remedy, God bee our good speede, and straight he kneeled upon his knees, and made a soft prayer to God Almighty, desiring his ayde, and to give him good successe in that (to see to) dangerous and strange Adventure, and then straightwayes hee cried aloud ; Oh thou Mistris of my actions and motions, most excellent, peerelesse Dulcinea del Toboso, if it be possible, that the prayers and requests of this thy happy Lover come to thine eares, harken, I beseech thee, by thy

CHAPTER
XXII

Of the famous Adventure of Montesinos Cave, which is in the heart of Mancha, which the valerous Don Quixote happily accomplished.

CHAPTER
XXII
Of the famous
Adventure of
Montesinos
Cave, which
is in the heart
of Mancha,
which the
valerous
Don Quixote
happily
accomplished.

unheard of beauty, deny not now unto me thy favour and protection, which I so much neede : I goe to cast my selfe headlong to a plunge, and sinke my selfe into the Abissus, that presents it selfe to me, that the world may know, that if thou favour me, there shall be nothing impossible for mee to undergoe and end.

And in saying this, hee came to the mouth, but saw he could not come neere to bee let downe, except it were by making way with maine force, or with cutting thorow, and so laying hand on his sword, hee began to cut and slash the weedes that were at the mouth of the cave ; at whose rushing and noyse, there came out an infinite Company of Crowes and Dawes, so thicke and so hastily, that they tumbled Don Quixote on the ground, and if hee had beene as superstitious, as good Christian, hee would have taken it for an ill signe, and not have proceeded.

Well, he rose, and seeing the Crowes were all gone, and that there were no other night-birds, as Bats, that came out amongst the Crowes, Sancho and the Scholler let him downe, to search the bottome of that fearefull Cave ; but Sancho first bestowed his benediction on him, and making a thousand crosses over him, sayd ; God and the Rocke of France, together with the Trinity of Gaeta, guide thee, thou Flower, Creame, and Scumme of Knights Errant : There thou goest, Hackster of the world, Heart of steele, and Armes of brasse, God againe be thy Guide, and deliver thee sound and without skarre, to the light of this world which thou leavest, to bury thy selfe in the obscurity which thou seekest.

The Scholler did (as it were) make the same kinde of wishes and deprecations. Don Quixote cried out, that they should yet give him more rope, which they gave by little and little : and when his voyce (that was stopt in the gutters of the Cave) could be no longer heard, and that they had let downe their hundred fathome of rope, they were of opinion to hoyst him up againe, since they could give him no more cord ; for all that, they stayed some halfe an houre, and then began easily to draw up the rope, and without any wait, which made them think Don Quixote was within, and Sancho

HISTORIE OF DON QUIXOTE

beleeving it, wept bitterly, and drew up apace, that he might
bee satisfied: but comming somewhat **neere** foure-score
fathome, they felt a waight, which made **them** very much
rejoyce.

At length when they came to ten, they plainely saw Don
Quixote: to whom Sancho cryed out, saying; You are well
returned, Sir, for we thought you had stayed there for breed.
But Don Quixote did not answer a word: but drawing him
altogether out, they saw that his eyes were shut, as if hee
were asleepe; they stretcht him on the ground, and unbound
him, and for all this he awaked not. But they so turned,
tossed and shaked him, that a pretty while after he came to
himselfe, lazing himselfe, as if he had wakened out of a great
and profound sleep, and looking wildely round-about him,
sayd; **God** forgive you, Friends, for you have raised mee
from **one of** the delicatest and pleasingest lives and sights
that **ever** was seene by humane eye: Now at length I perceive, that all the delights of this world doe passe like a
shadow or dreame, or wither like a flower of the field: Oh
unhappy Montesino's, oh ill wounded Durandarte, oh luck-
les Balerma, oh mournfull Guadiana, and you unfortunate
daughters of Ruydera, that shew by your waters, those your
faire eyes wept.

The Scholler and Sancho gave eare to these words which
Don Quixote spake, as if with great paine they came from
his very entrailes: They desired him to let them know his
meaning, and to tell them what he had seene in that hellish
place. Hellish, call ye it? sayd Don Quixote, well, call it not
so, **for** it deserves not the name, as straight you shall heare:
Hee desired them to give him somewhat to eat, for he was exceeding hungry. They layd the Schollers course wrapper upon
the greene grasse, and went to the Spence of their wallets, and
all three of them being set like good fellowes, eat their
Beavar, and supped all together. The cloth taken **up**
(Don Quixote sayd) Sit still Ho, let none of you
rise, and marke me attentively.

Of the famous
Adventure of
Montesinos
Cave, which
is in the heart
of Mancha,
which the
valerous
Don Quixote
happily
accomplished.

171

THE SECOND PART OF THE

CHAPTER XXIII

Of the admirable things, that the unparalel'd Don
Quixote recounted, which he had seene in Montesino's profound Cave, whose strangenesse
and impossibility makes this Chapter
be held for Apocrypha.

IT was well toward foure of the clocke, when
the Sunne, covered betweene two clouds,
shewed but a dimme light, and with his
temperate beames, gave Don Quixote
leave, without heat or trouble, to relate
to his two conspicuous Auditors, what he
had seene in Montesino's Cave; and he
began, as followeth: About a twelve or
fourteene mens heights in the profundity of this Dungeon,
on the right hand, there is a Concavity and Space able to
containe a Cart, Mules and all; some light there comes into
it by certaine chinks and loope-holes, which answer to it a
farre off in the Superficies of the earth; this Space and Concavity saw I, when I was weary and angry to see mee my
selfe, hanging by the rope, to goe downe that obscure region,
without being carried a sure or knowne way: so I determined
to enter into it, and to rest a little; I cryed out unto you,
that you should let downe no more rope, till I bad you; but
it seemed you heard me not: I went gathering up the rope
you let downe to me, and rolling of it up into a heape, sate
me downe upon it, very pensative, thinking with my selfe
what I might doe to get to the bottome; and being in
this thought and confusion, upon a sudden (without any
former inclination in mee) a most profound sleep came upon
me, and when I least thought of it, without knowing how,
nor which way, I awaked out of it, and found my selfe in the
172

HISTORIE OF DON QUIXOTE

CHAPTER
XXIII

Of the admirable things,
that the
unparalel'd
Don Quixote
recounted,
which he
had seene in
Montesino's
profound
Cave, etc.

middest of the fairest, most pleasant, and delightfull medow, that ever Nature created, or the wisest humane discretion can imagine; I snuffed mine eyes, wiped them, and saw that I was not asleepe, but really awake, notwithstanding I felt upon my head and my brest, to be assured, if I were there my selfe or no in person, or that it were some illusion, or counterfet; but my touching, feeling, and my reasonable discourse that I made to my selfe, certified me, that I was then present, the same that I am now.

By and by I saw a Princely and sumptuous Palace or Castle, whose wals and battlements seemed to bee made of transparent Cristall, from whence (upon the opening of two great gates) I saw that there came towards me a reverend olde man, clad in a tawny bayes frocke, that he dragged upon the ground; over his shoulders and brest, he wore a tippet of greene sattin, like your fellowes of Colledges, and upon his cap a blacke Milan bonet, and his hoary beard reached down to his girdle, he had no kind of weapon in his hand, but onely a Rosary of Beads, somewhat bigger then reasonable wal-nuts, and the Credo-Beads, about the bignesse of Ostrich egges, his countenance, pace, gravity, and his spreading presence, each thing by it selfe, and all together, suspended and admired.

He came to me, and the first thing he did, was to imbrace me straightly, and forthwith sayd; It is long since (renowned Knight, Don Quixote de la Mancha) that we, who live in these enchanted Desarts, have hoped to see thee, that thou mightst let the world know what is contained heere, and inclosed in this profound Cave, which thou hast entred, called Montesino's Cave: an exployt reserved onely to be attempted by thy invincible Heart, and stupendious Courage. Come with mee, thou most Illustrious Knight, for I will shew thee the wonders that this transparent Castle doth conceale, of which I am the Governour, and perpetuall chiefe Warder, as being the same Montesinos, from whom the Cave takes name.

Scarce had he told me that he was Montesinos, when I asked him, Whether it were true that was bruited heere in

173

CHAPTER
XXIII
Of the admirable things,
that the
unparalel'd
Don Quixote
recounted,
which he
had seene in
Montesino's
profound
Cave, etc.

the world above, that he had taken his great friend Durandartes heart out of the midst of his bosome with a little dagger, and carried it to the Lady Belerma (as he willed) at the instant of his death? Hee answered me, that all was true, but onely that of the dagger, for it was no dagger, but a little Stilleto, as sharpe as a Nawle.

Belike (quoth Sancho) it was of Ramon de Hozes the Sevillians making. I know not (sayd Don Quixote) but twas not of that Stilletto-maker, for he lived but the other day, and that battell of Roncesvalles, where this accident happened, was many yeeres since: but this averring is of no importance or let, neither alters the truth, or Stories text.

You say right (quoth the Scholler) for I harken with the greatest delight in the world. With no lesse doe I tell it you (sayd Don Quixote) and proceede; The venerable Montesinos brought me into the Cristalline Palace, where in a low Hall, exceeding fresh and coole, all of Alabaster, was a great Sepulcher of Marble, made with singular Art, upon which I saw a Knight layd at length, not of Brasse, Marble, or Iasper, as you use to have in other tombes, but of pure flesh and bone, hee held his right hand (which was somewhat hairy and sinowy, a signe that the owner was very strong) upon his heart-side, and before I asked Montesinos ought, that saw mee in suspence, beholding the tombe, he sayd:

This is my friend Durandarte, the flower and mirror of Chivalrie, of the enamoured and valiant Knights of his time: He is kept heere enchanted, as my selfe and many more Knights and Ladies are, by Merlin that French Enchanter; who, they say, was sonne to the Devill, but as I beleeve he was not so, only he knew more then the Devill. Why, or how he enchanted us, no body knowes, which the times will bring to light, that I hope are not farre off: all that I admire is, (since I know for certaine, as it is now day, that Durandarte dyed in my armes, and that after he was dead, I tooke out his heart, and surely it weighed above two pounds; for according to naturall Philosophy, he that hath the biggest heart, is more valiant then he that hath but

For so I translate it, to shew
the Authours
mistake.

174

a lesse: **which** beeing so, and that this Knight died really)
how he complaines and sighes sometimes as if **he** were alive?
Which said, the wretched Durandarte, crying out aloud,
said; Oh my Cousin Montesinos, the last thing that I
requested you when I was dying, and my soule departing,
was, That you would carry my heart to Belerma, taking it
out of my bosome, either with ponyard or dagger: which
when the venerable Montesinos heard, he kneeled before the
greeved Knight, and with teares in his eyes, said; Long
since, Oh Durandarte, long since my dearest Cousin, I did
what you en-joyn'd me in that bitter day of our losse; I
tooke your heart, as well as I could, without leaving the
least part of it in your brest: I wiped it with a laced handkerchiefe, and posted with it towards France, having first
layd you in the bosome of the earth, with so many teares as
was sufficient to wash my hands, or to wipe off the bloud from
them, which I had gotten by stirring them in your entrailes:
and for more assurance that I did it, my dearest Cousin, at
the first place I came to from Roncesvalle, I cast salt upon
your heart, that it might not stinke, and might be fresh,
and embalmed when it should come to the presence of the
Lady Belerma, who with you and me, Guadiana your Squire,
the waiting-woman Ruydera, and her seven Daughters, and
her two Neeces, and many other of your acquaintances and
friends, have beene enchanted heere by Merlin that Wizard
long since, and though it be above five hundred yeeres agoe,
yet none of **us** is dead; onely Ruydera, her Daughters and
Neeces **are** wanting, whom by reason of their lamentation,
Merlin **that** had compassion on them, turned them into so
many **Lakes now** living in the world: and in the Province of
Mancha **they are** called the Lakes of Ruydera; seven belong
to the Kings of Spaine, and the two Neeces to the Knights of
the most holy Order of Saint Iohn. Guadiana your Squire,
wailing in like **manner** this mis-hap, **was** turned into a River
that bore his owne name, who when **hee** came to the superficies of the earth, and saw the Sun in another heaven, such
was his griefe **to have** left you, that **he** straight plunged
himselfe into **the** entrailes of the earth: but, as it is not

**CHAPTER
XXIII**

Of the admir-
able things,
that the
unparalel'd
Don Quixote
recounted,
which he
had seene in
Montesino's
profound
Cave, etc.

175

CHAPTER XXIII

Of the admirable things, that the unparalel'd Don Quixote recounted, which he had seene in Montesino's profound Cave, etc.

possible for him to leave his naturall Current, sometimes he appeares and shewes himselfe, where the Sunne and men may see him. The aforesaid Lakes do minister their waters to him, with which, and many others, hee enters Portugall in pompe: but which way so-ere he goes, hee shewes his sorrow and melancholy, and contemnes the breeding of dainty fish in his waters, and such as are esteemed, but only muddie and unsavorie, farre differing from those of golden Tagus; and what I now tell you, Cousin mine, I have told you often, and since you answere mee nothing, I imagine you eyther beleeve me not, or not heare me; for which (God knowes) I am heartily sorry. One newes I will let you know, which, though perhaps it may not any way lighten your griefe, yet it will no way increase it: Know, that you have heere in your presence, (open your eyes and you shall see him) that famous Knight, of whom Merlin prophesied such great matters, that Don Quixote de la Mancha, I say, that now newly and more happily then former Ages, hath raised the long-forgotten Knight Errantry, by whose meanes and favour, it may be, that we also may be dis-inchanted; for great exploits are reserved for great Personages. And if it be otherwise (answered the grieved Durandarte) with a faint and low voyce, if it be otherwise, O Cousin, I say, *Patience and shuffle: and turning on one side, hee returned to his accustomed silence, without speaking one word.

By this wee heard great howling and moane, accompanied with deepe sighes, and short-breath'd accents: I turned mee about, and saw that in another roome there came passing by the Christall waters, a procession of a company of most beautifull Damozels, in two rankes, all clad in mourning, with Turbants upon their heads, after the Turkish fashion; at last, and in the end of the rankes, there came a Lady, who by her majesty appear'd so, clothed in like manner in blacke, with a white dressing on her head, so large, that it kissed the very ground. Her Turbant was twice as bigge as the biggest of the rest, shee was somewhat bettle-brow'd, flatte-nosed, wide-mouth'd, but redde lipped: her teeth, for sometimes she discovered them, seemed to be thin, and not

*Paciencia y barajar. A Metaphor taken from Cardplayers, who when they lose, cry to the dealer, Patience, and shuffle the Cards.

176

HISTORIE OF DON QUIXOTE

very-well placed, though they were as white as blancht
Almonds; in her hand shee carried a fine cloth, and within
it (as might be perceived) a Mommied heart, by reason of
the dry embalming of it: Montesinos told me, that all
those in that procession, were servants to Durandarte and
Belerma, that were there enchanted with their Masters, and
that shee that came last with the linnen cloth and the
heart in her hand, was the Lady Belerma, who, together
with hir Damozels, four daies in the weeke did make that
procession, singing or to say truer, howling their Dirges
over the body and greeved heart of his Cousin, and that
if now she appeared somewhat foule to mee, or not so faire
as Fame hath given out, the cause was; her bad nights, but
worse daies that she indured in that enchantment, as I
might see by her deepe-sunke eyes, and her broken complexion, and her monthly disease, is not the cause of these,
(an ordinary thing in women) for it is many moneths since,
and many yeeres, that she hath not had it, nor knowne what
it is; but the griefe that shee hath in her owne heart, for that
she carries in her hand continually, which renewes and brings
to her remembrance, the unfortunatenesse of her lucklesse
Lover; for if it were not for this, scarce would the famous
Dulcinea del Toboso equall her in beauty, wit, or livelinesse,
that is so famous in the Mancha, and all the world over.
Not too fast (then said I) Signior Don Montesinos, on with
your story as befits; for you know, all comparisons are odious,
and so leave your comparing, the peerelesse Dulcinea del
Toboso is what she is, and the Lady Belerma is what she
is and hath beene; and let this suffice.

To which he answered, Pardon me Signior Don Quixote,
for I confesse I did ill, and not wel to say, the Lady Dulcinea
would scarce equall the Lady Belerma, since it had beene
sufficient, that I understood (I know not by what aime)
that you are her Knight, enough to have made me bite
my tongue, before I had compared her with any thing but
heaven it selfe. With this satisfaction that Montesinos gave
me, my heart was free from that sodaine passion I had, to
heare my Mistresse compared to Belerma.

Of the admir-
able things,
that the
unparalel'd
Don Quixote
recounted,
which he
had seene in
Montesino's
profound
Cave, etc.

3 : Z   177

CHAPTER
XXIII
Of the admir-
able things,
that the
unparalel'd
Don Quixote
recounted,
which he
had seene in
Montesino's
profound
Cave, etc.

And I marvell (said Sancho) that you got not to the olde Carle and bang'd his bones, and pulled his beard, without leaving him a haire in it.

No, friend Sancho, said he, it was not fit for me to doe so; for wee are all bound to reverence our Elders, although they be no Knights, and most of all when they are so, and are enchanted. I know well enough, I was not behinde-hand with him in other questions and answeres that passed betweene us. Then said the Scholler, I know not, Signior Don Quixote, how you in so little time (as it is since you went downe) have seene so many things, and spoken and answered so much. How long is it (quoth he) since I went downe? A little more then an houre (said Sancho.) That cannot be (replyed Don Quixote) because it was morning and evening, and evening and morning three times; so that by my account, I have beene three daies in those parts so remote and hidden from our sight. Surely, my Master (quoth Sancho) is in the right; for as all things that befall him are by way of enchantment; so perhaps, that which ap-peares to us but an houre, is to him there, three nights and three dayes. He hath hit it (said Don Quixote.) And have you eat, Sir, in all this time (quoth the Scholler)? Not a bit (quoth Don Quixote) neyther have I beene hungry, or so much as thought of eating. And the enchanted, eat they? said the Scholler. No, said he, neyther are they troubled with your greater excrements, although it be probable that their nailes, their beards, and their haires grow. Sleep they haply? said Sancho. No indeed, said Don Quixote, at least these three daies that I have beene with them, not one of them hath closed his eyes, nor I neyther. That fits the Proverb, quoth Sancho, which sayes, You shall know the person by his company: you have beene amongst the enchanted, and those that watch and fast: no marvell therefore though you neyther slept nor eat whilest you were amongst them; but pray, Sir, pardon me, if I say, God (or the Devill I was about to say) take me, if I beleeve a word of all this you have spoken. Why not? said the Scholler, doe you thinke Signior Don Quixote would lye to us, for

HISTORIE OF DON QUIXOTE

though he would, hee hath **not** had time to compose or invent such **a** million **of** lies? I doe not beleeve (quoth Sancho) **that** my Master lies. But what doe you beleeve then (quoth Don Quixote)? Mary I beleeve (said Sancho) **that** that Merlin, or those Enchanters that enchanted all that rabble, that you say you have seene and conversed with there below, clapt into your apprehension or memory all this Machine that you have told us, and all that remaines yet to be told. All this may be, Sancho, said Don Quixote, but 'tis otherwise; for what I have told, I saw with these eyes, and felt with these hands: but what wilt thou say when I shall tell thee, that, amongst infinite other matters and wonders, that Montesinos shewed me, which at more leisure, and at fitting time in processe of our journey I shall tell thee: He shewed me three Country wenches, that went leaping and frisking up and downe those pleasant fields like Goats, and I scarce saw them, when I perceived the one was the peerlesse Dulcinea, and the other two the selfe-same that wee spoke to when wee left Toboso. I asked Montesinos whether hee knew them: who answered me, Not: but that sure they were some Ladies of quality there enchanted, that but lately appeared in those fields, and that it was **no** wonder; for that there were many others of former times and these present, that were enchanted in strange and different shapes, amongst whom hee knew Queene Guiniver, and her woman Quintaniona filling Lansarotes cups when he came from Britaine.

When Sancho heard his Master thus farre, it made him starke madde, and ready to burst with laughter; for by reason that he knew the truth of Dulcinea's enchantment, as having been himselfe the Enchanter, and the raiser of that tale, hee did undoubtedly ratifie his beliefe, that his Master was madde and out of his wittes; and so told him: In an ill time, and dismall day (Patron mine) went you downe into the other world, and at an ill season met you with Signior Montesinos, that hath returned you in this pickle: you were well enough heere above, in your right sences as God hath given them you, uttering sentences, and giving good counsaile

179

every foote, and not as now telling the greatest unlikelihoods that can be imagined.

Because I know thee, Sancho (quoth Don Quixote) I make no account of thy words. Nor I of yours, said hee: you may strike or kill me if you will, eyther for those I have spoken, or those I meane to speake, if you doe not correct and amend your selfe. But pray tell me, Sir, whilest we are quiet, how knew you it was our Mistris? spoke you to her? what said shee, and what answered you? I knew her, said Don Quixote, by the same clothes she had on at such time as thou shewd'st her me: I spoke to her, but she gave me not a word, but turned her backe, and scudded away so fast, that a flight would not have overtaken her: I meant to have followed her, and had done it, but that Montesinos told mee it was in vaine, and the rather, because it was now high time for me to returne out of the Cave. He told me likewise, that in processe of time, he would let me know the meanes of dis-enchanting Durandarte, and Belerma and himselfe; together with all the rest that were there: But that which most greeved me, was; that whilest I was thus talking with Montesinos, one of the unfortunate Dulcinea's companions came on one side of me (I not perceiving it) and with teares in her eyes, and hollow voyce said to me; My Lady Dulcinea del Toboso commends her to you, and desires to know how you doe: and withall, because she is in great necessity, she desires you with all earnestnesse, that you would be pleased to lend her three shillings upon this new Cotton Petticote that I bring you, or what you can spare; for she will pay you againe very shortly. This message held me in suspence and admiration: so that turning to Signior Montesinos, I asked him, Is it possible, Signior, that those of your better sort that be enchanted are in want? To which he answered, Beleeve me, Signior Don Quixote, this necessity rangeth and extends it selfe every where, and overtakes all men, neither spares shee the Enchanted; and therefore since the Lady Dulcinea demaunds these three shillings of you, and that the pawne seemes to bee good, lend them her, for sure shee is much straightned. I will take no pawne (quoth I)

180

neither can I lend what shee requires, for I have but two shillings: these I gave, which were the same, Sancho, that thou gavest me tother day, to give for almes to the poore that we met: and I told the Mayd, Friend, tell your Mistris that I am sorry with al my heart for her wants, and I would I were a *Fucar to releeve them; and let her know, that I neither can, nor may have health, wanting her pleasing company, and discreet conversation, and that I desire her, as earnestly as may be, that this her Captive Servant and Way-beaten Knight may see and treat with her.

You shall also say, that when she least thinkes of it, shee shall heare say, that I have made an oath and vow, such as was the Marquis his of Mantua, to revenge his Nephue Baldwine, when he found him ready to give up the ghost in the midst of the mountaine; which was, not to eat his meat with napkins, and other Flim-flams added therunto, till he had revenged his death: And so swear I, not to be quiet, till I have travelled all the seven partitions of the world, more punctually then Prince Don Manuel of Portugall, till I have dis-enchanted her. All this and more you owe to my Mistresse, said the Damozell; and taking the two shillings, in stead of making me a courtesie, she fetcht a caper two yards high in the ayre.

Blessed God! (Sancho cryed out) and is it possible that Enchanters and Enchantments should so much prevaile upon him, as to turn his right understanding into such a wilde madnes? Sir, Sir, for Gods love have a care of your selfe, and looke to your credit: beleeve not in these bubbles that have lessened and crazed your wits. Out of thy love, Sancho, thou speakest this (said Don Quixote) and for want of experience in the world, all things that have never so little difficulty seeme to thee to be impossible: but time will come (as I have told thee already) that I shall relate some things that I have seene before, which may make thee beleeve what I have said, which admits no reply, or controversie.

CHAPTER XXIII

Of the admirable things, that the unparalel'd Don Quixote recounted, which he had seene in Montesino's profound Cave, etc.

*Fucares, were a rich family, and name in Germany that maintained a banke of monies in Spain, and still used to furnish Philip the 2. with monies in his warres.

THE SECOND PART OF THE

CHAPTER XXIV

Where are recounted a thousand flim-flams, as
impertinent, as necessary to the understanding of this famous History.

HE Translator of this famous History out
of his Originall, written by Cid Hamete
Benengeli, sayes; That when hee came to
the last chapter going before, these words
were written in the Margin by the same
Hamete. I cannot beleeve or be perswaded, that all that is written in the
antecedent Chapter hapned so punctually
to the valerous Don Quixote: the reason is, because all
Adventures hitherto have beene accidentall and probable;
but this of the Cave, I see no likelihood of the truth of it,
as being so un-reasonable: Yet to thinke Don Quixote
would lye, being the worthiest Gentleman, and noblest
Knight of his time, is not possible; for he would not lye,
though he were shot to death with arrowes. On the other
side I consider, that he related it, with all the aforesaid circumstances, and that in so short a time, hee could not frame
such a Machina of fopperies, and if this Adventure seeme to
be Apocrypha, the fault is not mine: so that leaving it in-
different, I here set it downe. Thou, Oh Reader, as thou
art wise, judge as thou thinkest good; for I can doe no more,
though one thing be certaine, that when hee was upon his
death-bed, he disclaimed this Adventure, and said, That he
had onely invented it, because it suted with such as hee had
read of in his Histories: so he proceeds, saying:

The Scholler wondred, as well at Sancho's boldnesse, as his
Masters patience, but he thought, that by reason of the joy
that he received in having seene his Mistresse Dulcinea (though
enchanted) that softnesse of condition grew upon him; for
182

had it beene otherwise, **Sancho** spoke words that might have grinded him to powder: **for** in his opinion he was somwhat sawcy with his Master, to whom he said:

Signior Don Quixote, **I** thinke the journey that I have made with you, very wel employd, because in it I have stored up foure things. The first is, the having knowne your selfe, which I esteeme as a great happinesse. The second, to have knowne the secrets of this Montesinos Cave, with the transformations of Guadiana and Ruydera's Lakes, which may helpe me in my *Spanish Ovid* I have in hand. The third is, to know the Antiquity of Card-playing, which was used at least in time of the Emperor Charles the Great, as may be collected out of the words you say Durandarte used, when **after a** long speech betweene him and Montesinos, hee awakened saying; Patience, and shuffle: and this kind of speaking, he could not learne when he was enchanted, but when hee lived in France, in time of the aforesaid Emperor: and this observation comes in pudding time for the other booke that I am making, which is, My *supply to Polydore Vergil*, in the invention of Antiquities, and I beleeve, in his hee left out Cards, which I will put in, as a matter of great importance, especially having so authentike **an** author as Signior Durandarte. The fourth is, to have **knowne** for a certaine the true spring of the River Guadiana, which hath hitherto beene concealed.

You have reason (sayd Don Quixote :) but I would faine know of you, now that it pleased God to give you abilities **to** print your bookes, To whom will you direct them ? You have Lords and *Grandes in Spaine (sayd the Scholler) to whom I may direct them. Few of them (sayd Don Quixote) not because they doe not deserve the dedications, but because they will not admit of them, not to oblige themselves to the satisfaction, that **is** due to the Authors paines and courtesie. One Prince I know, that may supply the deserts of the rest, with such advantage, that should I speake of it, it might stirre up envy in some noble brests : but let this rest till some fit time, and let **us** looke out where we may lodge too night.

Not farre from hence (sayd the Scholler) there is a Hermi-

CHAPTER XXIV

Where are recounted a thousand flim-flams, as impertinent, as necessary to the understanding of this famous History.

*A name given to men of title, as Dukes, Marquisses, or Earles in Spaine, whose onely priviledge is to stand covered before the King.

CHAPTER
XXIV

Where are
recounted
a thousand
flim-flams, as
impertinent,
as necessary
to the under-
standing of
this famous
History.

tage, where dwels a Hermit, that they say hath been a
Souldior, and is thought to bee a good Christian, and very
discreet, and charitable. Besides the Hermitage, he hath a
little house, which he hath built at his owne charge, yet
though it be little, it is fit to receive ghests. Hath hee
any Hens, trow (sayd Sancho)? Few Hermits are without
um (quoth Don Quixote :) for your Hermits now adayes, are
not like those that lived in the Desarts of Ægypt, that were
clad in Palme-leaves, and lived upon the roots of the earth :
but mistake me not, that because I speake well of them, I
should speake ill of these, onely the penitency of these times
comes not neere those : yet for ought I know, all are good,
at least I think so, and if the worst come to the worst, your
Hypocrite that faines himselfe good, doth lesse hurt then he
that sinnes in publike.

As they were thus talking, they might espy a Foot-man
comming towards them, going apace, and beating with his
wand a Hee-Mule laden with Lances and Halberds ; when
hee came neere them, hee saluted them, and passed on : but
Don Quixote sayd to him ; Honest fellow, stay, for me
thinkes you make your Mule goe faster then needes.   I
cannot stay, Sir (sayd he) because these weapons that you
see I carry, must bee used to morrow morning : so I must
needs goe on my way, Farewell : But if you will know why I
carry them, I shall lodge to night in the *Vente above the
Hermitage, and if you goe that way, there you shall have me,
and I will tell you wonders : and so once more, Farewell. So
the Mule pricked on so fast, that Don Quixote had no leisure
to aske him, what wonders they were ; and as hee was curious,
and alwayes desirous of novelties, hee tooke order that they
should presently go and passe that night in the Vente, without touching at the Hermitage, where the Scholler would
have stayed that night.

So all three of them mounted, went toward the Vente,
whither they reached somewhat before it grew darke, and the
Scholler invited Don Quixote to drinke a sup by the way at
the Hermitage : which as soon as Sancho heard, he made
haste with Dapple, as did Don Quixote and the Scholler

*Ventas,
Places in
Spaine, in
barren un-
peopled parts
for lodging,
like our
beggerly Ale-
houses upon
the High-
wayes.

184

HISTORIE OF DON QUIXOTE

likewise : but as Sancho's **ill** lucke would have **it,** the Hermit
was not at home, as was **told** them by the Vnder-Hermit :
they asked him whether **he** had any of the dearer sort of
wine? who answered, His Master had none : but if they
would have any cheape water, hee would give it them with
a good will. If my thirst would bee quencht with water,
wee might have had Wels to drinke at by the way. Ah
Camacho's marriage, and Don Diego's plenty, how oft shal
I misse you? Now they left the Hermitage, and spurred
toward the Vente, and a little before them, they overtooke
a Youth, that went not very fast before them ; so they overtooke him : he had a sword upon his shoulder, and upon it,
as it seemed, a bundle of clothes, as breeches, and cloke, and
a shirt ; for he wore a velvet jerkin, that had some kinde of
remainder of sattin, and his shirt hung out, his stockings were
of silke, and his shooes square at toe, after the Court-fashion,
he was about eighteene yeeres of age, and active of body to
see to : to passe the tediousnesse of the way, he went singing
short pieces of songs, and as they came neere him, he made an
end of one, which the Scholler (they say) learnt by heart, and
it was this :

Where are
recounted
a thousand
flim-flams, as
impertinent,
as necessary
to the under-
standing of
this famous
History.

> To the warres I goe for necessity,
> At home would I tarry, if I had money.

Don Quixote was the first that spoke to him, saying ; You
go very naked, Sir Gallant. And whither, a Gods name?
Let's know, if it be your pleasure to tell us? To which the
Youth answered, Heat and poverty are the causes that I
walke so light, and my journey is to the wars. Why for
poverty (quoth Don Quixote)? for heat it may well be. Sir,
(sayd the Youth) I carry in this bundle a paire of slops,
fellowes to this Ierken, if I weare um by the way, I shall
doe my selfe no credit with them when I come to any towne,
and I have no money to buy others with, so as well for this,
as to aire my selfe, I goe till I can over-take certaine companies of Foot, which are not above twelve leagues from
hence, where I shall get me a place, and shall not want car-
riages to travell in, till I come to our imbarking place, which
(they say) must be in Cartagena, and I had rather have the

3 : AA   185

CHAPTER
XXIV
Where are
recounted
a thousand
flim-flams, as
impertinent,
as necessary
to the under-
standing of
this famous
History.

King to my Master, and serve him, then a beggerly Courtier.
And have you any extraordinary pay? sayd the Scholler.

Had I served any Grande, or man of quality (sayd the
Youth) no doubt I should; for that comes by your serving
good Masters, that out of the Scullery men come to bee
Lieutenants or Captaines, or to have some good pay: but I
always had the ill lucke to serve your Shag-rags and Vp-
starts, whose allowance was so bare and short, that one halfe
of it still was spent in starching me a ruffe, and it is a
miracle, that one ventring Page amongst an hundred, should
ever get any reasonable fortune. But tell me, Friend
(quoth Don Quixote) Is it possible, that in all the time you
served, you never got a Livery? Two (sayd the Page:)
But as he that goes out of a Monastery, before he professeth,
hath his habit taken from him, and his clothes given him
backe: so my Masters returned me mine, when they had
ended their businesses, for which they came to the Court
for, and returned to their owne homes, and with-held their
Liveries, which they had onely shewed for ostentation.

*Cullionry.

A notable * Espilorcheria, as saith your Italian (quoth
Don Quixote) for all that, thinke your selfe happy that you
are come from the Court, with so good an intention, for
there is nothing in the world better, nor more profitable,
then to serve God first, and next, your Prince and naturall
Master, especially in the practice of Armes, by which, if
not more wealth, yet at least, more honour is obtained, then
by Learning, as I have sayd many times, that though Learning hath raised more houses then Armes, yet your Sword-men
have a kind of (I know not what) advantage above Schollers,
with a kinde of splendor, that doth advantage them over all.

And beare in your minde what I shall now tell you, which
shall be much for your good, and much lighten you in your
travels, that is, not to thinke upon adversity; for the worst
that can come is death, which if it be a good death, the best
fortune of all is to die. Iulius Cæsar, that brave Romane
Emperour, being asked, Which was the best death? answered,
A sudden one and unthought of; and though he answered
like a Gentile, and voyd of the knowledge of the true God,

186

HISTORIE OF DON QUIXOTE

yet he sayd well, to save humane feeling a labour; for say you should bee slaine in the first skirmish, either with a Canon-shot, or blowne up with a Mine, What matter is it? All is but dying, and there's an end : And as Terence sayes, A Souldier slaine in the field, shewes better, then alive and safe in flight ; and so much the more famous is a good Souldiour, by how much hee obeyes his Captaines, and those that may command him ; and marke, childe, it is better for a Soldiour to smell of his gun-powder, then of civet ; and when olde age comes upon you in this honourable exercise, though you be full of scarres, maimed, or lame, at least, you shall not be without honour, which poverty cannot diminish ; and besides, there is order taken now, that olde and maimed Souldiers may be releeved ; neither are they dealt withall like those mens * Negars, that when they are olde and can doe their Masters no service, they (under colour of making them free) turne them out of doores, and make them slaves to hunger, from which nothing can free them but death, and for this time I will say no more to you, but onely get up behinde me till you come to the Vente, and there you shall sup with me, and to morrow take your journey, which God speede, as your desires deserve.

CHAPTER XXIV Where are recounted a thousand flim-flams, as impertinent, as necessary to the understanding of this famous History.

*He describes the right subtill and cruell nature of his damned Countrymen.

The Page accepted not of his invitement, to ride behinde him ; but for the supper hee did : And at this season (they say) Sancho sayd to himselfe ; Lord defend thee, Master ; And is it possible, that a man that knowes to speake such, so many, and so good things (as hee hath sayd heere) should say hee hath seene such impossible fooleries, as he hath told us of Montesino's Cave. Well, wee shall see what will become of it. And by this they came to the Vente just as it was night, for which Sancho was glad, because too his Master tooke it to be a true Vente, and not a Castle, as hee was wont. They were no sooner entred, when Don Quixote asked the *Venter for the man with the Lances and Halberds, who answered him, hee was in the stable looking to his Moyle: Sancho and the Scholler did the same to their Asses, giving Don Quixotes Rozinante the best manger and roome in the stable.

*Ventero, the Master of the Vente.

187

CHAPTER XXV

Of the Adventure of the Braying, and the merry
one of the Puppet-man, with the memorable
southsaying of the prophesying Ape.

ON QUIXOTE stood upon thornes, till
hee might heare and know the promised
wonders, of the man that carried the
Armes, and went where the Venter had
tolde him, to seeke him ; where finding
him, hee sayd ; That by all meanes he
must tell him presently, what hee had
promised him upon the way. The man
answered him, The story of the wonders requires more
leisure, and must not bee told thus standing: good Sir
let mee make an end of provandring my Beast, and I will
tell you things that shall admire you.

Let not that hinder you (quoth Don Quixote) for Ile
helpe you : and so he did, sifting his barley, and cleansing
the manger (a humility that obliged the fellow to tell him
his tale heartily :) thus sitting downe upon a bench, Don
Quixote by him, with the Scholler, Page, and Sancho,
and the Venter, for his complete Senate and Auditory, he
began :

You shall understand, that in a towne, some foure leagues
and an halfe from this Vente, it fell out, that an Alderman
there, by a trick and wile of a wench, his mayd-servant
(which were long to tell how) lost his Asse, and though
the sayd Alderman used all manner of diligence to finde
him, it was impossible. His Asse was wanting (as the publike voyce and fame goeth) fifteene dayes: when the Alderman that lost him, being in the market-place, another
Alderman of the same towne told him; Pay mee for my
newes, Gossip, for your Asse is forth-comming. I will

HISTORIE OF DON QUIXOTE

CHAPTER
XXV

Of the Adventure of the
Braying, and
the merry one
of the Puppet-
man, with the
memorable
southsaying
of the pro-
phesying Ape.

willingly, Gossip (sayd **the** other) but let me know where
he is? This morning (sayd the Second) I saw him upon the
mountaines without his pack-saddle, or any other furniture,
so leane, that it was pity to see him, I would have gotten
him before me, and have driven him to you, but hee is
so mountainous and wilde, that when I made towards him,
hee flew from mee, and got into the thickest of the wood :
If you please, wee will both returne and seeke him, let me
first put up this Asse at home, and Ile come by and by.
You shall doe me a great kindnesse (quoth he) and I will
repay you (if need be) in the like kinde.

With all these circumstances, just as I tell you, all that
know the truth, relate it : In fine, the two Aldermen, afoot
and hand to hand, went to the Hils, and comming to the
place where they thought to finde the Asse, they missed of
him, neither could they finde him, for all their seeking round-
about. Seeing then there was no appearance of him, the
Alderman that had seene him, sayd to the other ; Harke
you, Gossip, I have a tricke in my head, with which we shall
finde out this Beast, though hee bee hidden under ground,
much more if in the mountaine : Thus it is, I can bray
excellent well, and so can you a little : well, tis a match. A
little, Gossip (quoth the other) Verily, Ile take no ods of any
body, nor of an Asse himselfe. We shall see then (said the
second Alderman) for my plot is, that you goe on one side
of the hill, and I on the other, so that wee may compasse it
round, now and then you shall bray, and so will I, and it
cannot bee, but that your Asse will answer one of us, if hee
bee in the mountaine.

To this the owner of the Asse answered ; I tell you, Gossip,
the device is rare, and worthy your great wit : so dividing
themselves (according to the agreement) it fell out, that just
at one instant both brayed, and each of them coozened with
the others braying, came to looke another, thinking now
there had beene newes of the Asse : And as they met, the
Looser sayd ; Is it possible, Gossip, **that** it was not mine
Asse that brayed? No, twas I, sayd the other. Then
(replide the Owner) Gossip, betweene you and an Asse there

189

CHAPTER
XXV

Of the Adventure of the
Braying, and
the merry one
of the Puppet-
man, with the
memorable
southsaying
of the pro-
phesying Ape.

is no difference, touching your braying; for in my life I never heard a thing more naturall.

These praises and extollings (sayd the other) doe more properly belong to you then mee, for truely you may give two to one, to the best and skilfullest Brayer in the world; for your sound is lofty, you keepe very good time, and your cadences thicke and sudden: To conclude, I yeeld my selfe vanquished, and give you the prize and glory of this rare ability. Well (sayd the Owner) I shall like my selfe the better for this heereafter, and shall thinke I know something, since I have gotten a quality, for though I ever thought I brayed well, yet I never thought I was so excellent at it, as you say.

Let me tell you (sayd the other) there bee rare abilities in the world, that are lost and ill-imployed, in those that will not good them-selves with them. Ours (quoth the Owner) can do us no good, but in such businesses as wee have now in hand, and pray God in this they may.

This sayd, they divided themselves againe, and returned to their braying, and every foot they were deceived, and met; till they agreed upon a counter-signe, that to know twas themselves, and not the Asse, they should bray twice together: so that with this doubling their brayes, every stitch-while they compassed the hill, the lost Asse not answering so much, as by the least signe; but how could the poore and ill-thriving Beast answer, when they found him in the Thicket eaten with Wolves? And his Owner seeing him, sayd; I marvelled he did not answer; for if he had not been dead, he would have brayed, if he had heard us, or else he had beene no Asse: but i'faith, Gossip, since I have heard your delicate braying, I thinke my paines well bestowed in looking this Asse, though I have found him dead.

* Tis in a very good hand, Gossip (sayd the other:) And if the Abbot sing well,* the little Monke comes not behinde him. With this, all comfortlesse and hoarce, home they went, where they told their Friends, Neighbours, and Acquaintances, what had happened in the search for the Asse, the one exaggerating the others cunning in braying; all which was

*En buena
mano esta.
Alluding to
two, that
strive to make
one another
drinke first.

*The one as
very an Asse
as the other.

190

HISTORIE OF DON QUIXOTE

CHAPTER
XXV

Of the Adven-
ture of the
Braying, and
the merry one
of the Puppet-
man, with the
memorable
southsaying
of the pro-
phesying Ape.

knowne and spred abroad in the neighboring townes: And the Devill, that alwaies watcheth how he may sow and scatter quarrels and discord every where, raising brabbles in the aire, and making great Chimæra's of nothing, made the people of other townes, that when they saw any of ours, they should bray, as hitting us in the teeth with our Aldermens braying.

The Boyes at length fell to it, which was, as if it had falne into the jawes of all the Devils in Hell, so this braying spred it selfe from one towne to the other, that they which are borne in our towne, are as well knowne as the begger knowes his dish; and this unfortunate scoffe hath proceeded so farre, that many times those that were scoffed at, have gone out armed in a whole Squadron, to give battell to the Scoffers, without feare or wit, neither King nor Keisar being able to prevent them: I beleeve, that to morrow or next day, those of my towne will be in field (to wit, the Brayers) against the next towne, which is two leagues off, one of them that doth most persecute us; and because we might be well provided, I have bought those Halberds and Lances, that you saw. And these be the wonders, that I said I would tell you of: and if these bee not so, I know not what may.

And heere the poore fellow ended his discourse: and now there entred at the doore of the Vente, one clad all in Chamois, in hose and doublet, and called aloud; Mine Oast, have you any lodging? for here comes the prophesying Ape, and the Motion of *Melisendra*. Body of me (quoth the Venter) heere is Master Peter, we shall have a brave night of it (I had forgot to tell how this Master Peter had his left eye, and halfe his cheeke, covered with a patch of green Taffata, a signe that all that side was sore:) so the Venter proceeded, saying; You are welcome, Master Peter, Where's the Ape and the Motion, that I see um not? They are not farre off (quoth the Chamois-man) onely I am come before, to know if you have any lodging?

I would make bold with the Duke of Alva himselfe (sayd the Venter) rather then Master Peter should bee disap-

191

CHAPTER XXV

Of the Adventure of the Braying, and the merry one of the Puppet-man, with the memorable southsaying of the prophesying Ape.

poynted: let your Ape and your Motion come; for wee have ghests heere to night, that will pay for seeing that, and the Apes abilities. In good time (sayd hee of the Patch) for I will moderate the price, so my charges this night be payd for; and therefore I will cause the Cart where they are, to drive on: with this hee went out of the Vente againe. Don Quixote straight asked the Venter, What Master Peter that was, and what Motion or Ape those he brought?

To which the Venter answered; He is a famous Puppet-Master, that this long time hath gone up and down these parts of Aragon, shewing this motion of *Melisendra, and Don Gayferos,* one of the best histories that hath bin represented these many yeeres in this kingdom. Besides, he hath an Ape, the strangest that ever was; for if you aske him any thing, he marketh what you aske, and gets up upon his Masters shoulder, and tells him in his eare by way of answer, what he was asked: which Master Peter declares: he tells things to come, as well as things past, and though he doe not alwaies hit upon the right, yet he seldome erres, and makes us beleeve the Devill is in him. Twelve pence for every answer we give, if the Ape doe answer, I meane, if his Master answer for him, after hee hath whispered in his eare; so it is thought that Master Peter is very rich, he is a notable fellow, and (as your Italian saith) a boon companion; hath the best life in the world, talkes his share for sixe men, and drinks for a doozen, all at his Tongues charge, his Motion, and his Apes.

By this, Master Peter was return'd, and his Motion and Ape came in a smal carriage; his Ape was of a good bignesse, without a tayle, and his bumme as bare as a Felt, but not very ill-favoured. Don Quixote scarce beheld him, when hee demanded, Master Prophesier, What fish doe we catch? Tell us what will become of us, and heere is twelve-pence, which he commanded Sancho to give Master Peter; who answered for the Ape and said: Sir, this beast answeres not, nor gives any notice of things to come, of things past hee knowes something, and likewise a little of things present.

192

HISTORIE OF DON QUIXOTE

Zwookers (quoth Sancho) **Ile** not give a farthing to know what is past: for who **can** tell that better then my selfe? and to pay for what I **know**, is most foolish: but since you say hee knowes things present, heere 's my twelve-pence, and let good-man Ape tell me what my wife Teresa Pansa doth, and in what shee busies her selfe. Master Peter would not take his mony, saying; I will not take your reward before-hand, till the Ape hath first done his duty: so giving a clap or two with his right hand on his left shoulder, at one friske the Ape got up, and laying his mouth to his eare, grated his teeth apace, and having shewed this feat the space of a Creeds saying, at another frisk he leap'd to the ground, and instantly Master Peter very hastily ran and kneeled downe before Don Quixote, and embracing his legs, said: These legges I embrace, as if they were Hercules Pillars. O famous reviver of the long-forgotten Knight Errantry! Oh never sufficiently extolled Knight Don Quixote de la Mancha! raiser of the faint-hearted, propper of those that fall, the staffe and comfort of all the unfortunate! Don Quixote was amazed, Sancho confused, the Scholler in suspence, the Page astonisht, the Bray townes-man all in a gaze, the Venter at his wittes end, and all admiring that heard the Puppet-mans speech, who went on, saying:

And thou honest Sancho Pansa, the best Squire to the best Knight of the world, rejoyce, for thy wife Teresa is a good hous-wife, and at this time she is dressing a pound of flaxe; by the same token shee hath a good broken-mouth'd pot at her left side, that holds a pretty scantling of wine, with which she easeth her labour.

I beleeve that very well (sayd Sancho) for she is a good soule; and if she were not jealous, I would not change her for the Gyantesse Andandona, that, as my Master sayes, was a woman for the nonce: and my Teresa is one of those that will not pine her selfe, though her heyres smart for it.

Well, I say now (quoth Don Quixote) he that reades much, and travels much, sees much, and knowes much. This I say, for who in the world could have perswaded mee that Apes could prophesie? which **now** I have seene with

CHAPTER
XXV
Of the Adven-
ture of the
Braying, and
the merry one
of the Puppet-
man, with the
memorable
southsaying
of the pro-
phesying Ape.

THE SECOND PART OF THE

CHAPTER
XXV
Of the Adven-
ture of the
Braying, and
the merry one
of the Puppet-
man, with the
memorable
southsaying
of the pro-
phesying Ape.

mine owne eyes; for I am the same Don Quixote that this
beast speakes of, although he have bin somewhat too liberall
in my praise: but howsoever I am, I give God thanks that
he hath made me so relenting and compassionate; alwaies
enclined to do good to all, and hurt to no man.

If I had money (said the Page) I would aske Mr. Ape
what should befall me in the peregrination I have in hand.
To which Master Peter answered, that was now risen from
Don Quixotes foot, I have told you once that this little beast
foretels not things to come; for if he could, twere no matter
for your mony: for heere is Signior Don Quixote present,
for whose sake I would forgoe all the Interest in the world:
and to shew my duety to him, and to give him delight, I
will set up my Motion, and freely shew all the company in
the Vent some pastime gratis. Which the Venter hearing,
unmeasurably glad, pointed him to a place where he might
set it up; which was done in an instant.

Don Quixote liked not the Apes prophesying very well,
holding it to be frivolous, that an Ape should onely tell
things present, and not past, or to come. So whilest Master
Peter was fitting his Motion, Don Quixote tooke Sancho
with him to a corner of the stable, and in private said:

Looke thee, Sancho, I have very well considered of this
Apes strange quality, and finde that this Master Peter hath
made a secret expresse compact with the Devill, to infuse
this ability into the Ape, that he may get his living by it,
and when he is rich, he will give him his soule; which is
that, that this universall enemy of mankinde pretends: and
that which induceth me to this beliefe, is, that the Ape
answers not to things past, but onely present; and the
Devils knowledge attaines to no more, for things to come
he knowes not, only by conjecture: for God alone can dis-
tinguish the times and moments, and to him nothing is past
or to come, but all is present: Which being so, it is most
certaine that this Ape speakes by instinct from the Devill,
and I wonder he hath not beene accused to the Inquisition,
and examined, and that it hath not beene pressed out of him,
to know by what vertue this Ape prophesieth; for certainely,

194

HISTORIE OF DON QUIXOTE

neyther he nor his Ape are Astrologers, nor know how to
cast figures, which they call judiciary, so much used in
Spaine: for you have no paltry Woman, nor Page, nor
Cobler, that presumes not to cast a figure, as if it were one
of the knaves at Cards upon a table, falsifying that wondrous
Science with their ignorant lying.

Of the Adven-
ture of the
Braying, and
the merry one
of the Puppet-
man, with the
memorable
southsaying
of the pro-
phesying Ape.

I knew a Gentlewoman that asked one of these Figure-
flingers, if a little foysting-hound of hers should have any
puppies, and if it had, how many, and of what colour the
whelps should be. To which my cunning man (after hee had
cast his figure) answered: That the bitch should have young,
and bring forth three little whelps, the one Greene, the
other Carnation, and the third of a mixt colour, with this
proviso, that she should take the dogge betweene eleven and
twelve of the clocke at noone, or at night, which should
be on the Munday, or the Saturday; and the successe was,
that some two dayes after the bitch died of a surfet, and
Master figure-raiser was reputed in the towne a most perfect
Iudiciary, as all, or the greatest part of such men are. For
all that (said Sancho) I would you would bid Master Peter
aske his Ape, whether all were true that befell you in
Montesino's Cave; for I thinke (under correction) all was
cogging and lying, or at least but a dreame. All might be
(said Don Quixote) yet I will doe as thou dost advize me,
though I have one scruple remaining.

Whilest they were thus communing, Master Peter came
to call Don Quixote, and to tell him that the Motion was
now up, if he would please to see it, which would give him
content.

Don Quixote told him his desire, and wished that his Ape
might tell him, if certaine things that befell him in Montesino's Cave were true, or but dreames; for himselfe was
uncertaine whether. Master Peter, without answering a
word, fetcht his Ape, and putting him before Don Quixote
and Sancho, saide, Looke you, Master Ape, Signior Don
Quixote would have you tell him, whether certaine things
that hapned to him in Montesino's Cave were true or false?
and making the accustomed signe, the Ape whipt upon his

CHAPTER XXV

Of the Adventure of the Braying, and the merry one of the Puppetman, with the memorable southsaying of the prophesying Ape.

left shoulder, and seeming to speake to him in his eare, Master Peter straight interpreted. The Ape, Signior, saies that part of those things are false, and part of them true, and this is all he knowes touching this demand; and now his vertue is gone from him, and if you will know any more, you must expect till Friday next, and then he will answer you all you will aske, for his vertue will not returne till then.

Law ye there (quoth Sancho) did not I tell you that I could not beleeve that all you said of Montesinos Cave could hold currant? The successe heereafter will determine that (quoth Don Quixote) for time, the discoverer of al things, brings every thing to the Sunnes light, though it be hidden in the bosome of the earth: and now let this suffice, and let us goe see the Motion; for I beleeve we shall have some strange novelty. Some strange one? quoth Master Peter, this Motion of mine hath a thousand strange ones: I tell you Signior, it is one of the rarest things to be seene in the world; *operibus credite et non verbis*: and now to worke, for it is late, and we have much to doe, say, and shew.

Don Quixote and Sancho obeyed, and went where the Motion was set and opened, all full of little waxe lights, that made it most sightly and glorious. Master Peter straight clapped himselfe within it, who was hee that was to manage the artificiall Puppets, and without stood his boy to interpret and declare the mysteries of the Motion; in his hand hee had a white wand, with which he pointed out the severall shapes that came in and out. Thus all that were in the Vente being placed, and some standing over-against the Motion, Don Quixote, Sancho, the Scholler and the Page, placed in the best seates, *the Trudge-man began to speak what shall be heard or seene, by him that shall heare or read the next Chapter.

*El Trujaman. An Interpreter amongst the Turks, but here taken for any in generall.

196

CHAPTER XXVI

Of the delightfull passage of the Puppet-play, and other pleasant matters.

EERE Tyrians and Troyans were all silent, I meane, all the spectators of the Motion had their eares hanged upon the Interpreters mouth, that should declare the wonders; by and by there was a great sound of Kettle Drums, and Trumpets, and a volly of great shot within the Motion, which passing away briefly, the boy beganne to raise his voyce, and to say:

This true History which is here represented to you, is taken word for word out of the French Chronicles, and the Spanish Romants, which are in every bodies mouth, and sung by boyes up and downe the streets. It treats of the liberty that Signior Don Gayferos gave to Melisendra his wife, that was imprisoned by the Moores in Spaine, in the City of Sansuena, which was then so called, and now Saragosa; and looke you there, how Don Gayferos is playing at Tables, according to the song;

> Now Don Gayferos at Tables doth play,
> Vnmindfull of Melisendra away.

And that Personage that peepes out there with a Crowne on his head, and a Scepter in his hand, is the Emperor Charlemaine, the supposed father of the said Melisendra, who grieved with the sloth and neglect of his Sonne in law, comes to chide him: and marke with what vehemency and earnestnesse he rates him, as if he meant to give him halfe a doozen Connes with his Scepter. Some Authors there bee that say, hee did, and sound ones too: and after

THE SECOND PART OF THE

CHAPTER
XXVI
Of the
delightfull
passage of
the Puppet-
play, and
other pleasant
matters.

he had told him many things concerning the danger of his reputation, if he did not free his Spouse, twas said hee told him, I have said enough, looke to it. Looke ye Sir, againe, how the Emperor turnes his backe, and in what case hee leaves Don Gayferos, who all enraged flings the Tables and the table-men from him, and hastily calls for his Armour, and borrowes his Cousin Germane Roldan his sword Durindana; who offers him his company in this difficult enterprise. But the valorous enraged Knight would not accept it, saying; That hee is sufficient to free his Spouse, though she were put in the deepe Centre of the earth: and now hee goes in to Arme himselfe for his Iourney.

Now turne your eyes to yonder Tower that appeares, (for you must suppose it is one of the Towers of the Castle of Saragosa, which is now called the Aliaferia) and that Lady that appeares in the window, cladde in a Moorish habit, is the peerelesse Melisendra, that many a time lookes toward France, thinking on Paris and her spouse, the onely comforts in her imprisonment. Behold also a strange accident now that happens, perhaps never the like seene: see you not that Moore that comes faire and softly, with his finger in his mouth, behinde Melisendra? looke what a smacke he gives her in the midst of her lippes, and how sodainely shee begins to spit, and to wipe them with her white smocke sleeve, and how she laments, and for very anguish despiteously rootes up her faire hayres, as if they were to blame for this wickednesse. Marke you also that grave Moore, that stands in that open Gallery, it is Marsilius King of Sansuenna, who when he saw the Moores sawcinesse, although he were a kins-man, and a great favourite of his, hee commanded him straight to bee apprehended, and to have two hundreth stripes given him, and to be carried thorow the chiefe streets in the City, with minstrels before, and rods of Iustice behinde; and looke ye how the sentence is put in execution before the fault bee scarce committed; for your Moores use not (as we doe) any legall proceeding. Childe, childe (cried Don Quixote aloud) on with your story in a direct line, and fall not into your crookes and your trans-

HISTORIE OF DON QUIXOTE

versals : **for to** verifie a **thing I** tell you, there had need be
a Legall proceeding. **Then** Master Peter too said from
within ; Boy, fall not you **to** your flourishes, but doe as that
Gentleman commands you, which is the best course ; sing
you your plaine song, and meddle not with the treble, lest
the strings breake. I will, Master (said the boy) and proceeded, saying :

Of the
delightfull
passage of
the Puppet-
play, and
other pleasant
matters.

He that you see there (quoth he) on horsebacke, cladde in
a Gascoyne cloake, is Don Gayferos himselfe, to whom his
Wife (now revenged on the Moore for his boldnesse) shewes
her selfe from the battlements of the Castle, taking him to
bee some passenger, with whom shee passed all the discourse
mentioned in the Romant, that sayes ;

> **Friend, if toward France you goe,
> Aske if Gayferos be there** or no, etc.

The rest **I** omit, for all prolixity is irkesome, tis sufficient
that you **see** there how Don Gayferos discovers himselfe, and
by Melisendra's jocund behaviour, we may imagine shee
knowes him, and the rather, because now we see, she lets
her selfe down from a bay-window, to ride away behinde her
good Spouse : but alas, unhappy creature, one of the skirts
of her kirtle hath caught upon one of the yron barres of the
window, and she hovers in the ayre, without possibility of
comming to the ground : but see how pittifull heavens releeve
her **in her** greatest necessity ; for Don Gayferos comes, and
without any care of her rich Kirtle, layes **hold** of it, and
forcibly brings her downe with him, and **at one** hoist sets her
astride **upon** his **horses** crupper, and commands her to sit
fast, **and clap her** armes about him, **that** shee fall not ; for
Melisendra **was not** used to that kinde **of** riding. Looke you
how the horse **by** his neighing shewes **that** he is proud with
the burden **of his** valiant Master, and faire Mistresse. Look
how they turne their backes to the **City,** and merrily take
their way toward Paris. Peace **be with** you, O peerelesse
couple of true Lovers, safely may you arrive at your **de-**
sired Country, **without** Fortunes hindering **your** prosperous

199

Of the
delightfull
passage of
the Puppet-
play, and
other pleasant
matters.

*Mezquitas,
Moorish
Churches.

voyage: may your friends and kindred see you enjoy the rest
of your yeeres (as many as Nestors) peaceably.

Heere Master Peter cryed out aloud againe, saying;
Plainenesse, good boy, doe not you soare so high, this affec-
tation is scurvy. The Interpreter answered nothing, but
went on, saying, There wanted not some idle spectators that
pry into every thing, who saw the going downe of Melisendra,
and gave Marsilius notice of it, who straight commanded to
sound an Alarme; and now behold, how fast the City even
sinkes againe with the noyse of bels that sound in the high
Towers of the *Mesquits.

There you are out Boy (said Don Quixote) and Master
Peter is very improper in his belles; for amongst Moores
you have no bels, but Kettle-drummes, and a kinde of
Shaulmes that bee like our Waytes, so that your sounding
of bels in Sansuenna is a most idle foppery. Stand not upon
trifles, Signior **Don** Quixote, said Master Peter, and so
strictly upon every thing, for we shall not know how to
please you. Have you not a thousand Comedies ordinarily
represented, as full of incongruities and absurdities, and yet
they runne their Careere happily, and are heard, not only
with applause, but great admiration also? On, boy, say on,
and so I fill my purse, let there be as many improprieties as
moates in the Sunne. You are the right (quoth Don Quixote)
and the boy proceeded.

Looke what a company of gallant Knights go out of the
City in pursuit of the Catholike Lovers, how many Trumpets
sound, how many Shaulmes play, how many drummes and
kettles make a noyse, I feare me they will over-take them,
and bring them backe both bound to the same horses tayle,
which would be a horrible spectacle.

Don Quixote seeing and hearing such a deale of Moorisme,
and such a coyle, he thought fit to succour those that fled so
standing up, with a loud voyce he cryed out; I will never
consent while I live, that in my presence, such an outrage as
this, bee offred to so valiant, and so amorous a bold Knight,
as Don Gayferos: Stay, you base Scoundrels, doe not yee
follow or persecute him: if you doe, you must first wage
200

warre with mee: so doing and speaking, he unsheathed his sword, and at one friske he got to the Motion, and with an unseene and posting fury, he began to raine strokes upon the Puppetish Moorisme, overthrowing some, and beheading others, maiming this, and cutting in pieces that, and amongst many other blowes, he fetcht one so downe right, that had not Mr. Peter tumbled and squatted downe, hee had clipped his Mazard as easily, as if it had beene made of March-pane. Mr. Peter cryed out, saying; Hold, Signior Don Quixote, hold; and know that these you hurle downe, destroy and kill, are not reall Moores, but shapes made of paste-boord: Looke you, looke yee now (wretch that I am) hee spoyles all, and undoes me. But for all this, Don Quixote still multiplied his slashes, doubling and redoubling his blowes, as thicke as hops.

And in a word, in lesse then two Credo's, he cast downe the whole Motion (all the tackling first cut to fitters, and all the Puppets) King Marsilius was sore wounded, and the Emperour Charlemaine, his head and crowne were parted in two places, the Senate and Auditors were all in a hurry, and the Ape gat up to the top of the house, and so out at the window, the Scholler was frighted, the Page cleane dastarded, and even Sancho himselfe was in a terrible perplexity, for (as he sware after the storme was past) he never saw his Master so outragious.

The generall ruine of the Motion thus performed, Don Quixote began to bee somewhat pacified, and sayd; Now would I have all those heere at this instant before mee, that beleeve not, how profitable Knights Errant are to the world; and had not I beene now present, what (I marvell) would have becomne of Signior Don Gayferos, and the faire Melisendra? I warrant, ere this, those dogs would have overtaken, and shewed them some foule play: when all is done, long live Knight Errantry, above all things living in the world.

Long live it on Gods name (sayd Mr. Peter) agen with a pitifull voyce, and may I die, since I live to be so unhappy, as to say with King *Don Rodrigo, Yesterday I was Lord

CHAPTER XXVI

Of the delightfull passage of the Puppet-play, and other pleasant matters.

*Don Rodrigo was the last King of the Goths, that raigned in Spaine, conquered by the Moores.

THE SECOND PART OF THE

CHAPTER
XXVI

Of the
delightfull
passage of
the Puppet-
play, and
other pleasant
matters.

of all Spaine, but to day have not a Battlement I can call mine : Tis not yet halfe an houre, scarce halfe a minute, that I was Master of Kings and Emperours, had my stables, coffers, and bags full of horses and treasure : but now I am desolate, dejected and poore, and to adde more affliction, without my Ape, that before I can catch him againe, I am like to sweat for it, and all through the unconsiderate furies of this Sir Knight, who is sayd to protect the fatherlesse, to rectifie wrongs, and to doe other charitable works ; but to me onely, this his generous intention hath beene defective, I thanke God for it. In fine, it could bee none but The Knight of the Sorrowfull Countenance, that discountenanced me and mine. Sancho grew compassionate to heare Master Peters lamentation, and sayd ; Weepe not, nor grieve, Master Peter, for thou breakest my heart ; and let me tell thee, that my Master, Don Quixote, is so scrupulous and Catholicall a Christian, that if hee fall into the reckoning, that hee have done thee any wrong, hee knowes how, and will satisfie it with much advantage. If (sayd Master Peter) Signior Don Quixote would but pay mee for some part of the Pieces that he hath spoyled, I should bee contented, and his Worship might not bee troubled in conscience : for hee that keepes that, that is another mans, against the Owners will, and restores it not, can hardly be saved.

That 's true (quoth Don Quixote :) But hitherto, Master Peter, I know not whether I have detained ought of yours. No ? not ? said Master Peter, why these poore relikes that lie upon the hard and barren earth, who scattered and anni-hilated them, but the invincible force of that powerfull arme ? And whose were those bodies, but mine ? And with whom did I maintaine my selfe, but with them ? Well, I now (sayd Don Quixote) verily beleeve, what I have done often, that the Enchanters that persecute me, doe nothing but put shapes really, as they are before mine eyes, and by and by trucke and change them at their pleasures. Verily, my Masters, you that heare me, I tell you, all that heere passed, seemed to me to be really so, and immediately that that Melisendra was Melisendra ; Don Gayferos, Don Gayferos ;

202

HISTORIE OF DON QUIXOTE

and Marsilius, Marsilius; and Charlemaine, Charlemaine:
And this was it that stirred up my choller; and to accomplish my Profession of Knight Errant, my meaning was to
succour those that fled, and to this good purpose I did all
that you have seene, which if it fell out unluckily, twas no
fault of mine, but of my wicked persecutors: yet for all this
errour (though it proceeded from no malice of mine) I my
selfe will condemne my selfe in the charge; let Master Peter
see what hee will have for the spoyled pieces, and I will pay
it all in present currant coyne of Castile.

Of the
delightfull
passage of
the Puppet-
play, and
other pleasant
matters.

Master Peter made him a low leg, saying; I could expect
no lesse from the unheard of Christianity of the most valorous Don Quixote de la Mancha, the true Succourer and
Bulwarke of all those that be in neede and necessity, or
wandring Vagamundes, and now let the Venter and the
Grand Sancho bee Arbitratours, and Price-setters betweene
your Worship and me, and let them say what every torne
piece was worth. The Venter and Sancho both agreed:
and by and by Mr. Peter reached up Marsilius King of Saragosa headlesse, and sayd; You see how impossible it is for
this Prince to returne to his first being, and therefore, saving
your better judgements, I thinke fit to have for him two
shillings and three-pence.

On then, quoth Don Quixote. Then for this (quoth
Master Peter) that is parted from head to foot, taking the
Emperour Charlemaine up, I thinke two shillings seven-
pence halfe-peny is little enough. Not very little, quoth
Sancho. Nor much (sayd the Venter:) but moderate the
bargaine, and let him have halfe a crowne. Let him have
his full asking (sayd Don Quixote) for, for such a mishap as
this, wee'l nere stand upon three halfe-pence more or lesse;
and make an end quickly, Master Peter, for it is neere
supper-time, and I have certaine suspitions that I shall eat.
For this Puppet (sayd Mr. Peter) without a nose, and an eye
wanting, of the faire Melisendra, I aske, but in Iustice foureteene pence halfe-penny.

Nay, the Devil's in it (sayd Don Quixote) if Melisendra
bee not now in France, or upon the borders, at least, with

203

CHAPTER
XXVI
Of the
delightfull
passage of
the Puppet-
play, and
other pleasant
matters.

her Husband; for the horse they rode on, to my seeming, rather flew then ran; and therefore sell not me a Cat for a Coney, presenting me heere Melisendra nose-lesse, when shee (if the time require it) is wantonly solacing with her Husband in France. God give each man his owne, Mr. Peter, let us have plaine dealing; and so proceed. Master Peter, that saw Don Quixote in a wrong vaine, and that he returned to his olde Theame, thought yet he should not escape him, and so replied; Indeede this should not be Melisendra, now I thinke on't; but some one of the Damozels that served her, so that five pence for her will content me.

Thus he went on prizing of other torne Puppets, which the Arbitrating Iudges moderated to the satisfaction of both parties, and the whole prices of all were, twenty-one shillings and eleven pence, which when Sancho had disbursed, Master Peter demanded over and above twelve-pence for his labour, to looke the Ape. Give it him, Sancho (sayd Don Quixote) not to catch his Ape, *but a Monkey, and I would give five pound for a reward, to any body that would certainely tell me, that the Lady Melisendra and Don Gayferos were safely arrived in France, amongst their owne people.

*As we say,
To catch a
Fox.

None can better tell then my Ape (said Master Peter) though the Devill himselfe will scarce catch him; yet I imagine, making much of him, and hunger, will force him to seeke me to night, and by morning we shall come together. Well, to conclude; the storme of the Motion passed, and all supped merrily, and like good fellowes, at Don Quixotes charge; who was liberall in extremity. Before day, the fellow with the Lances and Halberds was gone, and somewhat after, the Scholler and the Page came to take leave of Don Quixote, the one to returne homeward, and the other to prosecute his intended voyage, and for a releefe Don Quixote gave him six shillings.

Master Peter would have no more to doe with him; for hee knew him too well. So he got up before the Sunne, and gathering the relikes of the Motion together, and his Ape,

204

he betooke him to his Adventures. The Venter that knew not Don Quixote, wondred as much at his liberality, as his madnes. To conclude, Sancho payd him honestly, by his Masters order, and taking leave, about eight of the clocke they left the Vente, and went on their way, where wee must leave them ; for so it is fit, that we may come to other matters pertaining to the true de-claration of this famous History.

CHAPTER XXVII

Who Master Peter and his Ape were, with the ill successe that Don Quixote had in the Adven-ture of the Braying, which ended not so well, as he would, or thought for.

ID HAMETE, the Chronicler of this famous History, beginnes this Chapter with these words: I sweare like a Catholike Christian. To which the Translatour sayes, That Cid his swearing like a Catholike Christian, hee being a Moore, as undoubtedly he was, was no otherwise to be understood, then that as the Catholike Christian, when hee sweares, doth or ought to sweare truth, so did he, as if he had sworne like a Catholike Christian, in what hee meant to write of Don Quixote, especially in recounting who Mr. Peter and the prophesying Ape were, that made all the Countrey astonisht at his fore-telling things. He sayes then, that hee who hath read the former part of this History, will have well remembred that same Gines de Passamonte, whom Don Quix-ote, amongst other Gally-slaves, freed in Sierra Morena, a benefit for which afterward hee had small thankes, and worse payment, from that wicked and ungratefull Rowt.

This Gines de Passamonte, whom Don Quixote called

CHAPTER
XXVII

Who Master
Peter and his
Ape were,
with the ill
successe that
Don Quixote
had in the
Adventure of
the Braying,
etc.

Ginesillo de Parapilla, was hee that stole Sancho's Dapple; which, because neither the manner nor the time were put in the first part, made many attribute the fault of the Impression, to the Authours weakenesse of memory. But true it is, that Gines stole him, as Sancho slept upon his backe, using the same tricke and device of Brunelo's, when as Sacripante being upon the siege of Albraca, he stole his horse from under his legs; and after Sancho recovered him againe, as was shewed.

This Gines, fearefull of being found by the Iustices that sought after him, to punish him for his infinite villanies and faults, that were so many and so great, that him selfe made a great volume of them, determined to get him into the Kingdome of Aragon, and so covering his left eye, to apply himselfe to the office of a Puppet-man; for this and juggling hee was excellent at. It fell out so, that hee bought his Ape of certaine captive Christians that came out of Barbary, whom hee had instructed, that upon making a certaine signe, hee should leape upon his shoulder, and should mumble, or seeme to doe so, at least, something in his eare.

This done, before he would enter into any towne with his Motion or Ape, he informed himselfe in the neerest towne, or where hee best could, what particulars had happened in such a place, or to such persons, and bearing all well in minde, the first thing he did, was to shew his Motion, which was sometimes of one Story, otherwhiles of another: but all merry, delightfull, and familiarly knowne.

The sight being finisht, hee propounded the rarities of his Ape, telling the people that hee could declare unto them, all things past and present; but in things to come, he had no skill: For an answer to each question hee demanded a shilling; but to some hee did it cheaper, according as hee perceived the Demanders in case to pay him; and sometimes he came to such places, as he knew what had happened to the Inhabitants, who although they would demand nothing, because they would not pay him; yet he would straight make signes to the Ape, and tell them, the Beast had told him this or that, which fell out just by what hee had before

206

HISTORIE OF DON QUIXOTE

heard, and with this hee got an unspeakable name, and all men flocked about him, and at other times (as he was very cunning) he would reply so, that the answers fell out very fit to the questions : and since no body went about to sift, or to presse him, how his Ape did prophesie, hee gulled every one, and filled his pouch.

As soone as ever he came into the Vente, hee knew Don Quixote and Sancho, and all that were there : but it had cost him deare, if Don Quixote had let his hand fall somewhat lower, when hee cut off King Marsilius his head, and destroyed all his Chivalry, as was related in the antecedent Chapter. And this is all that may be sayd of Master Peter and his Ape.

And returning to Don Quixote de la Mancha, I say, that after hee was gone out of the Vente, hee determined first of all to see the bankes of the river Heber, and all round-about, before hee went to the City of Saragosa, since betweene that and the Iusts there, he had time enough for all. Heereupon hee went on his way, which he passed two dayes without lighting on any thing worth writing, till the third day, going up a Ridge-way, hee heard a sound of Drummes, Trumpets, and Guns ; at first, hee thought some Regiment of Souldiers passed by that way : so, to see them, he spurred Rozinante, and got up the Ridge, and when he was at the top, he saw (as he ghessed) at the foot of it, neere upon two hundred men, armed with different sorts of Armes, to wit, Speares, Crosse-bowes, Partizans, Halberds, and Pikes, and some Guns, and many Targets. He came downe from the high ground, and drew neere to the Squadron, insomuch that he might distinctly perceive their Banners, judged of their Colours, and noted their Impreses, and especially one, which was on a Standard or Shred of white Sattin, where was lively painted a little Asse, like one of your Sardinian Asses, his head lifted up, his mouth open, and his tongue out, in act and posture just as he were braying, about him were these two verses written in faire letters ;

CHAPTER
XXVII
Who Master
Peter and his
Ape were,
with the ill
successe that
Don Quixote
had in the
Adventure of
the Braying,
etc.

> Twas not for nought that day,
> The one and t' other Iudge did bray

207

CHAPTER XXVII

Who Master Peter and his Ape were, with the ill successe that Don Quixote had in the Adventure of the Braying, etc.

By this device Don Quixote collected, that those people belonged to the Braying Towne, and so he told Sancho, declaring likewise what was written in the Standard; hee told him also, that hee that told them the Story, was in the wrong, to say they were two Aldermen that brayed: for by the verses of the Standard, they were two Iudges. To which Sancho answered, Sir, that breakes no square, for it may very well be, that the Aldermen that then brayed, might come in time to be Iudges of the Towne, so they may have beene called by both titles. Howsoever, tis not materiall to the truth of the story, whether the Brayers were Aldermen, or Iudges, one for another, be they who they would, and a Iudge is even as likely to bray as an Alderman.

To conclude, they perceived and knew, that the towne that was mocked, went out to skirmish with another that had too much abused them, and more then was fitting for good neighbours. Don Quixote went towards them, to Sancho's no small griefe, who was no friend to those enterprizes. Those of the squadron hemmed him in, taking him to be some one of their side. Don Quixote lifting up his Visor, with a pleasant countenance and courage, came toward the Standard of the Asse, and there all the chiefest of the Army gathered about him to behold him, falling into the same admiration as all else did the first time they had seene him. Don Quixote that saw them attentively looke on him, and no man offering to speake to him, or aske him ought, taking hold on their silence, and breaking his owne, hee raised his voyce, and said:

Honest friends, I desire you with all earnestnesse, that you interrupt not the discourse that I shall make to you, till you shall see that I eyther distaste or weary you; which if it be so, at the least signe you shall make, I will seale up my lips, and clappe a gagge on my tongue. All of them bade him speake what hee would, for they would heare him willingly.

Don Quixote having this licence, went on, saying, I, my friends, am a Knight Errant, whose exercise is Armes, whose profession, to favor those that need favor, and to helpe the distressed. I have long knowne of your misfortune, and the cause that every while moves you to take Armes to bee revenged on your enemies. And having not once, but many times pondered your businesse in my understanding, I finde (according to the Lawes of Duell) that you are deceived to thinke your selves affronted; for no particular person can affront a whole Towne, except it be in defying them for Traitors in generall, because he knowes not who in particular committed the Treason, for which he defied all the Towne.

CHAPTER XXVII

Who Master Peter and his Ape were, with the ill successe that Don Quixote had in the Adventure of the Braying, etc.

We have an example of this in Don Diego Ordonnez de Lara, who defied the whole towne of Zamora, because hee was ignorant, that onely Vellido de Olsos committed the treason in killing his King; so he defied them all, and the revenge and answer concerned them all: though howsoever Don Diego was somewhat too hasty and too forward; for it was needlesse for him to have defied the dead, or the waters, or the Corne, or the children unborne, with many other trifles there mentioned: but let it goe, for when Choller over-flowes, the **tongue** hath neyther father, governour, or guide that may correct it. This being so then, that one particular person cannot affront a Kingdom, Province, City, Common-wealth, or Towne onely, it is manifest, that the revenge of defiance for such as affront is needlesse, since it is none; for it were a goodly matter sure that those of the towne of Reloxa should every foot go out to kill those that abuse them so: Or that your *Cazoteros, Verengeneros, Vallenatos, Xanoneros, or others of these kindes of Nicknames, that are common in every boyes mouth, and the ordinary sort of people: twere very good, I say, that all these famous Townes should bee ashamed, and take revenge, and **runne with** their swords continually drawne like Sackbuts, for **every** slender quarrell. No, no, God forbid: Men of wisedome **and** well-governed Common-wealths, ought **to** take Armes **for** foure things, and so to endanger their persons, lives, and estates. First, **to** defend the Catholike Faith. Secondly, their lives, which **is** according to Divine and Naturall Law. Thirdly, to defend their honour, family, **and** estates. Fourthly, to serve their Prince in a lawfull

CHAPTER
XXVII
Who Master
Peter and his
Ape were,
with the ill
successe that
Don Quixote
had in the
Adventure of
the Braying,
etc.

warre, and if we will, we may adde a fift (that may serve for a second) to defend their Country. To these five capitall causes, may be joyned many others, just and reasonable, that may oblige men to take Armes: but to take them for trifles, and things that are rather fit for laughter and pastime then for any affront, it seemes that he who takes them, wants his judgement. Besides, to take an unjust revenge, (indeed nothing can be just by way of revenge) is directly against Gods Law which wee professe, in which we are commanded to doe well to our enemies, and good to those that hate us; a Commandement that though it seeme difficult to fulfill, yet it is not onely to those that know lesse of God then the world, and more of the flesh then the Spirit; for Iesus Christ, true God and man, who never lyed, neyther could, nor can, being our Law-giver, said that his yoke was sweet, and his burden light: so he would command us nothing that should be unpossible for us to fulfill. So that, my masters, you are tied both by Lawes Divine and humane to be pacified.

The Devill take mee (thought Sancho to himselfe at this instant) if this Master of mine be not a Divine, or if not, as like one as one egge is to another.

Don Quixote tooke breath a while, and seeing them still attentive, had proceeded in his discourse, but that Sancho's conceitednesse came betwixt him and home, who seeing his Master pawse, tooke his turne, saying:

My Master Don Quixote de la Mancha, sometimes called The Knight of the sorrowfull Countenance, and now The Knight of the Lyons, is a very judicious Gentleman, speakes Latin and his mother-tongue as well as a Bachelor of Arts, and in all he handleth or adviseth, proceeds like a man of Armes, and hath all the Lawes and Statutes of that you call Duell, *ad unguem*: therefore there is no more to bee done, but to governe your selves according to his direction, and let mee beare the blame if you doe amisse. Besides, as you are now told, tis a folly to be ashamed to heare one Bray; for I remember when I was a boy, I could have brayed at any time I listed, without any bodies hinderance,

HISTORIE OF DON QUIXOTE

which I did so truly and cunningly, that when I brayed, all the Asses in the Towne would answer me; and for all this, I was held to be the sonne of honest parents, and though for this rare quality I was envied by more then foure of the proudest of my parish, I cared not two strawes; and that you may know I say true, doe but stay and hearken, for this science is like swimming, once known, never forgotten, so clapping his hand to his nose he began to bray so strongly, that the vallies neere-hand resounded againe. But one of them that stood neerest him, thinking hee had flouted them, lifted up a good Batte he had in his hand, and gave him such a blow, that he tumbled him to the ground.

Don Quixote, that saw Sancho so evill intreated, set upon him that did it, with his Launce in his hand; but there came so many betwixt them, that it was not possible for him to bee revenged: rather seeing a cloud of stones comming towards himselfe, and that a thousand bent Crosse-bowes began to threaten him, and no lesse quantity of gunnes; turning Rozinantes reines, as fast as he could gallop, he got from among them, recommending himselfe heartily to God, to free him from that danger, and fearing every foot, lest some bullet should enter him behinde, and come out at his brest: so he still went fetching his breath, to see if it failed him. But they of the squadron were satisfied when they saw him flie, and so shot not at him. Sancho they set upon his Asse, (scarce yet come to himselfe) and let him go after his Master, not that he could tell how to guide him: but Dapple followed Rozinantes steppes, without whom he was nobody.

Don Quixote being now a pretty way off, looked backe, and saw that Sancho was comming, and marked that nobody followed him. Those of the squadron were there till darke night, and because their enemies came not to battell with them, they returned home to their towne, full of mirth and jollity: and if they had knowne the ancient custome of the Grecians, they would have raised a Trophy in that place.

THE SECOND PART OF THE

CHAPTER XXVIII

Of things that Benengeli relates, which he that reades shall know, if he read them with attention.

HEN the Valiant man turnes his backe, the advantage over him is manifest, and it is the part of wise men to reserve themselves to better occasions. This truth was verified in Don Quixote, who giving way to the fury of the people, and to the ill intentions of that angry squadron, tooke his heeles, and without remembring Sancho, or the danger he had left him in, got himselfe so farre as he might seeme to be safe. Sancho followed layd a-thwart upon his Asse, as hath been said. At last he overtook him, being now come to himself, and comming neere, he fell off his Dapple at Rozinantes feet, all sorrowfull, bruised and beaten. Don Quixote alighted to search his wounds, but finding him whole from top to toe, very angrily he said, You must Bray with a plague to you, and where have you found that tis good naming the Halter in the hanged mans house ? to your braying musick, what counterpoint could you expect but Bat-blowes ? And, Sancho, you may give God thankes, that since they blessed you with a cudgell, they had not made the *Per signum crucis* on you with a Scimitar.

I know not what to answer (quoth Sancho) for me-thinkes I speake at my backe, pray let's bee gone from hence, and Ile no more braying : yet I cannot but say, that your Knight Errants can flye, and leave their faithfull Squires to bee bruised like Privet by their enemies.

212

HISTORIE OF DON QUIXOTE

To **retire, is** not to flye (said Don Quixote) for know, Sancho, that Valour that is not founded upon the Basis of Wisedome, is stiled Temerity, and the rash mans actions are rather attributed to good fortune, then courage. So that I confesse I retired, but fledde not, and in this have imitated many valiant men, that have reserved themselves for better times; and Histories are full of these, which because now they would be tedious to me, and unprofitable to thee, I relate them not at present.

CHAPTER XXVIII

Of things that Benengeli relates, which he that reades shall know, if he read them with attention.

By this time Sancho, with Don Quixote's help, got to horse; and Don Quixote mounted Rozinante, and by little and little, they had gotten into a little Elme-grove, some quarter of a league off: now and then Sancho would fetch a most deep Heigho, and dolorous sighes. And Don Quixote demanding the reason of his pittifull complaints, he said, that from the point of his backe-bone, to the top of his crowne, he was so sore, that he knew not what to doe. The cause of that paine undoubtedly (quoth Don Quixote) is, that as the cudgell with which they banged thee was long and slender, it lighted upon those parts of thy backe all along, that greeve thee; and if it had beene thicker, it had grieved thee more. Truely (quoth Sancho) you have resolved mee of a great doubt, and in most delicate tearmes declared it to me. Body of me, was the cause of my griefe **so** concealed, that you must needs tell me that all of me was sore where the cudgell lighted? If my ankles did paine **me,** I warrant, you would riddle the cause of it; but tis **poore** riddling to tell that my brusing grieves me. Yfaith, **yfaith,** Master mine, other mens ills are slightly regarded, and **every day I** discover land, and see how little I can expect **from** your service; for if at this time you suffered me to be dry-beaten, we shal come a hundred and a hundred times to the Blanket-tossing you wotte of, and other childish trickes, which if they now lighted on my shoulders, they will after come out at mine eyes. It were a great deale better for mee, but that I am a beast, and shall never do ought well while I live. It were a great deale better (I say againe) for me to get mee home to my Wife and Children, to main-

213

CHAPTER
XXVIII

Of things that
Benengeli
relates, which
he that reades
shall know, if
he read them
with atten-
tion.

taine and bring them up with that little God hath given
me, and not to follow you up and downe these by-waies,
drinking ill, and eating worse. And for your bedde, good
honest Squire, even count mee out seven foot of good earth;
and if you will have any more, take as many more; for you
may feed at pleasure, stretch your selfe at your ease. I
would the first that made stitch in Knight Errantry were
burned, or beaten to powder, or at least hee that first would
be Squire to such fooles, as all your Knight-Errants in
former times have beene, of the present I say nothing; for
your selfe being one, I respect them, and because I know
that you know an Ace more then the Devill in all you
speake or thinke.

I durst venter a good wager with thee, Sancho, quoth
Don Quixote, that now thou talkest and no body controules
thee, thou feelest no paine in all thy body: Talke on, childe
mine, all that is in thy minde, or comes to thy mouth, for
so thou beest not griev'd, I will be pleased with the distaste that thy impertinencies might give mee. And if you
desire so much to bee at home with your wife and children,
God forbid I should gainesay it: you have money of mine,
and see how long tis since our third sally from home,
and how much is due to you for every moneth, and pay
your selfe.

When I served (quoth Sancho) Tomè Carrasco, Father to
the Bachelor Carrasco, whom you know well, I had two
Ducats a moneth besides my victuals: of you I know not
how much I shall have, though I am sure it is a greater
toyle to be a Squire to a Knight Errant, then to serve a
rich Husbandman; for indeed, we that serve Husbandmen,
though wee labour never so much in the day time, if the
worst come to the worst, at night we sup with the Pottage-
pot, and lye in a bed, which I have not done ever since I
served you, except it were that short time wee were at Don
Diego de Miranda's house, and after when I had the cheere
of the skimmings of Camacho's pots, and when I ate and
drunke and slept at Basilius his house; all the rest hath
been upon the cold ground, to the open ayre, and subject,

214

HISTORIE OF DON QUIXOTE

as you **would** say, to the inclemencies of the heavens, onely living upon bits of cheese, and scraps of bread, and drinking water, sometimes of brookes, sometimes of springs, which we met withall by the waies we went.

I confesse, Sancho, (quoth Don Quixote) that all thou sayest may be true; how much more thinkest thou should I give thee, then Tomè Carrasco?

You shall please me (quoth Sancho) with twelve-pence more a moneth, and that concerning my wages for my service; but touching your word and promise you gave mee, that I should have the Government of an Iland, it were fit you added the tother three shillings, which in all make up fifteene.

It is very well, **said** Don Quixote, **and** according to the wages that you have allotted unto your selfe, it is now twenty **five** daies since our last sallie, reckon, Sancho, so much for so much, and see how much is due to you, and pay your selfe, as I have bidden you.

Body of mee (said Sancho) you are cleane out of the reckoning; for touching the promise of governing the Iland, you must reckon from the time you promised, til this present. Why, how long is it (quoth hee) since I promised it? If I be not forgetfull (said Sancho) it is now some twenty yeeres, wanting two or three dayes. Don Quixote gave himselfe a good clappe on the forehead, and began to laugh heartily, saying, Why, my being about Sierra Morena, and **our** whole travels were in lesse then two Moneths, and dost thou say it was twenty yeeres since I promised thee the Iland? I **am** now **of** opinion, that thou wouldst have all the mony thou **hast of** mine, consumed in paying thee wages: which if it **be so, and** that thou art so minded, from hence-forward take it, much good may it doe thee; for so I may not be troubled with such a Squire, I shall be glad to be poore, **and** without a farthing. But tell mee, thou Prevaricator of **the** Squirely lawes of Knight-Errantry, where hast thou ever seene or read of any Squire belonging to Knight Errant, that hath capitulated with his Master, to give him thus much or so much? Lanch, lanch, thou base lewd fellow,

CHAPTER
XXVIII
Of things that
Benengeli
relates, which
he that reades
shall know, if
he read them
with atten-
tion.

215

CHAPTER
XXVIII

Of things that
Benengeli
relates, which
he that reades
shall know, if
he read them
with atten-
tion.

*A Tricke to
give a tucke
with the
thumbe upon
ones lip, as
fresh men
are used in a
Vniversity.

thou Hobgoblin; Lanch, I say, into the *Mare magnum*
of their Histories; and if thou finde that any Squire have
sayd, or so much as imagined, what thou hast sayd, I will
give thee leave to brand my fore-head, and to boot, to seale
me with *foure tuckes in the mouth: Turne thy reines, or
thine Asses halter, and get thee to thy house, for thou shalt
not goe a step further with me. Oh ill-given bread, and
ill-placed promises! Oh man more beast then man! now
when I thought to have put thee into a fortune, and such
a one, that in spite of thy wife, thou shouldest have beene
stiled, 'My Lord': Thou leavest me? Now doest thou goe,
when I had a purpose to have made thee Lord of the best
Iland in the world? Well, well, as thou thy selfe hast sayd
many times; The hony is not for the Asses mouth: An Asse
thou art, an Asse thou wilt be, and an Asse thou shalt die,
and till then wilt thou remaine so, before thou fallest into
the reckoning that thou art a beast.

Sancho beheld Don Quixote earnestly, all the while hee
thus rated him, and was so mooved, that the teares stood in
his eyes, and with a dolorous low voyce hee sayd; Master
mine, I confesse that, to be altogether an Asse, I want nothing but a taile: if you will put one on me, I will be contented, and will serve you like an Asse all dayes of my life.
Pardon me, Sir, and pitty my youth, and consider my folly;
for if I speake much, it proceedes rather out of simplicity
then knavery. 'Who erres and mends, to God himselfe
commends.'

I would be sorry, little Sancho, (quoth Don Quixote)
but that thou shouldst mingle some by-pretty Proverb
in thy Dialogue. Well, Ile pardon thee for this once,
upon condition heereafter thou mend, and shew not thy
selfe so covetous, but that thou rouze up thy spirits, and
encourage thy selfe with hope of the accomplishment of
my promise; For better late then not at all. Sancho
answered him, he would; though it were to make a vertue
of necessity.

Heereupon they put into the Elme-grove, and Don
Quixote got to the foot of an Elme, and Sancho to the

foot of a Beech; for these kind of trees and such like, have
alwaies feet, but no hands. Sancho had an ill night on
it; for his Bat-blow made him more sensible in the cold.
Don Quixote fell into his usuall imaginations: yet they
both slept, and by day-peepe they were on their way,
searching after the famous bankes of Heber, where
they happened upon what shall be told in
the ensuing Chapter.

CHAPTER XXIX

Of the famous Adventure of the Enchanted
Barke.

 ON QUIXOTE and Sancho, by their com-
putation, two dayes after they were out
of the Elme-grove, came to the River
Heber, whose sight was very delightsome
to Don Quixote; for first he contem-
plated on the amenity of those bankes,
the cleernesse of the water, the gentle
current, and the abundancy of the liquid
Cristall, whose pleasing sight brought a thousand amorous
thoughts into his head, especially hee fell to thinke what he
had scene in Montesino's Cave: for though Master Peters
Ape had told him, that part of it was true, and part false,
he leaned more to the truth then to the other, contrary to
Sancho, who held all, as false as Falshood it selfe.

As they were thus going on, Don Quixote might see a
little Boat, without oares or any other kinde of tackling,
which was tied by the brinke of the River, to a trees stump
on the banke. Don Quixote looked round-about him, but
could see no body; so, without more adoe, hee alighted from
Rozinante, and commanded Sancho to doe the like from
Dapple, and that he should tye both the Beasts very well,

CHAPTER
XXIX

Of the famous
Adventure
of the
Enchanted
Barke.

to the root of an Elme or Willow there. Sancho demanded of him the cause of that sudden lighting, and of that tying. Don Quixote made answer; Know, Sancho, that this Boat thou seest directly (for it can bee nothing else) cals and invites me to goe and enter into it, to give ayde to some Knight, or other Personage of ranke and note, that is in distresse: for this is the stile of bookes of Knight-hood, and of Enchanters that are there intermingled, that when any Knight is in some danger, that he cannot bee freed from it, but by the hand of some other Knight, although the one bee distant from the other, two or three thousand leagues or more, they either snatch him into a cloud, or provide him a Boat to enter in, and in the twinkling of an eye, either carry him thorow the aire, or thorow the sea, as they list, and where his assistance is needfull; so that, Sancho, this Boat is put heere to the same effect, and this is as cleare as day, and before wee goe, tye Dapple and Rozinante together, and let's on in Gods Name: for I will not faile to imbarke my selfe, though Bare-foot Friers should intreat me.

Well, seeing tis so (sayd Sancho) and that you will every foot run into these (I know not what I shall call them) fopperies, there's no way but to obey, and lay downe the necke, according to the Proverbe; Doe as thy Master commands thee, and sit downe at Table with him: But for all that, for discharge of my conscience, let me tell you, that (me thinkes) that is no Enchanted Boat, but one that belongs to some Fisher-men of the River; for heere the best Saboga's in the world are taken.

This he spoke whilst he was tying his Beasts, leaving them to the protection and defence of Enchanters, which greeved him to the soule. Don Quixote bad him he should not bee troubled for the leaving those beasts; for hee that should carry them thorow such longinque wayes and regions, would also looke to the other. I understand not your Lognicke (quoth Sancho) neither have I heard such a word in all the dayes of my life. Longinque (sayd Don Quixote) that is, farre, remote: and no marvell thou understandest not that word, for thou art not bound to the understanding of Latin,

218

HISTORIE OF DON QUIXOTE

though yee have some that presume to know when they are ignorant. Now they are bound (sayd Sancho) what shall we doe next?

CHAPTER
XXIX
Of the famous
Adventure
of the
Enchanted
Barke.

What? (sayd Don Quixote) blesse our selves and weigh anchor, I meane, let us imbarke our selves, and cut the rope by which this boat is tyed: so leaping into it, and Sancho following him, he cut the cord, and the Boat faire and softly fell off from the Banke; and when Sancho saw himselfe about a two rods length within the River, hee began to tremble, fearing his perdition: but nothing so much troubled him, as to heare Dapple bray, and to see that Rozinante struggled to unloose himselfe: and hee told his Master; Dapple brayes and condoles for our absence, Rozinante strives to bee at liberty, to throw himselfe after us. Oh most deare friends, remaine you there in safety, and may the madnesse that severs us from you, converted into repentance, bring us back to your Presence: and with that he began to weep so bitterly, that Don Quixote, all moody and cholericke, began to cry out; What makes thee feare, thou cowardly Impe? what cryest thou for, thou heart of curds? who persecutes thee? who baites thee, thou soule of a Milk-sop? or what wantest thou in the middest of all abundance? art thou happily to goe bare-foot over the Riphæan mountaines? Rather upon a seat like an Arch-Duke, thorow the calme current of this delightfull River: from whence we shall very quickly passe into the maine sea but hitherto wee have gone and sayled some seven or eight hundred leagues, and if I had an Astrolabe heere, to take the height of the Pole, I could tell thee how farre wee have gone, though, either my knowledge is small, or wee have now, or shall quickly passe the Æquinoctiall Line, which divides and cuts the two contraposed Poles in equall distance.

And when you come to this Line you speake of, how farre shall we have gone? A great way (answered Don Quixote:) For of three hundred and sixty degrees, which the whole Globe containeth of Land and water, according to Ptolomies Computation, who was the greatest Cosmographer knowne, we shall have gone the halfe, when we come to the Line I

CHAPTER
XXIX
Of the famous
Adventure
of the
Enchanted
Barke.

*Mistakes of
the words,
Ptolomeo and
Computo : for
so it is in the
Spanish.

have told you of. Verily (quoth Sancho) you have brought
me a pretty witnesse, to confirme your saying, *To ly my
and Comtation, and I know not what. Don Quixote
laught at Sancho's interpretation he had given to the name,
and to the Computation and account of the Cosmographer
Ptolomeus, and sayd to him ; You shall understand, Sancho,
that when the Spanyards, and those that imbarke themselves at Cadiz, to goe to the East Indies, one of the greatest
signes they have, to know whether they have passed the
Æquinoctiall, is, that all men that are in the ship, their
Lice dye upon them, and not one remains with them, nor
in the Vessell, though they would give their waight in
gold for him : so that, Sancho, thou mayst put thy hand to
thy thigh, and if thou meet with any live thing, we shall be
out of doubt ; if thou findest nothing, then we have passed
the Line.

I cannot beleeve any of this, quoth Sancho : but yet I will
doe what you will have mee, though I know no necessity for
these trials ; since I see with these eyes, that we have not
gone five rods lengths from the Banke ; for there Rozinante
and Dapple are, in the same places where we left them, and
looking well upon the matter, as I now doe, I sweare by Me,
that wee neither moove nor goe faster then an Ant.

Make the triall that I bade you, and care for no other ;
for thou knowest not, what Columnes are, what Lines, Paralels, Zodiacks, Clipticks, Poles, Solstices, Æquinoctials,
Planets, Signes, Poynts, and Measures, of which the Celestiall and Terrestriall Spheres are composed : for if thou
knewest all these, or any part of them, thou mightst plainely
see what Paralels wee have cut, what Signes we have seene,
and what Images we have left behinde, and are leaving now.
And let me wish thee againe, that thou search and feele thy
selfe : for I doe not thinke, but that thou art as cleane as a
sheet of white smooth paper.

Sancho began to feele, and comming softly and warily
with his hand to the left side of his necke, hee lifted up
his head, and sayd to his Master ; Either your experience
is false, or else we are not come neere the place you speake

220

HISTORIE OF DON QUIXOTE

CHAPTER
XXIX
Of the famous
Adventure
of the
Enchanted
Barke.

of, by many leagues. **Why** (quoth Don Quixote) hast thou met with some thing? I, with some things, (sayd hee) and shaking his fingers, hee washed his whole hand in the river; by which, and in the Current, the boat softly slid along, without being mooved by any secret influence, or hidden Enchantment, but the very course it selfe of the water, as yet soft and easie.

By this they discovered two great water-mils in the midst of the River: and Don Quixote, as soone as hee saw them, cried aloud to Sancho; Seest thou, Friend, that City, Castle, **or** Fortresse that shewes it selfe, where some Knight is sure oppressed, or some Queene or Princesse in ill plight, for whose succour I am brought hither?

What the Devill of City, Castle, or Fortresse, Sir, doe you talke of (quoth Sancho)? doe you not see that those are water-mils in the River to grinde corne? Peace, Sancho (sayd hee) for though they looke like Water-mills, yet they **are** not, and I have told thee already, that these Enchant-**ments** chop and change things out of their naturall being: I say **not** that they change them out of one being into another really, but in appearance, as was seene by experience in the transformation of Dulcinea, the onely refuge of my hopes.

Now the Boat being gotten into the middest of the Current, began to moove somewhat faster then before. They of the Mills, that saw the Boat come downe the river, and that it was now even gotten into the swift streame of the wheeles, many of them came running out with long poles to stay it: and as their faces and clothes were all covered with meale-dust, they made a strange shew, and cryed out, saying; Devils of men, whither goe you? Are you mad to drowne your selves, **or** bee beaten to pieces against these wheeles?

Did not I **tell** thee, Sancho (sayd Don Quixote) then, that we should come where I should shew the force of mine Arme? look what wicked uncouth fellowes come to encounter mee; looke what a troope of Hobgoblins oppose themselves against mee; looke what ugly visages play the

CHAPTER
XXIX
Of the famous
Adventure
of the
Enchanted
Barke.

Bull-beggers with us : Now you shall see, you Rascals ; and standing up in the Boat, he began aloud to threaten the Millers, saying ; You base Scumme and ill-advised, free and deliver that person, which is in your Fortresse or Prison opprest, bee hee high or low, or of what sort or quality soever ; for I am Don Quixote de la Mancha, otherwise called, The Knight of the Lyons, for whom the happy ending of this Adventure is reserved by order of the high Heavens : and this sayd, hee layd hand to his sword, and beganne to fence in the aire against the Millers, who hearing, but not understanding those madnesses, stood with their poles to stay the Boat, which was now entring the source and channell of the wheeles. Sancho kneeled devoutly upon his knees, praying Heaven to free him from so manifest a danger, which succeeded happily, by the quicknesse and skill of the Millers, who opposing their staves to the Boat, stayd it : but so, that they overturned it, and Don Quixote and Sancho topted into the River : but it was well for Don Quixote, who could swimme like a Goose, though the waight of his Armes carried him twice to the bottome, and had it not beene for the Millers, who leaped into the water, and pulled them out both, as if they had waighed them up, there they had both perished.

When they were both on land, more wet then thirsty, Sancho, upon his knees, with joyned hands, and his eyes nailed to Heaven, prayed to God with a large and devout prayer, to free him from thence-forward, from the rash desires and enterprizes of his Master. And now the Fishermen came, the Owners of the Boat, which was broken to pieces by the wheeles, who seeing it spoyled, began to disrobe Sancho, and to demand payment of Don Quixote, who very patiently, as if he had done nothing, sayd to the Millers and Fisher-men, that hee would very willingly pay for the Boat, upon condition they should freely deliver him, without fraud or guile, the person or persons that were oppressed in their Castle.

What person, or what Castle mad-man ? (sayd one of the Millers) will you, trow, carry away those that came hither

HISTORIE OF DON QUIXOTE

to grinde their corne? Enough, thought Don Quixote to himselfe, here a man may preach in a wildernes, to reduce a base people to a good worke. In this Adventure two deep Enchanters have met, and the one disturbes the other: the one provided me the Barke, and the other overthrew me out of it; God helpe us, all this world is tricks and devices, one contrary to the other; I can doe no more: and raising his voyce, he went on, saying; Friends, whosoever you are, locked up in this prison, pardon mee; for, by my ill fortune and yours, I cannot deliver you from your pain: this Adventure is kept and reserved for some other Knight. When he had said this, he agreed with the fishers, and paid 25 shillings for the boat, which Sancho gave with a very good will, saying, With two of these boat-trickes we shall sinke our whole stocke.

The Fishermen and the Millers were in a great admiration, to see two such strange shapes, quite from the ordinary fashion of other men, and never understood to what purpose Don Quixote used all those discourses to them; so holding them for maddemen, they left them, and got to their Milles, and the Fishers to their quarters. Don Quixote and Sancho like beastes turne to their beasts: and this end had the Adventure of the Enchanted Barke.

CHAPTER XXX

What happened to Don Quixote with the faire Huntresse.

ERY melancholy and ill at ease went the Knight and Squire to horse-backe, especially Sancho, for it grieved him at the soule to meddle with the stocke of their money; for it seemed to him, that to part with any thing from thence, was to part with his eye-balls. To be briefe, without speaking a word, to horse they went, and left the famous river. Don Quixote, buried in his amorous cogitations, and Sancho in those of his preferment; for as yet hee thought he was farre enough off from obtaining it: for although he were a foole, yet hee well perceived, that all his Masters actions, or the greatest part of them were idle; so hee sought after some occasion, that without entring into farther reckonings, or leave-taking with his Master, hee might one day get out of his clutches, and goe home, but fortune ordered matters contrary to his feare. It fell out then, that the next day about Sun-setting, and as they were going out of a wood, Don Quixote spreads his eyes about a green meadow, and at one end of it saw company, and comming neere, he saw they were Falconers; he came neerer, and amongst them beheld a gallant Lady upon her Palfrey, or milke-white Nagge, with greene furniture, and her Saddle-pummell of silver. The Lady her selfe was all clad in greene, so brave and rich, that bravery it selfe was transformed into her. On her left hand shee carried a Soare-Falcon, a signe that made Don Quixote think she was some great Lady, and Mistresse to all the rest, as true it was: so hee cried out to Sancho; Runne,

224

sonne Sancho, and tell **that** Lady on the Palfrey with the Soare-hawke, that I, **The** Knight of the Lyons, doe kisse her most beautifull hands ; and if her magnificence give me leave, I will receive her commands, and be her servant to the uttermost of my power, that her highnesse may please to command mee in; and take heede, Sancho, how thou speakest, and have a care thou mixe not thy Ambassage with some of those Proverbs of thine. Tell me of that ? as if it were now the first time that I have carried Embassies to high and mighty Ladies in my life? Except it were that thou carriedst to Dulcinea (quoth Don Quixote) I know not of any other thou hast carried, at least whilest thou wert with mee. That's true, said Sancho ; but a good pay-master needs no surety : and where there is plenty, the ghests are not empty, I meane, there is no telling nor advising mee ought; for of all things I know a little. I beleeve it (said Don Quixote) get thee gone in good time, and God speed thee.

Sancho went on, putting Dapple out of his pace with a Careere, and comming where the faire Huntresse was, alighting, he kneeled downe, and said ; Faire Lady, that Knight you see there, called The Knight of the Lyons, is my Master, and I am a Squire of his, whom at his house they call Sancho Pansa ; this said Knight of the Lyons, who not long since was called, The Knight of the sorrowfull Countenance, sends me to tell your Greatnesse, That you be pleased to **give** him leave, that with your liking, good will, and consent, he put in practice his desire, which is no other (as he sayes, and I beleeve) then to serve your *lofty high-flying beauty ; and if your Ladiship give him leave, you shall doe a thing **that** may redound to your good, and hee shall receive a most remarkeable favour and content.

Truely, honest Squire, said the Lady, thou hast delivered thy Ambassage with all the circumstances that such an Ambassage requires : rise, rise, for the Squire of so renowned a Knight as he **of** the sorrowfull countenance (of whom **wee** have heere speciall notice) tis not fit should kneele : rise up friend, and tell your Master that he come neere on Gods

3 : FF

THE SECOND PART OF THE

CHAPTER
XXX

What hap-
pened to Don
Quixote with
the faire
Huntresse.

name, that the Duke my Husband and I may doe him service
at a house of pleasure we have heere.

Sancho rose up astonisht, as well at the good Ladies
beauty, as her court-ship and courtesie, especially for that
shee told him she had notice of his Master, The Knight of
the sorrowfull Countenance ; for in that she called him not
Knight of the Lyons, it was because it was so lately put
upon him.   The Duchesse asked him (for as yet we know not
of what place shee was Duchesse) tell me, Sir Squire, is not
this your Master, one, of whom there is a History printed,
and goes by the name of, *The ingenious Gentleman, Don
Quixote de la Mancha*, the Lady of whose life is likewise, one
Dulcinea del Toboso?   The very self-same (said Sancho)
and that Squire of his, that is, or should be in the History,
called Sancho Pansa, am I, except I were changed in my
cradle, I mean that I were changed in the Presse.   I am glad
of all this (quoth the Duchesse :) goe, brother Pansa, and
tell your Master that he is welcome to our Dukedome, and
that no newes could have given me greater content.   Sancho
with this so acceptable an answer, with great pleasure returned to his Master, to whom he recounted all that the
great Lady had said to him, extolling to the heavens her
singular beauty, with his rusticall tearmes, her affablenesse
and courtesie.   Don Quixote pranked it in his saddle, sate
stiffe in his stirrops, fitted his Visor, rowsed up Rozinante, and
with a comely boldnesse went to kisse the Duchesses hands,
who causing the Duke her husband to be called, told him,
whilest Don Quixote was comming, his whole Embassie : so
both of them having read his first part, and understood by
it his besotted humour, attended him with much pleasure
and desire to know him, with a purpose to follow his humour,
and to give way to al he should say, and to treat with him
as a Knight Errant, as long as he should be with them, with
all the accustomed ceremonies in bookes of Knight Errantry,
which they had read, and were much affected with.

By this, Don Quixote came with his Visor pulled up, and
making shew to alight, Sancho came to have held his stirrop :
but he was so unlucky, that as hee was lighting from Dapple,

226

HISTORIE OF DON QUIXOTE

one of his feet caught upon a halter of the packe-saddle, so that it **was** not possible for him to dis-intangle himself, but hung by it, with his mouth and his brest to the ground-ward. Don Quixote, who used not to alight without his stirrops being held, thinking Sancho was already come to hold it, lighted sodainely downe, but brought saddle and all to ground, (belike being ill-girt) to his much shame, and curses inwardly layd upon the unhappy Sancho, that had still his legge in the stockes. The Duke commanded some of his Falconers to helpe the Knight and Squire, who raised Don Quixote in ill plight with his fall, and limping, as well as he could, he went to kneele before the two Lordings : but the Duke would not by any meanes consent, rather alighting from his horse, he embraced Don Quixote, saying :

I am very sorry, Sir Knight of the sorrowfull Countenance, that your first fortune hath beene so ill in my ground ; but the carelesnesse of Squires is oft the cause of worse successes. It is impossible, valerous Prince, that any should be bad, since I have seene you, although my fal had cast me to the profound Abisme ; since the glory of seeing you would have drawne mee out, and raised mee up. My Squire (a curse light on him) unties his tongue better to speake maliciously, then hee girts his horses saddle to sit firmely : but howsoever I am downe or up, on foot or on horsebacke, I will alwaies bee **at** yours, and my Lady the Duchesses service, your worthy Consort, the worthie Lady of beauty, and universall Princesse of courtesie. Softly, my Signior (Don Quixote de la Mancha) quoth the Duke, for where my Lady Dulcinea del Toboso is present, there is **no reason** other beauties should be praised.

Now **Sancho** Pansa was free from **the** noose, and being at hand, **before his** Master could answer a word, he said, It **cannot be denied,** but affirmed, that my Lady Dulcinea del **Toboso is very faire** ; but where we least thinke, there **goes the Hare away** : for I have heard say, that shee you **call Nature, is like a** Potter that makes vessels of Clay, **and he that makes a handsome** vessell, may also make two **or three, or an hundred : this I** say, that you may know, **my Lady**

CHAPTER
XXX
What happened to Don Quixote with the faire Huntresse.

227

CHAPTER
.XXX
What hap-
pened to Don
Quixote with
the faire
Huntresse.

the Dutchesse comes not a whit behinde my Mistresse the Lady Dulcinea del Toboso. Don Quixote turned to the Duchesse, and said, Your Greatnesse may suppose that never any Knight in the world had ever such a prater to his Squire, nor a more conceited then mine, and he will make good what I say, if your Highnesse shall at any time be pleased to make triall. To which (quoth the Duchesse) that honest Sancho may be conceited, I am very glad, a signe hee is wise ; for your pleasant conceits, Signior, as you very wel know, rest not in dull braines, and since Sancho is witty and conceited, from hence-forward I confirme him to be discreet : And a Prater, added Don Quixote. So much the better (said the Duke) for many conceits cannot be expressed in few words : and that we may not spend the time in many, come, Sir Knight of the sorrowfull Countenance : of the Lyons, your Highnesse must say (quoth Sancho :) for now we have no more sorrowfull countenance. And now let the Lyons beare countenance. The Duke proceeded : I say let the Knight of the Lyons come to my Castle, which is neere heere, where he shall have the entertainment that is justly due to so high a personage, and that, that the Duchesse and I are wont to give to Knights Errant that come to us.

By this time Sancho had made ready and girded Rozinantes saddle well ; and Don Quixote mounting him, and the Duke upon a goodly horse, set the Duchesse in the middle, and they went toward the Castle. The Duchesse commanded that Sancho should ride by her, for she was infinitely delighted to heare his discretions. Sancho was easily entreated, and weaved himselfe betweene the three, and made a fourth in their conversation. The Duke and Duchesse were much pleased, who held it for a great good fortune, to have lodged in their Castle such a Knight Errant and such a Squire Erred.

CHAPTER XXXI

That treates of many and great affaires.

REAT was the joy that **Sancho** conceived to see himselfe a favourite to the Duchesse, as he thought ; **for it** shaped out unto him, that he should finde in her Castle, as much as in Don Diego's, or that of Basilius : for he was alwaies affected with a plentifull life, and so layd hold upon Occasions locke, ever when it was presented. The History then tells us, that before they came to the house of pleasure or Castle, the Duke went before, and gave order to all his followers how they should behave themselves towards Don Quixote, who as he came on with the Duchesse to the Castle gates, there came out two Lackeyes, or Palfrey-boyes, clothed down to the feete in coates like night-gownes, of fine Crimson Sattin, and taking Don Quixote in their armes, without hearing or looking on him, they said, Goe, and let your Greatnesse help my Lady to alight. Don Quixote did so, and there was great complementing betwixt both about it : but in the end, the Duchesses earnestnesse prevailed, and shee would not descend or alight from her Palfrey, but in the Dukes armes, saying ; That shee was too unworthy to bee so unprofitable a burden to so high a Knight. At length the Duke helped her, and as they entred a great Base Court, there came two beautiful Damozels, and cast upon Don Quixote's shoulders, a faire mantle of finest Scarlet, and in an instant all the leads of the Courts and entries were thronged with men and maide-servants of the Dukes, who cried aloud ; Welcome, oh Flower and Creame of Knights Errant, and all or most of them sprinkled pots of sweet water upon Don Quixote, and upon the Duke, all which made Don Quixote admire, and never till then did he truly

believe that he was a Knight Errant, really and not fantasti-
cally, seeing that he was used just as hee had read Knights
Errant were in former times.

Sancho, forsaking Dapple, shewed himselfe to the Duchesse,
and entered into the Castle, but his conscience pricking him,
that he had left his Asse alone, he came to a reverend old
waiting woman, that came out amongst others to wait upon
the Duchesse, and very softly spoke to her, Mistresse Gon-
salez, or what is your name forsooth ? Donna Rodriguez de
Grishalva, said the waiting woman, what would you have,
brother, with me ? To which (quoth Sancho) I pray will
you doe me the favour as to goe out at the Castle-gate,
where you shall finde a Dapple Asse of mine, I pray will you
see him put, or put him your selfe in the stable ; for the
poore wretch is fearefull, and cannot by any meanes endure
to be alone. If the Master (quoth she) be as wise as the man,
we shall have a hot bargaine on it : get you gone with a
Murrin to you, and him that brought you hither, and looke
to your Asse your selfe, for the waiting women in this house
are not used to such drudgeries. Why truly (quoth Sancho)
I have heard my Master say, who is the very Wizard of
Histories, telling that story of Lanzarote, when he came
from Britaine, that Ladies looked to him, and waiting
women to his Courser : and touching my Asse in particular,
I would not change him for Lanzarotes horse. Brother
(quoth she) if you be a Iester, keepe your witte till you have
use of it, for those that will pay you ; for I have nothing but

this *figge to give you. Well yet (said Sancho) the figge
is like to be ripe, for you will not lose the *Prima vista* of
your yeeres by a peepe lesse. Sonne of a whore, said the
waiting-woman all incensed with choller, whether I am olde
or no, God knowes, I shall give him account, and not to thee,
thou rascall, that stinkest of Garlicke : all this shee spoke so
loud, that the Duchesse heard her, who turning, and seeing
the woman so altered, and her eyes so bloudy red, she asked
her with whom she was angry ?

Here (said shee) with this Ideot, that hath earnestly
entreated me to put up his Asse in the stable, that is at the

HISTORIE OF DON QUIXOTE

Castle-gate, giving mee for **an** instance, that they have done so I know not where, that certaine Ladies looked to one Lanzarote, and waiting women to his horse, and to mend the matter, in mannerly tearms cals me *old one. That wold more disgrace me (quoth the Duchesse) then all he should say, and speaking to Sancho, shee said, Looke you friend Sancho, Donna Rodriguez is very young, and that Stole she weares, is more for authority, and for the fashion, then for her yeeres. A pox on the rest of my yeeres I have to live (quoth Sancho) if I meant her any ill, I onely desired the kindnesse, for the love I beare to mine Asse, and because I thought I could not recommend him to a more charitable person, then Mistris Rodriguez. Don Quixote, that heard all, sayd; Are these discourses, Sancho, fit for this place? Sir (sayd Sancho) let every man expresse his wants wheresoere he be. Heere I remembred my Dapple, and heere I spoke of him, and if I had remembred him in **the** stable, there I would have spoken.

**Vieja:* a
name that a
woman in
Spain can not
endure to
heare though
shee were as
old as Methu-
salem.

To this (quoth the Duke) Sancho is in the right, and there is no reason to blame him. Dapple shall have provander, as much as he will, and let Sancho take no care, he shall be used as well as his owne person. With these discourses, pleasing unto all but Don Quixote, they went up staires, and brought Don Quixote into a goodly Hall, hung with rich cloth of Gold and Tissue, six Damozels un-armed him, and served for Pages, all of them taught and instructed by the Duke and Dutchesse, what they should doe, and how they should behave themselves towards Don Quixote, that hee might imagine and see they used him like a Knight Errant.

Don Quixote once un-armed, was in his straight trouses and doublet of Chamois, dry, high, and lanke, with his jawes, that within and without bussed one another; a picture, that if the Damozels that served him, had not had a care to hold in their laughter (which was one of the precise orders their Lords had given them) had burst with laughing. They desired him to unclothe himselfe, to shift a shirt: but he would by no meanes consent, saying; That honesty was as

231

CHAPTER XXXI

That treates of many and great affaires.

proper to a Knight Errant, as valour. Notwithstanding, hee bad them give a shirt to Sancho : and locking himselfe up with him in a chamber, where was a rich bed, hee pluckt off his clothes, and put on the shirt ; and as Sancho and he were alone, he thus spoke to him :

Tell me (moderne Iester and old Iolt-head) is it a fit thing, to dishonour and affront so venerable an old waiting-woman, and so worthy to be respected, as she ? Was that a fit time to remember your Dapple ? Or thinke you, that these were Lords to let Beasts fare ill, that so neatly use their Masters? For Gods love, Sancho, looke to thy selfe, and discover not thy course thred, that they may see thou are not woven out of a base web. Know, Sinner as thou art, that the Master is so much the more esteemed, by how much his servants are honest, and mannerly ; and one of the greatest advantages that great men have over inferiours, is, that they keep servants as good as themselves. Know'st thou not, poore fellow, as thou art, and unhappy that I am, that if they see thee to bee a grosse Pesant, they will thinke that I am some Mountibanke, or shifting Squire ? No, no, friend Sancho, shun, shun these inconveniencies ; for he that stumbles too much upon the Prater and Wit-monger, at the first toe-knocke fals, and becomes a scornefull Iester : bridle thy tongue, consider and ruminate upon thy words, before they come from thee, and observe, that wee are now come to a place, from whence, with Gods helpe and mine armes valour, we shall goe bettered three-fold, nay, five-fold in fame and wealth.

Sancho promised him very truely, to sow up his mouth, or to bite his tongue, before he would speake a word that should not be well considered and to purpose, as he had commanded ; and that he should not feare, that by him they should ever bee discovered. Don Quixote dressed himselfe, buckled his sword to his belt, and clapped his skarlet mantle upon him, putting on a Hunters cap of greene sattin, which the Damozels had given him : and thus adorned to the great chamber he went, where he found the Damozels all in a row, six on one side, and six on the other, and all with provision

232

HISTORIE OF DON QUIXOTE

for him **to** wash, which **they** ministred to him with many courtesies and ceremonies.

Betwixt them straight they got him full of pompe and Majesty, and carried him **to** another roome, where was **a** rich table, with service for foure persons. The Duke and Dutchesse came to the doore to receive him, and with them a grave Clergy-man, *one of those that governe great mens houses, one of those, that as they are not borne nobly, so they know not how to instruct those that are : one of those that would have great mens liberalities, measured by the straightnesse of their mindes : of those, that teaching those they governe, to bee frugall, would make them miserable : such a one, I say, this grave Clergy-man was, that came with the Duke to receive Don Quixote ; there passed a thousand loving complements, and, at last, taking Don Quixote betweene them, they sate downe to dinner.

The Duke invited Don Quixote to the upper end of the table, which, though he refused ; yet the Duke so importuned him, that he was forced to take it. The Clergy-man sate over against him, and the Duke and Duchesse on each side. Sancho was by at all, gaping in admiration, to see the honour those Princes did to his Master, and seeing the many ceremonies and intreaties, that passed betwixt the Duke and him, to make him sit downe at the tables end, he sayd, If your Worships will give mee leave, Ile tell you a tale that happened in our towne, concerning places. Scarce had Sancho sayd this, when Don Quixote began to shake, beleeving certainely he would speake some idle speech. Sancho beholding, understood him, and sayd, Feare not, Sir, that I shall be unmannerly, or that I shall say any thing that may not bee to the purpose ; for I have not forgotten your counsell, touching speaking much or little, well or ill.

I remember nothing, Sancho (quoth Don Quixote) speake what thou wilt, **so** thou speake quickly. Well, what I shall speake (quoth Sancho) is as true, as my Master, Don Quixote, will not let me **lie,** who is heere present. For me (replide Don Quixote) lie **as** much as thou wilt, for Ile not hinder thee : but take heede what thou speakest. I have so heeded

3 : GG

CHAPTER
XXXI
That treates
of many and
great affaires.
and re-heeded it, that you shall see I warrant yee. Twere very fit (quoth Don Quixote) that your Greatnesses would command this Coxcombe to bee thrust out ; for he will talke you a thousand follies.

Assuredly (quoth the Duchesse) Sancho shall not stirre a jot from me; for I know, hee is very discreet. Discreet yeeres live your Holinesse (quoth Sancho) for the good opinion you have of me, although I deserve it not, and thus sayes my tale : A Gentle-man of our towne, very rich and well borne ; for hee was of the bloud of the Alami of Medina del Campo, and married with Donna Mencia de Quinnones, that was daughter to Don Alonso de Maranon, Knight of the order of Saint Iacques, that was drowned in the Herradura, touching whom that quarrell was not long since in our towne; for, as I remember, my Master, Don Quixote, was in it, where little
After he had
begun a tale
without head
or foot, hee
askes a
question.
Thomas the Mad-cap, sonne to Balvastro the Smith, was wounded. Is not all this true, Master mine? Say by your life, that these Lords may not hold me for a prating Lier.

Hitherto (sayd the Clergy-man) I rather hold thee for a Prater, then a Lier: but from henceforward, I know not for what I shall hold thee. Thou givest so many witnesses, and so many tokens, Sancho, that I cannot but say (quoth Don Quixote) thou tellest true: on with thy tale, and make an end; for I thinke thou wilt not have ended these two dayes. Let him goe on (quoth the Duchesse) to doe me a pleasure, and let him tell his tale, as he pleaseth, though hee make not an end these six dayes; for if they were so many yeeres, they would bee the best that ever I passed in my life.

I say then, my Masters, that the sayd Gentle-man I told you of at first, and whom I know, as well as I know one hand from another (for, from my house to his, tis not a bow-shoot) invited a poore, but honest Husband-man. On, Brother (sayd the Clergy-man) for, mee thinkes, you travell with your tale, as if you would not rest till the next world. In lesse then halfe this, I will, if it please God (quoth Sancho) and so I proceed : The sayd Husband-man comming to the

234

HISTORIE OF DON QUIXOTE

said Gentle-man Inviters house, (God be mercifull to him, for he is now dead) and for a further token, they say, died like a Lambe; for I was not by: for at that time I was gone to another towne to reaping.

I prethee (quoth the Clergy-man) come backe from your reaping, and without burying the Gentle-man (except you meane to make more obsequies) end your tale. The businesse then (quoth Sancho) was this, that both of them being ready to sit downe at table; for, me thinkes, I see them now, more then ever. The Dukes received great pleasure, to see the distaste that the Clergy-man tooke, at the delayes and pawses of Sancho's tale. And Don Quixote consumed himselfe in choller and rage. Then thus (quoth Sancho) both of them being ready to sit downe, the Husband-man contended with the Gentle-man not to sit uppermost, and he with the other, that he should, as meaning to command in his owne house: but the Husband-man presuming to be mannerly, and courteous, never would, till the Gentleman very moody, laying hands upon him, made him sit downe perforce, saying, Sit downe, you Thresher; for where-soere I sit, that shall be the Tables end to thee: and now you have my Tale, and truely I beleeve, it was brought in heere pretty-well to the purpose.

Don Quixote's face was in a thousand colours, that Iaspered upon his browe. The Lords dissembled their laughter, that Don Quixote might not be too much abashed, when they perceived Sancho's knavery: and to change discourse, that Sancho might not proceed with other fooleries, the Duchesse asked Don Quixote what newes he had of the Lady Dulcinea, and if hee had sent her for a Present lately, any Gyants, or Bug-beares, since he could not but have overcome many. To which Don Quixote answered, Lady mine; my misfortunes, although they had a beginning, yet they will never have ending: Gyants, Elves, and Bug-beares I have over-come and sent her; but where should they finde her that is enchanted, and turned into the foulest creature that can be? I know not (quoth Sancho) me-thinkes she is the fairest creature in the world, at least

CHAPTER XXXI

That treates of many and great affaires.

235

CHAPTER
XXXI
That treates
of many and
great affaires.

*A good
mistake.

I know well, that for her nimblenesse and leaping, *sheel'e give no advantage to a Tumbler: In good faith, my Lady Duchesse, shee leapes from the ground upon an Asse, as if she were a Catte. Have you scene her enchanted, Sancho? said the Duke. How? seene her? (quoth Sancho) Why, who the Devill but I was the first that fell into the tricke of her Enchantment? shee is as much Enchanted as my Asse.

The Clergy-man that heard them talke of Gyants, Elves, and Bug-beares, and Enchantments, fell into reckoning, that that was Don Quixote de la Mancha, whose story the Duke ordinarily read, and for which hee had divers times reprehended him, telling him, twas a madnesse to read such fopperies, and being assured of the certainty which he suspected, speaking to the Duke very angerly, hee said: Your Excellency ought to give God Almighty an account for this mans folly. This Don Quixote, or Don Coxe-combe, or how doe you call him, I suppose hee is not so very an Ideot as your Excellency would make him, giving him ready occasions to proceed in his empty-brain'd madnesse. And framing his discourse to Don Quixote, he said:

And who, good-man Dull-pate hath thrust into your braine, that you are a Knight Errant, that you overcome Gyants, and take Bug-beares? get you in Gods name, so be it spoken, return to your house, and bring up your children if you have them, and looke to your stocke, and leave your ranging thorow the world, blowing bubbles, and making all that know you, or not know you, to laugh. Where have you ever found with a mischiefe, that there have beene, or are Knights Errant? where any Gyants in Spaine? or Bug-beares in Mancha? or Enchanted Dulcinea's, with the rest of your troope of simplicities?

Don Quixote was very attentive to this Venerable mans discourse, and seeing him now silent, without any respect of the Dukes, with an angry countenance, he stood up and said, But his answer deserves a Chapter by it selfe.

HISTORIE OF DON QUIXOTE

CHAPTER XXXII

Of Don Quixotes answer to his Reprehender, with other successes as wise as witty.

ON QUIXOTE being thus upon his legges, and trembling from head to foot, like a man filled with quicke-silver, with a hasty and thicke voyce, said, The place, and Presence before whom I am, and the respect I have, and alwaies had to men of your Coat, do binde and tye up the hands of my just wrath; so that as well for what I have said, as for I know, all know that women, and gowned mens weapons are the same, their tongues: I will enter into single combat with you with mine, though I rather expected good counsaile from you, then infamous revilings; good and well-meant reprehensions require and aske other circumstances, other points; at least, your pub-like and so bitter reprehensions have passed all limits, and your gentle ones had beene better: neyther was it fit that without knowledge of the sinne you reprehend, you call the sinner without more adoe, Cox-combe and Ideot. Well, for which of my Coxcombries seene in mee, doe you con-demne and revile mee, and command me home to my owne house, to looke to the governing of it, my wife and children, without knowing whether I have any of these? Is there no more to be done, but in a hurry to enter other mens houses, to rule their owners? nay one that hath beene a poore Pedagogue, or hath not seene more world then twenty miles about him, to meddle so roundly to give Lawes to Chivalry, and to judge of Knights Errant? Is it happily a vaine plotte, or time ill spent, to range thorow the world, not seeking it's dainties, but the bitternesse of it, whereby good men aspire to the seat of immortality? If

Of Don
Quixotes
answer to his
Reprehender,
with other
successes as
wise as witty.

your Knights, your Gallants, or Gentlemen should have
called me Cox-comb, I should have held it for an affront
irreparable: but that your poore Schollers account mee a
madde-man, that never trod the paths of Knight Errantry,
I care not a chip; a Knight I am, a Knight Ile die, if it
please the most Highest. Some goe by the spacious field
of proud ambition, others by the way of servill and base
flattery, a third sort by deceitfull hypocrisie, and few by
that of true Religion: but I by my starres inclination goe
in the narrow path of Knight-Errantry; for whose exercise I
despise wealth, but not honor. I have satisfied grievances,
rectified wrongs, chastised insolencies, overcome Gyants,
trampled over Sprites; I am enamoured, onely because there
is a necessity Knights Errant should bee so, and though I
be so, yet I am not of those vicious Amorists, but of your
chaste Platonicks. My intentions alwaies aime at a good
end, as, to doe good to all men, and hurt to none: If he
that understands this, if he that performes it, that practiseth
it, deserve to be called foole, let your Greatnesses judge,
excellent Duke and Duchesse.

Well, I advise you (quoth Sancho) Master mine, speake no
more in your owne behalfe, for there is no more to bee said,
no more to be thought, no more persevering in the world:
besides, this Signior, denying as he hath done that there
neyther is, nor hath beene Knight Errant in the world, no marvell though hee knowes not what he hath said. Are you trow
(quoth the Clergy man) that Pansa, whom they say your
Master hath promised an Iland? Marry am I (said he) and
I am hee that deserves it, as well as any other, and I am he

*He blunders
out proverbs
as usually to
no purpose,
which is
Sancho's part
alwaies.

that *keepe company with good men, and thou shalt be as
good as they: and I am one of those that: Not with whom
thou wert bred, but with whom thou hast fedde: and of
those that: Leane to a good tree, and it will shadow thee:
I have leaned to my Master, and it is many moneths since I
have kept him company, and I am his other selfe. If God
please, live he, and I shall live, hee shall not want Empires
to command, nor I Islands to governe.

No surely, friend Sancho, straight, said the Duke, for I in
238

HISTORIE OF DON QUIXOTE

CHAPTER
XXXII

Of Don
Quixotes
answer to his
Reprehender,
with other
successes as
wise as witty.

Signior **Don Quixote's name,** will give thee **an** odde one of mine, of **no small worth.** Kneele downe, Sancho, quoth Don Quixote, **and kisse** his Excellencies foot, for the favour hee hath done thee: which Sancho did: but when the Cleargy-man saw this, **hee** rose up wonderfull angry, saying; By my holy Order, I am about to say, Your Excellency is as mad as one of these sinners, and see if they must not needs be madde, when wise men canonize their madnesse; your Excellency may doe well to stay with them, for whilest they be heere, Ile get mee home and save a labour of correcting what I cannot amend, and without any more adoe, leaving the rest of his dinner, he went away, the Duke and the Duchesse not being able to pacifie him, though the Duke said not much to him, **as** being hindred with laughter at his unseasonable choller.

When he had ended **his** laughter, **he** said to **Don** Quixote, Sir Knight of the Lyons, you have answered **so** deeply for **your** selfe, that you left nothing unsatisfied **to** this your **grievance,** which though it seeme to be one, yet **is** not; for **as women have** not the power to wrong, neyther have Church-men, **as** you best know. 'Tis true (quoth Don Quixote) **the** cause is, that hee who cannot be wronged, can doe no wrong to any body; women, children, and Churchmen, as they cannot defend themselves, when they are offended, so they cannot suffer an affront and a grievance, there is this difference (as your Excellency best knowes:) The affront comes from one that may doe it, and be able to make it good, the grievance **may** come from eyther party without affronting. For ex-**ample.** One stands carelesly in the street, some ten men come armed, and bastonadoing him, he claps hand to his sword, and doth his devoir: but the multitude of his assail-ants hinder him of his purpose, which is **to** bee revenged; this **man** is wronged, but **not** affronted, and this shal be confirmed by another example. One stands with his backe turned, another comes and strikes him, and when he hath done, runnes away, th'other followes, but overtakes him not: he that received the blow, is wronged, but not affronted, because the affront ought to have beene maintained: if he

239

CHAPTER
XXXII
Of Don
Quixotes
answer to his
Reprehender,
with other
successes as
wise as witty.

that strooke him (though he did it basely) stand still and face his enemy, then hee that was strooke is wronged and affronted both together: wronged, because he was strooke cowardly; affronted, because he that strooke him, stood still to make good what he had done: and so according to the Lawes of cursed Duel, I may be wronged, but not affronted; for children nor women have no apprehension, neyther can they flye, nor ought to stand still: and so is it with the Religious; for those kindes of people want Armes offensive and defensive, so that though they be naturally bound to defend themselves, yet they are not to offend any body and though even now I said I was wronged, I saw now I am not; for hee that can receive no affront, can give none: for which causes I have no reason to resent, nor doe I, the words that that good man gave me; onely I could have wished he had stayed a little, that I might have let him see his error, in saying or thinking there have beene no Knights Errant in the world; for if Amadis had heard this, or one of those infinite numbers of his linage, I know it had not gone well with his Worship.

Ile sweare that (quoth Sancho) they would have given him a slash, that should have cleaved him from head to foot, like a Pomegranate, or a ripe Muske Melon; they were pretty Youths to suffer such jests. By my Holidam, I thinke certainely if Renaldos de Montalvan had heard these speeches from the poore knave, he had bung'd up his mouth that he should not have spoken these three yeeres; I, I, hee should have dealt with them, and see how he would have scaped their hands.

The Duchesse was ready to burst with laughter at Sancho, and to her minde, she held him to be more conceited, and madder then his Master, and many at that time were of this opinion.

Finally, Don Quixote was pacified, and dinner ended, and the cloth being taken away, there came foure Damozels, one with a silver Bason, the other with an Ewre, a third with two fine white Towels, the fourth with her arms tucked up to the middle and in her white hands (for white they were)

240

HISTORIE OF DON QUIXOTE

CHAPTER
XXXII

Of Don
Quixotes
answer to his
Reprehender,
with other
successes as
wise as witty.

a white Naples washing ball. Shee with the Bason came very mannerly, and set it under Don Quixote's chinne, who very silent, and wondring at that kinde of ceremony, taking it to bee the custome of the Country, to wash their faces in stead of their hands, he stretcht out his face as far as he could, and instantly the Ewre began to rain upon him, and the Damozell with the soape ran over his beard apace, raising white flakes of snow, for such were those scowrings, not only upon his beard, but over all the face and eyes of the obedient Knight, so that he was forced to shut them.

The Duke and Duchesse that knew nothing of this, stood expecting what would become of this Lavatory. The Barber Damozell, when she had soaped him well with her hand, feined that she wanted more water, and made her with the Ewre, to goe for it, whilest Signior Don Quixote expected; which shee did, and Don Quixote remained one of the strangest pictures to move laughter that could be imagined. All that were present (many in number) beheld him, and as they saw him with a neck halfe a yard long, more then ordinary swarthy, his eyes shutte, and his beard full of soape, it was great marvell, and much discretion, they could forbeare laughing. The Damozels of the jest cast downe their eyes, not daring to looke on their Lords; whose bodies with choller and laughter even tickled againe, and they knew not what to doe; eyther to punish the boldnes of the girles, or reward them for the pastime they received to see Don Quixote in that manner.

Lastly, she with the Ewre came, and they made an end of washing Don Quixote, and straight she that had the towels, wiped and dried him gently, and all foure of them at once making him a low courtesie, would have gone: but the Duke, because Don Quixote should not fall into the jest, called to the Damozell with the bason, saying, Come and wash me too, and see that you have water enough. The wench, that was wily and carefull, came and put the bason under the Duke, as she had done to Don Quixote, and making haste, they washed and scowred him very well, and

3 : HH   241

CHAPTER
XXXII

Of Don
Quixotes
answer to his
Reprehender,
with other
successes as
wise as witty.

leaving him dry and cleane, making curtesies, they went away. After, it was knowne that the Duke swore, that if they had not washed him as well as Don Quixote, he would punish them for their lightnesse, which they discreetly made amends for, with soaping him.

Sancho marked all the ceremonies of the Lavatory, and said to himselfe; Lord (thought he) if it be the custome in this Countrie to wash the Squires beards, as well as the Knights? for of my soule and conscience I have need of it, and if they would, to runne over me with a Rasor too.

What saist thou to thy selfe, Sancho? said the Duchesse. I say, Madam, (quoth he) that I have heard that in other Princes Palaces they use to give water to wash mens hands when the cloth is taken away, but not lie to scowre their beards, and therefore I see tis good to live long, to see much; although tis said also, that he that lives long, suffers much, though to suffer one of these Lavatories, is rather pleasure then paine.

Take no care Sancho, quoth the Duchesse, for Ile make one of my Damozels wash thee, and if need be, lay thee a bucking. For my beard (quoth Sancho) I should bee glad for the present, for the rest, God will provide hereafter. Looke you, Carver, said the Dutchesse, what Sancho desires, doe just as hee would have you. The Carver answered, that Signior Sancho should be punctually served, and so he went to dinner, and carried Sancho with him, the Dukes and Don Quixote sitting still, and conferring in many and severall affaires, but all concerning the practice of Armes and Knight Errantry.

The Duchesse requested Don Quixote, to delineate and describe unto her (since he seemed to have a happy memory) the beauty and feature of the Lady Dulcinea del Toboso, for according to Fames Trumpet, she thought that shee must needs be the fairest creature in the world, and also of the Mancha.

Don Quixote sighed at the Duchesses command, and sayd, If I could take out my heart, and lay it before your Great-

HISTORIE OF DON QUIXOTE

nesses eyes, upon this table in a dish, I would save my tongue
a labour **to** tell you that, which would not be imagined; for
in my heart, your Excellency should see her lively depainted :
but why should I be put to describe and delineate exactly,
piece for piece, each severall beauty of the peerelesse Dulcinea, a burden fitter for other backes then mine; an enterprize, in which the pensils of Parrasius, Timantes, and
Apelles, and the tooles of Lisippus, should indeed be employed, to paint and carve her in tables of Marble and
Brasse, and Ciceronian and Demosthenian Rhetoricke to
praise her.

CHAPTER
XXXII

Of Don
Quixotes
answer to his
Reprehender,
with other
successes as
wise as witty.

What meane you by your Demosthenian, Signior Don
Quixote? quoth the Duchesse. Demosthenian Rhetoricke
(quoth hee) is as much to say, as the Rhetoricke of De-
mosthenes, as Ciceronian of Cicero, both which were the
two greatest Rhetoricians in the world. Tis true (quoth
the Duke) and you shewed your ignorance in asking that
question: but for all that, Sir Don Quixote might much
delight us, if he would paint her out; for Ile warrant,
though it bee but in her first draught, shee will appeare so
well, that the most faire will envy her. I would willingly
(sayd he) if mis-fortune had not blotted out her Idæa, that
not long since befell her, which is such, that I may rather
bewaile it, then describe her; for your Greatnesses shall
understand, that as I went heeretofore to have kissed her
hands, and receive her benediction, leave and licence, for this
my third sally, I found another manner of one then I looked
for, I found her enchanted, and turned from a Princesse to
a Countrey-wench, from faire to foule, from an Angell to
a Devill, from sweet to contagious, from well-spoken to
rusticke, **from** modest to skittish, from light to darknesse,
and finally **from** Dulcinea del Toboso, to a Pesantesse of
Sayago.

Now God **defend** us (quoth the Duke) with a loud voyce,
who is he that **hath** done so much hurt to the world? Who
hath taken away **the** beauty that cheered it? the quicknesse
that entertained it? and the honesty that did credit it?
Who? sayd hee, who but some cursed Enchanter? one of

243

THE SECOND PART OF THE

**CHAPTER
XXXII**

Of Don
Quixotes
answer to his
Reprehender,
with other
successes as
wise as witty.

those many envious ones that persecute mee? This wicked
race borne in the world, to darken and annihilate the
exployts of good men, and to give light and raise the deedes
of evill. Enchanters have me persecuted: Enchanters me
persecute: and Enchanters will mee persecute, till they cast
me and my lofty Chivalry, into the profound Abisme of
forgetfulnesse, and there they hurt and wound mee, where
they see I have most feeling; for to take from a Knight
Errant, his Lady, is to take away his eye-sight, with which
hee sees the sunne that doth lighten him, and the food
that doth nourish him. Oft have I sayd, and now I say
againe, that a Knight Errant without a Mistris, is like a
tree without leaves, like a building without cement, or a
shadow without a body, by which it is caused.

There is no more to be sayd (quoth the Duchesse:) but
yet if we may give credit to the *History of Don Quixote*,
that not long since came to light, with a generall applause,
it is sayd (as I remember) that you never saw Dulcinea, and
that there is no such Lady in the world; but that she is a
meere fantasticall creature ingendred in your braine, where
you have painted her with all the graces and perfections that
you please.

Here is much to be sayd (quoth he), God knowes, if there
be a Dulcinea or no in the world, whether she be fantasticall, or not: and these be matters, whose justifying must
not be so far searcht into. Neither have I ingendred or
brought foorth my Lady, though I contemplate on her, as is
fitting, she being a Lady that hath all the parts that may
make her famous thorow the whole world: as these; faire,
without blemish; grave, without pride; amorous, but honest;
thankfull, as courteous; courteous, as well-bred: And finally,
of high descent; by reason that beauty shines and marcheth
upon her noble bloud, in more degrees of perfection, then in
meane-borne beauties.

Tis true (sayd the Duke:) but Don Quixote must give
mee leave, to say what the *History*, where his exployts are
written, sayes; where is inferred, that though there be a
Dulcinea in Toboso, or out of it, and that she bee faire in

244

the highest **degree, as** you describe her, yet **in** her highnesse of birth **shee is not** equall to your *Oriana's, your Alastraxarea's, or your Madasima's, with others of this kinde, of which **your** Histories are full, as you well know. To this I answer you (quoth Don Quixote) Dulcinea is vertuous, and Vertue addes to Linage, and one that is meane and vertuous, ought to be more esteemed, then another noble and vicious: besides, Dulcinea hath one shred that may make her Queene with Crowne and Scepter: for the merit of a faire and vertuous woman, extends to doe greater miracles, and although not formally, yet vertually shee hath greater fortunes layd up for her.

CHAPTER XXXII

Of Don Quixotes answer to his Reprehender, with other successes as wise as witty.

*Names of fained Ladies in bookes of Knight-hood.

I say, Signior Don Quixote (quoth the Duchesse) that in all you speake, you goe with your leaden plummet, and, as they say, with your sounding line in your hand, and that hence-forward I will beleeve, and make all in my house beleeve, and my Lord the Duke too, if neede be, that there is a Dulcinea in Toboso, and that at this day she lives, that she is faire, and well-borne, and deserves that such a Knight, as Don Quixote, should serve her, which is the most I can, or know how to endeere her. But yet I have one scruple left, and, I know not, some kind of inckling against Sancho: the scruple is, that the History sayes, that Pansa found the sayd Lady Dulcinea (when he carried her your Epistle) winnowing a bag of wheat, and for more assurance, that it was red wheat, a thing that makes mee doubt of her high birth.

To which Don Quixote replide: Lady mine, you shall know, that all or the most part of my affaires, are cleane different from the ordinary course of other Knights Errant, whether they bee directed by the unscrutable will of the Destinies, or by the malice of some envious Enchanter, and as it is evident, that all, or the most of your famous Knights Errant, one hath the favor not to be inchanted; another, to have his flesh so impenetrable, that he cannot be wounded, as the famous Roldan, one of the twelve Peeres of France, of whom it was sayd, that hee could not bee wounded, but upon the sole of his left foot; and that this too must be with **the** poynt of a great Pin, and with no other kinde of weapon;

245

THE SECOND PART OF THE

CHAPTER
XXXII

Of Don
Quixotes
answer to his
Reprehender,
with other
successes as
wise as witty.

so that when Bernardo del Carpia did kill him in Ronces-valles, seeing he could not wound him with his sword, he lifted him in his armes from ground, and stifled him, as mindefull of the death that Hercules gave Anteon, that horrid Gyant, that was sayd to be the sonne of the earth. From all this I infer, that it might be I might have had some of these favours, as not to be wounded; for many times, experience hath taught mee, that my flesh is soft and penetrable, or that I might have the power not to be enchanted; but yet I have seene my selfe clapt in a cage, where all the world was not able to inclose me, had it not been by vertue of Enchantments; but since I was free, I shall beleeve that no other can hinder me: So that these Enchanters, who see, that upon me they cannot use their sleights, they revenge themselves upon the things I most affect, and meane to kill me, by ill-treating Dulcinea, by whom I live: and so I beleeve, that when my Squire carried my Ambassage, they turned her into a Pesant, to bee im-ployed in so base an office, as winnowing of wheat: but I say, that wheat was neither red, nor wheat; but seedes of Orientall Pearles, and for proofe of this, let me tell your Magnitudes, that comming a while since by Toboso, I could never finde Dulcinea's Palace; and Sancho, my Squire, having seene her before in her owne shape, which is the fairest in the world, to me she then seemed a foule course Country-wench, and meanly nurtured, being the very Dis-cretion of the world: And since I am not enchanted, neither can I be in all likely-hood, she is she that is enchanted, greeved, turned, chopped and changed, and my enemies have revenged themselves on me in her, and for her I must live in perpetuall sorrow, till shee come to her pris-tine being.

All this have I spoken, that no body may stand upon what Sancho sayd, of that sifting and winnowing of hers: for since to me she was changed, no marvell though for him shee were exchanged. Dulcinea is nobly borne, and of the best bloud in Toboso, of which, I warrant, she hath no small part in her: and for her, that towne shall be famous in after-

246

HISTORIE OF DON QUIXOTE

ages, as Troy for Helen, **and** Spaine for * Cava, though with more honour and reputation: On the other **side,** I would have your Lordships know, that Sancho Pansa is one of the prettiest Squires that ever served Knight Errant: sometimes he **hath** such sharpe simplicities, that to thinke whether he be Foole or Knave, causeth no small content: hee hath malice enough to be a Knave; but more ignorance to bee thought a foole; hee doubts of every thing, and yet beleeves all: when I thinke sometimes hee will tumble headlong to the foot, hee comes out with some kinde of discretion that lifts him to the clouds.

Finally, I would not change him for any other Squire, though I might have a City to boot; therefore I doubt, whether it bee good to send him to the Government, that your Greatnesse hath bestowed on him, though I see in him a certaine fitnesse for this you call governing; for, trimming his understanding but a very little, hee would proceede with his government, as well as the King with his customes: besides, wee know by experience, that a Governour needes not much learning, or other abilities: for you **have a** hundred, that scarce can read a word, and yet they governe like Ier-Falcons: the businesse is, that their meaning be good, and to hit the matter aright they undertake; for they shall not want Counsellours, to teach them what they shall doe, as your Governours that be Sword-men, and not Schollers, that have their Assistants to direct them. My counsell should bee to him: That neither bribe he take, nor his due forsake, and some other such toyes as these, that I have within mee, and shall bee declared at fit time to Sancho's profit, and the Ilands which hee shall governe.

To this poynt of their discourse came the Duke, Duchesse, and Don Quixote, when straight they heard a great noise of people in the Palace: and Sancho came in, into the Hall, unlookt for, all in a maze, with a strainer in stead of a Bib, and after him many Lads, or to say better, Scullions of the kitchin, and other inferior people, and one came with a little kneading-tub with water, that seemed, by the colour and sluttishnesse, to bee dish-water, who followed and

Of Don Quixotes answer to his Reprehender, with other successes as wise as witty.

*Daughter to the Earle, that betrayed Spaine to the Moores. *Vide Mariana. Hist. de Reb. Hisp.*

CHAPTER
XXXII

Of Don
Quixotes
answer to his
Reprehender,
with other
successes as
wise as witty.

persecuted **Sancho,** and sought by all meanes to joyne the **vessell to his** chinne, and another would have washed him.

What's the matter, Hoe (quoth the Duchesse)? What doe yee to this honest man? What? doe yee not know hee is Governour-Elect? To which the Barber-Scullion replide, This Gentle-man **will** not suffer himselfe to bee washed, according **to** the custome, as my Lord the Duke, and his Master were. Yes marry will I (sayd Sancho) in a great huffe: but I would have cleaner towels, and cleerer sudds, and not **so** sluttish hands; for there is no such difference betweene my Master and mee, that they should wash him with rose-water, and me with the Devils lie: the customes of great mens Palaces are so much **the** better, by how little trouble they cause: **but** your Lavatory custome heere, is **worse then** Penitentiaries, my **beard** is cleane, and I neede **no such** refreshing; and hee that **comes to** wash mee, or **touch a** haire of my head (of my beard, I say) sir-reverence **of the** company, Ile give him such **a** boxe, that Ile set **my** fist in his skull; for these kinde of ceremonies and **soape-**layings, are rather flouts, then entertainers of ghests.

The Duchesse was ready to die with laughter, **to** see Sancho's choller, and to heare his reasons; but Don Quixote was not very well pleased **to** see **him** so ill dressed with his jasperd towell, and hemmed in by **so** many of the Kitchin Pensioners; **so** making a low legge **to** the Dukes, as if he intended to speake, with a grave **voyce** he spoke to the skoundrels:

Harke, ye Gentlemen, pray let **the Youth** alone, and get you gone as ye came, if you please, **for my** Squire is as cleanly **as** another, and these troughs **are as** straight and close for him, as your little red clay drinking cups: take my counsaile **and** leave him, for neither he nor I can abide jests. Sancho **caught** his words out of his mouth, and went on, saying; No, **let** um come to make sport with the setting dogge, and Ile **let** um alone, as sure as it is now night; let um bring a comb hither, or what they wil, and curry my beard, and if they finde any thing foule in it, let um sheare

248

me to fitters. Then quoth the Duchesse (**unable to** leave laughing) Sancho sayes well, he is cleane, **as he** sayes, and needes **no** washing: and if our custome please **him** not, let him **take his** choyce, besides, you ministers **of** cleanlinesse **have beene** very slacke and carelesse, I know not whether I may say, presumptuous to bring to such a personage and such a Beard, in stead of a Bason and Ewre of pure gold, and Diaper towels, your kneading-troughes and dish-clouts; but you are unmannerly raskals, and like wicked wretches must needs shew the grudge you beare to the Squires of Knights Errant.

CHAPTER
XXXII

Of Don
Quixotes
answer to his
Reprehender,
with other
successes as
wise as witty.

The raskall regiment, together with the Carver that came with them, thought verily the Duchesse was in earnest: so they tooke the sive-cloth from Sancho's necke, and even ashamed went their waies, and left him, who seeing himselfe out of that (as he thought) great danger, kneeled before the Duchesse, saying, From great Ladies, great favors are still expected, this that your worship hath now done me, cannot be recompenced with lesse, then to desire to see my self an armed Knight Errant, to employ my selfe all daies of my life in the service of so high a Lady. I am a poore Husbandman, my name is Sancho Pansa, children I have, and serve as a Squire, if in any of these I may serve your Greatnesse, I will be swifter in obeying, then your Ladiship in commanding.

Tis well seene, Sancho, quoth the Duchesse, that you have learnt to be courteous in the very schoole of courtesie: I meane, **it** seemes well, that you have been nursed at Don Quixote's brest, who is the Creame of complement, and the flower **of** ceremonies: well fare such a Master, and such **a** Servant; **the** one for North-starre of Knight Errantry, the other for **the** Starre of Squire-like fidelitie: Rise, friend Sancho, **for I** will repay your courtesie, in making my Lord the **Duke as** soone as he can, performe the promise he hath made **you**, of being Governor of the Iland.

With this, **their** discourse ceased, **and** Don Quixote went to **his** after-noones sleepe, and the Duchesse desired Sancho, that **if** he were not very sleepie, hee would passe the afternoone

CHAPTER
XXXII
Of Don
Quixotes
answer to his
Reprehender,
etc.

with her and her Damozels in a coole roome. Sancho answered, that though true it were, that he was used in the afternoones to take a some five houres nappe, yet to doe her goodnesse service, hee would do what he could, not to take any that day, and would obey her command: so he parted. The Duke gave fresh order for Don Quixote's usage, to be like a Knight Errant, without differing a jot from the ancient stile of those Knights.

CHAPTER XXXIII

Of the wholesome discourse that passed betwixt the Duchesse and her Damozels with Sancho Pansa, worthy to be read and noted.

ELL the Storie tells us, that Sancho slept not that day, but according to his promise, came, when he had dined, to see the Duchesse, who for the delight shee received to heare him, made him sit downe by her in a low chaire, though Sancho, out of pure mannerlinesse would not sit: but the Duchesse bade him sit as he was Governour, and speake as hee was Squire, though in both respects he deserved the very seate of Cid Ruydiaz the Champion.

*The
Spaniards
lowsie
humility.

Sancho * shrunke up his shoulders, obeyed and sate downe, and all the Duchesses Waiting-women and Damozels stood round about her, attending with great silence to Sancho's discourse: but the Duchesse spake first, saying;

Now that we are all alone, and that no body heares us, I would, Signior Governor would resolve me of certaine doubts I have, arising from the printed *History of the Graund Don Quixote*, one of which is, that since honest Sancho never saw

250

HISTORIE OF DON QUIXOTE

Dulcinea, I say, the Lady Dulcinea del Toboso, neither carried her Don Quixotes letter, for it remained in the note-booke in Sierra Morena, how he durst feigne the answer, and that he found her sifting of wheat; this being a mocke and a lye, and so prejudiciall to the Lady Dulcinea's reputation, and so unbefitting the condition and fidelity of a faithfull Squire.

Here Sancho rose without answering a word, and softly crooking his body, and with his finger upon his lippes, he went up and downe the roome, lifting up the hangings: which done, he came and sate downe againe, and said, Now I see, Madam, that nobody lies in wait to heare us, besides the by-standers, I will answer you without feare or fright, all that you have asked, and all that you will aske mee. And first of all I say, that I hold my Master Don Quixote, for an incureable Madde-man, though sometimes he speakes things, that, in my opinion, and so in all theirs that heare him, are so discreet, and carried in so even a tracke, that the Devill himselfe cannot speake better; but truely and without scruple, I take him to be a very Franticke; for so I have it in my mazard, I dare make him beleeve that, that hath neither head nor foot, as was the answer of that letter, and another thing that hapned some eight dayes agoe, which is not yet in print, to wit, the Enchantment of my Lady Dulcinea; for I made him beleeve she is enchanted, it being as true, as the Moone is made of greene cheese.

The Duchesse desired him to tell her that Enchantment and conceit: which he did, just as it passed: at which the hearers were not a little delighted. And prosecuting her discourse, the Duchesse sayd, I have one scruple leapes in my minde, touching what Sancho hath told mee, and a certaine buzze comming to mine eares, that tels me; If Don Quixote de la Mancha be such a shallow mad-man and Widgin, and Sancho Pansa his Squire know it; yet why for all that, he serves and followes him, and relies on his vaine promises; doubtlesse, hee is as very a Mad-man and Block-head, as his Master, which being so as it is, it will bee very unfitting for my Lord the Duke, to give Sancho an Iland

Of the whole-some dis-course that passed be-twixt the Duchesse and her Damozels with Sancho Pansa, worthy to be read and noted.

THE SECOND PART OF THE

Of the whole-
some dis-
course that
passed be-
twixt the
Duchesse and
her Damozels
with Sancho
Pansa, worthy
to be read
and noted.

to governe; for hee that cannot governe himselfe, will ill governe others.

By 'r Lady (quoth Sancho) that scruple comes in pudding-time: but bid your Buzze speake plaine, or how hee will; for I know he sayes true; and if I had beene wise, I might long since have left my Master: but twas my lucke, and this wilde Errantry, I cannot doe withall, I must follow him, wee are both of one place, I have eaten his bread, I love him well, he is thankfull, hee gave me the Asse-colts, and above all, I am faithfull, and it is impossible any chance should part us, but death: and if your Altitude will not bestow the Government on mee, with lesse was I borne, and perhaps, the missing it might bee better for my conscience; for though I be a foole, yet I understand the Proverbe that sayes, The Ant had wings to doe her hurt, and it may bee, Sancho the Squire may sooner goe to Heaven, then Sancho the Governour. Heere is as good bread made, as in France; and in the night Ione is as good as my Lady; and unhappy is that man, that is to breake his fast at two of the clocke in the after-noone; and there's no heart a handfull bigger then another; and the stomacke is filled with the coursest victuals; and the little Fowles in the aire, have God for their Provider and Cater; and foure yards of course Cuenca cloth, keepe a man as warme, as foure of fine *Limiste wooll of Segovia; and when wee once leave this world, and are put into the earth, the Prince goes in as narrow a path as the Iourney-man; and the Popes body takes up no more roome then a Sextons, though the one be higher then the other; for when we come to the pit, all are even, or made so in spite of their teethes, and good-night.

*Their
Limiste breed
came first out
of England.

Let mee say againe, If your Lady-ship will not give mee the Iland, as I am a foole, Ile refuse it, for being a wise-man: for I have heard say, The neerer the Church, the further from God; and, All is not gold that glistreth; and that from the oxen, plough and yokes, the Husband-man Bamba was chosen for King of Spaine: and that Rodrigo, from his tissues, sports, and riches, was cast out to be eaten by snakes (if we may beleeve the rimes of the old Romants, that Iye not.)

252

HISTORIE OF DON QUIXOTE

CHAPTER
XXXIII

Of the whole-
some dis-
course that
passed be-
twixt the
Duchesse and
her Damozels
with Sancho
Pansa, worthy
to be read
and noted.

Why, no more they doe not (sayd Donna Rodriguez, the Wayting-woman, that was one of the Auditours) for you have one Romant that sayes, that Don Rodrigo was put alive into a Tombe full of Toades, Snakes, and Lizards, and some two dayes after, from within the Tombe, hee cryed with a low and pitifull voyce, 'Now they eat, now they eat me in the place where I sinned most': and according to this, this man hath reason to say, he had rather be a Labourer then a King, to bee eaten to death with vermine.

The Duchesse could not forbeare laughing, to see the simplicity of her woman, nor to admire to heare Sancho's proverbiall reasons, to whom she sayd; Honest Sancho knowes, that when a Gentle-man once makes a promise, he will performe it, though it cost him his life. My Lord and Husband the Duke, though he be no Errant, yet hee is a Knight, and so hee will accomplish his promise of the Island, in spight of envy or the worlds malice. Be of good cheere, Sancho; for when thou least dreamest of it, thou shalt be seated in the Chayre of thy Iland, and of Estate, and shalt claspe thy Government in thy robes of Tissue. All that I charge thee, is, that you looke to the governing your Vassals, for you must know, they are all well-borne and loyall.

For governing (quoth Sancho) there's no charging mee; for I am naturally charitable and compassionate to the poore, and of him that does well they will not speake ill, and by my Holidam they shall play me no false play: I am an old dog, and understand all their Hist, hist: and I can snuffe my selfe when I see time, and I will let no cobwebs fall in my eyes, for I know where my shoo wrings me: this I say, because honest men shall have hand and heart, but wicked men neyther foot nor fellowship. And me-thinkes for matter of Government, there is no more but to begin, and in fifteene daies Governour, I could manage the place, and know as well to governe, as to labour, in which I was bredde. You have reason, Sancho, quoth the Duchesse, for no man is borne wise, and Bishops are made of men, and not of stones. But turning to our discourse that wee had touching the Lady Dulcinea's Enchantment, I am more

253

**CHAPTER
XXXIII**

Of the whole-
some dis-
course that
passed be-
twixt the
Duchesse and
her Damozels
with Sancho
Pansa, worthy
to be read
and noted.

then assured, that that imagination that Sancho had to put
a tricke upon his Master, and to make him thinke the
Country wench was Dulcinea, that if his Master knew her
not, all was invented by some of those Enchanters that persecute Signior Don Quixote; for I know partly, that that
Country wench that leapt upon the Asse-colt, was, and is
Dulcinea, and Sancho thinking to be the deceiver, is himselfe
deceived; and there is no more to be doubted in this, then
in things that we never saw: and know, Sancho, that here
we have our Enchanters too, that love, and tell us plainely
and truly, what passeth in the world, without trickes or
devices; and beleeve me, Sancho, that leaping wench was,
and is Dulcinea, who is enchanted as the Mother that
brought her forth, and when we least thinke of it, we shall
see her in her proper shape, and then Sancho will thinke he
was deceived.

All this may be (quoth Sancho) and now will I beleeve all
that my Master told me of Montesino's Cave, where he said
he saw our Mistresse Dulcinea, in the same apparell and
habit, that I said I had seene her in, when I enchanted her
at my pleasure; and it may be, Madam, all is contrary
(as you say) for from my rude witte, it could not be pre-
sumed that I should in an instant make such a witty lye;
neyther doe I beleeve that my Master is so madde, that
with so poore and weake a perswasion as mine, he should
beleeve a thing so incredible: but for all that, good Lady,
doe not thinke me to be so malevolent, for such a Leeke as
I am, is not bound to boare into the thoughts and malicious-
nesse of most wicked Enchanters. I fained that, to scape
from my Masters threats, and not with any purpose to hurt
him, and if it fell out otherwise, God is above that judgeth
all harts. Tis true, said the Duchesse, but tell me, Sancho,
what is that you said of Montesinos Cave? I should be glad
to heare it. Then Sancho began to tell word for word, all
that passed in that Adventure. Which when the Duchesse
heard, shee said, Out of this successe may be inferred, that
since the **Grand Don Quixote** sayes that he saw there the
same labouring wench that Sancho saw at their comming

254

HISTORIE OF DON QUIXOTE

CHAPTER
XXXIII
Of the whole-
some dis-
course that
passed be-
twixt the
Duchesse and
her Damozels
with Sancho
Pansa, worthy
to be read
and noted.

from Toboso, without **doubt it** is Dulcinea, and that in this
the Enchanters heere are very listning and wary. This I
said (quoth Sancho) that if my Lady Dulcinea del Toboso
be enchanted, at her peril bee it, for Ile have nothing to doe
with my Masters Enemies, who are many, and bad ones.
True it is, that she that I saw was a Country wench, and so
I held her, and so I judged her to be; and if that were
Dulcinea, Ile not meddle with her, neyther shall the Blowze
passe upon my account. I, I, let's have giving and taking
every foot. Sancho said it, Sancho did it, Sancho turned,
Sancho return'd, as if Sancho were a dish-clout, and not the
same Sancho Pansa that is now in Print all the world over,
as Samson Carrasco told mee, who at least is one that is
Bachelorized in Salamanca, and such **men** cannot lye, but
when they list, or that it much concernes **them**: so there is
no reason any man should deale with me, **since** I have a
good report, and as I have heard my Master say, Better
have an honest name then much wealth. Let um joyne mee
to this Government, and they shall see wonders: for hee that
hath **beene a** good Squire, will easily be a good Governour.

Whatsoever Sancho hitherto hath said (quoth the Duchesse)
is Catonian sentences, or at least taken out of the very entrailes of Michael Verinus, *Florentibus occidit annis.* Well,
well, to speake as thou dost, a badde cloake often hides a
good drinker. Truly Madam, said Sancho, I never drunke
excessively in my life, to quench my thirst sometimes I have,
for I am no hypocrite, I drinke when I am dry, and when I
am urged too, for I love not to be nice or unmannerly; for
what heart of marble is there, that will not pledge a friends
carowse? but though I take my cup, I goe not away drunke:
besides, your Knight Errants Squires ordinarily drinke water,
for they alwaies travell by Forrests, Woods, Medowes, Mountaines, cragy Rockes, and meete not with a pittance of wine,
though they **would** give an eye for it.

I beleeve it, said the Duchesse, and now, Sancho, thou
maist repose thy selfe, and after we will talke at large, and
give order how thou maist be joyned, as thou saist, to the
Government.

255

THE SECOND PART OF THE

CHAPTER
XXXIII

Of the whole-
some dis-
course that
passed be-
twixt the
Duchesse and
her Damozels
with Sancho
Pansa, worthy
to be read
and noted.

Sancho againe gave the Duchesse thankes, but desired her
she would doe him the kindnesse, that his Dapple might
bee well lookt to. What Dapple (quoth shee)? My Asse
(said Sancho) for not to call him so, I say my Dapple: and
when I came into the Castle, I desired this waiting woman
to have a care on him, and she grew so loud with me, as
if I called her ugly or old, for I held it fitter for them to
provender Asses, then to authorize Roomes: Lord God, a
Gentleman of my towne could not endure these waiting
women. Some Pesant, quoth Donna Rodriguez the waiting woman; for if he had beene a Gentleman, and well
bredde, hee would have extolled them above the Moone.
Goe too, no more (quoth the Duchesse) Peace Rodriguez,
and be quiet, Sancho, and let mee alone to see that Sancho's
Asse bee made much of; for being Sancho's houshold-stuffe,
I will hold him on the Apples of mine eyes. Let him be in
the stable (quoth Sancho) for neither hee nor I am worthy
to be so much as a minute upon those Apples of your Greatnesse eyes, and I had as liefe stabbe my selfe, as consent to
that; for although my master sayes, that in courtesies one
should rather lose by a card too much, then too little; yet
in these Asse-like courtesies, and in your Apples, it is fit to
bee wary and proceed with discretion. Carry him Sancho
(quoth the Duchesse) to thy Government, for there thou
maist cherish him at thy pleasure, and manumit him from
his labour. Doe not thinke you have spoken jestingly, Lady
Duchesse, (quoth Sancho) for I have seene more then two
Asses goe to Governments, and 'twould be no novelty for
me to carry mine.

Sancho's discourse renewed in the Duchesse more laughter
and content, and sending him to repose, shee went to tell
the Duke all that had passed betweene them, and both
of them plotted and gave order, to put a jest upon Don
Quixote that might be a famous one, and suting to his
Knightly stile, in which kind they played many prankes
with him, so proper and handsome, that they are
the best conteined amongst all the Adventures of this Grand History.

256

CHAPTER XXXIV

How notice is given for the dis-enchanting of
the peerelesse Dulcinea del Toboso, which
is one of the most famous Adventures
in all this booke.

REAT was the pleasure the Duke and
Duchesse received with Don Quixote and
Sancho Pansa's conversation, and they resolved to play some trickes with them,
that might carry some twi-lights and
appearances of Adventures. They tooke
for a Motive that which Don Quixote had
told unto them of Montesinos Cave, be-
cause they would have it a famous one: but that which the
Duchesse most admired at, was, that Sancho's simplicity
should be so great, that he should beleeve for an infallible
truth, that Dulcinea was enchanted, hee himselfe having
beene the Enchanter, and the Impostor of that businesse:
So giving order to their servants for all they would have
done, some weeke after they carried Don Quixote to a Boare-
hunting, with such a troope of wood-men and hunters, as
if the Duke had beene a crowned King. They gave Don
Quixote a hunters sute, and to Sancho one of finest greene
cloth: but Don Quixote would not put on his, saying; That
shortly hee must returne againe to the hard exercise of
Armes, and that therfore he could carry no Wardrobes or
Sumpters. But Sancho tooke his, meaning to sell it with
the first occasion offered.

The wisht-for day being come, Don Quixote armed himselfe, and Sancho clad himselfe, and upon his Dapple, (for
hee would not leave him, though they had given him a
horse) thrust himselfe amongst the troope of the Wood-

3 : KK   257

THE SECOND PART OF THE

CHAPTER
XXXIV
How notice
is given
for the dis-
enchanting of
the peerelesse
Dulcinea del
Toboso, which
is one of the
most famous
Adventures in
all this booke.

men. The Duchesse was bravely attired, and Don Quixote out of pure courtesie and manners, tooke the reines of her Palfrey, though the Duke would not consent: at last they came to a wood that was betweene two high mountaines, where taking their stands, their lanes and paths, and the hunters devided into severall stands, the chase began with great noyse, hooting and hollowing, so that one could scarce heare another, as well for the cry of the dogges, as for the sound of the Hornes. The Duchesse alighted, and with a sharpe Iavelin in her hand, shee tooke a stand, by which she knew some wilde Boares were used to passe. The Duke also alighted and Don Quixote, and stood by her. Sancho stayed behinde them all, but stirred not from Dapple, whom hee durst not leave, lest some ill chance should befall him, and they had scarce lighted, and set themselves in order with some servants, when they saw there came a huge Boare by them, baited with the dogges, and followed by the hunters, gnashing his teeth and tuskes, and foaming at the mouth: and Don Quixote seeing him, buckling his shield to him, and laying hand on his sword, went forward to encounter him: the like did the Duke with his Iavelin; but the Duchesse would have beene formost of all, if the Duke had not stopped her. Onely Sancho, when he saw the valiant Beast, left Dapple, and began to scudde as fast as hee could, and striving to get up into a high Oake, it was not possible for him, but being even in the middest of it, fastned to a bough, and striving to get to the toppe, he was so unlucky and unfortunate, that the bough broke, and as he was tumbling to the ground, he hung in the ayre fastned to a snagge of the Oake, unable to come to the ground, and seeing himselfe in that perplexity, and that his greene coat was torne, and thinking, that if that wilde beast should come thither, he might lay hold on him, be began to cry out and call for helpe so outragiously, that all that heard him, and saw him not, thought verily some wilde beast was devouring him.

Finally, the Tuskie Boare was laid along, with many javelins points, and Don Quixote turning aside to Sancho's

258

HISTORIE OF DON QUIXOTE

CHAPTER
XXXIV

How notice
is given
for the dis-
enchanting of
the peereiesse
Dulcinea del
Toboso, which
is one of the
most famous
Adventures in
all this booke.

noyse, that knew him by his note, he saw him hanging on
the Oake, and his head downward, and Dapple close by him,
that never left him in all his calamity, and Cid Hamete
sayes, that hee seldome saw Sancho without Dapple, or
Dapple without Sancho, such was the love and friendship
betwixt the couple.

Don Quixote went and unhung Sancho, who seeing himselfe free, and on the ground, beheld the torne place of his
hunting sute, and it grieved him to the soule, for hee thought
hee had of that sute at least an inheritance. And now they
layed the Boare athwart upon a great Mule, and covering
him with Rose-mary bushes, and Myrtle boughes, he was
carried in signe of their victorious spoiles, to a great field-
Tent, that was set up in the midst of the wood, where
the Tables were set in order, and a dinner made ready, so
plentifull and well drest, that it well shewed the bounty and
magnificence of him that gave it.

Sancho, shewing the wounds of his torn garment to the
Duchesse, said, If this had beene hunting of the Hare, my
coate had not seene it selfe in this extremity: I know not
what pleasure there can be in looking for a beast, that if
he reach you with a tuske, he may kill you: I have often
heard an olde song, that sayes, 'Of the Beares maist thou
be eat; as was Favila the great.' He was a Gothish King
(quoth Don Quixote) that going a hunting in the mountaines, a Beare eate him. This I say (said Sancho) I would
not that Kings and Princes should thrust themselves into
such dangers, to enjoy their pleasure; for what pleasure can
there be to kill a beast that hath committed no fault?

You are in the wrong, Sancho, quoth the Duke; for the
exercise of beast-hunting is the necessariest for Kings and
Princes that can bee. The chase is a shew of Warre, where
there be stratagems, crafts, deceits, to overcome the enemy
at pleasure; in it you have sufferings of cold and intolerable
heates, sleepe and idlenesse are banisht, the powers are
corroborated, the members agilitated. In conclusion, tis
an exercise that may be used without prejudice to any
body, and to the pleasure of every body, and the best of

CHAPTER
XXXIV

How notice
is given
for the dis-
enchanting of
the peerelesse
Dulcinea del
Toboso, which
is one of the
most famous
Adventures in
all this booke.

it is, that it is not common, as other kindes of sports are, except flying at the fowle, onely fit for Kings and Princes. Therefore (Sancho) change thy opinion, and when thou art a Governour, follow the chase, and thou shalt be a hundred times the better.

Not so, quoth Sancho, tis better for your Governour, to have his legges broken, and be at home: twere very good that poore suiters should come and seeke him, and hee should be taking his pleasure in the woods: 'twould bee a sweet Government yfaith. Good faith sir, the Chase and Pastimes are rather for idle companions then Governours: My sport shall be Vyed Trumpe at Christmas, and at Skettle pinnes Sundaies and Holidaies; for your hunting is not for my condition, neyther doth it agree with my conscience.

Pray God, Sancho it be so (quoth the Duke) for to doe and to say, goe a severall way. Let it be how 'twill, (said Sancho) for a good paymaster needes no pledge, and Gods helpe is better then early rising, and the belly carries the legges, and not the legges the belly; I meane, that if God helpe mee, and I doe honestly what I ought, without doubt I shall governe as well as a Ier-Falcon, I, I, put your finger in my mouth, and see if I bite or no.

A mischiefe on thee, cursed Sancho, quoth Don Quixote, and when shall wee heare thee (as I have often told thee) speake a wise speech, without a Proverbe? My Lords, I beseech you leave this Dunce, for he will grinde your very soules, not with his two, but his two thousand Proverbs, so seasonable, as such be his health or mine, if I hearken to them.

Sancho's Proverbs (quoth the Duchesse) although they bee more then Mallaras, yet they are not lesse to be esteemed then his, for their sententious brevity. For my part, they more delight mee then others, that bee farre better, and more fitting.

With these and such like savoury discourses, they went out of the tent to the wood, to seeke some more sport, and the day was soone past, and the night came on, and not so

HISTORIE OF DON QUIXOTE

light and calme as the time of the yeere required, it being about Mid-summer: but a certaine dismalnesse it had, agreeing much with the Dukes intention, and so as it grew to be quite dark, it seemed that upon a sudden, all the wood was on fire, thorow every part of it, and there were heard heere and there, this way and that way, an infinite company of Cornets, and other warlike instruments, and many troopes of horse that passed thorow the wood; the light of the fire, and the sound of the warlike instruments, did as it were blinde, and stunned the eyes and eares of the bystanders, and of all those that were in the wood. Straight they heard a company of *Moorish cryes, such as they use when they joyne battell, Drums and Trumpets sounded, and Fifes, all, as it were, in an instant, and so fast, that he that had had his sences, might have lost them, with the confused sound of these instruments.

CHAPTER XXXIV
How notice is given for the disenchanting of the peerelesse Dulcinea del Toboso, which is one of the most famous Adventures in all this booke.

*Lelilies, like the cries of the wilde Irish.

The Duke was astonisht, the Duchesse dismayd, Don Quixote wondred, Sancho trembled: And finally, even they that knew the occasion, were frighted: their feare caused a generall silence, and a Post in a Devils weede passed before them, sounding, in stead of a Cornet, a huge hollow Horne, that made a hoarce and terrible noyse. Harke you, Post, quoth the Duke, What are you? Whither goe you? And what men of warre are they that crosse over the wood? To which the Post answered, with a horrible and free voyce; I am the Devill, I goe to seeke Don Quixote de la Mancha, and they which come heere, are six troopes of Enchanters, that bring the peerelesse Dulcinea del Toboso upon a triumphant Chariot, she comes here enchanted with the brave French man Montesinos, to give order to Don Quixote, how she may be dis-enchanted.

If thou wert a Devill, as thou sayest (quoth the Duke) and as thy shape shewes thee to bee, thou wouldst have knowne that Knight Don Quixote de la Mancha: for hee is heere before thee. In my soule and conscience (quoth the Devill) I thought not on it; for I am so diverted with my severall cogitations, that I quite forgot the chiefe, for which I came for. Certainely (sayd Sancho) this Devill is an honest

261

THE SECOND PART OF THE

CHAPTER XXXIV

IIow notice is given for the dis-enchanting of the peerelesse Dulcinea del Toboso, which is one of the most famous Adventures in all this booke.

fellow, and a good Christian; for if he were not, he would not have sworne by his soule and conscience: And now I beleeve, that in Hell you have honest men. Straight the Devill, without lighting, directing his sight toward Don Quixote, sayd; The unlucky, but valiant Knight Montesinos, sends mee to thee, O Knight of the Lyons (for mee thinkes now I see thee in their pawes) commanding mee to tell thee from him, that thou expect him heere, where he will meet thee; for he hath with him Dulcinea del Toboso, and meanes to give thee instruction, how thou shalt dis-enchant her; and now I have done my message, I must away, and the Devils (like me) be with thee: and good Angels guard the rest. And this sayd, he winds his monstrous Horne, and turned his backe, and went, without staying for any answer.

Each one began afresh to admire, especially Sancho and Don Quixote. Sancho, to see that in spite of truth, Dulcinea must be enchanted: Don Quixote, to thinke whether that were true that befell him in Montesino's Cave, and being elevated in these dumps, the Duke sayd to him; Will you stay, Signior Don Quixote? Should I not? quoth he. Heere will I stay couragious and undanted, though all the Devils in Hell should close with mee. Well (quoth Sancho) if I heare another Devill and another Horne, I 'le stay in Flanders as much as heere.

Now it grew darker, and they might perceive many lights up and downe the wood, like the dry exhalations of the earth in the skie, that seeme to us to be shooting-stars: besides, there was a terrible noyse heard, just like that of your creaking wheeles of Oxe-waines, from whose piercing squeake (they say) Beares and Wolves doe flye, if there be any the way they passe. To this tempest, there was another added, that increast the rest, which was, that it seemed, that in all foure parts of the wood, there were foure encounters or battels in an instant: for there was first a sound of terrible Canon-shot, and an infinite company of Guns were discharged, and the voyces of the Combatants seemed to bee heard by and by a farre off, the Moorish cries reiterated.

262

HISTORIE OF DON QUIXOTE

Lastly, the Trumpets, Cornets, and **Hornes**, Drums,
Canons, and Guns, **and above** all, the fearefull noyse of
the Carts, **all** together made **a** most confused **and** horrid
sound, which tried Don Quixotes uttermost courage, to
suffer it : but Sancho was quite gone, and fell **in a** swound
upon the Duchesses coats, who received him, and commanded they should cast cold water in his face ; which
done, he came to himselfe, just as one of the Carts of those
whistling wheeles came to the place, foure lazie Oxen drew
it, covered with blacke clothes ; at every horne they had
a lighted Torch tyed, and on the top of the Cart there
was a high seat made, **upon which a** venerable old man sate,
with a beard **as white as snow, and so** long, **that** it reached
to his girdle : his **garment was a long gowne** of blacke
buckoram ; for **because the Cart was full of** lights, all
within it might **very well bee** discerned **and seene: two**
ugly spirits guided it, **clad in** the said **buckoram, so mon-**
strous, that Sancho, **after hee** had **seene them, winked,**
because he would see **um no** more : **when the Cart drew**
neere **to their** standing, the venerable **olde** man **rose from**
his seat, **and** standing up **with** a loud voyce, sayd ; **I** am the
wise Lyrgander : and the **Cart** passed on, hee not speaking
a word more.

After this, there passed another Cart **in** the same manner
with another olde man inthronized ; who making the Cart
stay, with a voyce no lesse lofty then the other, sayd ; I am
the wise Alquife, great friend to the ungratefull Vrganda ;
and on he went : and straight another Cart came on, the
same pace ; but hee that sate **in** the chiefe seat, was no
old man (as the rest) but **a good** robustious fellow, and ill-
favoured, who when hee **came** neere, rose up, as the rest ;
but with a voyce more hoarce and divellish, sayd ; I **am**
Archelaus the Enchanter, mortall enemy to Amadis **de**
Gaule, **and all his** kindred : And so on hee passed, all three
of these **Carts** turning **a** little forward, made a stand,
and the troublesome noyse of their wheeles ceased, and
straight there **was** heard no noyse, but a sweet and con-
senting **sound of** well-formed musike, which comforted

263

CHAPTER
XXXIV
How notice
is given
for the dis-
enchanting of
the peerelesse
Dulcinea, etc.

Sancho, and hee held it for a good signe, and hee sayd thus to the Duchesse, from whom hee stirred not a foot, not a jot.

Madam, where there is musike, there can bee no ill. Neither (quoth the Duchesse) where there is light and brightnesse. To which (sayd Sancho) the fire gives light, and your bon-fires (as we see) and perhaps might burne us: but musike is always a signe of feasting and jollity.

You shall see that (quoth Don Quixote) for he heard all, and he sayd well, as you shall see in the next chapter.

CHAPTER XXXV

Where is prosecuted the notice, that Don Quixote had, of dis-enchanting Dulcinea, with other admirable accidents.

HEN the delightfull musike was ended, they might see one of those you call triumphant chariots come towards them, drawne by six dun Mules, but covered with white linnen, and upon each of them came a Penitentiary with a Torch, clothed like-wise all in white: the Cart was twice or thrice as big as the three former, and at the top and sides of it, were twelve other Penitentiaries, as white as snow, all with their torches lighted, a sight that admired and astonisht joyntly: and in a high throne sate a Nymph, clad in a vaile of cloth of silver, a world of golden spangles glimmering about her, her face was covered with a fine cloth of Tiffany, for all whose wrinkles the face of a most delicate Damozell was seene thorow it, and the many lights, made them easily distinguish her beauty and yeeres, which (in likely-hood) came not to twenty, nor were

HISTORIE OF DON QUIXOTE

under seventeene: Next her came a shape, clad in a gowne of those you call Side-garments, downe to her foot, her head was covered with a blacke vayle: but even as the Cart came to bee just over-against the Dukes and Don Quixote, the musike of the Hoboyes ceased, and the Harps and Lutes that came in the Cart began, and the gowned shape rising up, unfolding her garment on both sides, and taking her vaile off from her head, shee discovered plainely the picture of raw-boned Death, at which Don Quixote was troubled, and Sancho afrayd, and the Dukes made shew of some timorous resenting. This live Death standing up, with a drowzie voice, and a tongue not much waking, began in this manner:

I Merlin am, he that in Histories,
They say, the Devill to my Father had,
(A tale by age succeeding authorized)
The Prince and Monarch of the Magicke Art,
And Register of deepe Astrologie,
Succeeding ages, since, me emulate,
That onely seeke to sing and blazon foorth
The rare exployts of those Knights Errant brave,
To whom I bore, and bare a liking great.

And howsoever of Enchanters, and
Those that are Wizards or Magicians be,
Hard the condition rough and divellish is,
Yet mine is tender, soft, and amorous,
And unto all friendly, to doe them good.

In the obscure and darkest Caves of Dis,
Whereas my soule hath still beene entertain'd
In forming Circles and of Characters,
I heard the lamentable note, of faire
And peerelesse Dulcinea del Toboso.

I knew of her Enchantment and hard hap,
Her transformation, from a goodly Dame
Into a Rusticke wench, I sorry was,
And shutting up my spirit within this hollow,
This terrible and fierce Anatomy,
When I had turn'd a hundred thousand bookes
Of this my divellish Science and uncouth,
I come to give the remedy that's fit.
To such a griefe, and to an ill so great.

Verses made
on purpose
absurdly, as
the subject required, and so
translated *ad
verbum*.

3 : LL   265

THE SECOND PART OF THE

Where is prosecuted the notice, that Don Quixote had, of disenchanting Dulcinea, with other admirable accidents.

Oh Glory thou of all, that doe put on
Their coats of steele and hardest Diamond,
Thou light, thou Lanthorne, Path, North-star, and Guide
To those that casting of their sluggish sleepe,
And feather-beds, themselves accommodate
To use the exercise of bloody Armes,
To thee, I say, oh never prais'd enough,
Not as thou ought'st to be : oh Valiant !

Oh joyntly Wise ! to thee, oh Don Quixote,
The Mancha's Splendour, and the Star of Spain,
That to recover to her first estate,
The peerelesse Dulcinea del Tobos.
It is convenient that Sancho thy Squire,
Himselfe three thousand, and three hundred give
Lashes, upon his valiant buttocks both
Vnto the aire discover'd, and likewise
That they may vex, and smart, and grieve him sore ;
And upon this, let all resolved be,
That of her hard misfortunes Authors were
My Masters, this my cause of comming was.

By Gad (quoth Sancho) I say not three thousand; but I will as soone give my selfe three stabs, as three ; the Devill take this kinde of dis-enchanting. What have my buttocks to doe with Enchantments? Verily, if Master Merlin have found no other meanes to dis-enchant the Lady Dulcinea del Toboso, shee may goe enchanted to her grave.

Good-man Rascall (quoth Don Quixote) you Garlicke stinkard; I shall take you, and binde you to a tree, as naked as your mother brought you forth, and let mee not say three thousand and three hundreth, but Ile give you sixe thousand and sixe hundred, so well layd on, that you shall not claw them off at three thousand and three hundred plucks, and reply not a word, if thou dost, Ile teare out thy very soule.

Which when Merlin heard, quoth he, It must not be so, for the stripes that honest Sancho must receive, must bee with his good will, and not perforce, and at what time hee will, for no time is prefixed him: but it is lawfull for him, if he will redeeme one halfe of this beating, he may receive it from anothers hand that may lay it on well.

266

HISTORIE OF DON QUIXOTE

No **other**, nor laying on (quoth Sancho) no hand shall come **neere** me: am I Dulcinea del Toboso's Mother trow ye? that my buttocks should pay for the offence of her eyes? My Master indeed, he is a part of her, since every stitch while, hee calls her, My life, my soule, my sustenance, my prop; hee may bee whipped for her, and doe all that is fitting for her dis-enchanting, but for me to whip **my** selfe, I *bernounce.

Sancho scarce ended his speech, when the silver Nymph that came next to Merlins Ghost, taking off her thin vaile, she discovered her face, which seemed unto al to be extraordinary faire, and with a manly grace, and voice not very amiable, directing her speech to Sancho, she said, Oh thou unhappy Squire, soul of lead, and heart of corke, and entrailes of flint, if thou hadst bin bidden, thou face-flaying theefe, to cast thy selfe from a high towre downe to the ground: if thou hadst been wisht, enemy of mankinde, to eat a dozen of Toads, two of Lizardes, and **three** of Snakes: if thou hadst beene perswaded to kill thy wife and children with some truculent and sharpe Scimitar no marvel though thou shouldst shew thy selfe nice and squeamish? but to make a doe for three thousand and three hundred lashes (since the poorest schoole-boy that is, hath them every moneth) admires, astonishes, and affrights all the pittifull entrailes of the Auditors, and of all them that in processe of time shall come to the heare **of** it: Put, oh miserable and flinty brest: put, I say, thy skittish Moyles eyes, upon the bals of mine, compared to shining stars, and thou shalt see them weep drop after drop, making furrowes, careeres and paths, upon the faire fields **of my** cheekes. Let it moove thee, knavish and untoward Monster, that my flourishing age (which is yet but in it's ten, and **some** yeeres; for I am nineteene, and not yet twenty) doth consume and wither under the barke of a rusticke Labourer: and if now I seeme not so to thee, tis a particular favour that Signior Merlin hath done me who is heere present, onely that my beauty may make thee relent; **for** the teares of an afflicted fairenesse, turne rockes into

Where is prosecuted the notice, that Don Quixote had, of dis-enchanting Dulcinea, with other admirable accidents.

*Mistaken instead of renounce, for so it goes in the Spanish.

267

THE SECOND PART OF THE

CHAPTER
XXXV
Where is pro-
secuted the
notice, that
Don Quixote
had, of dis-
enchanting
Dulcinea,
with other
admirable
accidents.

cotton, and Tygres into Lambes. Lash, lash that thicke flesh of thine, untame beast, and rowze up thy courage from sloth, which makes thee onely fit to eat till thou burst, and set my smooth flesh at liberty, the gentlenesse of my condition, and the beauty of my face, and if for my sake thou wilt not bee mollified, and reduc't to some reasonable termes, yet doe it for that poore Knight, that is by thee; for thy Master (I say) whose soule I see is traversed in his throte, not ten fingers from his lips, expecting nothing, but thy rigid or soft answer, either to come out of his mouth, or to turne backe to his stomacke.

Don Quixote hearing this, felt to his throte, and turning to the Duke, sayd; Before God, Sir, Dulcinea hath sayd true; for my soule indeed is traversed in my throte, like the nocke of a crosse-bow. What say you to this, Sancho? quoth the Duchesse. I say what I have sayd (quoth Sancho) that the lashes I bernounce. Renounce thou wouldst say, Sancho, sayd the Duke. Let your Greatnesse pardon me, sayd Sancho, I am not now to looke into subtilties, nor your letters too many, or too few; for these lashes that I must have, doe so trouble mee, that I know not what to doe or say: but I would faine know of my Lady Dulcinea del Toboso, where shee learnt this kinde of begging shee hath: shee comes to desire mee to teare my flesh with lashes, and cals mee Leaden Soule, and Vntamed Beast, with a Catalogue of ill names, that the Devill would not suffer. Doz shee thinke my flesh is made of brasse? Or will her dis-enchantment bee worth any thing to me or no? What basket of white linnen, of shirts, caps, or socks (though I weare none) doth shee bring with her, to soften me with? onely some kinde of railing or other, knowing that the usuall proverbe is, An Asse laden with gold, will go lightly up hill; and that Gifts doe enter stone-wals; and Serve God, and work hard; and, Better a bird in the hand, then two in the bush. And my master too, that should animate mee to this task, and comfort me, to make me become as soft as wool, he saies, that he will tye me naked to a tree, and double the number of my lashes, and
268

HISTORIE OF DON QUIXOTE

therefore these compassionate Gentles should consider, that they **doe** not onely wish **a** Squire to whip himselfe, but a Governour also, as **if** it were no more, but drinke to your Cherries, let um learne, let um learne with a pox, to know how to aske, and to demand ; for all times are not alike, and men are not alwayes in a good humor : I am now ready to burst with greefe, to see my torne coat, and now you **come** to bid mee whip my selfe willingly, I being as farre from it, as to turne *Cacicke.

By my faith, Sancho (quoth the Duke) if you doe not make your selfe as **soft** as a ripe fig, you finger not the Government. Twere good indeede, that I should send a cruell flinty-hearted Governour amongst my Ilanders, that will not bend **to the** teares of afflicted Damozels, nor to the intreaties, of **discreet**, imperious, ancient, wise Enchanters. To conclude, **Sancho**, either **you must** whip your selfe, **or** bee **whipt, or not bee Governour.**

Sir (quoth Sancho) may I not have two dayes respite **to consider ? No,** by no meanes, quoth Merlin, **now at this** instant, and in this place this businesse must bee dispatcht, or Dulcinea shall returne to Montesino's Cave, and to her pristine being of a Country-wench, or as she is, she shall be carried to the Elyzian fields, there to expect till the number of these lashes be fulfilled. Goe to, honest Sancho, sayd the Duchesse, be of good cheere, shew your love for your Masters bread that you have eaten, to whom all of us are indebted **for** his pleasing condition, and his high Chivalry. Say I, **sonne,** to this whipping-cheere, and hang the Devill, and let **feare** goe whistle, a good heart **conquers** ill fortune, as well **thou** knowest.

To this, Sancho yeelded these foolish speeches, speaking **to Merlin :** Tell me, Signior Merlin, sayd he, when the Devill-**Post passed** by heere, and delivered his message to my Master **from Signior** Montesinos, bidding him from him hee should **expect him** heere, because he came to give order, that my **Lady Dulcinea** should be dis-enchanted, where is he, that **hitherto wee have** neither seene Montesinos, or **any** such **thing ?**

CHAPTER XXXV

Where is prosecuted the notice, that Don Quixote had, of dis-enchanting Dulcinea, with other admirable accidents.

*Caciques, are great Lords amongst the West-Indians.

269

THE SECOND PART OF THE

CHAPTER XXXV

Where is prosecuted the notice, that Don Quixote had, of disenchanting Dulcinea, with other admirable accidents.

To which, said Merlin, Friend Sancho; The Devill is an Asse, and an arrant Knave, I sent him in quest of your Master: but not with any message from Montesinos, but from me, for he is still in his Cave, plotting, or to say truer, expecting his dis-enchantment, for yet he wants something toward it; and if hee owe thee ought, or thou have any thing to doe with him, Ile bring him thee, and set him where thou wilt: and therefore now make an end, and yeeld to his disciplining, and beleeve me it will doe thee much good, as well for thy minde as for thy body: for thy minde, touching the charity thou shalt performe, for thy body, for I know thou art of a sanguine complection, and it can doe thee no hurt to let out some bloud.

What a company of Physicians there be in the world, said Sancho, even the very Enchanters are Physicians. Well, since every body tells me so, that it is good (yet I cannot thinke so) I am content to give my selfe three thousand and three hundred lashes, on condition that I may bee giving of them as long as I please, and I will be out of debt as soone as tis possible, that the world may enjoy the beauty of the Lady Dulcinea del Toboso, since it appeares, contrary to what I thought, that shee is faire. On condition likewise that I may not draw bloud with the whip, and if any lash goe by too, it shall passe for currant: Item, that Signior Merlin, if I forget any part of the number (since he knowes all) shall have a care to tell them, and to let me know how many I want, or if I exceed. For your exceeding, quoth Merlin, there needs no telling, for comming to your just number, forth-with Dulcinea shall be dis-enchanted, and shall come in all thankefulnesse to seeke Sancho, to gratifie and reward him for the good deed. So you need not bee scrupulous, eyther of your excesse or defect, and God forbid I should deceive any body in so much as a haires breadth.

Well (quoth Sancho) a Gods name bee it, I yeeld to my ill fortune, and with the aforesaid conditions accept of the penitence.

Scarce had Sancho spoken these words, when the Waites began to play, and a world of guns were shot off, and Don
270

HISTORIE OF DON QUIXOTE

Quixote hung about Sancho's necke, kissing his cheekes and
forehead a thousand times. The Duke, the Duchesse, and
all the by-standers, were wonderfully delighted, and the
Cart began to go on, and passing by, the faire Dulcinea
inclined her head to the Dukes, and made a low courtsie
to Sancho, and by this the merry morne came on apace, and
the flowers of the field began to bloome and rise up, and
the liquid Cristall of the brookes, murmuring thorow the
gray pebbles, went to give tribute to the Rivers, that expected them, the sky was cleere, and the ayre wholesome,
the light perspicuous, each by it selfe, and all together
shewed manifestly, that the day, whose skirts Aurora came
trampling on, should be bright and cleere.

And the Dukes being satisfied with the Chase, and to
have obtained their purpose so discreetly and happily,
they returned to their Castle, with an intention to
second their jeast; for to them there was no earnest
could give them more content.

CHAPTER
XXXV
Where is pro-
secuted the
notice, that
Don Quixote
had, of dis-
enchanting
Dulcinea,
with other
admirable
accidents.

EDINBURGH

T. & A. CONSTABLE

Printers to Her Majesty

1896

www.ingramcontent.com/pod-product-compliance
Lightning Source LLC
Chambersburg PA
CBHW060528030726
47498CB00004B/1119